MIRAGE

MIRAGE

•••●•••

Cody Dillon

MIRAGE

Author Credits: CORY BERINGER

This is a work of fiction. All of the characters, names, incidents, organizations, and dialogue in this novel are either the products of the author's imagination or are used fictitiously.

iUniverse books may be ordered through booksellers or by contacting:

iUniverse
1663 Liberty Drive
Bloomington, IN 47403
www.iuniverse.com
1-800-Authors (1-800-288-4677)

ISBN: 978-1-4917-5447-4 (sc)
ISBN: 978-1-4917-5448-1 (hc)
ISBN: 978-1-4917-5449-8 (e)

Library of Congress Control Number: 2014921363

Printed in the United States of America.

iUniverse rev. date: 12/4/2014

Prologue

It was a calm, yet hot day in Mirage, Arizona. Hell, truth be told most days in September were hot in Southern Arizona. The only positive thing about this particular day was that the normally scalding wind was not tearing through the desert. Tolerable was one way to describe it, but to most normal people it was just plain hot and miserable.

Mirage formed by the cooling of the earth billions of years ago and hasn't changed much to this day. The barren dirt and lava rock landscape is only occasionally interrupted by the odd cactus or creosote bush. The surrounding area featured a dreary terrain with very little change in the primarily flat topography. Considering all of the monotony of the landscape and the constant heat waves visible in the distance, it was easy to get lost there if you weren't careful.

Scorpions, snakes, and lizards thrived in and around the miniscule town which boasted a population of more or less than two hundred people. Several small houses, dilapidated trailers, and lonely mercantile shops dotted the barren landscape along Arizona State Highway thirty three. It is fair to say that this was not a destination, but rather a place you had to get through to get where you were going.

Sullivan Mills sat on a broken down green camper's chair, rubbing a pronounced two inch scar at the outside corner of his left eye, in front of "THE LAST STOP." The establishment was an eighty year old run down gas station with an adobe structure and storefront that was in desperate need of repair and paint. The small shop sold fuel, beef jerky, and silly desert trinkets for the few vacationers from other parts of the country that happened to stop. Most of Sully's customers simply needed gas and/or driving directions The Last Stop was situated on a small, barren knoll on the far eastern edge of town. Sully could see anyone coming or going, and it was one of the primary reasons he had bought the place.

Mirage was a town that just about everyone passed by, without a second thought. One of the only temptations to stop in the anti-metropolis was a crumbling service station on the edge of town with two lonely full serve gas pumps in front. Sully had thought that, in this day and age, full-service fuel for the same high price as self-service might attract more business. Still he was continually a witness to the parade of humanity passing him by. Very much like Sully's life.

Sully was in his mid-thirties but looked very much older. He was almost six feet tall with an athletic build that he barely even had to try to maintain. Short light brown hair was usually covered by a hat, most often his favorite straw cowboy hat of ten years. The hat showed the wear and tear of every one of those years, not unlike Sully. He had deep lines around his eyes and mouth that he tried to hide with a continual three day beard. He was best described as not quite handsome, but rugged and well-built.

The few residents of Mirage that Sullivan had cause to deal with called him "Milly", a nickname given to him early in life that he had wanted desperately to shed, but could not. "Sully" sounded much cooler and infinitely more manly, but try as he might he could never quite shake the moniker of "Milly".

"*To hell with it*" he thought, as he made circles in the dust with the toe of his well-worn cowboy boots. The boots were beyond repair and in long in need of replacement. "*If they only knew*" Sully mused to himself, and the thought allowed an extraordinarily rare grin to creep across his face.

Mirage was located seventy miles in either direction from what the locals considered a major city, and roughly two miles from the Border of Mexico. A good day at the dilapidated gas stop granted no more than four or five customers, and so far this day had yielded only one. But that one customer had haunted Sully.

An unremarkable mini-van had stopped for a "top-off" early in the morning. What had been remarkable to Sully was the driver of the van. A beautiful brunette wearing large, dark sunglasses had made his heart skip a beat, and then jump into his throat. It could have been his lost love if hadn't known better, but other than the hair being short, and the wrong color it was her ten years after her disappearance / death.

She had paid with cash and not given Sully more than a glance, but when she drove off Sully felt a shiver run down his spine. This wasn't unusual for Sully because he saw Zoe reflected in just about every woman he came into contact with.

His mid-morning daydream about the wonderful life he had lived with Zoe was interrupted by the loud ding that preceded his second customer of the day. Sully tipped back the brim of his cowboy hat with his right index finger, and stood from the chair. He was quite wary as he approached the dusty Black sedan that was so obviously a government vehicle they might as well have written it on the sides.

His hope was that all they wanted was fuel. Sully was not the slight bit afraid of what he was certain were government agents in the sedan, for Christ's sake he was once one of the best agents the United States Government had ever seen.

Sully unconsciously touched the Ruger LCP .380 Auto that was always at home in his right back pocket as he walked slowly toward the driver's door of the agent mobile. As he approached the driver's side door the blacked out window slid down three inches and the Driver barked "fill it up fast" at Sully, and the window slid back up.

"You got it Ace" Sully said quietly aloud to no one and suppressed an urge to smile. Sully thought he should have saluted the arrogant son of a bitch. He pumped the gas and returned to "Ace" to collect.

"Thirty eight fifty" he said. The window rolled down slightly as Sully approached the door, so he knew that he was being watched. This was standard operating procedure for any field agent. The agent handed him a pre-paid gas card and again barked at Sully "make it snappy!" Hot blood now rose to Sully's face and he was suppressing several urges as he walked at his preferred speed toward the office to complete the transaction. Not one of the urges that he was feeling was to smile this time.

As Sully was nearing the door of the station an explosion with no sound threw Sully into the office, smashing his right shoulder unmercifully against the door frame. He came to his unconscious rest fully across the small shop with his head resting on a bag of Mexican pork rinds - Chicharones.

[illegible] didn't know. He was better than the [illegible], and the [illegible] appearance of death.

She hadn't [illegible] with [illegible] more than a [illegible], but when the drove of [illegible] her [illegible] for Sully [illegible] Zoe [illegible] women [illegible] into contact with.

He had [illegible] wondered [illegible] life he had [illegible] with Zoe was interrupted by the loud [illegible] of [illegible]. Sully tapped [illegible] of his [illegible] was [illegible] as he [illegible] that was [illegible] when [illegible].

[illegible] Sully was [illegible] what he [illegible] the [illegible]. [illegible]

[illegible] CB [illegible] that [illegible] in the [illegible] pocket [illegible] with [illegible] and [illegible] the [illegible] window [illegible] and [illegible] up [illegible] Sully [illegible] window [illegible].

[illegible] Sully said [illegible] to [illegible] and [illegible] to [illegible] Sully [illegible] he [illegible] the [illegible].

[illegible]," he said. The window [illegible] and [illegible] that he was being watched. [illegible] agent. [illegible] Sully [illegible] walked [illegible] toward [illegible] office [illegible] of the [illegible] he was feeling [illegible] this time.

As Sully was [illegible] the door of the [illegible] with [illegible] into the [illegible] right shoulder [illegible] the door [illegible] across the small shop with his [illegible] resting on a bag of Mexican [illegible] Chicharrones.

Chapter 1

Sully's childhood was very ordinary, too ordinary. It wasn't an abusive, or terrible childhood, it just kind of happened. Sully never knew a Father, and his Mother, Donna, was a kind woman who worked hard to provide for the both of them. He never knew of any relatives, and really had no friends because Mirage was populated primarily by Native Americans and Mexican Americans. Both ethnicities tended to shun the few white kids in town. Sully barely noticed the indifference, and it had never bothered him.

Sully spent most of his free time as a child prowling the desert with his old single shot twenty two rifle. At seven years old he had started working for a local Llama rancher doing all of the shitty chores that the rancher needed done and didn't want to do himself. How did the old joke go? The work sucks, but at least the pay is shitty, or something to that effect. The job kept him busy and let him contribute a small bit. His only luxury, if you could call it that, was the used rifle bought from Levi the rancher for twenty bucks.

Young Sully enjoyed hunting for the very few Jack-rabbits that managed to survive in the desert, and his Mother could cook them up into a feast. It was always a welcome addition to the meager board of fare that was the norm in the Mills home.

Sully's Mother Donna was a waitress / hostess at the only Diner in town, Smitty's. The pay she received for her twelve plus hour days was meager at best, and the tips were nearly non-existent.

Sully was never quite comfortable calling her Mother or Mom because he grew up virtually devoid of any type of a loving relationship. He had always called her "D" as far back as his memory allowed.

Thinking back on it Sully recalled that in her early life "D" was quite pretty, but life in Mirage had beaten her down. In his formative years he could only recall her as bitter and distant. Their relationship was more as partners involved in keeping the household going than what most would consider a normal Mother / Son relationship.

The only feeling he had ever recalled for "D" was pity, especially when he often heard her crying in her room late at night. For whatever reason Sully never felt the urge, or need to go and comfort her.

It seemed that Sully could never remember a time that he did not think that there was a hell of a lot more of the world to see than the deserts of Arizona, and a hell of a lot more life to be lived. Quite early in his life, Sully had vowed to leave his hometown as soon as possible.

After an interminably mundane four years of High School, where none of his thirty two classmates wanted anything to do with a painfully quiet guy called "Milly", Sully ran for the place he had thought that he was sure to be accepted unconditionally, the U.S. Marine Corps.

His decision was rewarded from the start. It was the only place that Sully ever felt like he truly belonged in his young life.

Marine Boot Camp turned out to be the best time of Sully's life. The drill instructors constantly screaming in his face had never even fazed him. It turned out that Sully had more than enough aptitude, and the perfect disposition for Military training. Climb that wall – no problem. One hundred push-ups – bring it on. Crawl through that mud pit – easy. It was the first time in his life that he was truly excelling at something and he was intoxicated with the feeling.

Here Sullivan was on his own terms and no-one even dared try to call him Milly, at least not twice. He had gone from a skinny kid from nowhere Arizona into the epitome of a lean mean fighting machine. Even here he found it easier not to have friends. After a short time the others pretty much stopped trying to befriend him. That suited Sully just fine; he acted as if he was a better Marine than all of them put together. It was most likely that his arrogance and aloofness put most people off.

Sully applied for all forms of military training available to him. From medic to bomb disposal Sully wanted to learn each and every task the Marines were willing to teach him. He had breezed through boot camp, and several other specialty training camps in his first year as a "Jar-Head".

Sully's eagerness and willingness to learn and take on new tasks did not go un-noticed. When his orders came through to be deployed to Germany, Master Sergeant Dixon called him to his office.

"Get your ass in here!!" Dixon bellowed.

Sully had liked Dixon from the moment they had met. He was a no nonsense career Marine with a "kick ass, take names" attitude that was almost as tough as his, and it didn't hurt his aura any that he was a six foot eight heavily muscled black man. Even his bald misshaped head was intimidating.

"Aye-Aye Sir" Sully yelled back with apparent respect.

Entering Dixon's office Sully saw "Sarge" comfortably behind his khaki steel Government desk with the cliché half cigar smoldering in the corner of his mouth. To Dixon's right was a man in his late forties wearing an ill fitted, dark blue, cheap suit. Other than the three men in the room, it was devoid of personality. He marched in smartly with razor sharp turns, and stood exactly three feet from the desk, dead center. He saluted smartly and then stood at an attention so rigid you could have mistaken him for a mannequin.

"Corporal, I am sure you know your orders were cut." Dixon said not looking up at him but rather shuffling papers on his desktop.

"Yes Sir" Sully yelled back. Dixon had a history of testing the metal of young Marines in hundreds of sadistic ways, and would fuck with them by not issuing the at ease command until he was damned good and ready.

"What the fuck good is a highly trained Marine stationed at a country club base in fuckin' Germany? Did you put in for this cupcake duty Corporal?" Dixon was now looking him straight in the eye and it was quite clear to Sully that these were deliberate questions that he wanted deliberate answers to.

Sully replied "Sir, the Marine does not know what good he would be in Germany Sir, and the Marine left his application for deployment preference blank, Sir." The only thing moving was his mouth. His statement was true. Sully did not care where he was deployed, as long as it wasn't back to Southern Arizona.

"At ease Mills, and permission to speak freely." Dixon replied with a small grin creeping across his face. He seemed to have satisfied himself by fucking with yet another young Marine.

"Mills, this is James Weathers." Dixon said as he almost imperceptibly nodded his head in the general direction of the man in the bad suit. "He has a different assignment he wants to talk to you about, and I want you to consider it seriously Mills, get me?" Dixon had snarled the "*get me*" at him.

"Yes Sir" Sully replied still wondering what in the hell was going on, but tingling with the prospect of what might happen next.

Dixon stood and started leaving the room, but at the door he turned and added "Mills, as far as you know Weathers carries no rank, but I expect you to show him the same respect you would show me. Get me Corporal?" Dixon said as he reached the door pointing the stogie at him.

"Yes Sir" Sully replied, now really confused.

As Dixon left, Weathers pulled an industrial steel chair from the corner and noisily dragged it next to Sully. He moved briskly to Dixon's chair and said "how would you like to be more than you can be." Weathers paused a long moment to let his comment sink in, then said "have a seat Sullivan."

Sully sat down in a crisp military fashion and said "thank you Sir." Maybe a little bit too aggressively. He did as he was instructed to by Dixon and gave Weathers the respect he had yet to earn from him.

Weathers loosened his tie and undid the top button of his shirt as he said "Mills, you have to understand that everything said here is highly sensitive, and I am only talking to you because Sergeant Dixon recommended you as a candidate for the duty I am about to discuss with you." Weathers seemed about as serious as Sully had ever seen someone, and he considered himself a serious man.

Sully immediately got excited about the possibility to have his duty changed to something this motivating. His response was too hasty when he blurted "I'm your man Sir".

Weathers retorted "Whoa, whoa there Corporal, how's about we talk about my project a little bit before you go volunteering for it."

It was apparent to Sully by both the man's body language and facial expression that his overly enthusiastic response had really irritated Weathers.

Weathers continued with "your enthusiasm is admirable son, but you best check it at the door before you end up volunteering for something that could ruin your life." Sully noticed the Fatherly tone of his voice and immediately resented it.

Now Weathers looked him straight in the eye and said "listen very closely to what I'm gonna tell you right now Mills." It was needless to say that he had Sully's full attention at this point. Weathers continued "what I am offering you is not for every service man and there will be no negative reflection in your file if you choose not to accept this assignment." Well, with that said, Sully was on the edge of his seat with wonderment.

Weathers very seriously continued "we need a new batch of covert operatives for a government agency that I can't disclose to you right now."

Sully realized that he was sweating with excitement and wiped his forehead as Weathers said "you were chosen because you apparently have no known relatives, other than your Mother, you are a loner that has few or no friends, and you have shown your aptitude for military training."

Weathers was now paging through what Sully could only guess was his classified personnel file as he went on with "this assignment involves years of training, aliases, and the possibility that we would fake your death and erase your identity. Think long and hard about this for the next few hours. I will meet with you again at eighteen hundred hours." He had uttered the last part as if he had rehearsed it and said it a lot.

Sully stood and said "Yes Sir, eighteen hundred, here Sir?" Sully asked now thinking Weathers might deserve the respect Dixon had ordered him to give.

Without hesitation Weathers said "don't worry Corporal, we can find you any time we want to."

His mind and body a buzz, Sully said "Yes Sir."

It was ten minutes before eighteen hundred hours that Sully heard a knock on his private barracks door. Two men wearing suits that were equally as cheap as Weathers' were at his door. They were both wearing sunglasses, and had large bulges under their left arms. Sully thought to himself that even Carl Childers from "Sling Blade" could have spotted these Bozos as agents from over a hundred yards away.

Bozo number one said "you Mills?" in a very un-polite manner.

Sully replied "yeah, unless you didn't mean Sullivan Mills, there are six Mills on this base dumb-ass." Sully said condescendingly.

"Come with us! Weathers wants to see you." Bozo number two shouted as he shook his head in disgust at his partner's idiocy.

The Bozos led Sully to a black Hummer parked behind his barracks. The windows of the Hummer were totally blacked out, and it had chrome wheels. Sully was sure that this was not a vehicle from any government agency that he knew of.

The passenger side back door of the hummer opened and Bozo number one tried to shove him inside, instead Sully did a quick spin move sweeping Bozo one's feet from under him. As Sully climbed on top of him with a clenched fist ready to bust Bozo's nose, then he heard a shout from inside the Hummer that stopped him. "That's enough Mills!" Sully heard Weathers command.

Sully immediately backed off and stood at attention in front of the open Hummer door.

"Get in Mills, and for God's sakes dial it down a notch." Weathers said as he slouched back into his luxurious leather seat.

Mills was impressed by the vehicle even more as he climbed in. The Hummer had it all. Satellite tracking equipment, phones and faxes, and a full p.c., wow. "Yes Sir, sorry Sir" Sully said in the least threatening tone he could muster.

He sat straight across from Weathers and said "can you tell me more Sir?"

Weathers was typing furiously at the pc to his left, but stopped and looked directly at Mills when he said "Mills, you're going to have to get used to working on a "need to know" basis if you are willing to join my team. By the way, you've had sufficient time to make a decision. What is it?"

Sully's head was swimming in a pool of possible answers to this question. He had thought about it all day, and as excited as he was, the job description he was given was quite vague. He was still reluctant when he answered with a firm "Sir, even though I would like to know more, I have decided to join your team, Sir."

Weathers had a big smile on his face now as he said, "welcome aboard Mills, when we get to Langley tomorrow I will fill in all the gaps and I think then you will know that you made the right move."

Sully thought, man I hope so, as he said "thank you Sir."

Sully returned to his barracks to find he had been robbed. The place had literally been turned up-side down. He was many things, but not stupid. Weathers had taken the opportunity of their meeting to send more Bozos here to check up on him. "Dammit" Sully yelled. It was going to take him until dawn to get this mess cleaned up.

He was about ten minutes into straightening the room when he heard a noise from behind him. Sully spun around quickly, expecting an attack, only to see good ole' Bozo number two standing in what was left of the door frame smoking a cigarette. He chuckled and said "looks like you had a problem here Mills."

Sully advanced quickly toward him ready to wring his neck when he heard Weathers' voice in the distance yelling "that's enough Mike!" Mike, a.k.a. Bozo number two, said to Sully "here" as he tossed a large black duffel bag in Sully's direction. "Grab your personal shit, and change into some civilian clothes" Mike said and continued with "you got about seven minutes, so make it snappy. The Lear leaves in twenty." When he finished his order he walked outside after crushing his cigarette out symbolically on Sully's floor.

It took Sully less than three minutes to change and grab his personal things. All he took was his three other sets of civilian clothes, a small picture of his Mother, and the six pistols he had bought over the last year. The Bozos hadn't found them because he had built a false floor in his wall locker to hide them.

Sully walked out of the barracks wearing loose fitting blue jeans, a tan Eddie Bauer long sleeved button down shirt, hiking boots, a San Diego Padres ball cap, and a nine millimeter Beretta safely tucked in the rear of his waistband.

He walked at a quick pace toward Weathers' black Hummer and when he was almost there he threw the duffel bag right at Bozo number one. As the duffle hit him in the gut, it doubled him over there was an audible "oof". Sully walked casually past him and quietly said "stick that somewhere ass-hole."

Weathers stepped out of the Hummer just as Bozo number one dropped the bag and starting heading towards Sully. He yelled "if you kids don't learn to play nice this is gonna be a long fuckin' trip. So lock it up and act like Soldiers."

The ride to the base Airport took only a few minutes, a not a word was uttered until they stopped and the Bozo twins got out. As Sully was moving toward the door Weathers grabbed his arm and said "once we take off I will brief you privately, away from Mike and Duane."

This just keeps getting better and better Sully thought. He was on cloud nine.

Sully had been on all forms of military transportation, and most civilian, but never a Lear jet. As he walked up the four stairs that folded in and became part of the fuselage he was not disappointed. *So this is how the rich live* Sully thought as he settled into the overstuffed chair closest to him. *The cost of the décor of this one little jet is probably worth more than the entire town of Mirage,* he continued musing.

Not long after takeoff Weathers came to him and said "follow me to the command center in the back."

The command center was a small office crammed with an oak desk; several televisions tuned to all of the big news networks, a wall sized dry erase board, and several computers.

"Sit down Sullivan" Weathers said motioning to a chair bolted to the floor in front of the desk. Because of how plush the Lear was Sully had forgotten that he was on an airplane. Weathers had walked around the desk and sank into an oversized burgundy leather arm chair. He opened a desk-top humidor and grabbed a small cigar. As he clipped the end with a gold cigar trimmer he had produced from the breast pocket of his jacket he said "Want one Sullivan, Macanudos?" His voice inflected upward as he said the last word.

Sully was wary now because Weathers had never called him by his first name and now he had done it twice. He said "no thank you Sir" calmly.

Weathers produced a large crystal ashtray from a desk drawer took his time preparing his cigar and then lit it with a wooden match. It wasn't until he had taken several draws that he again looked at Sully and said "you don't know what you're missing Son, best cigars ever made."

Sully thought '*wait a minute Sullivan twice and now Son? What was next ole' buddy?*' Sully was now very suspicious, but trying to go with the flow as he said "I only smoke cheap cigars anything that fancy would be wasted on me Sir."

Weathers raised an eyebrow and said "have it your way, let's get to it then." Weathers was back in business mode now as he said. "You have been recruited by the SSO, which stands for Special Sanctions Organization, and yeah it is exactly what it sounds like, we are assassins. The Feds gave up being cute with naming covert groups a long time ago, but they are still hung up on having the three letter acronyms." Weathers leaned back in his chair now to gauge Sully's reaction as he puffed away on his cigar.

Sully was excited now, "Holy shit I'm gonna be an assassin" he thought. He tried to curb his noticeable excitement when he said "understood Sir, what's next, who do you want me to kill!" Sully had blurted the statement out like he was throwing it up. He knew that excitement was written all over his face.

Weathers laughed aloud and said "slow down there Son, you have quite a bit of training ahead of you before we get to any of that." He was smiling broadly apparently knowing that he had a new recruit, and that Mills would work out well. "You've got to assure me at this point that you are in."

Sully blurted out "without a doubt Sir!" *"Man this is cool!"* Sully thought.

All business now Weathers said "you need to understand that we are a black-ops group, and officially we don't exist, and if you sign on neither will you." He continued with "I report directly to the Secretary of Defense and if you or anyone fucks up, he is gonna pull the plug on all of this.

We do what needs to be done. What the Government can't do with the press everywhere nowadays." He continued with "We are ghosts, and if you sign on you will be too. I have decided that we aren't doing the norm with you, and we will keep your identity alive, it might be useful to us in the future." Weathers finished sternly.

Weathers continued with "Dixon is gonna keep you alive by making the Marines think you are still there as his private secretary. It really only takes a couple of forms a month."

Weathers asked Sully a direct question now, with "it's okay to say no Mills, many of our recruits don't make it this far."

Sully thought for a second then realized what Weathers was referring to. He quietly asked "What about my Mother?"

Weathers replied "You will be issued a non-traceable cell phone upon landing that will be your contact with us, as well as the outsiders. You can make any calls you want to, but realize they are all monitored and recorded."

It was sinking in now to Sully that this was a well-run and extremely well-funded unit, and it was best to stop being so eager and to let things happen as they were supposed to. He replied to Weathers "Yes Sir, just tell me what you need me to do, and I'll do it."

Weathers furrowed his brow and said "I need a direct answer to this next question for the record, and take a minute to think about your answer. Are you willing to be an agent for the United States Special Sanction Organization knowing all of the facts given to you that affect your life going forward?"

A twenty year old kid from a miniscule town in southern Arizona did think this time. "What life do I have to care about other than "D", and continued thinking with; "This opportunity is more than I could ever get out of the Marine Corps."

Sully was stone cold in his reply when he said "Sir I am ready, willing, and able to become an agent of the SSO."

Weathers was visibly pleased when he sat forward in his chair and offered his right hand out to Sullivan as a gesture to shake hands as he said "well then, welcome aboard agent Mills."

Sully had taken his hand and shook it with a possibly too firm grip and said "Thank you Sir, you won't be disappointed."

Weathers' smile turned rapidly into a frown and he said "I better not be Mills, I spent a lot of time researching you before we even made contact." He continued with "you are obviously willing, but you have a shit load of training to do before you are ready and able."

Sully smiled, a thing he did rarely, and said "I won't let you down Sir." He was smiling because he had already been through some of the toughest training the Marines had to offer, and it all had come naturally to him, almost too easy at times. "How could this be any tougher" he thought.

Weathers said "I hope you don't let the SSO down Mills, I would hate to have to order a sanction on you."

This got Sully' full attention, "*holy shit, I better not fuck this up*" he thought as he said "I always do my best Sir, you get me, you get one hundred percent at all times."

Weathers' frown turned back to a small smile when he said "good." He continued with "in the SSO you will be trained to look and act like a civilian at all times, so cut the military courtesy. You can start by calling me Jim, hell Weathers isn't even my real name."

Sully stammered "yes Sir, I mean okay Jim." He had been in the Marines almost two years now and calling Weathers by his first name was very awkward for him.

Weathers chuckled and said "don't worry Mills, we will train that out of you."

Chapter 2

And they did. Sully had spent twenty seven months training with the SSO. It was a lot tougher than the Corps. Not so much physically, Sully was still rock hard and ripped, but mentally.

The training had encompassed everything. He was given training to know how to use tons of weaponry, vehicles, boats, planes, helicopters, and jets. Martial arts training was mandatory. He was instructed in computer use to the point that he could hack into anything. Cellular phones and all forms of micro-technology were given to him as toys. The SSO had access to forms of technology not even available to the public, and he was trained on the use of all of them. Dress codes to blend in anywhere were at his disposal, and he studied hard to know all of them.

Sully had always been a good student, average to good grades in all subjects in high school, but the SSO had tons of technical stuff for him to download. Sully struggled at times, but as usual gave one hundred ten percent, and passed with flying colors. Nearing the end of training Sully felt that he knew it all, and could do it all. This was a somewhat dangerous attitude for a trained assassin.

The SSO had assigned Sully a fully furnished apartment close to the training campus, and it was extremely comfortable. Most nights he was found holed up there pouring over manual after manual.

Weathers followed his training closely, and they met bi-weekly to discuss his progress. Their meetings were becoming more and more casual, and Sully was surprised to find that he was considering him as a mentor, rather than a superior officer.

Weathers would counsel Sully at each meeting. Some were held at local bars, others at the nearby "Appleby's", and some at Weathers' office. The meetings always changed, and the public ones were designed to teach Sully to blend into the background, not wear a t-shirt with Government Assassin emblazoned on the front and back.

Sully was surprised to find that he was truly happy here, a feeling he had never felt before. Mirage had been okay, but never to the level of happiness had he felt now. He constantly caught himself noticing the weather, trees blowing in the wind, and everything happening in his "world."

Sully was at Weathers office for a meeting. He had started looking forward to his meetings with "Jim". He walked casually into his office, sat in the chair in front of his desk as a civilian would and said "Good morning, Sir." He still could only call Weathers Sir, no matter how many times he had asked him to call him Jim. He did in public settings, of course, but it never sat well with him. To him Weathers deserved respect, and Sully gave it.

Weathers was not his jovial self this day and replied "Hi Sully." Although he never coached him, Weathers had started calling him Sully only a few weeks into his training. It pleased Sully that someone finally got it right. "Milly" was dead.

Sully had been trained by the best to be casual, and that was almost reflected when he said "what's up Sir?" smiling a crooked smile.

"I got a directive from Bob that we need to activate you sooner than expected." "Bob" was Robert McMillan, the current Secretary of Defense.

Weathers continued seriously with "Before we can activate you we have to send you on one last training assignment. You are being sent to Phoenix tomorrow for a team building class."

"Team building" Sully said with a smart ass tone to his voice. "Isn't that for corporate assholes?" he said even more sarcastically.

Weathers snapped back "its SSO policy, and it has to be completed successfully before we can activate any agent, refuse and I'll boot your ass out of here personally, got me Mills." He was obviously not joking.

Sully had never seen Weathers so irritated, so in an attempt to diffuse the situation he replied "hey, if it needs to be done I'll do it, you know me Boss." Sully had taken to calling Weathers "Boss" shortly after he had starting calling him Sully. "Just get it done and get your ass back here Sully." Weathers said seemingly calmed a little now.

After their meeting was finished Sully went back to his apartment and packed what he would need for the trip. Weathers had given him his trip voucher, and all of the instructions needed for the training exercise.

Sully spent the afternoon reading over the manual, and when he finished threw it at his duffel bag and said aloud to no one "what a crock of shit."

The plane landed at Sky Harbor airport at four p.m. on an August afternoon. Sully had almost forgotten how oppressive the heat was. It was one hundred nine when he walked out of the terminal to get a cab.

The cab ride to his hotel was uneventful, and ended at a Radisson in downtown Phoenix. The room was just fine by Sully's standards, and convenient because the stupid class was being held in a conference room here.

Sully ignored the invitation to the Friday night "meet and greet" in the hotel bar, and opted to stay in his room, order a pizza, and re-read the manual for tomorrow's "festivities".

When he could no longer stand the dribble written in the manual he turned on the television. All that did was irritate him further. When he could no longer stand that, and knew the "meet and greet" would be over, he headed down to the hotel bar for a drink. Hopefully they would be open at one in the morning.

"Mulligans", the hotel bar was open until two as luck would have it. The Irish pub theme was way overdone, and Sully liked it. He walked deliberately to a spot at the rail where the bartender was standing and said "double scotch rocks with a Heineken chaser." The bartender looked at him and knew right away he was not to be messed with. Sully's order was there within thirty seconds. "Run a tab" Sully said as he surveyed the room. Mulligan's policy was no tabs, but the bartender was intimidated and said "fine Sir."

Only five people occupied the bar at this early hour including Sully. There was a sloppy drunk salesman at the end of the bar, and two guys drinking pitchers of beer. He knew that he was sure to see them tomorrow at the class. They were betting that one was better than the other at throwing darts. Then Sully turned and saw the most stunning blonde he had ever seen sitting alone in a corner booth reading a romance novel.

Call it fate, or what you will, but Sully was drawn to the blonde in the booth. He slugged down his scotch rocks, grabbed his Heineken, and headed towards the booth in the corner.

Sully was shocked that as he approached her he had butterflies in his stomach and he started sweating. Sully had "had" plenty of girls, but all were as a sexual need, never as a love interest, hell he had never felt anything for any of them, much less love.

He approached the booth and uttered "reading anything interesting?"

She looked up and laughed at him and replied "top ten in the worst come-on lines ever cowboy, want to try again?"

Sully was taken aback by her sarcasm but still mustered the courage to reply. He said "sorry to have bothered you, I just thought you might want to talk. I couldn't sleep, so I came down here for a drink. I wasn't coming-on to you, I just thought I'd say hello. Again, I am sorry to have bothered you." Sully turned to walk away and was shocked to hear a reply from her.

She had said "go on and sit down with me, but I'm telling you that I am not interested in anything but maybe a chat with you to pass some time, this book stinks." She continued with "it might be better to talk to you than reading this shit, but we'll see." As she said it she had a sarcastically wry smile on her face.

Sully did an about face and sat in the booth in the smoothest way he knew how to. He opened with "sorry that you thought I was coming-on to you, heck you're not even my type" He smiled a broad fake smile and winked at her as he said it.

They both laughed honest laughs, and that is how Sully and Zoe met.

Zoe Millstad had grown up in rural West Virginia. She was quite pretty, but always considered herself as plain. She grew up as the only child in a poor, abusive home where she was constantly beaten by her Mother and sexually abused by her Step-Father. These circumstances had molded her into a shy and reclusive girl.

She tried her best to make friends at school, but the other girls considered her "trailer trash" and would have little, or nothing, to do with her.

The few people that saw it fit to talk to her called her "Milly" as a nick-name, and it infuriated her. Her name was Zoe and that was what she wanted to be called.

She was a very good student, and her academic excellence alienated her even further. Zoe was living a sad existence and knew it was up to her to change the circumstances.

When she was twelve years old she decided she had enough. One night, while her Mother was at work, she killed her Step-Father with his own shotgun while he was trying to rape her.

When he had walked into her room Zoe pulled the shotgun from under her "Strawberry Shortcake" comforter and pointed it squarely at his chest. He continued to advance and laughed as he said "I know you ain't got the guts to use that girl, so put it down."

The noise from the blast of a shotgun in the small room was deafening, but Zoe had expected that. Her ears ringing she jumped swiftly out of the bed, shotgun in hand, and stood over him. It was clear, even to a twelve year old girl, that he was mortally wounded. As she straddled what was left of his chest she said "any last request asshole?" The only response was a bloody gurgle. She shot him in the face, and knew he was dead.

This was not an impulse killing, Zoe had a plan. She had a bag packed, and the seventy two dollars she found in her now late Step Father's wallet, combined with her savings of eighty three dollars, was sure to be enough to get her a bus ticket to Canada. Zoe said "thanks jerk-off" as she stuffed his cash into her bag. Zoe spat on him as she left, symbolically. She was apprehended at the Greyhound station two hours later.

After she was caught, and told the local authorities her story, the Judge sentenced her to five years in a female juvenile detention facility, and lifetime probation.

"Juvy Jail," as the detainees called it, was even worse for Zoe than home. She was one of the youngest girls there and constantly had to fight to establish her position. She won some fights, but lost most. Her nose had been broken several times, and it had made her pretty face less so. All she wanted was to get out of this horrible place. When she was fourteen she was told that her Mother had been shot and killed in a drug raid. *Good riddance to bad baggage,* Zoe thought.

When she was finally released at sixteen, she was sent to a foster home that had nine foster kids including Zoe. The Bartowski's were nice enough people, but obviously into foster care only for the money. Life for her wasn't getting much better. Zoe never went back to school, but got her GED at seventeen.

She had jumped from dead end job to dead end job until her eighteenth birthday. Now she was considered an adult according to society, and enlisted in the Army that same day.

Without her noticing, Zoe had grown from an awkward teenager into a beautiful woman. She was now five foot seven with a lean, muscular frame. No matter what she wore, it looked good on her. Her extremely light brown hair was constantly mistaken for blonde, and her eyes were so green they made emeralds envious. If she knew how hauntingly beautiful she had become it would have made her arrogant, but she still saw herself as plain. The rough childhood she had endured had made her a cold and distant woman.

Zoe followed her plan and joined the Army. It wasn't long after that she found that she was now in an element where she was in charge. For Zoe it was true that you got out of the military exactly what you put into it, and Zoe always gave it her all. She was close to the best in her company at any, and all, training they threw at her. By the time she was twenty one Zoe was a Sergeant, and in charge of her life for the first time.

Zoe had just gotten her wings, after completing Airborne training, when she met a man who called himself "Weathers". He had approached her and simply said "how would you like to be more than you can be?"

Zoe breezed through the long and complicated SSO training program, and had one last task to complete before being deployed. Team building in Arizona.

The team building class was as dull as a butter knife. Sully was looking in his soft sided black leather briefcase for toothpicks to keep his eyes open until Zoe walked in. Now he was wide awake and didn't hear a word the speaker was saying.

He couldn't help staring at her, and looked down at his paperwork like a fifth grader whenever she caught him looking at her.

They had spent the whole night, well actually morning, talking, both of them making sure to stick to their cover stories. It was certain that neither of them had slept. While Sully looked in need of sleep, a shave, and shower, Zoe was radiant in Sully's eyes, looking better than he had ever remembered someone looking.

Sully didn't know what was happening to him. His normally steel exterior had been penetrated. He was drunk, not with the spirits, but with love. "How the hell can I be in love after a four hour chat" Sully thought. But there was no denying it, he was smitten.

The agent running the class looked more like a troll than an SSO agent, and Sully only paid attention when he said "now you will be placed in teams of two to complete this training exercise. To be fair we will team up alphabetically."

Sully's heart leapt! What were the odds that Mills and Millstad wouldn't be a pairing? He tried to look calm until the pairings got to the M's, and his patience was rewarded with "Mills, Millstad table number nine."

They sat across from one another at table nine just like at Mulligans; Zoe broke the ice with "long time no see, tough guy."

Sully replied "do I know you?" as he smiled the biggest smile of his life. They both laughed softly, but uncontrollably.

Sully was shocked to receive an "A" in the class because he hadn't remembered a word of what was said by any of the instructors. It must have been that he had read the manual five times that got him a high mark. The speakers had turned into a buzz of background noise, as he stared at Zoe and day dreamed about her without clothing.

Sully thought "Get a fucking grip man! You're acting like a dog in heat for Christ's sake." But there was no breaking the spell that Zoe had placed him under. Sully's mind had been racing all day trying to come up with the right words to ask her to dinner. He thought he finally had it as they were being dismissed from the class when Zoe said "want to get something to eat with me?" Her slight West Virginian accent was like honey to Sully's ears, and he was shocked that she has taken the initiative. He said "meet you in the lobby in an hour?"

Zoe replied "sounds good" with a genuine smile on her pretty face.

Zoe parted with him and went up to her room. She had goose-bumps, and there were about a million butterflies in her stomach. In her room she sat on the bed for a minute and thought "what the heck is going on here? You've known this man less than a day, and you think you are falling in love with him?" This was not at all Zoe's style, and her feelings were so strong they frightened her.

Zoe got ready franticly, and before she finally dressed she had tried on everything she had brought to Phoenix. Nothing seemed right. She finally settled on jeans, a light green Oxford shirt, and black high heels. Although she rarely wore make-up, she applied some eye-liner and rouge. "Keep it casual girl" she said aloud to herself as she finished primping in the mirror.

Sully had the same dilemma of his own. He felt incredibly stupid as he frantically looked at all of the clothes he had, trying to decide what to wear. He finally settled on blue jeans, his customary cowboy boots, and a red and white striped Roper shirt. He was so jazzed up that he had cut himself deeply while shaving. He had changed the toilet paper dressing three times, and the bleeding hadn't stopped. He resigned himself to the reality that he would have to meet Zoe with a piece of toilet paper stuck on his face. "Well, at least it's a conversation starter" Sully thought.

They met in the lobby exactly one hour after they had parted. As they walked up to one another Zoe snickered and said "razor a little dull big guy?"

Sully replied "guess so, sorry." They were so obviously awkward with one another that a blind man could have seen that they were falling in love.

"You made the date lady, where are we off to?" Sully said, having rehearsed the line in the elevator ride to the lobby.

Zoe said "normally I would suggest a walk until we found something, but it's still over a-hundred degrees out, so let's get a cab." She too had rehearsed this line.

There were cabs waiting outside of the hotel, and when they climbed in Zoe said to the cabby "Lonestar steakhouse please." Sully was thrilled that she chose his kind of place, but was worried that she did so for him.

Sully said "we can go any place you want you know, don't pick a steakhouse just for me." He was trying his best to be charming.

Zoe replied "Don't flatter yourself Mills, I've heard great things about this place and it's where I want to go." Zoe said with a firm emphasis on the "I". She continued with "I didn't think you were the vegetarian type Sully."

They both laughed, and chatted like they were old friends for the duration of the cab ride.

The meal was perfect for them. Sully was shocked when she had ordered a large Porterhouse rare, and he did the same. "This lady can eat!" Sully thought. Zoe had finished more of her massive steak than he had. All of the side dishes were great too.

After dinner they went to the crowded bar and sat at a corner booth. Zoe had a black Russian, and Sully sipped a beer.

After a little chit chat and flirting Zoe, who quite apparently had no problem being forward looked Sully straight in the eye and said "Where is this going between us Sully?" There was a huge lump in her throat as she continued "if this is just one of those seminar romances, that lasts one weekend, I'm not interested."

Sully was shocked at her statement. As silly as it seemed, he had thought that they were onto something special, but obviously Zoe didn't. Sully said "hold that thought, I need to use the Men's room." He stood and left the booth.

As Sully turned militarily and left he faintly heard Zoe saying "hurry back." He walked briskly past the Men's room and left the restaurant. He was relieved to find a cab waiting outside. He hadn't wanted to have to steal a car tonight. Sully got in the cab and ordered "airport Radisson, and step on it." The cab driver never said a word and started driving.

Sully pressed and held the number two on his cell phone to speed dial the SSO. A dispatcher answered with "Cuyahoga sheet metals, how may I direct your call?"

Sully quickly gave his access code and when the SSO dispatch agent answered he said. "Mills, I'm coming back tonight and I need a flight."

The dispatchers at the SSO that Sully had dealt with in the past were all extremely well trained and efficient. This agent was no different. She simply said "Hold please," and transferred him.

Typically he would have been transferred to the Operations Section, and they would swiftly give him his flight information. Not this time.

After several minutes, the phone on the other end of the line connected and Sully was somewhat surprised to hear Weathers' voice saying "what's going on Mills?"

Sully's mind was racing as he tried to calmly say "Nothing Boss, I completed the stupid class and I think I should get out of here before someone recognizes me and compromises me." Sully was lying, and hoped Weathers bought it.

Sully considered Weathers as a mentor but still was not comfortable calling him Jim, or James. He had settled on "Boss". He didn't like lying to him, but felt he had to get as far away from Zoe as possible right now.

Weathers simply said "fine Mills, I can have a Lear there in an hour, but I want to debrief you personally as soon as you get back." There was rarely any outward emotion in Weathers' voice, but Sully had been around him long enough to detect certain tones and deflections. Sully knew without a doubt that he was pissed-off.

Sully simply replied "yes Sir."

When Sully arrived back at SSO headquarters he instructed the driver of his pick-up car to go directly to Weathers' office. He walked in carrying his large duffel bag and Weathers' secretary, who knew him well now, said with a wanting smile and bedroom eyes "he's not here Sully, but I'll call him for you," with an emphasis on the "you". The secretary, Stephanie, had flirted with Sully from the first time they met.

Sully had no interest in Stephanie or any other female at the moment, so he walked casually past her, dropping his bag by her desk. He continued past her and into Weathers' office as he said coldly "I'll wait, watch the bag."

Weathers' office was overly extravagant and Sully plunked down on the overstuffed leather couch and closed his eyes to wait for the "Boss". He hadn't had time to change so he was still in the outfit he had worn to dinner with Zoe only five hours ago. It dawned on Sully for the first time that it was two in the morning and Weathers must have instructed Stephanie to be here in expectation of his arrival. His eyes opened as he thought, "two a.m. and he's prepared for me, I'm in deep shit this time".

Sully heard the door to Weathers' office slam closed to wake him from a nap, dreaming of making love to Zoe, and arose from the sofa to watch Weathers striding rapidly toward his desk.

Before he even sat down Weathers said "you want to explain to me why I had to divert a Lear to pick your ass up?"

Sully sat down quietly in the right armchair facing Weathers' too big desk without saying a word, but now absolutely certain that he was pissed. The erection that the dream about Zoe had given Sully rapidly faded.

Weathers continued with "if you think the Lear jets we have are your private fleet you're wrong." The blood was rising to his face as he had said this and Sully knew immediately that he had made a big mistake when Weather raised his voice a notch and said "You had a First Class commercial ticket for tomorrow, well shit today at this point. What, that's not good enough for you now?"

As Sully started to open his mouth to answer Weathers quickly stopped him with a finger pointed at him and said loudly "just shut up and let me finish Mills, and when I do finish, you had best have a better explanation for me than the bullshit you gave me on the phone." Weathers continued his tirade with "I don't think you know that I have to explain every unscheduled flight directly to the Secretary of Defense. Most are warranted, this isn't. If you don't give me a damned good explanation for this, I'm gonna bust your ass all the way down to dispatcher."

Sully was getting a little pissed-off now too, having been chastised like a teenager who took the family car without permission. He waited until Weathers was done, but had already dug his heels in as he replied with no emotion "It's just like I told you Sir."

Weathers was visibly displeased with the response, but now leaned back in his chair when he said calmly "If that's the way you want to play it Mills your ass is in my hands and I will forward your bullshit along." As he finished he looked disappointedly at his protégé. He finally looked down at the papers on his desk as he said "be back here at twelve hundred hours and I will decide what to do with you, now get out of my sight." He said as if scolding a child.

Sully walked the mile back to his apartment, carrying his heavy duffel, thinking the whole way. His first thought was to just keep walking, but he knew that if he did, the SSO would hunt him down and kill him no matter where he went. He finally decided to keep his appointment with Weathers no matter what it meant for him. Then his thoughts rambled back to Zoe. He had hated to run out on her like that, but he had finally finished his training and needed no distractions on the eve of his first assignment.

Chapter 3

When Sully didn't return to their table for over twenty minutes Zoe truly cried for the first time in her life. She allowed herself to sob for a full two minutes, and then vowed to never cry again.

She paid the bill that the louse had skipped on with cash, and then got a cab back to the hotel. When she was somewhat settled in her room she called into the SSO and asked about getting an earlier flight back. When she was finally connected to Operations, they quickly said no.

Zoe went to the bathroom and washed the stupid make-up from her face that had ran all over with her asinine crying, packed all of her things, and went to bed, thinking of Sully. She was trying her best not to cry again.

Sully had spent the whole day thinking about what to do about his meeting with Weathers. He had no defense for his lie, and finally decided he would not lie any further. He chose to remain silent and let Weathers do whatever he must.

Sullivan Mills arrived at James Weathers office ten minutes before their scheduled meeting with all of his personal belongings packed into a small tattered suitcase. The only things that he owned were his weapons, and by now he had acquired quite a few. And that was the contents of the suitcase it was the same suitcase he had left Mirage Arizona carrying years ago. He was certain he was headed for the bus to nowhere again.

He entered the outer office wearing the only clothes he owned. Worn out blue jeans with holes in them, an old flannel shirt, and an old pair of cowboy boots. All of his other clothing was Government Issue. He wasn't even wearing underwear so he couldn't be accused of stealing. He had never "gone commando" before, and the lack of support was uncomfortable for him. He set his case by the door as Stephanie said "they are in there waiting for you." She had never looked at him, and was definitely not flirting with him today.

Sully knew that the "they" Stephanie had said was not a good sign. Sully had always met with Weathers one on one. When he walked in to the main office Weathers was behind his desk smoking one of his prized cigars. Standing to his right was a man Sully had met only once, Fred Spyes, SSO Director of Operations.

Sully had come to grips with his current situation, and walked in casually and sat down as he thought a civilian would, without saying a word.

Weathers raised an eyebrow and said "I hope you are willing to treat this meeting more seriously than you decided to dress Mills." He continued with "Spyes is here to help me make you understand what's going on for you right now."

Sully had always thought that it was ironic that a man named Spyes was second in charge of a group of spies and assassins.

Spyes took the lead now and said "Normally when a rookie agent breaks protocol, like you did, we bust them hard." He said in a businesslike manner. Spyes continued with "the only thing saving you right now is that I have an assignment that is necessary, and you are the best agent for the job. Spyes nodded toward Weathers and quickly left the room.

Weathers looked Sully squarely in the eyes and said "that qualifies as strike two and a half. Don't even breathe in the wrong direction from this point forward, Mills."

It was quite clear to Sully that his actions had caused irreparable damage to his relationship with Weathers. He stood, in his old military manner, and said "yes Sir." He was relieved to not be in that much trouble and excited at the same time when he had heard Weathers say assignment.

Weathers was less serious now as he said "this assignment requires you to have a partner, and for the both of you to look like a married couple." Weathers pushed the intercom button on his phone and said "send her in now Stephanie."

When Sully turned to see Zoe Millstad walk into the room to report to Weathers he wanted to run away again. Instead he fell into his chair awkwardly and was only able to look at her shoes when he stammered "you, you're an agent?" He had no idea that Zoe was thinking the exact same thing.

Weathers interrupted their reunion saying "come sit down agent Millstad." He motioned to the armchair next to Sully. He continued with "I would think by now that you two might have figured out that your meeting one another was not an accident." He said as Zoe sat down.

Sully's mind was racing, and he barely heard Weathers continue with "sometimes the oldest tricks are the best. We had satellite trackers on both of you and know exactly how much time you spent together" Weathers said smugly.

"If you want to see the transcripts of your conversations I can provide them to both of you" Weathers said now, having fun at their expense. He continued with "if you like romance novels, it's a good read."

Both Sully and Zoe were mad as hell at the invasion of privacy and it showed. Sully was ready to yell at him when Weathers said "before either of you shout at me about your privacy, let me explain."

Weathers played with and lit one of his cigars before continuing with "this mission was in the works long before that bullshit team building thing. I needed to know if you two would fit together as the right team for this assignment. I don't think that I have to tell you two that my little trick worked out a lot better than I had expected. You two have been very carefully separated during your training for just this kind of situation. Now, can we all talk calmly about the assignment?" He finished looking sternly at both of them.

Weathers' last statement had snapped both of them out of their train of thoughts about all of this, and there was an almost simultaneous "yes Sir" spoken loudly from both Sully and Zoe.

Weathers said "good, then let's get to work." Sully thought he looked smug, but didn't care because his first assignment was finally here, and he was becoming intoxicated with the pheromones emanating from Zoe.

Weathers said "I want both of you to go to your apartments. Your dossiers will be there waiting. Give them a quick once over, and be ready at nineteen hundred hours. I am sending a car for both of you, and we will meet at the bar at the Outback Steakhouse to continue this briefing. Do either of you have a problem with that?" Weathers had uttered the question with a tone of "you had better not have a problem".

It was an almost simultaneous response of "no Sir", but this time there was trepidation in both voices.

Weathers said "good, now get the hell out of here. I need a nap because someone got my ass down here at two in the morning." He was looking angrily at Sully when he said the last part.

As they left Weathers' office, Sully grabbed his bag. When they got outside there were cars and drivers waiting for both of them.

At the SSO field agents were treated like royalty, and even the rookies had the respect of all of the lower agents. They were on the top rung of the SSO ladder, and had earned it with their years of training. No one messed with a field agent at the SSO.

Before she could get away, Sully grabbed Zoe by the arm and said pleadingly "Zoe, let me explain."

Zoe ripped her arm from his grasp turned to face him and said "you hurt me Mills. You made me cry for the first time in my life, and I can never forgive you for that!" She had almost yelled her rehearsed statement at him. She turned quickly and got in her car. The driver of the car sped away as he had been instructed to by Zoe.

Sully was crushed. He walked slowly to his car and got in. When the driver got in he turned around, looked at Sully with a grin and simply said "women?"

Sully grimaced at him and angrily said "just shut the fuck up, and take me to my apartment."

The driver did as he was told without uttering a sound the whole way.

Chapter 4

Zoe needed time to think, and unpack when she got to her apartment. She thought while she unpacked "why did you chastise him like that? It gave you chills to find out that he was an agent, just like you, and you pushed away the only man you have ever wanted to spend time with. He was going to try to explain and you emasculated him. So what so you cried over him leaving, that's no excuse to push him away when he obviously wants to come back to you". After finishing these thoughts she was furious with herself.

Zoe sat for an hour reading the dossier, and was more excited than she had ever been in her life. They were going to Monaco to pose as a married couple, to befriend a couple that needed to be sanctioned. The procedure had been drilled into her. Never ask why they needed to be killed, just do it.

She read on, Benjamin and Jan Dallman were the targets. They were a young wealthy couple that traveled Europe and lived on their extravagant yacht. They looked nice enough, but they had stepped on the wrong side of the Government hard enough to deserve death.

Zoe put the dossier in her safe, and started getting ready for dinner. 'Knock his socks off' she thought as she picked an outfit to wear.

When Sully got back to his apartment he threw the suitcase at the closet. He ducked quickly remembering it was filled with loaded weapons and ammo. Luckily none had fired and he was safe.

He immediately noticed the dossier on his coffee table, and sat on the couch to begin pouring over it. He had excelled in his training by reading, and re-reading, and re-reading every manual he was given. He was determined that the sanctions would be no different. He set his cell phone alarm to make sure he saved time to dress for dinner.

When Sully's cell phone alarm went off it startled him. He was so deeply entranced with the dossier that a bomb could have gone off without his knowing. It was time to get ready for dinner with Zoe.

As he showered he was running scenario after scenario through his mind on how to approach Zoe. He stopped thinking deliberately as he shaved carefully, trying not to repeat his earlier embarrassment.

He dressed in light brown khaki slacks, a black Marino turtleneck sweater to show off his muscular build, and dark brown boat shoes, sans socks.

Sully had never been vain, but he wanted desperately to look his best for Zoe. He combed his hair in the mirror for the fifth time, and said to his reflection "be charming asshole."

On the ride to dinner he instructed the driver to stop at a flower shop. The driver had a Q-14 earpiece so that he could talk directly to the SSO. The driver was talking to thin air as far as anyone else knew, when Sully said "I need an open flower shop near my route." No time at all passed when he said again to no one "roger, I see it on my GPS.

Sully went into the flower shop and bought a single red rose with baby's breath adornment wrapped in gold cellophane. He felt awkward as he walked back to the car with it.

The side trip for the rose had made him ten minutes late. He was hoping Weathers hadn't arrived yet as he walked into the bar with the rose safely tucked in his waistband behind him.

Zoe had arrived at the bar ten minutes early. She ordered a white wine spritzer and stood purposely with her back to the door, but she could see the door in the windows across from her. She was dressed in a tight black dress that showed her every curve, and it was just short enough to show her sculpted, athletic legs. The black high heels she wore made her calves flex, and it finished the look.

At exactly nineteen hundred hours Zoe's phone rang and when she answered it was Weathers. Weathers said "I am unavoidably detained, and can't meet the two of you. Please have a nice dinner on me, I will call the restaurant and arrange it. Tell Mills that we will meet tomorrow in my office at O nine hundred."

Zoe said “yes Sir”, and heard him hang up. She knew this was a ploy to get herself and Mills together, and she didn’t mind. At the very least she wouldn’t have to explain her outfit to him.

When Mills walked through the door, and she saw him in the glass reflection, her heart fluttered. He was the most handsome thing she had ever seen. It was all she could do to contain herself from turning and running into his arms.

Sully walked into the Outback and when he looked to his right he almost fainted. He saw Zoe standing at the bar alone looking gorgeous. She wasn’t facing him, but he had memorized every curve of her body, and the fabulous dress she was wearing showed every one of them. He tried to keep himself from running, as he walked up to her. When he was ten feet from her she turned around, and Sully stopped in his tracks. She looked like a goddess to him and he didn’t know if he should bow to her or continue forward. Her broad smile summoned him forward.

As Sully closed the last ten feet he reached behind himself to gather the rose he had bought for her. When he reached out to give her the rose she threw herself at him and they had their first kiss. He held her tightly and they both kissed like neither had ever been kissed before. Sully pulled her so tightly to him that he broke the stem of the rose in his right hand.

When they finally separated she looked deeply into his eyes and said “I’ve been waiting for you for a long time Sullivan Mills.” They were still so close that her words were breathed to him rather than spoken.

It was all Sully could do to reply. He swallowed hard and said softly “I’ll never leave you again Zoe, unless you ask me to.” Now Zoe grabbed him hard and they kissed again.

Zoe backed away finally and said “wanna know a secret?”

Sully was on cloud forty seven when he replied “sure, what is it?” They were acting like teenagers, and Sully loved it because he had never had any romance in his life before this.

Zoe leaned forward kissed him lightly once and slid to his ear nibbled for a second then whispered “Weathers isn’t coming, I’m not hungry, there is a motel across the street, and I brought my own car.”

Sully grabbed her lightly by the arm as she grabbed her purse and started for the door before he even responded. When they were at the door he stopped and said "I'm not sure, I could really go for a blooming onion."

Zoe shoved him out the door as they both laughed.

They made love most of the night. At first they were both frantic and wanting, later slow and loving.

When they took breaks they talked truthfully to one another.

During one break Sully told her about his boring life in Arizona, and what had led him to this point. When he finished it was clearly Zoe's turn, and she left the bed wrapping her glistening body in a sheet.

Zoe sat at the small table by the door of the motel room and said "I need you to just sit there and not say anything while I try to tell you about my childhood. You are the only person I have ever felt comfortable enough to tell this to so please don't interrupt me." Zoe was shaking now.

Sully softly said "you don't have to tell me anything you don't want to Zoe." He was confused now.

Zoe continued with "I have to Sully, so you really know who I am, and what I've been through, before you decide to move forward with our relationship." She couldn't stop shaking, and continued with "just please listen and try to understand."

Zoe finally let it out, after years of holding it in. She let all of her past flow out of her and into Sully's ears. She explained the sexual abuse by her step-father, her subsequent murder of him, her horrible time in the juvenile penal system, and finished with the death of her mother. She turned to look at Sully and said "could you have a serious relationship with a monster like me?"

Sully moved off the bed and quickly to her, held her tightly and said "Zoe, our pasts don't define us they only mold us into who we are today." He kissed her lightly on the forehead and then said "hold onto your sheet lady, but you are most definitely not a monster, and I love you. I think I have from the first time I met you."

She held him so tightly she cracked his back, and she sobbed uncontrollably for a minute. When she finished she looked up and kissed him deeply. Then she said "I love you too Sully, but could you please stop making me cry you bastard."

Sully chuckled, picked her up and carried her back to the bed. He snuggled closely to her and softly said "sleep my love."

And they did.

Sully and Zoe awoke in each other's arms as the dawn broke through the cracks in the window shades. Sully tried to sneak his numb right arm from beneath Zoe without waking her, but failed.

Zoe grabbed his arm and moved tightly into him. Sully said "Good morning beautiful" and nuzzled the back of her neck with his nose. He continued with "My arm is asleep, and I need to use the bathroom, just wait right here, and I'll be right back."

Zoe relented and let his arm slip from under her. She watched as he crossed the room butt naked and said "nice ass agent Mills" and whistled a cat call at him. Sully stuck his tongue out at her as he closed the bathroom door, and she giggled.

Sully urinated, brushed his teeth with complimentary motel toothpaste using his index finger and washed up quickly. He stepped out of the bathroom wearing a towel tucked around his waist.

He knew it was going to be a great day when he saw Zoe standing fully naked in front of him. She threw her arms around his neck and kissed him deeply. As his towel began to rise in the front she stepped back and said "no fair you brushed your teeth, and I haven't." She grabbed her purse and said "give me a minute to brush mine, then come and take a shower with me."

Sully didn't even wait thirty seconds, and joined her in the bathroom. As she finished brushing her teeth, he got the shower warm. When she finished she sexily said "what's that?" Pointing at the towel around his waist that now looked like a pup tent.

Sully winked and said "get that gorgeous body in the shower and I will show you." She kissed him again, grabbed him by the hand and said "come on" as she stepped into the shower. Sully barely had time to drop the towel as they entered the shower.

They made slow passionate love in the shower after soaping one another thoroughly. When they finished and toweled one another off Sully said "we had better get dressed, or we're gonna be late for the meeting with Weathers." Sully smiled at her and continued with "besides, if you keep running around naked, we're gonna have to find out if this motel has a monthly rate."

He was sitting on the edge of the bed starting to pull his underwear on when she ran over and tackled him on the bed. Zoe kissed him and said "tell me you love me again."

Sully said very seriously "Zoe you are my first and only love." She smiled a broad genuine smile and said "same goes for me cowboy." She playfully kissed him on the nose, jumped off of the bed, and started getting dressed.

Zoe gave Sully a ride back to his apartment and they agreed upon the way that they would try their best not to show their feelings for one another anywhere around the SSO campus.

Sully left her car quickly and ran into his building. He only had an hour before the meeting with Weathers, and he had to change, and read his dossier again.

As Zoe drove to her apartment she was happier than she had ever been in her life. She turned up the radio and sang along loudly and off key. Sully seemed to be the perfect man, and she was suddenly deeply in love with him. During the last twelve hours it seemed that she had a constant smile on her face. Sully was right though, they had to keep their love private for now. Zoe raced home, changed, and started reading her dossier again.

When Zoe was ushered into Weathers office Sully was already there talking with him. She walked in and sat down in the armchair next to Sully.

Weathers said "good, now that both of you are here we can get down to business. This sanction is very important, but there are elements not covered in the dossier."

Sully said "seems straightforward enough, we act as a couple, befriend them, then kill them."

Weathers said "yes, but you need to get information out of them first. We need to know where they are getting all of their money. The Government has enough reasons to sanction the Dallmans, but they want to know more.

Zoe said "what kind of information are you looking for?"

Weathers said "good question agent Millstad, we need any kind of financial information you can get. How they came to have their wealth, and where they hide all the money. We are sending you two very well-funded. You will have fifty thousand dollars in cash, and a million dollar account to draw on, but before you get any ideas, we have a tracer on the account, and we will need expenditure reports filled out for all cash transactions."

Sully said "it sounds a little like you don't trust us Boss." Sully was jokingly sarcastic.

Weathers smiled and said "you two better get used to it because whenever you are out on a sanction you are still on a very short leash."

Zoe said "fine, I think we understand Sir, when do we leave?" She was as excited as Sully to finally be active in the field.

Weathers said "we are still trying to work that out; we are giving you a Lear with a crew that will be at your disposal, but it is not to be abused." He had directed this last comment at Sully, for good reason. Weathers continued "we currently have a logistical problem with the Lear, but as soon as it is ready you will go.

Zoe asked "does that mean hours or days Sir?" Zoe was always very straight forward with Weathers.

Weathers replied "looks more like days at this point, but I want you two ready at a moment's notice." Weathers continued "Operations has your clothing, luggage, and I.D. packages ready. There is a car waiting outside to take both of you."

Weathers finished with "this is the first field assignment for both of you, and I have the highest expectations. Don't disappoint me. Now get out of my office, I have work to do on getting that Lear ready to go."

They left together and got into the car to go to Operations. They were given all of their gear, and were driven separately to their respective apartments.

When Sully got into his apartment with all of his gear for the operation, he rifled through it. All fancy clothes and then a large brick of money. He put the money in his safe, and called Zoe.

Zoe answered her phone and was ecstatic when she heard Sully's voice. She said very sexily "well agent Mills, why would you be calling this morning."

Sully replied coldly "I will be over in ten minutes to pick you up, can you be ready that quickly?"

Zoe felt a little put off by Sully's tone but said "I will be ready and waiting for you big boy."

Sully said simply "fine." He was playing it cool for right now. He needed to talk to Zoe A.S.A.P

When Zoe got into Sully's SSO issued agent mobile, she was more beautiful than ever he thought. As soon as she entered the vehicle Sully said "hello agent Millstad" coldly and held a finger to his lips, the international signal to be quite. He handed her a note and put the car in gear.

Zoe was very confused now, and the smile on her face quickly turned into a frown. She said frigidly "hello Sullivan" and opened the note. The note read:

THERE ARE EYES AND EARS EVERYWHERE WATCHING US. I AM DRIVING OFF CAMPUS SO WE CAN TALK OPENLY. FOR NOW JUST TALK ABOUT THE MISSION, I LOVE YOU ZOE.

Zoe folded the note carefully and put it in her purse. "*Hell of a first love note*" she thought. Zoe was as smart as Sully, and just as highly trained, but now she blushed at how stupid she had been. Love had clouded her judgment, and she had been acting like a fool, she thought.

She looked at Sully and nodded in understanding at him, and he nodded back and winked at her. They drove in silence for a while.

Sully finally broke the silence and said "I thought we could get some breakfast at the Denny's in town" his tone was all business.

Zoe coldly replied "that sounds fine Mills, it will give us a chance to work on our cover stories."

When they reached the Denny's, they walked in silence toward the entrance when Sully said "you know what, I'm not really that hungry, and would you rather just walk and talk?" He winked at her.

Zoe smiled and said "That would be fine Mills, I'm not a big breakfast person anyhow." She understood the circumstances now. She thought "*it's a good thing I wore flats*".

When they were about four hundred yards from the Denny's, they had walked behind a small strip mall. Sully grabbed her hand and said "we are about as safe as we can be now, you look beautiful Zoe. I'm didn't mean to be so cold to you, but I hope you understand." He grabbed her and gave her a deep kiss.

Zoe felt a rush of sexual excitement when he kissed her. When the kiss ended she looked down at her feet and said "I'm so sorry I have been such a fool Sully, but this is the first time I've been in love and it overwhelms me at times."

Sully gently lifted her chin so that her could kiss her lightly, then he said "Zoe, I am having the same feelings, and it's hard for me to control too." He continued "we just have to try to be more careful than we have been. I'm pretty sure our cars and apartments are bugged and I know our cell phones have GPS tracers on them."

She nodded at him signifying that she understood, then wrapped her arms around him and hugged him tightly. Zoe whispered in his ear "you are a dream come true for me Sullivan Mills."

Sully whispered back "I never dared to dream that a woman as wonderful as you are would love me." Sully's cellular phone rang and ruined their tender moment. He broke their embrace and dug the phone out of his pocket.

Sully pushed the send button on the phone to connect the call and simply said "Mills."

It was Weathers on the other end of the line and he said "the Lear will be ready to go at thirteen hundred hours. Your weapons and ordinance will be on board. Are you ready Mills?"

Sully replied with an eager "yes Sir, one hundred percent!"

Weathers continued "good, is agent Millstad with you?" there was an odd tone in his voice, but Sully was too excited to notice.

Sully said "yes Boss."

Weathers said "fine, then you can tell her. You will be leaving from hangar number nine and don't be late, or I will have both your asses. I'm not going to see either of you before you go, but I will be in contact. Good luck Mills, and tell agent Millstad the same." Weathers hung up with a loud click.

Sully turned to Zoe and said excitedly "we leave at thirteen hundred!" They slapped hands in a high five, then kissed deeply again.

Chapter 5

The Lear was airborne at five minutes past thirteen hundred hours. The expected flight time to Monaco was nine hours.

Sully and Zoe were both enamored with the luxury of the Lear. They worked mostly, but took breaks for the five star meals they were served.

During a dinner of filet mignon and lobster tails, Zoe said "I could get used to this." She was smiling at Sully as she said it, giving him a look so hot look that it could have melted the butter on the table.

They had been exchanging loving and suggestive looks the whole flight. They could hardly wait to be alone together.

Sully smiled back at her and said "well you had better act like you are used to it for the next couple of weeks. Remember we are now Brian and Patricia Nelson, wealthy investors."

Zoe said "don't worry about me Mills, when we land I am fully into being Trish Nelson." She was smiling when she said this, but it was obvious that she was quite serious.

The plane landed in Monaco at six thirty local time. Sully and Zoe had showered and changed on the plane. Zoe was wearing a Chanel floral print sheer dress with a wide tan matching belt at the waist, Ferragamo high heels, large dark Lauren sunglasses, and a cabana hat with a band that matched her dress.

When she was fully primped she walked out of the master suite located in the back end of the Lear. She twirled to let the bottom of her dress fluff out, and said to Sully "like it?"

She had taken Sully's breath away, he was speechless. Sully wanted to tell her what a vision of loveliness she was, but they were still on a plane that was certain to be bugged, so he tried his best to calmly say "looks like a perfect portrayal of Trish Nelson to me."

Sully was wearing an off white Christian Dior linen suit with a tan silk shirt, Dior light brown boating shoes, an oversized gold Rolex watch, and small Dakota Smith sunglasses.

Zoe said "you look like a pretty good Brian Nelson to me too." She wanted to tell him he looked very handsome, but she had gotten the hint of his response that they had to be careful about what they said.

They had each repacked the bags that they wanted taken to the resort, and the copilot/valet/driver, Julian, had already loaded them into their limousine.

As they rode to the five star resort in the limo Zoe had a bubbly look on her face and Sully knew she was about to speak casually. He put a finger to his mouth and gently shook his head. Zoe got the hint, and knew it was not yet time to speak her mind.

When they arrived at the fabulous Arriba resort that was sitting high on a hilltop overlooking the Ligurian Sea, they were both very impressed. It was an incredible setting.

A bell-hop dragging a large golden cart was ready to take their bags even before Julian had popped the trunk lid open. Sully/Brian got out of the driver's side and walked around the front of the car to the rear passenger door. He opened the door and gave his hand to Zoe/Trish. As he helped her out he said jovially "we're here Trish, just like you wanted." When she was out of the car he grabbed her, held he closely, and gave her the true kiss he had been longing to give her for the entire length of the trip. Sully/Brian whispered in her ear "I'm sorry I couldn't tell you how fabulous you look on the plane, I hope you understand"

Zoe's knees went weak, and if Sully hadn't been holding her closely she might have fallen. Zoe/Trish managed to whisper back a breathless "I love you."

Julian interrupted them saying "please wait in the lobby, I will check you in."

They walked holding hands into the lobby and were impressed. Although it was way overdone in its Polynesian / Spanish theme, all of the décor appeared to be very expensive.

Sully and Zoe waited outside the door to their villa as the bell-hop took their luggage inside. When he came out with an empty cart, Sully tipped him an American twenty dollar bill and said "thank you."

Sully grabbed Zoe and kissed her again, a long slow deep kiss this time. Then he again whispered to her "wait here a few minutes and I will sweep the place." Zoe nodded her head to him knowing that he was going in the villa to check for listening devices and video cameras.

Sully walked into the villa and straight to his suitcase. He took out what would look to anyone as a small tape recorder, and it actually worked as one, but its true purpose was as a high frequency detector. It took Sully a full ten minutes to sweep the large villa before he could deem it as clean.

Sully returned to Zoe outside and stated "as far as I can tell it's clean." He smiled genuinely at her now, knowing they were on their first assignment together, and were finally alone.

Before Zoe could even respond Sully swept her up into his well-built arms and carried her into the villa. He kicked the door closed behind them and carried her straight to the bedroom. He set her gently down on the humongous bed and said to her "I hate to be so cliché, but I wanted to carry you across the threshold on our first "married" assignment."

Zoe pulled him onto the bed beside her, rolled over on top of him, and straddled him. She looked deeply into his eyes and lovingly asked "how did you get to be the sweetest man in the world?"

Sully playfully said "I've had years of practice with lots of other women." And then he laughed.

Zoe fell down on top of him a tried her best to be serious, and looking him squarely in the eyes she said "I want names."

They laughed together, and the tension had been dissolved. A night of lovemaking ensued, and they both felt as if they had found a love that would last a lifetime.

It had been prearranged, by the SSO, for them to meet Ben and Jan Dallman the day after they landed for brunch at the resort at ten thirty.

Brian and Trish, at least for this mission, had overslept and were running more than fashionably late.

They arrived at the entrance to the main dining room at five minutes to eleven. When Zoe asked the hostess for the Dallmans' table they were led across the room to a large table overlooking the water.

Luckily the Dallmans hadn't ordered yet, and Ben Dallman stood up and offered his hand to Sully/Brian. Sully/Brian shook his hand as Ben said "sorry we were so late, I thought you might have given up on us." He said with a grin.

The Dallmans were both in their early forties and in reasonably good shape. Ben had a small gut, and Jan could stand to lose a few pounds. They seemed nice enough, but Sully couldn't wait to get them in the sights of his sniper rifle.

Sully/Brian didn't skip a beat, and conveniently lied as he said "not a problem at all Ben, we took the time to browse the resort's gift shop, and I got to watch Trish spend a lot of money." He laughed a big fake laugh and Ben joined in.

Ben said "my broker said we should get together and "do lunch" sometime, then he said you were going to be here in Monaco, so I thought what the heck."

Sully/Brian was getting his use out of his studying of the dossier when he replied "yeah, I've golfed with Steve a few times, he said the same to me, and here we are." Sully had never touched a golf club in his life, and had no idea who Steve was.

Sully/Brian nodded at Jan and said "I am truly sorry, this is my beautiful wife Trish, and I am Brian Nelson."

Zoe/Trish interrupted him with "he thinks the "beautiful" part will make me forget what he said about my spending money." She said it with a smile that would have engaged anyone.

They all laughed together, and Ben said "meet my beautiful wife Jan." They all started laughing again.

Sully was very pleased, it had taken them all of fifteen seconds to disarm and befriend the Dallmans. Zoe was truly an asset on this mission and it had showed already.

The brunch was wonderful and full service would be an understatement. Omelets were made to order table side, the prime rib was cut to order, and crepes of any want were available. It was apparent to Sully that if he wasn't careful, he would gain twenty pounds on this mission.

Sully was thinking of a way to approach Ben about his earnings, when Ben said "so what is it that you do for a living Brian?"

Sully/Brian said "Trish and I are investors, mostly pharmaceuticals, but we are open to anything with a high rate of return. He wanted to ask Ben the same question, but checked himself. They had plenty of time to get the information they needed. There was no need to rush things.

Zoe/Trish was selling her role and said "we got in on the ground floor of Viagra, and could have retired on that return alone. Brian was smart enough to get a lifetime two percent profit share" she was sipping on her umbrella drink as she said this.

Jan Dallman laughed and said "I've never had brunch before with a couple who made their fortune in dick drugs"

They all laughed again.

Ben took the lead now and said "after brunch we are all going to Ajaccio on my yacht."

Zoe/Trish said "oh no, there is no way we could impose on you for a trip like that." Zoe was in full character and doing it perfectly.

Sully/Brian said "as much as I hate to say it, Trish is right, we couldn't impose."

Jan Dallman jumped in and said "nonsense, what good is gobs of money if you can't show it off to new friends."

Ben Dallman followed up with "we won't take no for an answer, and besides, the boat leaves in two hours. So let's finish up here and you guys can go get into some sea togs, and pack for a wonderful, overnight adventure." Ben was smiling like a used car salesman as he said this.

Zoe/Trish said "I guess it's no use fighting honey, I think it sounds like fun." She winked at Sully.

Jan said "that's the spirit Trish, let's go have some fun!"

Sully/Brian acted like he was finally relenting and let out a heavy sigh before he said "as long as you are sure we aren't imposing, we're in."

Ben said "great, then it's settled, we cast off in two hours." He was smiling at the prospect of new friends.

If he only knew that the "Nelsons" were here to kill him and his wife.

Sully noticed that when Zoe was in character as Trish she had dropped the West Virginian accent that he loved. He thought it was a risky move. Something like that could easily trip her up and expose them.

Sully hailed a resort golf cart for a ride back to their villa. On the ride he called Julian on his cell phone and told him what was going on.

Julian said "not a problem Sir, I will have you packed and ready in fifteen minutes, and I will lay out a change of clothes for you both."

Sully said "thank you Julian, and by the way, find out where the hell Ajaccio is." and ended the call. Sully was getting more and more impressed with the efficiency of the SSO.

When they got back to their villa Julian was just finishing laying out their clothes.

Julian said "you're all set here, I will back in a few minutes with your bags, and Ajaccio is a small resort town on the Italian island of Corsica." Julian had been given his own villa on the resort property and they had loaded it with all of Sully and Zoe's gear.

Sully said "thanks Julian" and had to suppress the urge to tip him as he left.

When they were finally alone he turned to Zoe and said "you were awesome!" He walked to her and gave her a hug.

When their embrace ended Zoe said "me, you were perfect, are you sure this is your first mission?" She was beaming at him.

Sully grabbed her again and kissed her deeply, then whispered "I could tell you, but then I'd have to kill you, so no comment." Sully had a wry grin on his face.

Zoe laughed, and it was like a symphony to Sully's ears whenever she did.

Sully and Zoe talked strategy about the mission for an hour. They finally decided that the best plan to get the financial information they needed was for Zoe to hang close to Jan and marvel at all of the luxuries of the Dallmans yacht, then try to get some information out of her.

They decided that Sully should be casual with Ben for the time being so it didn't seem like they were there to get information out of them.

After Julian came back with their bags, they dressed into their boating attire.

Zoe was dressed in a short white silk Nicole Miller skirt, light pink Fendi flats, and a matching Nicole Miller pink and white floral print blouse.

Sully said "you look incredible Zoe." And she did.

Sully had on weaved leather Dior sandals, a way over the top Tommy Bahama print short sleeved silk shirt, and light cotton Tommy Bahama pants with a matching jacket that he had slung over his right shoulder. To top off the look he was wearing a Tommy Bahama cabana hat with a band to match the silly shirt. He felt ridiculous.

Zoe looked at him fully dressed, suppressed a giggle, and said "If that was the look you were going for, you sure nailed it."

Sully looked at the floor shook his head and said "I look like an idiot." And he did.

Zoe walked over to him and rubbed his right shoulder saying in a motherly voice "awww poor baby looks stupid."

They both laughed uncontrollably for a minute.

As they walked to the door to leave Zoe stopped and said "would you promise me one thing?"

Sully turned to her and said very seriously "of course, anything, you should know that by now."

Zoe smiled and said "promise to sing Copacabana to me in that get-up sometime."

They were both laughing again as Sully said "I promise."

The Dallmans yacht was spectacular, Sully couldn't even begin to guess how much it cost. The yacht was at least sixty feet long and had a crew of seven. Everything they saw was perfection.

The Dallmans were waiting for them on the front deck, and a steward guided them to it.

Their bags had been taken from them and delivered to their state room. Sully was praying that the crew was reliable, because both his and Zoe's bag contained a silenced nine millimeter Berretta.

When they reached the front deck of "Jan's Folly" the Dallmans were already comfy and sunning themselves. Jan Dallman apparently didn't want tan lines. She had a light robe next to her upholstered deck chair, and it must have been her cycle to tan the front of her body. Sully thought she must have been a good girl, because Santa had bought her some of the biggest breast implants he had ever seen.

Ben was on an identical chair on his stomach wearing only a waaay to small yellow Speedo.

The sight of both of them was justification enough to kill them, Sully thought.

The steward that had led them to the front deck announced their presence. He said "Mr. and Mrs. Dallman, the Nelsons are here."

Jan jumped up and grabbed her robe to cover herself, Ben on the other hand simply stood up and walked over to them.

Ben came over and shook Sully's hand. He said "welcome aboard Brian, but I gotta tell you that we don't have a stage on this boat so if you are planning to perform, you will have to settle for the dining room.

Again Sully/Brian looked at his shoes and shook his head.

Zoe/Trish jumped in and said "awe come on, I think he looks cute." Laughing as she said it.

She continued with "excuse me boys, but I am going over to Jan. It's a little too loud here standing here next to Brian.

Ben was laughing and Sully said "that's it, last straw!" he threw his jacket on the deck, stripped out of the stupid shirt, stuffed it in the ridiculous hat, and threw them overboard. He put the jacket on and remained bare chested, and he definitely had the build to pull it off.

They all laughed, and the planned ice breaker had worked to perfection.

Zoe/Trish went to Jan Dallman and said "why would you try to cover up that beautiful body? I always wanted breasts as big as yours." Zoe/Trish could feel the bile rising in her throat as she said it, but she smiled and tried to look sincere.

Jan closed the distance to her and said softly "your breasts are the absolute perfect size for your body, and to tell you the truth, these bad boys only cost me one blow job." Then she laughed loudly, juggling her breasts.

Ben said to Sully/Brian they look like they will be okay with one another, let's go do some man stuff.

The yacht was underway and just leaving the harbor when Ben shouted "Matt!"

Matt was a small Spaniard, almost a dwarf, with a pushed in face, a severe hair lip, one eye, and a noticeable limp. Sully thought he would be a shoe-in if there was ever a casting call for a Hispanic Quasimodo.

Matt said "si senor Dallman" from the upper deck.

Ben said to Matt "tell Juan that we are going to the back deck to shoot trap." He continued to Sully/Brian "I found poor little Matt being beaten in an alley in Madrid. Jan said we should try to help his sorry little ass, so I paid his hospital bill and gave him a job.

Matt yelled down from the upper deck "si senor Dallman, Juan will be ready for you."

Ben said to Matt again "and Matt, find a large tee shirt for my guest, his shirt seems to have fallen overboard."

Again the diminutive Matt said "si senor Dallman."

Meanwhile Jan was giving Zoe/Trish a tour of the yacht. Jan stopped constantly to point out expensive items she had bought, how much they cost, and where she had purchased them.

Zoe/Trish was getting bored and irritated by her bragging, but played along smiling and acting fascinated by her silly belongings. Zoe thought that she was really going to enjoy killing her.

Suddenly a gunshot rang out and Zoe/Trish crouched into a fighting position. Jan laughed at her and said "honey don't fret, it's just the boys playing with guns.

Juan had given him a bright orange tee shirt still wrapped in plastic, Sully/Brian took his jacket off and started to slip it on when he noticed that it was emblazoned with "Jan's Folly" across the front in black. He put it on anyway.

Ben was in his element, he had a three thousand dollar over and under Bennelli shot gun and was showing Sully/Brian hot to shoot clay pigeons. He looked absurd in a light brown Cabelas trap vest and the Speedo. Sully almost drooled at the thought of killing this blowhard. Instead he smiled and said "wow Ben you are a really good shot."

Ben said condescendingly "want to try, it's easy."

Sully/Brian said "no thanks, guns scare me." If he only knew Sully thought.

Ben laughed at him and said "have it your way Alice" He turned and yelled "pull." Two clay pigeons were thrown and he missed them both. As he was reloading Sully thought oh yeah I'm gonna enjoy killing this guy without a doubt.

Zoe/Trish and Jan had changed into bathing suits and were chatting by the pool when the men found them.

Zoe greeted him by coming over and holding him tightly and giving him a big kiss. Sully thought thank god she held me, because his knees went weak when he saw her in a small, lime green Chanel bikini that made her eyes look perfect, with a sheer white cover up. Sully was starting to doubt whether or not he was worthy of this goddess and her love.

He whispered to her "you look amazing Zoe." And she did.

Sully/Brian went to change into swim attire and said he would be back shortly.

Zoe/Trish took the opportunity to work on getting information from Jan. Zoe/Trish said "Jan this yacht is absolutely wonderful, and I love everything you've done with it. Brian and I are doing very well, but I don't think we will ever come close to having something like this."

Jan responded "Thank you Trish, and I can tell you that it takes a lot of risk to get this kind of reward."

They had both been lying on their backs, but now Zoe/Trish half sat up and leaned toward her on one elbow. She asked "what kind of risk?"

Jan said "we learned a long time ago that weapons were the way to go. We can buy one thousand AK-47's for around five thousand dollars, and the return is about five hundred percent. Besides, the kickbacks from the competing buyers is sometimes more than what we make off of the sale." She said it as if she were selling glassware.

Zoe/Trish said with a tone of fear in her voice "isn't it dangerous?"

Jan said "oh no dear we are just the money people, we have loads of people who do the dangerous stuff."

Zoe/Trish didn't want to push it too far right now, so she changed the subject and said to Jan "What is the best poolside drink we could have right now?"

Jan sat up and said "hmmm let me think." And a moment later she said loudly "Javier, a pitcher of Pina Colada's for me and the lady!"

As the girls drinks arrived, so did Sully/Brian ready to take a quick swim before the sun went down. Ben walked over to Jan's chair and took her drink, after he did he said "mmm Pina Colada's, want one Brian?"

Sully/Brian had walked over to Zoe/Trish, and while blowhard Ben was stealing his wife's drink had given her a light kiss.

Sully said "no thanks, but I will have a Dos Equis dark if you got one."

Ben yelled "Javier, bring a glass for my wife and a Dos Equis dark for Brian!"

Sully/Brian and Ben sat at a small table facing the girls, and Jan's glass and Sully/Brian's drinks arrived within thirty seconds. After Javier filled both Jan's new glass and Zoe/Trish's, Ben raised his stolen glass and said "a toast, to new friends." They all raised their glasses and then took a drink.

Sully/Brian looked at Zoe/Trish and said "I never knew you liked Pina Coladas, do you like getting caught in the rain?" Sully/Brian smiled broadly as he said it.

There was a collective groan, and Jan said "that line was almost as bad as the shirt you wore when you came aboard." She said it with an emphasis on the almost.

They all laughed.

When Sully and Zoe got back to their state room to prepare for dinner, Zoe put a finger to her lips and quickly swept the small room again for recording devices. Sully watched her bending and stretching to look for signals in the small bikini and was very aroused. He hadn't bothered to tell her that he had done the sweep himself when he came to change into his swim trunks.

When she came back to him she said "I am pretty sure it's clean" and gave him a hug. She backed away a little and pointed to his swim trunks and said "what's that?"

Sully said "I would have to be ninety years old and dead for three months not to get aroused by you looking for bugs in that bikini."

Zoe said "want to take a shower with me handsome?" she was untying the top of her bikini as she said it.

Sully said "did you really think you had to ask?"

Zoe grabbed his hand and led him to the small bathroom. She said "and by the way, I'm not into health food, I am into champagne." She laughed at him and said "The Pina Colada song, you really need to update your act Mills."

Sully laughed also and said "give me a break Zoe, everyone thought it was cute."

They contributed to saving the ships water supply by squeezing into the small shower stall together. They made love awkwardly in the close quarters, but it was still satisfying for both of them.

As they dressed for dinner Sully walked up behind Zoe grabbed her around the waist and said "wherever you go, whatever you do, don't ever get rid of the bikini you were wearing today."

Zoe turned and kissed him on the nose and said seriously "do you think I need bigger boobs?"

Sully said "let me see them again and I will tell you" he was smiling and so was she.

Zoe, who was only wrapped in a towel, said "if I do that we will be late for dinner, Cowboy, and you know it." She turned and continued drying her hair.

Dinner was served in the main dining room. Sully and Zoe had been told to dress casually.

Sully, without Julian's help thankfully, was dressed in tan Dockers, an off white Polo, and his weaved leather Dior sandals.

Zoe wore a simple off white Chanel dress with black Fendi high heels.

The Dallmans were dressed similarly. As they walked in, Jan, who obviously needed something to eat said with a slight slur "hi guys, ready for dinner?"

Sully/Brian thought why the hell else would we be here, but instead politely said "yes we are both hungry, and something smells good."

Ben said "I took the liberty of having the chef prepare his specialty, seafood paella. I hope neither of you are allergic to shellfish." Ben almost sounded like a gracious host.

Zoe/Trish said glowingly "of course not, that sounds wonderful."

Sully knew Zoe was as well trained as he was, but couldn't help himself from being proud of her, she was utter perfection.

Ben said "great, you'll love it, it truly is wonderful. When dinner arrives we all need to pair it with the Shiraz I picked out."

Matt, the troll, came out of the kitchen wearing a cheap white waiter's tuxedo carrying a tray containing four large shrimp cocktails. He very carefully handed them out and then said directly to Ben "what will everyone have to drink Sir?"

Ben who clearly thought he was in charge said "let's have pink ladies for the ladies, and the men will have two bottles of Dos Equis dark."

Matt said "very good Sir" and turned to go.

Sully/Brian had finally had enough of Ben calling the shots and said "wait one second Matt, Trish what would you like to drink?"

Zoe/Trish said "actually I would like a glass of Chablis"

Sully/Brian said "fine Trish, Matt the lady will have a glass of Chablis, and I will have a double scotch rocks, with a Heineken chaser." He thought fuck it if I have to be with this asshole for two days I am not going to let him run the whole show.

Ben said "sorry to have offended you Brian, I just thought you would be comfortable with me placing the drink orders for us."

A drunken Jan slurred "bravo Brian, it's about time someone stood up to him." After she said it she shrunk into her seat like a four year old in trouble.

Sully/Brian stood from the table and said "sorry if I have offended you Ben, and I am especially sorry to you Jan, but I can call for a helicopter pickup as soon as we reach Ajaccio." He and Zoe had planned this move carefully, and he hoped like hell it was going to work.

Ben had a shocked look on his face, and said "sit down Brian, it's been a long time since I've been bawled out like that, and apparently it's been long overdue."

Sully/Brian didn't sit but stood his ground and said "Ben I like you, and I appreciate your hospitality, and I know you could buy and sell me without losing sleep, but Trish and I have spent the whole day with both of you and by now you should know that we aren't children or some of your lackeys. If you aren't ready to show us a little respect, we are ready to leave."

Sully/Brian stood and waited for a response.

After a long pause Ben finally said "point taken Brian, It was rude of me to order dinner and drinks for the both of you. I can have the chef make anything you would like. I am sorry."

Sully/Brian sat down with a scowl on his face and didn't say a word.

Zoe/Trish jumped in and said "I'm excited about the paella, it sounds wonderful, and the Shiraz sounds like a great pairing."

Jan slurred "that's the spirit Trish let's make lemons out of lemonade."

Ben screamed toward the galley "make that a virgin pink lady!"

The dinner was very tense, the food and service were great, but the conversation was cordial at best.

As soon as the dessert plates were cleared Zoe/Trish stood and said "thank you for a wonderful day" coldly.

Sully/Brian, who hadn't uttered a word during dinner, simply stood and nodded toward them.

Sully and Zoe went back to their room without saying a word.

When the door was closed behind them Sully said quietly to Zoe "I think it's best if we whisper, I think these walls are pretty thin."

Zoe's face flushed with embarrassment because of the way she usually yelled and moaned loudly when she and Sully made love.

Sully grabbed her and whispered "you were great Trish."

Zoe caught on and after she kissed him whispered "you were pretty damn good yourself Brian, I think Ben will treat you as an equal going forward." She was smiling as Sully reached around her and unzipped her dress.

It was odd to Zoe that she felt as if she knew this man all of her life, and trusted him implicitly. She had never trusted any one before.

Sully whispered "I think at the very least Ben will show us a little more respect tomorrow." He slowly slid Zoe's dress off and to the floor.

Zoe pulled his shirt over his head, kissed his bare chest, and said softly "would you still love me if my body looked like Jan's?"

Sully was unlatching her bra as he said quietly in his best redneck impression "long as you get you them big old store bought titties I'll foller you around like a lovesick hound dog."

They both laughed quietly as Zoe unzipped Sully's pants and slid them and his underwear to the floor.

After Sully kicked his shoes off and stepped out of the pants pile, they moved in unison toward the bed as they were kissing one another ravenously.

Sully sat her on the bed and softly said "I think we are one hell of a team Zoe" as he gently slid off her lace panties.

A minute later, Zoe looked up at him after taking his fully erect penis out of her mouth, and said "just tell me you Love me"

Sully pulled her to her feet, picked her up, and laid her down gently onto the bed. He was between her legs when he looked up at her and said "my turn, lie back and relax my love"

Zoe had never had oral sex before, and she did relax and let herself enjoy every second of it, she put a pillow over her face to muffle her moans and screams of ecstasy. After Zoe had climaxed several times, she pulled Sully up to her face and said "please make love to me now." And he complied with her request enthusiastically. When she kissed him deeply during their lovemaking, Zoe could taste the musky fluid of her most private part on Sully's lips and tongue. She was pleasantly surprised to discover that she loved it.

They were so sexually compatible it scared Sully. He thought "how have I fallen so deeply in love so quickly, and why would this perfect woman love me back"?

They fell asleep in each other's arms smiling contently.

When Zoe awoke early the next morning she looked out of the porthole and saw land. She dove onto the bed to wake Sully up. She said "time to wake up sleepy head, we've arrived to Corsica."

Sully opened his eyes and gave her a big yawn in response. He said "good for Corsica", rolled over and closed his eyes.

Zoe jumped on top of him and teasingly tried to tickle his ribs.

Sully didn't even open his eyes and said "Zoe I am not ticklish, and right now you are starting to piss me off."

Zoe laughed, kissed him on the shoulder, and said "my, aren't we the grumpy Gus" she pinched his ass really hard and jumped off the bed.

Sully sat up and yelled "Ouch, god dammit Zoe that hurt!" He was definitely awake now.

Zoe was naked, and in a fighting stance and said "what are you gonna do about it big boy?" she had a big playful smile on her face.

Sully had a furious look on his face and was rubbing his ass where Zoe had pinched him. He shook his head in disgust, and said "great, I have fallen head over heels in love with a damned morning person." He tried to be mad at her, but smiled and lightly laughed at her silly naked fighting stance he continued with "and a naked ninja to boot."

Zoe laughed cheerfully, jumped back onto the bed, took over rubbing his ass, and said in a mommy voice "did I hurt the little baby?" smiling at him.

Sully pouted and said "yeah you did, I'm gonna have a huge bruise."

Zoe smiled and sarcastically said "well then I guess you will have to put off that photo shoot for Playgirl for a while" and she giggled.

Sully laughed and grabbed her into a bear hug style embrace. He whispered in her ear "I'm not sure, but I don't think that this is the way that Government assassins usually act."

Sully tried to give her a kiss. Zoe pulled away and said "yuck, go brush your teeth stinky."

They met the Dallmans for breakfast, as instructed, on the main floor front deck at eight. The deck had been set up with a large patio table covered with a white tablecloth, and an umbrella that was flapping in the light breeze. There was a large insulated coffee carafe, place settings for four, and a large fruit try on the tabletop.

Ben and Jan were already there. Ben was enamored with a laptop computer, reading online news, and drinking coffee. Jan had large dark Ray Ban sunglasses on to hide her weary, bloodshot eyes, and was feeding her hang over with a mimosa.

When they reached the table Zoe/Trish took the lead, smiled and said "good morning Dallman's" with an engaging lilt in her voice.

Ben slapped his laptop closed and swept his hand toward the beautiful coastline squarely in front of them and said "welcome to Corsica. Come sit down and have some coffee." He was trying too hard to put the confrontational dinner behind them.

Javier had popped out seemingly from nowhere and stood next to the table quietly.

Zoe/Trish poured herself a cup of coffee and sipped it.

Jan groggily said "would you like cream or sugar Trish?"

Zoe/Trish said very seriously "no thank you, I take my coffee like my men, hot and black."

Ben spewed coffee from his mouth, and they all laughed, and the tension had been broken.

Ben was still laughing, wiping his mouth as he said "Javier is here to take your breakfast order, anything you would like."

Of course Ben ordered first and said "Javier tell Manuel I would like eggs Benedict with the eggs lightly poached, the Canadian bacon blackened, the English muffins lightly toasted, the Hollandaise sauce made with lots of pepper added, served on the side, and I want an extra spicy bloody Mary with two stalks of freshly pickled asparagus served with the meal."

All Sully/Brian could do was drop his jaw at the longwinded complicated order and think "what a pompous asshole, I can't wait to kill this jerk off".

Jan Dallman, who was in no shape to make such a complicated order simply said "I'll have the same, but make my bloody Mary a triple and bring it now."

Sully/Brian thought "*guess Jan wants a little more hair of the dog that bit her*" as he nodded at Zoe/Trish to indicate that it was her turn to order.

Zoe/Trish politely said "Javier if you have it I would like a half of a grapefruit." It was her normal breakfast.

It was Sully/Brian's turn to order, and he said "just a large glass of milk for me Javier, but please bring it when everyone's food arrives. Right now I would like a bottle of water." He had Ray Ban Frog skins resting on his head, and now covered his eyes with them.

Jan said "no wonder you two are so trim and fit. You don't eat."

Sully/Brian gave kudos to Javier, even with blowhard Ben's complicated order Javier wrote nothing down, and when they were all done ordering he simply nodded and left for the galley.

As they were waiting for their breakfasts to arrive, Ben said "what I had planned for the day was that the ladies could go shopping in town, I have a limo waiting for them, and Brian and I could tour the town on the Vespas I just purchased."

Sully/Brian said "that sounds fine to me Ben, what do you think Trish?"

Zoe/Trish said "Brian have you ever heard me say no to shopping?" She was flashing a dazzling smile, and playing her part extremely well.

Jan said "great, it's settled then. Trish you are going to love the shops in Ajaccio." She seemed impressed that Brian had asked Trish for her opinion, something she had quite obviously never experienced.

Ben said "we have one more option. We can take the launch to shore, or I have four top of the line Sea Doo Jet Ski's that we could ride in to shore. We can change there in a small villa I have rented."

Zoe/Trish said "oh definitely the Jet Ski's for my vote. She was truly excited about the prospect, and it showed.

Sully/Brian said "the Jet Ski's sound good to me." He was only concerned that there was no way to bring any weapons with this format. He knew how well he had been trained to kill without armaments.

Jan who was extremely hung over said "I will guard our bags, and go with Juan in the launch."

Ben shook his head in his outwardly apparent disgust at his wife and said "it's settled then. You will have fun on the Jet Ski's Trish. We are anchored two miles out, and the porpoises will ride next to us the whole way."

Zoe/Trish excitedly said "this sounds wonderful." She was genuine when she said it.

Breakfast arrived, and they ate. Zoe/Trish enjoyed her grapefruit. Ben was dissatisfied with the preparation of his eggs, big surprise. Jan ate very little, but was on her third triple bloody Mary, and seemed to perk up a little with the booze. Sully/Brian was content to sip his milk and strategize.

They met later in the lowest level of the ship at the stern. They had all changed, packed day bags, and given them to Matt, the troll.

Zoe/Trish had once again donned the fabulous itty bitty green bikini, but wore a Lauren sleeveless peach colored Oxford over it.

Sully/Brian had on a pair of faded black Levi's board shorts, and a dark green short sleeved Hilfiger Henley. Ben and Jan were dressed similarly. Ben with red and white swim trunks and a red "Jan's Folly" tee shirt, and Jan in a Teal one piece, backless Speedo swimsuit with a dangerously low cut neckline, to show off her best assets, with a white cotton beach cover up.

The weather was perfect, middle seventies with a few scattered puffy clouds, and a soft sea breeze that smelled fresh.

Ben pushed a button and the back end of the boat opened. They were all standing on a gangway next to the machines. The yacht had an interior wet dock for all of the Jet Ski's, the launch, and room for much more. Juan drove the launch out in reverse, with all the bags aboard, and left. The Jet Skis were ready and waiting.

Jan had apparently changed her mind, or more likely had been bullied, and was going with them. They were all given Speedo life vests, and Gargoyle wrap-around sunglasses with elastic bands attached.

Manuel, the chef, was apparently doing double duty and instructed them on the use of the personal watercrafts.

The Jet Ski's had no reverse gear so they were individually pushed backward until they cleared the boat by Manuel with the aid of what appeared to be little more than a long broomstick. As they were instructed they floated in the Ligurian Sea until they were well clear of the yacht.

Sully/Brian hit the gas and was surprised at the power the Sea Doo had, he slowed down to get a feel for the craft and Zoe/Trish flew by him at full throttle. He thought "*alright, if that's how you want to play I'm game.*"

Sully/Brian pushed the thumb throttle all the way down and tried to catch her. He hunched down over the handlebars to be more aerodynamic, but it was no use. He knew he was eighty pounds heavier, and she had the advantage, as long as she didn't let off the throttle. And she didn't.

Zoe/Trish was having a blast on the watercraft. She was speeding across the water with porpoises leaping in and out of the water alongside of her, she thought "*four years ago you were in a dreary foster home in nowhere West Virginia with no hope of a future, now you are flying over the waves in the Ligurian Sea off the coast of Corsica, you found love with a wonderful man who seems to adore you. Way to go girl, I don't care if you have to kill a thousand people who deserve it, this is worth it, and you finally have a life*".

Sully/Brian had given up on catching Zoe/Trish, and slowed down with the intention of joining up with Ben and Jan. Before he could look over his shoulder to see where they were, they went whizzing past him. Sully/Brian thought "*damn, these things need rearview mirrors*".

Sully/Brian was comfortably in the rear, and even at full throttle he estimated at least fifteen minutes before they reached shore. He had a team of no less than six porpoises diving in and out of the water by his side as his wingmen. He thought "*four years ago you were in a dead end town in nowhere Arizona, now you are a trained Government assassin skipping across the waves off the coast of Corsica, chasing the incredible woman you love on a Jet Ski. What a change of fortune*".

They were close to shore and Zoe/Trish slowed down to let Sully/Brian catch up, when he did they both let off the throttle and coasted to a floating stop.

Zoe bent to her side as far as she could to kiss him, and he did the same.

Sully/Brian whispered "just stick to the plan" and winked at her.

Zoe/Trish softly said "I love you Sullivan Mills. Race you to shore." She immediately hit the throttle to full speed.

Sully/Brian laughed and knew he couldn't catch her so he went half throttle to shore looking at the stunning coastline of Corsica, and the anciently quaint town of Ajaccio.

When he got to shore they had all gotten off their Jet Ski's, and shed their life vests. He saw the launch and Juan to his left, the bags had already been unloaded from the launch and it was ready to head back to the yacht. Sully/Brian beached his watercraft and jumped off and shed his life vest all in one smooth motion.

Ben said "you have to let me know if there is a problem with that Jet Ski, and if there is I can have the yacht's engineer look at it.

Sully half smiled and said "the machine is just fine, I'm just slow I guess."

Jan laughed and said "we can't all go as fast as Trish. She must weigh all of ninety five pounds." Jan was apparently over her hang over and well on her way to another.

Zoe/Trish snickered and said "ninety five, don't I wish. It's more like." She paused for a long moment, then continued "well let's just say it's more than that."

There were two valets waiting for them, and they attached ropes to all four Jet Skis and then to the launch. As the launch left the Jet Skis followed in a single file line.

Ben chuckled and said "well that does it, we are officially castaways now."

Sully/Brian quickly grabbed Zoe/Trish around the waist and said "I got dibs on Ginger"

They all laughed.

Jan said "great I get stuck with Gilligan again." She looked at Ben and shook her head.

Ben said "Lovey please tell me you're not sleeping with Gilligan" in a really bad Thurston Howell impression.

Zoe/Trish said "I think that should close the book on this bad joke."

They all nodded in agreement and laughed.

Sully was scanning the coastline in awe of the scenery, and happened to look at the nearest beach house and saw Julian standing next to it. Julian tugged on his ear and Sully ran his fingers through his hair. Julian turned and walked away.

Sully knew that was the signal to call in right away, and the response signal he gave was that he understood.

Sully/Brian said "what's next on the agenda Ben?"

Ben said "I got this covered." He waved and arm over his head vigorously, and two sand rails raced toward them.

When the sand rails arrived in a matter of seconds, the drivers leapt out and loaded their bags and they all climbed into them. The men got in one, and the ladies into the other. Before the ladies sand rail left Zoe/Trish turned to Jan and asked "do you think it would be all right if I drove?"

Jan said "you are an inspiration Trish, yes I would love it if you drove."

Zoe/Trish went to the driver and said "move over Ace, you've been demoted to navigator." The driver did as he was told and climbed into the passenger seat. Zoe/Trish turned to him and said "where are we going?"

The former driver said in broken English "well we turn round, and we go south on beach for two mile and three quarters half."

Zoe/Trish said "sounds easy enough. Jan I think we all had better buckle up."

Jan said "don't worry about it Trish, the beach is pretty smooth as long as you stay close to the water, and I know the way."

Jan and "Ace" scrambled to put on their belts as Zoe/Trish did the same. Zoe/Trish hit the gas hard throwing sand at the other sand rail. She drove forward about one hundred yards as fast as the sand rail would go in that short distance, turned the steering wheel quickly to the left, and pushed the gas pedal to the floor. Zoe/Trish executed a perfect slide U-turn and roared back toward the other sand rail. When she got back to the "boys" she slammed on the brakes and executed a perfect slide stop and ended up within inches of them.

Ben almost had to jump out of the way. He said "holy shit! Who the hell is, oh Trish it's you driving that thing like a maniac."

Sully/Brian said "pretty fancy driving there honey. Like Mario Andretti in a light green bikini, only with way better tits."

They all laughed, including the drivers.

Zoe/Trish switched the engine off in the sand rail and said "Ben, want to race to the villa?" she really wanted to race Sully, but Ben was the host.

Ben's eyes smiled before his mouth as he said "really, are you serious?"

Zoe/Trish said "you bet your sweet ass Benny boy, and a hundred bucks says I whoop ya." She flashed a suggestive smile at Sully, not Ben, as she said it but no one could tell because she still had the dark Gargoyles on.

Ben was smiling broadly now and said "You're on little lady, just let me get this thing turned around." Ben almost threw his now former driver into the passenger seat.

Before Ben started his sand rail Zoe/Trish said "Ben, if you want a head start just let me know."

Ben put his sunglasses back on and said "same goes for you Trish." Then he said over his shoulder "better buckle up Brian this might end up being a wild ride."

Sully/Brian said to Ben while casually putting on the four point seat buckle "kick her ass for the way she embarrassed me on the Jet Ski's, and I'll kick in a hundred of my own." He knew Ben would be motivated by money, and he was.

Ben hit the gas and did almost the same slide turn that Zoe did. Sully was impressed. He slid to a stop within two inches of the second sand rail.

Zoe/Trish said "have your navigator count to ten silently, then yell go." Zoe/Trish said and continued with "don't worry Brian, if I get so far ahead I can't see you I'll stop and wait." And she smiled at him again.

Sully/Brian Said to Ben "let's make it a thousand from me to shut her up." He made sure to say it loudly enough so that Zoe could hear him.

Zoe/Trish turned to look at Sully/Brian and said with a shocked look on her face "honey are you betting against me?"

Sully/Brian simply said "yep!" and gave her a toothy grin.

Zoe/Trish turned to Jan and said "silly boys, when will they ever learn." They both laughed.

Jan chimed in and said "would you like a side bet Ben?" they were all having fun with the little race.

Ben said to Jan "who's your money on?"

Jan said "why Trish of course, I've seen your driving Ben." She was laughing as she said it and added "how does five thousand sound to you?"

Ben was flexing his bank account as he said "like chump change, but you're on." He revved his engine several times to signify that the betting window was now closed.

Ben turned to his former driver and quietly said "count, but only to five, when I say so then yell go." He nodded at Brian, and Sully nodded back. He was cheating to get a head start. Sully remembered clearly how comprehensive the SSO driver training he and Zoe had gone through, and Ben was going to need a head start.

Ben turned to Zoe/Trish and said "Ready Trish?" Ben said smugly thinking his plan was the advantage he needed.

Zoe/Trish simply nodded he head and flashed him a winning smile.

Ben nodded back at her and said "countdown starts now!"

They both revved their engines and at the count of five Ben's former driver yelled "GO!"

Zoe/Trish stomped the accelerator to the floor of the sand rail and said aloud "shit, Ben you cheating son of a bitch!" They were caught in a cloud of sand and exhaust and were already thirty feet behind.

Ben was laughing aloud as his trick had worked, and yelled over the roar of the said rail's engine "we've got this in the bag Brian!"

Sully thought don't be so sure asshole, but said loudly "give her hell Ben."

Ben was driving straight toward a small lifeguard platform and Sully could tell that his plan was to get as close to it has he could without hitting it. Ben's motive was to keep Trish behind him closely enough so that when he swerved to miss the platform she would have to brake to miss it. At these speeds it was going to be a tricky maneuver.

Zoe was closing the gap rapidly, and was going to pass him soon if the circumstances didn't change.

When Ben reached the tower Zoe was way too close to them.

Suddenly Sully felt something he had never felt before, he realized that he was afraid. Not for himself, but for Zoe. Sully's mind was racing almost as fast his heart. He thought "what if Zoe hits the platform she might get hurt, or even killed at this speed". He could not believe that he was truly frightened for the first time in his life.

Sully turned around to look at the other sand rail. Zoe was way too close. He only had a split second to think and act. Sully unbuckled his seatbelt and let himself "fall" out of the sand rail. He was hoping for the best at over fifty miles an hour. Sully felt himself roll five or six times and then the lights went out.

Zoe had just about caught up to Ben's sand rail and was planning her pass when luckily she saw Sully fall out. Visibility was almost zero being behind due to the amount of sand and dust that these machines kicked up.

Zoe/Trish screamed "oh my god!" She shoved the brake pedal to the floor and turned the steering wheel to the right as hard and fast as she could. She missed hitting him by only two feet. Zoe/Trish threw the sand rail into park, unbuckled her seat belt and leapt from the sand rail in virtually one motion. She ran to Sully/Brian and dropped to his side. He was motionless.

Ben had no idea he was missing a passenger even after he saw the other sand rail come to a quick stop. Ben laughed and said loudly "see Brian, it worked!" Ben continued for another mile until he looked at his back seat to find that Brian was gone.

Zoe/Trish's years of training paid off greatly in this situation where most people would have panicked. She lightly pressed on his chest shouting "Brian, Brian!" Zoe/Trish had remembered both her medical training, and her cover story.

Jan had finally exited the vehicle, ran over to Trish and the twisted heap of a human that was Brian. Jan said "Oh my God, Trish is he all right?"

Zoe/Trish ignored her. She continued yelling to him and thought *"please God don't take this wonderful man away from me. How dare you finally give me love and then snatch it away from me you son of a bitch, haven't I suffered enough to suit you*" She wasn't even aware that tears were streaming down her face. Zoe/Trish started pounding on his chest with her fists now screaming his fake name over and over.

Sully/Brian coughed twice, then he blinked several times and when the darkness turned to bright light he said weakly "am I dead?"

Zoe/Trish collapsed onto his chest and said "no, no you're not Brian, but I thought you might be, you jerk." She was fully crying now.

Sully/Brian said "I thought I was, when I saw an angel kneeling over me in a fabulous little green bikini. I'm sorry I broke my promise honey." He put his arms around her and held her as she sobbed. Sully took a personal inventory and thought that, other than a massive headache, he was okay. He stroked Zoe's hair and said "I'm fine Trish, please don't cry" He called her Trish so that she knew he was mentally okay.

Jan had been clutching her heart at the tender moment. She finally said "what the heck happened Brian?"

Sully/Brian sat up and shook some of the sand out of his hair before he said "I couldn't see out of the back of the sand rail because of the sand and dust it was kicking up, so I unbuckled and leaned out to see where you guys were, next thing I knew there was an angel in a green bikini kneeling over me."

Zoe/Trish threw her arms around him and gave him a huge hug. She said "please don't scare me like that you creep."

Sully/Brian hugged her back a little too tightly and whispered in her ear "I'll tell you what really happened later please don't cry Zoe."

They broke their embrace and both of them stood up, Sully/Brian a whole lot more slowly than Zoe/Trish. Zoe/Trish's former driver came over and gave him a bottle of water.

Sully/Brian said "Thank you, I'm sorry, I never got your name."

He said in a thick Italian accent "They call me Cheeto, and my brother over there is called Chago. You are very welcome for the water Sir." He had pointed toward the other driver when identifying his Brother.

Sully/Brian said "well then thank you Cheeto." He took a long drink of water, then handed the bottle to Zoe/Trish.

All four of them climbed into the sand rail. Zoe/Trish and Sully/Brian were in the back, and Jan and Cheeto were in front with Cheeto driving. They all took extra care in buckling their seat belts. They had just started back toward the villa when the other sand rail showed up.

Ben said “what the hell happened?”

Jan was fuming at him and said “obviously nothing you cared too much about. You almost killed Brian you asshole!”

They arrived at the Dallman’s rented Corsican villa just after noon. Cheeto said “wait here, I will go get the Polaris, and Chago will ferry you all up to the house with your bags.” Cheeto jogged up the asphalt path toward the huge villa with his older brother Chago right behind him.

Ben turned to Sully/Brian, who was the only one seated, and said “what happened Brian?”

Jan, who was still fuming, said “he fell out of the fucking sand buggy and you just kept going, that’s what happened you buffoon.” She stormed off up the path towards the villa.

Sully/Brian jumped in and said “Ben don’t sweat it, it was my fault, I couldn’t see the girls, so I unbuckled my seatbelt and leaned out to try to see how far behind they were, and fell out. Simple as that Ben, you didn’t do anything wrong.” Sully/Brian stood gingerly and continued saying “maybe you should go after Jan and tell her what I just told you before she explodes.”

Ben said “good idea buddy, Chago will be back in a couple of minutes for you and the bags.” He started running up the asphalt path and yelled “Jan please wait up for me, we need to talk!”

When they were alone Zoe went to Sully and hugged him hard and started to cry again. She said through tears “what really happened, I doubt you just fell out?”

Sully said “later, Julian is here and I need my cell phone. He gave me a signal to call in, so we had better right away.”

Zoe found Sully’s cell phone quickly and he powered it up, he pushed and held two to speed dial the SSO. The phone connected, Sully gave his code, and it immediately rang again. Weathers picked up on the first ring and said “Mills I need an update.” He sounded surly and Sully didn’t like it.

Sully said “yes Sir, but it has to be fast until later.” He motioned to Zoe to come over, and tipped the phone away from his ear so they both could participate in the call, he wasn't confident enough right now to put it into speakerphone mode.

Weathers said "fine Sully, tell me how it's going." He didn't sound happy at all.

Sully said "agent Millstad has been trying to get the Intel you wanted from the female target, and she has found out that the bulk of the money the Dallmans make is from arms dealing. I think we have a good shot this afternoon to both get much more, Sir."

Weathers said "good work so far we suspected that, but this is the first confirmation. The sanction has been changed to an A.S.A.P. situation by the SOD, so get it done. You have thirty hours. I want a call as soon as possible when you get back to Monaco.

Sully said "yes Sir." And the phone disconnected.

Zoe said "are you sure you are alright Sully?" She had wiped the tears from her face but still looked very concerned.

Sully grabbed Zoe, kissed her deeply and said "as long as I have you I'm perfect."

They finished their embrace when Chago returned with the Polaris Ranger to take them to the villa. He loaded the bags into the back, and they rode with him up to the house.

The villa was beautiful. Done tastefully in a Tuscan theme and fit perfectly for the Corsican setting. It literally looked like it was worth millions.

When Chago stopped the ranger as close to the front door as he could, Zoe/Trish jumped out and said "this is a wonderful place."

Chago politely said "please don't worry about the bags, Cheeto has been told to which rooms they go, and will handle them with much carefulness."

Sully/Brian said "Thank you Chago, make sure that you and Cheeto see me later for a big tip."

Zoe/Trish began to walk toward the front door and Sully/Brian was hypnotized by the sight. Sully/Brian said "come here once."

Zoe/Trish turned, walked back to him and said "what?" with a smile on her face.

Sully/Brian said "nothing, you looked so good walking away, I wanted to see it again." He pulled her close and squeezed her butt as he kissed her. Then he said "I don't think God ever made a more beautiful ass, and trust me I know because I have studied them all." He said it with a loving smile on his face.

Zoe/Trish smiled and said "if you hadn't fallen out of a sand buggy half an hour ago, you know I would slap you silly, don't you"

Sully/Brian looked at the ground and said "yes dear, I was counting on that."

They were both laughing when Zoe said "come on, let's go take a shower together and change."

Sully/Brian said "that sounds really good." Sully's eyes were drooping since the adrenalin had worn off.

Zoe/Trish walked to the front door again purposely swinging her ass wildly. She was close to the door when Sully/Brian whistled at her. She went inside with a humongous smile on her face.

Sully/Brian got off the seat of the Ranger, and almost went to his knees in pain. He had purposely let Zoe go into the villa first so he could limp a few steps to loosen up. After he got a few steps under his belt he was able to walk somewhat normally, but stiffly.

He found everyone at the kitchen counter, he was guided by blowhard Ben's voice. When he had gotten his phone out of his bag earlier he had grabbed his roll of SSO cash, counted out fifteen hundred dollars, and put it in his pocket.

When he reached the group he cheerfully said "hey, what did I miss?" He was ready to collapse from the pain, but he managed a half smile.

Ben and Jan had apparently patched things up, and Jan said "are you sure you're okay Brian?" She sounded truly concerned.

Sully said "I'm fine Jan, just a little sore, and besides a triple scotch rocks, I could use some aspirin and a shower. He walked stiffly over to Ben and took one thousand dollars out of his pocket. He slapped it down on the table in front of him, smiled and said "right or wrong, you won Ben."

Cheeto had changed into a white suit and when he heard Sully/Brian's order it was there in twenty seconds. Cheeto came over with a silver tray with his drink and a bottle of aspirin.

Sully/Brian opened the bottle and shook out six aspirin. He popped them in his mouth and drank them down with the scotch in one drink. He said if someone could show me where, I'd like to take a shower.

Chago showed up seemingly out of nowhere, and said "please follow me Sir."

Sully/Brian said simply "thanks for the drink." He turned and followed Chago to his room.

Zoe/Trish said "please excuse me", and left with Sully/Brian. She seemed very concerned about Sully/Brian.

When they got to their suite Sully/Brian gave Chago a one hundred dollar bill. He said "split that with Cheeto."

Zoe was in the bathroom getting the shower warm and he went in to be with her.

The large bathroom had a stall shower and an oversized tub with jets. Sully went to the tub, sat on the edge, and turned the faucet on to get it really hot. When the water was scalding he pulled up the lever to close the drain. As the tub filled he said to Zoe "please turn that shower off and come here."

Zoe immediately turned off the shower and crossed the room to sit next to him. He whispered in her ear "you need to sweep the room, the frequency detector is in my bag."

Zoe quickly and efficiently swept their suite. She came back to him minutes later and said "it's clean Sully, are you sure you are okay?"

Sully pulled his tee shirt painfully over his head and said "I'll be fine after a good soak, especially if you join me." He winked at her and found that even that hurt.

The jet tub was surrounded by mirrors that were purposely made to look old and Zoe could see what Sully felt. Zoe covered her mouth, and tried to mask her look of horror and her eyes welled up with tears. She said "oh my God Sully your back is one giant bruise."

Sully said "well then it looks like it feels. I kind of bounced of some rocks when I dove out of the sand rail, and I think I might have cracked a couple ribs, but I will be good as new after a soak with you. Did you see any bubble bath? I've never had a bubble bath." Sully was doing his best to lighten the mood.

Zoe ran to him crying and said "we have to get you to a hospital, you could have internal injuries."

Sully said "calm down, it's been almost two hours, if I had any internal injuries, I would already be dead."

Zoe had caught Sully's slip up and said "wait a second, you ""dove"" out of the sand rail? What does that mean?"

Sully knew he had fucked up and was hoping she had not noticed. He said "Ben was heading straight for that lifeguard tower and was going to swerve to make you brake, but you were so close I was afraid you would crash into it, or flip over, trying to avoid it at the last second, so I dove out to make you stop."

Zoe said quite loudly "what?, WHAT?, you jumped out of a sand rail going sixty miles an hour, and risked your life to save mine?"

Sully couldn't look at her so he looked at the floor. He said "please let me finish before you say or do anything." Sully continued, with a slight shakiness to his voice "Zoe, for the very first time in my life I got scared, really scared. I have never been afraid of anything in my life, ever. But today I was, I was afraid of losing you. I had a flash through my mind of life without you, and I didn't like it one bit. So I jumped out of the sand rail to try to help you. Now that I finally found you, I don't think that I could ever be happy without you."

Zoe just stared at him with her eyes full. After a long moment she blinked, and the tears began to flow. She said "I already thought you were wonderful, but I think you just elevated yourself to extra super wonderful. Are you done?"

Sully said lovingly "no Zoe Millstad, one more thing. I love you more than you could possibly imagine. More than I ever thought possible. Now I'm done."

Zoe rushed over to hold him, and they both fell into the tub with an awkward splash.

Sully tried not to, but winced from the pain. The he said "what, no bubbles?" It had been a poor attempt at trying to lighten the mood.

Zoe stood up in the tub and did a quick striptease, sexily taking her bikini off. She did a slow turn for him and then lay in the huge tub next to him. They kissed for a while, and then Zoe said "why not just call me Bubbles, then we can call this a Bubble bath."

Sully tried desperately not to wince in pain as he took his board shorts off, but he failed.

Zoe noticed and said "stop being such a hero and let me help you." Zoe slid off his shorts and underwear and left the tub to throw their wet clothes into the shower stall.

Sully said "come back over here Bubbles."

Zoe rushed to him, and they made love in the tub slowly and more carefully than they ever had.

When Sully was in too much pain to continue Zoe got out of the tub and covered herself with a towel.

Zoe said "I'm sorry, I got a little carried away, I hope I didn't hurt you.

Sully said "the pain will go away and I will forget it, but that was the best 'Bubble' bath I could have ever dreamed of having, and I will never forget it." Then he told her he loved her again.

They talked seriously about mission strategy for about ten minutes. As they talked Zoe dressed and Sully toweled off and gingerly laid down on the bed. Sully said "I think I'll try to take a nap." His eyelids were already drooping. He had found a bottle of Ibuprofen in the bathroom and had taken six.

Zoe said "Well you're certainly not going riding around town on any stupid Vespa with that asshole young man." Zoe said in a stern Motherly tone, wagging a finger at him, smiling.

Sully smiled and started to laugh, then his laugh quickly stopped and he grimaced in pain. He said "Zoe don't make me laugh, it hurts."

Zoe had a true look of concern on her face now and said "I think I should stay with you Sully."

Sully was shaking his head when he said "I wish you could Zoe, but we need to finish this mission. Don't worry about me I will be fine after a little nap. Just stick to the plan."

Zoe/Trish returned to the kitchen clean, refreshed, relaxed and sexually satisfied. Seeing only Ben there made her blood pressure rise and she wasn't quite as relaxed as she was moments ago.

Zoe/Trish walked up to Ben and asked "where is Jan?" She said it as coldly as an iceberg. She was especially cold to him now that she knew that this asshole's actions had caused Sully to hurt himself to help her.

Ben replied, looking squarely at her breasts "Jan went up to shower and change her clothes. You look nice Trish." His eyes never left her breasts.

Zoe/Trish was wearing a Hermes green and yellow peasant skirt, a white sleeveless Lauren blouse, a Hermes scarf that matched the skirt, tied loosely around her neck like a tie, and black Stewart Weitzman flats.

Zoe/Trish frostily said "thank you Ben, I think you should make different plans, because I'm not allowing Brian to go anywhere for the rest of the day. He would never admit it, but he is banged up badly because of you. So you can plan on just playing with yourself. I'm quite sure you can manage that easily"

Ben seemed pissed at being chastised, and started to leave, but stopped and said "what the hell do you mean because of me?" Ben was angry and trying to intimidate her.

Zoe/Trish was in no mood to be messed with and said "just how fucking stupid do you think I am Ben? Don't you think I saw the lifeguard platform you wanted me to crash into? Brian didn't fall out of your sand rail you fucking idiot he jumped out so your wife, that you care so much about, and I wouldn't get seriously injured or killed in a race that supposed to be fun you asshole!"

Zoe had planned this tirade with Sully, and went into her purse and pulled out the five thousand dollars she had counted out in their room. Zoe had rolled the fifty one hundred dollar bills and put a rubber band around them. She threw the roll at Ben's face and he ducked. She said "That's the five thousand your wife bet you, and I'm paying it because I might have killed her too because of your actions, you fucking jerk off."

Zoe/Trish had noticed that Jan was on the bottom stair halfway through her speech. Ben stooped to pick the money up and the asshole put it in his pocket and smiled at her. He turned to leave and saw Jan on the stairs.

Jan now had a furious look on her face and as Ben approached her he said "now what's your problem Jan?" He said it indignantly with emphasis on the "your".

Jan said "you don't even give a shit that you could have hurt or killed me, do you, you prick?" Jan was fuming, and her face was red with rage.

Ben just chuckled at her and tried to pass her to go up the stairs. Jan slapped him so hard it almost knocked him off of his feet.

Ben looked shocked that Jan had the nerve to slap him. He started to raise a hand to retaliate.

He heard a voice from behind Zoe/Trish say loudly "lay one finger on her and I'll beat the living shit out of you!" It was Sully/Brian who had heard the yelling and threw on only sweat pants, with his silenced Berretta tucked in the small of his back of course.

He had heard the last two minutes of Zoe's tirade from the hallway. Now he walked out and stood next to Zoe/Trish. Sully/Brian glared at Ben with a look that was virtually daring him to make a move.

Jan walked away from Ben and crossed the room to Zoe/Trish and Sully/Brian. The three of them stood as one facing Ben.

Jan said "don't go away mad, Ben, just go away." She was brave now that she had backup.

Ben, trying to save face, said "I'm going to the casino to spend your money Trish." Taking the roll out of his pocket and waving it at her.

Zoe/Trish said "money well spent if I don't have to look at you Ben." The stare she was giving him could have burned through lead.

Ben harrumphed and turned from the group and went up the stairs. When Ben was gone Jan threw her arms around Sully/Brian and gave him a great big hug.

Sully/Brian almost passed out from the pain the hug caused him. Zoe/Trish tried to stop her but was too slow. Zoe/Trish quickly pulled Jan off of him.

Sully/Brian was thankful that they were by the kitchen counter. If he hadn't been able to hold onto it he would have hit the floor.

Jan looked confused and said to Zoe/Trish "it was just a platonic thank you hug Trish."

Zoe/Trish said to Jan "look at his back, and you will understand. We think he may have a couple cracked ribs too." Zoe was very serious, and worried about Sully.

Jan looked at Sully/Brian's back and gasped. Her eyes were wide, and Zoe didn't think she was breathing until she said "oh my God, Brian I am so sorry." Jan started to cry and sobbed "you saved my life, and saved me from a beating, and I repay you by hurting you further."

They all heard the buzzing of a Vespa, and Sully saw Ben leaving on it through the window by the front door. It was time for him and Zoe to enact their plan, and for them both to cross their fingers.

Sully/Brian looked at Zoe/Trish, raised his eyebrows as if to say "now or never" and said "I can get you away from Ben permanently, and save your life for certain if you are willing to play ball." Sully/Brian knew they were taking a huge risk, but he thought she would work with them. If not he would shoot her in the head right here and now.

Sully/Brian said to Zoe/Trish "I need to make a phone call. You explain our position to Jan, and Trish don't let Ben near her, or me, kill him if you have to. Tell Jan what's going on. I'll be in our room." Sully/Brian half-limped, half-ran, down the hallway toward their room, and was lost from sight.

Jan chuckled uneasily, and said to Zoe/Trish "kill him, he was joking, right?" Jan had a pensive half smile on her face.

Zoe/Trish looked at Jan stone cold, and said with no emotion "no Jan he was completely serious. As hard as this is going to be for you to comprehend right now, you are going to have to try. Brian and I are Government agents and our current mission is to terminate Ben and Jan Dallman with extreme prejudice." Zoe waited for a reaction from Jan before she continued.

Jan looked like she had just seen her life flash before her, and didn't like the ending. Zoe would remember that look of true horror on a sanction's face for the rest of her life.

After she took in what Zoe/Trish had just said she opened her mouth as if she was going to try to speak, but nothing came out.

Zoe/Trish grabbed her arm firmly, maybe a little too much so, and said pleasantly "Why don't we go sit at the table before you fall down." Jan was shaking and Zoe/Trish held her arm as they moved to the table.

When Zoe/Trish sat her down Jan said shakily "you're gonna kill me?" She was afraid and it showed.

Zoe/Trish was back in agent mode and said coldly "Jan if we wanted to kill you, you would already be dead. Now we wait for Brian." She couldn't say any more to her without a tape recorder, and a witness.

When Sully got to their room he went into their bags and grabbed a light brown Eddie Bauer long sleeved Oxford, his and Zoe's silenced Berretta nine millimeter semi-automatic pistols, the shoulder holsters that fit them, black jeans, black socks, black tennis shoes, a dark green Lauren jacket for Zoe, and a dark blue Hilfiger wind breaker for himself.

He threw all of the gear onto the bed and pushed two on his cell phone and was connected to the SSO. He gave his code and when he was connected he said "get me Weathers fast no matter where he is. He was dressing frantically while he waited, and it hurt like hell, but he was fully dressed and ready by the time Weathers picked up.

Weathers wasn't happy when he picked up and said "This better be good Mills its zero three thirty here." Sully knew by the sound of his voice that he had roused him with this call.

Sully said "it is Sir, potentially very good. We have turned the woman and I think she will tell you anything you want in exchange for a deal. She is being detained by agent Millstad as we speak."

Weathers was awake now, and excited when he said "you better not be joking Mills."

Sully said "no Sir the male target has been abusing her and we pushed the situation to a head. I'm ninety nine percent sure that she will deal. I'm going after the male right now, consider him sanctioned."

Weathers said "I'm sending Julian and a helicopter as soon as we hang up to pick up agent Millstad and the woman. Call when your sanction is completed and I will arrange a pick up for you Mills. One last thing Sully, I don't care how you did it but this is the best possible job you two could have done." There was pride in his voice at his new agents coming through big.

Sully said "thank you Sir. Expect the same from us always Boss." Weathers Hung up.

Sully racked a round into the chamber of his Berretta, and ran back to the kitchen.

Zoe and Jan were at the table sipping tea when Sully got back to the kitchen. Sully was in a hurry to get after Ben, so he pulled no punches and made it quick.

He walked in briskly and handed Zoe her pistol and shoulder holster. Jan looked at him, and now he had a stone cold stare on his face. Before she could speak Sully said "Mrs. Dallman I need to make this quick, so pay attention, think carefully, and give me only clear concise answers. Do you understand me Mrs. Dallman?" Sully had the tape recorder / bug detector in his hand.

Jan meekly said "Yes Brian, I understand." She looked very confused as she said it.

Sully handed the recorder to Zoe and continued with "Mrs. Dallman, Trish and I are Government agents, and we are in a position to help you. If you cooperate with us and answer all the questions we ask you truthfully we can make sure that the Justice department will show you quite a bit of leniency. Do you understand me Mrs. Dallman?"

Jan was shaking now when she said "I always knew this day would come, yes I understand Brian, and I will cooperate. I have a detailed log book on the yacht that contains all of our contacts and transactions for the last seven years." When she finished she started crying.

Sully said "perfect Mrs. Dallman, you have helped us more than we could have hoped for." When Sully finished he made a throat slashing gesture to Zoe and she turned off the tape recorder.

Now off the record Sully said "Trish, Julian will be here with a chopper any minute to pick the both of you up. After you are on board tell him to land on the yacht's helipad so Jan can get a few things but make sure to get the journal and our bags, and get our gear from here when I leave."

Zoe said "can I talk to you in the hallway quickly?" She looked sad.

Sully said "as long as we can keep a pistol trained on Mrs. Dallman, I don't see why not." Sully was in a hurry to kill Ben and showed no emotion.

Before they both went to the hallway Sully said "Jan there is a motorcycle in the garage, do you know where the keys to it are, and how do I get to the casino?"

Jan said "yes, Brian they are hanging on a hook inside the door of the first cabinet to your right as you walk out, and just go left out of the driveway and the casino is about eight miles down on that road." Jan was wiping tears from her face as she said it.

Sully said "thank you for everything Jan." Sully and Zoe's went into the hallway. While he had been talking to Jan, Zoe had slipped into her Shoulder Holster and put the jacket on.

Sully whispered "this is not the way I wanted to leave you Zoe, but I will see you back at headquarters soon." He kissed her and turned to go.

Zoe grabbed him and said "be careful Sullivan, I think Ben could be dangerous, and remember you promised me you wouldn't make me cry." She kissed him deeply, then said I love you.

Sully said "I love you more." He smiled his most charming smile and left before she could respond.

Zoe went back to the kitchen to take Jan with her to get her and Sully's gear, change her clothes, and then go outside to wait for Julian, and the helicopter. When she got to the room Zoe went into the bathroom and grabbed the handcuffs she had kept in her make-up bag. She crossed the room quickly to Jan and cuffed her to a heavy armchair.

Zoe said "sorry, while I change and pack you'll just have to sit there and wait." Zoe tried to be polite, but was so intense that it came off as cold.

Zoe changed quickly into black Lauren pencil pants, a black Jovine turtleneck, her shoulder holster and weapon, the same dark green Lauren jacket, and the black Weitzman flats.

She quickly threw all of the gear and clothes into the two bags, and was ready. She went over to Jan and unlocked her from the chair then cuffed her in the front.

Zoe grabbed the bags and gave one to Jan to carry. She said "carry that bag, and we will go outside to meet the helicopter.

She had heard a motorcycle roar to life ten minutes ago, and knew Sully had left.

Jan frowned and asked "Trish where did Brian go?" She was pretty sure she knew the answer to her question.

Zoe/Trish said coldly "to kill your Husband Jan."

Sully found the keys to the motorcycle and a black and silver striped Shoei full faced helmet. He put the helmet on and started the bike. Sully raced out the garage and onto the road. He knew Ben had turned to the left out of the driveway and that was the way Jan told him to go.

Sully was hoping to catch Ben before he reached the Casino. He was going way too fast on roads that curved wildly. On the few straight sections of road he pushed the bike well over one hundred miles per hour. Motorcycle training had been one of Sully's favorites in the SSO program, and he was taking full advantage of that training now.

Not long after he left the villa a jet black helicopter with no markings or lights flew right over Sully. He was thrilled to see it so soon, and he knew now that Zoe would be safe.

Sully pushed the bike harder and faster. He was determined to catch Ben and kill him.

Sully's determination paid off when he caught up to Ben about a mile from the casino. Sully flew past him and stopped about four hundred yards ahead. He threw the kick stand down and quickly dismounted the motorcycle. Sully took the helmet off and set it on the seat so Ben could see who was going to kill him. The adrenaline pumping through him, combined with the Ibuprofen, had taken virtually all of his pain away.

Sully was trained extensively to be a cold hard killer with no emotion, but this was different. This man's actions could have hurt Zoe, and that was unacceptable.

Sully stood in the road with his weapon in his right hand hidden behind his back.

As Ben got close to Sully he had a quizzical look on his face. He recognized that it was Sully/Brian standing in the road next to his motorcycle. He came to a stop ten yards from him. Ben was pissed off at the world, and especially at Sully/Brian for threatening him.

Ben got off of the silly little Vespa and said to Sully/Brian "you have the nerve to threaten me in my house when you are a guest, you steal my motorcycle, and now YOU want to confront ME."

Sully coldly said "your actions could have seriously hurt the woman I love, and it's time for you to pay for your actions."

Ben opened his mouth to retort, and the first bullet went right through it smashing his teeth and blowing the back of his throat out. He fell to the ground.

Sully walked calmly over to him and said "you've been sanctioned asshole." He shot him in the forehead, then took the roll of hundred dollar bills equaling five thousand dollars out his pocket, stripped the body of any and all identification, and turned to leave. Ben Dallman was most definitely dead.

A thought of Zoe ran through his mind, and he turned back and shot him tree more times in the chest. The weapon was fabulous. The sound of the slide moving a new shell into the chamber was louder than the soft puff that the actual shot made with the silencer attached. Sully policed the area for his brass.

Sully quickly called Julian and told him to hold the helicopter at the villa. He said he would be back shortly.

Sully donned the helmet, jumped on the bike and hurried back to the Dallman's rented villa.

Sully got back to the villa, and the helicopter had landed in the road, blocking his path. He parked the motorcycle on the side of the road and put the keys in his pocket. He ran to the chopper and climbed in.

The Lear pilot, Luke, was at the main controls, and Julian was in his usual spot as co-pilot. They lifted off and headed for the yacht.

After Sully got in he closed the helicopter door, and went right to Zoe and kissed her deeply. Sully had thought to hell with it. He didn't care right now if Julian, Luke, and Jan saw. He sat next to her and tried to cover his tracks by saying "That was for a job well done agent Nelson. They had to keep their cover up as much as possible around Jan.

Zoe said "thank you agent Nelson, but this mission is about over, and it is no longer necessary for us to act as a married couple." Privately she was incredibly happy he was safe, and her heart leapt when he kissed her, but she also knew they had to keep their cover for a while longer.

Sully said to Zoe "when we get to the yacht you take Jan and get the journal. I will go get our gear. Trish, if you encounter any resistance, don't hesitate. Zoe knew that Sully meant that if any of the crew, or Jan gave her any trouble she should kill them.

It took the helicopter only ten minutes to get to the yacht.

They all piled out of the chopper and Sully went one way and Zoe took Jan the other.

Sully flew down the stairs and was jogging to their former State room when he encountered Matt the troll. Matt looked at him with the silenced Berretta in his hand and said "Hey!" It was the last word he would ever utter. Sully wasn't in the mood for any shit, so he put the troll out of his misery. He stopped for one second aimed and shot him through his good eye. As Sully jogged by the remains of Matt he noticed the mural of blood, brain matter, and bits of skull on the wall.

Zoe kept having to push Jan in the back to keep her moving faster. She finally stopped, turned her around and looked her squarely in the eyes with a cold hard stare. Zoe/Trish said harshly "Jan if you don't move your ass, I have no problem killing you right here and finding that book myself, do you get me?" As she said the last part she grabbed Jan by the front of her shirt and pulled her so close to her that she could see the pores in her face.

"Now let's move out Jan double time or death time, your choice." Zoe said it so ruthlessly that it scared her.

They were on the move again at a good pace. Zoe/Trish and Jan reached the master cabin and went inside. Jan hustled to the large closet and went swiftly to the safe. As she worked the combination Zoe Pulled her Berretta out of its holster and pressed the tip of it behind Jan's left ear. She said icily "Jan most people keep pistols in their safe for just this kind of situation, now you weren't thinking of doing something stupid I hope." She pressed the mussel more tightly against her skull.

Jan was shaking as she opened the safe and said with fear "of course not Trish."

As soon as Jan turned the lever and Zoe/Trish heard the locks disengage she pushed Jan away from the safe and rudely said "what does this journal look like?"

Sully reached the door to their old state room door, and it was locked. His mind ran quickly through all the reasons it could be locked, and settled on the assumption that someone was in the room.

He stood back and kicked the flimsy door in with his gun raised. Juan, the launch driver, appeared from behind the corner of the hallway that led to the walk in closet. Sully shot him in the heart three times rapidly, and he fell into the bathroom. Sully ran over to him and holstered his gun. There was no need to shoot again.

He ran back and closed what was left of the door and slid a heavy armchair in front of it. He grabbed a duffel bag that Juan must have brought and headed for the safe. It was already open, and Sully silently thanked Juan for saving him the trouble. All Sully grabbed was the money, their cover passports, and the good jewelry that was given to them as props. He stopped at Juan's body and frisked him and found that he already had two bundles of the money, and was wearing the gold Rolex. He threw them in the duffel.

Sully just happened to look up and saw Zoe's green bikini. He smiled and stepped over Juan's body to retrieve it from the shower rod. The SSO was not getting this back.

Zoe was grabbing everything out of the safe and tossing it into a leather overnight bag that she had found on a shelf in the closet. There was a lot of cash, bonds, jewelry, and books she threw all five books at Jan's feet and said "which one is the journal you were talking about. Jan pointed to a thick red book that was smaller than the others.

Zoe/Trish picked it up and the cover said bible. She looked at Jan and said "real cute." Zoe/Trish scanned a couple of pages quickly and knew that Jan had been telling the truth. She threw all of the books in the bag and zipped it up. She said to Jan "that's it let's get back to the chopper.

Sully and Zoe made it back to the helicopter at virtually the same time. Sully helped her and Jan in, and then climbed in himself. He closed the door and said loudly "Let's get out of here!"

Julian shouted over the din of the chopper blades "I had Luke fly the Lear to Corsica yesterday. We have a crew there getting her fueled and ready as we speak. We should be stateside in about nine and a half hours.

Zoe/Trish yelled "good work Julian!"

When the Lear landed back at the SSO airfield there were at least twenty agents waiting at the hangar. They took Jan into custody, Zoe to debriefing, and Sully to the hospital.

He had spent the his first day back in the hospital being treated for four broken ribs, one of which had caused a small tear in his liver, and stress fractures in his clavicle and pelvis.

Zoe came to visit him in the hospital, but it had been a sterile conversation because they were on the base. He couldn't believe that in ten hours of not seeing her she got ten times more beautiful. He squeezed her hand and gave her a loving look before he insisted that she leave him.

After Zoe left, he was debriefed in the hospital, and then released with a set of instructions for his convalescence. He crumpled the instructions and threw them away without even reading them.

He got a ride back to his apartment, and threw away the arm sling he was given. He saw that his gear had been brought over in one large duffel bag sitting on his kitchen table. He quickly rifled through it and found what he was looking for, Zoe's green bikini. He folded it carefully and put it in his sock drawer. He turned out the lights, and then went to bed sad and sore. He missed Zoe terribly, and didn't know when they would be together again. This was the first time Sully had ever felt lonely in his life.

Two days later Sullivan Mills walked into James Weathers office feeling much better. Weathers had a big smile on his usually passive face, he said "come on and sit down Sully." It wasn't until he started toward the armchairs in front of Weathers' desk that he saw Zoe. Now Sully was smiling too.

Weathers said to both of them "I don't know how it is going to be possible for either of you to top this mission, and it's the first for both of you. Janice Dallman is singing like a bird, and Justice is busting gun running rings all over the World. I am giving you both the bonus money for two sanctions, as a reward for the excellent job you both did.

Zoe said thank you Sir, but Sully said nothing. He was looking past him and at all of the walls in Weathers' office. Weathers had a quizzical look on his face and said "Sully what the hell are you looking for?"

Sully suppressed a smile and said "Zoe and my picture on the wall with the big 'ASSASSINS OF THE MONTH' sign underneath." Now he gave Weathers a big smile.

They all laughed and then Weathers said "in case you haven't noticed yet Sully, this isn't Burger King. The best I can do is the bonus, and three weeks off for both of you before your next assignment.

Weathers stopped and said "give me your cellular phones."

They both did, and had the same confused look on their faces.

Weathers quickly took the back off of Zoe's phone, took the battery out, and pulled a small circuitry device out. He did the same to Sully's. He then said with a small self-satisfied smile on his face "this is a one way transmitter that works with your phone. Standard issue for new agents, remember that short leash I told you about. We had a tech agent listening to and transcribing since you were issued these phones. Having reassembled the phones while speaking, Weathers handed them back.

Zoe had a look of shame on her face when she said "what is the transmit range?"

Sully just looked mad as Weathers said "don't worry Zoe the transcripts come directly to me, and the transcribing agent is not bright enough to tell anyone.

Weathers finished with "just keep your phones charged and with you at all times just in case. Now get out of my office, both of you."

When they got outside they stopped and looked at each other. Zoe whispered sexily "I am not hungry, I brought my own car, and there is a motel not too far from here."

Sully smiled and whispered back "I don't know, I could really go for a blooming onion."

And they both laughed.

Zoe and Sully drove in silence to the blue cloud motel that was the closest hotel or motel that they could find after leaving the SSO campus. It was a dive of a motor court but they didn't care as long as they could be alone together. Zoe ran into the office and paid for their room.

She drove to lucky number seven and parked right in front of the door. They both got out like the car was on fire. When Zoe opened the door and they were finally alone together in the room Sully grabbed her and gave her a huge long series of kisses. Zoe was afraid to hug Sully too tightly because of his ribs, and it caused Sully to stop their frenzied kissing. He said "what is wrong Zoe, did I do something wrong?"

Zoe seriously said "are you kidding me, you are my white knight. I am just afraid to hurt you."

Sully quickly took off his shirt to show her how he was tightly wrapped with Ace bandages and tape. He said "I feel good as new, really Zoe I'm fine."

She put her hand on the bandages and her eyes welled up as she said "They said that you broke your collar bone and your pelvis too."

Sully grabbed her by the arms and said "I told you I'm fine, just some bumps and bruises, now make love to me and don't hold back.

Zoe pulled away from him and sat in a tattered chair and said "I have been dying to be alone with you because I do want to make love to you and not hold back, but there is ton of things I have been thinking about, and I need to talk to you openly or I will explode."

Sully looked confused and said "You should know you can tell me anything you want to. There isn't anything you could say to me that would make me love you less, unless you say that you don't love me, and if you don't I will walk out that door and you will never see me again.

Zoe was doing her best to hold back tears when she said "that's nowhere near what I want to say to you Sullivan. The problem I am having is that I care too much. When I saw you lying in that hospital bed in pain because of me, well it was incredibly hard. It's not like we are stock brokers Sully, it's clear to me now how much danger we are going to be in. Sullivan you opened my heart to love, and if I lost you it would close forever."

Sully took it the wrong way and said "I get it, I'll call a cab." He reached for the cell phone in his pocket, and headed for the door.

Zoe headed him off and said "Sully, what the hell is wrong with you? I tell you that I love you so much it scares me and you think I want you to leave? Please sit on the bed and talk to me." She grabbed his arm gently and guided him to the bed. She continued with "I don't know what you thought I was saying, but there was nothing vaguely resembling a request for you to leave."

Sully looked down and said "I feel exactly how you feel, but I promised not to ever make you cry again, and meant it." He looked at her and kissed her gently and continued "like you said, we aren't stock brokers, and this is a very dangerous profession we are in. If I could just quit and work at a gas station I would, but we don't have that option. You don't quit the SSO at this level, they quit you, or you get killed doing your job. Any way you look at it we are in this until it ends. The only way I can keep my promise to you is to get assigned to a different sector, or just try to avoid you. I had a stone cold heart before I met you, and I can always let it freeze again." As he finished he looked down again.

Zoe grabbed him and hugged him. They just held one another for a few minutes. When Zoe was sure she wouldn't cry she said "How did you get to be the sweetest man in the world?"

Sully let out one laugh and said "years of practice, with lots of other women."

Zoe kissed him gently and whispered "I want names."

They both smiled loving smiles at one another.

They made slow passionate love most of the day, ordered in pizza and beer, napped together, and after making love in the shower Zoe re-wrapped his ribs tightly.

Sully said “so we've got three weeks, and I have a hundred thousand to spend on you, where do you want to go?”

Zoe was thrilled and jumped on the bed next to him and said excitedly “really, we can go on a real vacation, I've never been on one, I wouldn't know how to act.”

Sully smiled broadly at her excitement and said “neither have I, so I guess we will just have to wing it”

Zoe could hardly contain herself and jumped up and down on the bed still kneeling next to him naked. Sully was entranced by her breasts bouncing up and down and became aroused again.

Sully grabbed her to stop the jumping, and kissed her.

Zoe felt his erection rub against her and said “How about we decide where to go a little later.”

Chapter 6

They finally settled on two and a half weeks in Hawaii. They found a secluded resort on the island of Kauai and Zoe made all of the arrangements online. The plan was that they would leave tomorrow at fourteen hundred.

After they left the Blue Moon, Zoe went to get some things from her apartment, and Sully took a cab to the nearest bank, withdrew thirty thousand dollars in cash, and then took the cab to a used car dealership in town.

Sully bought a nineteen ninety five Ford four door Crown Victoria for six thousand dollars. It had a lot of miles, but the banged up body made up for it. Nondescript, exactly what he was looking for.

Sully drove the car to a local real estate office and rented a small fully furnished house on the edge of town sight unseen. He paid with cash for six months. He gave them false, but verifiable personal information and they in turn gave him two sets of keys.

He drove toward his apartment and saw Zoe heading back. Sully flashed his lights at her and she pulled over. Sully got out and crossed the road to meet her.

Zoe chuckled and said "nice car you found for us tough guy. They didn't have a Yugo on the lot?"

Sully said "I thought it would do for now, besides the salesman said it was driven by a little old lady, and only to church on Sunday's."

Zoe laughed and said "and you bought it, and the car. Follow me back to my apartment, and then we can go together to our new palace."

Zoe dropped her agent mobile at her apartment and Sully loaded her things into the back seat of granny's car. She got in and gave him a kiss and said "let's get your stuff, and start our first vacation officially." Zoe was beaming with pleasure.

When they got to Sully's apartment it only took them five minutes to get what he needed just a few department aliases, complete with passports, and guns. Sully had started acquiring weapons when he was in the Marines, and had not stopped. The one bedroom in his apartment contained five large Cabelas gun safes that were full, and a small cot.

Although he sent seven hundred dollars a month home to his mother, he had amassed quite a bank account. All he had done for the past five years was study and train. Until Zoe, he had no friends or any reason to spend money. His uniforms and issued clothing were fine with him.

Zoe said "kind of bleak in here Sully, not even a television or radio. I guess you spent all of your time waiting for me." She playfully pinched his butt and smiled at him.

Sully was serious in his reply as he said "I think you might be more right than you could ever know." Then he kissed her. He said "wait there's one thing we can't forget." He went into a kitchen drawer and pulled out a package wrapped in newspaper.

Sully handed the package to Zoe and said "open it."

Zoe smiled at him and said "what is it?" as she tore into the package. She pulled out the green bikini from the Dallman sanction and threw her arms around him. She said "you get points for saving this." And she kissed him deeply.

They got lost twice trying to find their rental house, and it was almost dark when they finally did.

The house was an old two bedroom ranch, in need of paint, in the middle of nowhere. Zoe opened the door and the smell of must hit them both immediately. She had paused at the front door thinking Sully might make the romantic gesture he had before and carry her in, but he didn't.

After they had toured the small house hand in hand, Zoe laughed and said "did you get a package deal from the little old lady who owned the car?"

Sully laughed with her, saying "I guess so, let's open some windows and go shopping while this place airs out."

They drove twenty miles to the nearest Super Wal-Mart and outfitted themselves for their trip. Sully put Zoe in charge, and they both pushed carts in anticipation of the amount they needed to purchase.

Zoe picked out luggage, shoes, socks, undergarments, swimwear, and clothing for both of them. She especially had fun picking out Sully's clothes. He told her not to get too much because they planned on shopping on vacation, but she did. They were like newlyweds, grabbing at one another and kissing their way through the store.

When they were confident they had more than they needed for the trip Zoe said "let's eat in tonight, but I don't want pizza again. If we buy a cheap microwave, we could buy some frozen Chinese food. What do you think?"

Sully said "sounds great. I'll get the microwave and some wine and beer, you pick out the food." Zoe kissed him and they split up.

Sully met her as she was leaving the frozen food section and they checked out.

On the ride home Zoe said happily "that was fun Sully, I feel like we've been together forever." She put her head on his shoulder as he drove.

Sully replied "I hope it will always be like this Zoe." He put his arm around her and they drove the crappy car to their crummy rented home.

It took them half an hour to unload the car and most of it they just threw in the living room with the intention of packing tomorrow. On the last trip from the car to the house Sully led and blocked the door. He turned to Zoe and said "I bet you think I forgot." Sully dropped his bags and swept her up into his arms. He kissed her as he carried her across the threshold.

Zoe said "I love you Sullivan Mills." She kissed his nose and laughed.

Sully simply said "I love you too" and set her down onto her feet.

They had a satisfying, candlelit dinner and went to bed.

Sully said teasingly "you better get some sleep, you have a lot of packing to do tomorrow, and I hope you bought something to cook me for breakfast or you will have to run out."

Zoe punched him hard in the shoulder, giggled and said "if I thought you were serious, I would leave right now."

Sully rubbed his shoulder and in a hurt child voice said "that really hurt."

Zoe sexily said "don't worry baby, you will forget all about it in a minute.

They made love several times and on one break Zoe said "I'll be right back" she left the bed and went to the kitchen swinging her ass provocatively. She came back moments later with a quart of rocky road ice cream and two spoons. Zoe held the ice cream between her breasts and said "see anything you like?"

Sully laughed and said "oh boy ice cream!"

Zoe laughed and came to him.

They ate some of the ice cream and Sully went and put it away. Instead of going back to the bedroom he went to start their packing. It was a daunting task, considering the amount of stuff they had bought.

Sully waded through the sea of bags, and found the luggage. He opened the large bag they planned to check, threw it on the couch and started going through the bags.

It took him two hours to get them packed and he had laid out his clothes for the flight on the loveseat. He had found some of the boxer brief underwear that Zoe had bought for him and put a black pair on.

He went back to the bedroom and stood in the doorway for a long while watching Zoe sleeping curled up in the sheet. He was thinking "how have I been so lucky to have fallen in love with this perfect woman". It scared him how attached he already was to her.

Sully went to the back room closet and picked out some weapons for them to take with them. He grabbed the two Berettas that they had used on the Dallman mission with silencers and the shoulder rigs, two matching Taurus three fifty seven magnums with four inch barrels, and a snub nose Smith and Wesson thirty eight special. He grabbed two boxes of ammunition for each weapon.

He individually wrapped each weapon carefully in a pillow case, and took them and the boxes of ammunition to the large carry on suitcase. As he carefully packed them into the suitcase he was thinking that this wasn't the way Ozzie would pack for Harriet. He closed the large case, carried it to the back bedroom, and locked it in the closet.

Sully was not tired so he went to the kitchen and got a large glass of milk. He sat at the kitchen table sipping his milk, staring at the wall, and thinking. All kinds of thoughts ran through his mind.

Sully thought about his mother and wondered how she was, he wondered why he felt nothing about the three people he had killed, and he thought mostly about Zoe. He wondered how she would react when he told her he never wanted to get married, and he never wanted to have children.

Sully's thoughts were interrupted when Zoe came into the kitchen wrapped in the sheet from the bed and said "is there something wrong Sully?"

Sully said "not a thing Zoe, I just wanted some milk to wash down that ice cream. Let's go to bed." He felt bad at kind of lying to her but let it go and swept Zoe up into his arms and carried her to the bedroom.

The trip was wonderful for both of them, the resort was five stars in every way. The part of tourist seemed to come naturally to Zoe, and it pleased Sully to see her so happy.

In the first week Zoe had purchased so many trinkets and items of clothing for both of them that Sully was certain they would need at least two more pieces of luggage for the return trip. Sully didn't mind as long as Zoe was happy, he was.

They had snorkeled, para sailed, whale watched on a large sailboat, and even attempted surfing. They acted as newlyweds did, and usually started their daily adventures late because Zoe was a morning person and they made love daily until late morning. They were having the time of their lives until the eighth day.

They had come home from a fabulous dinner at the resort and were going to change clothes because Zoe wanted to go dancing. Sully had resisted this every evening when Zoe had asked him to, but finally relented.

There was a manila envelope addressed to Sully that had been slid under the door.

Sully picked it up and said "go ahead and change Zoe, I will see what this is all about." As Sully opened the envelope he thought "I hope whatever this is will get me out of going dancing".

Sully spent five minutes going over the contents of the envelope. Because it was in code it took him a while to translate. He had no idea how he was going to explain to Zoe that he had been activated, immediately, for a new sanction.

Zoe came out of the bedroom looking fabulous. She was wearing black high heels, and the same tight black dress she had worn the night they fell in love. Zoe did a slow provocative turn, and blew him a kiss then she said "What do you think?"

Sully's jaw had dropped when she walked into the room, and he could smell her essence from across the room. He was definitely, positively in love with this goddess, and had no idea how to tell her he had to leave.

Sully smiled and said "the greatest artist in the history of mankind couldn't have painted anything more beautiful than you look right now." He continued "it's too bad I sprained my ankle coming over to sit on the couch. I think dancing is definitely out for tonight."

Zoe laughed, came over to him sat on the couch and kissed him. She said "the kiss was for that wonderful comment, but if you think I am gonna buy the ankle bit your crazy." Zoe smiled, kissed him again and said "come on Sully, you agreed to go dancing with me, finally."

Sully kissed her neck and moved up and nibbled her ear he whispered to her "your smell great and taste even better, but the envelope poses us a problem, I don't think I have time to go dancing."

Zoe pulled away from him and said "what the hell are you talking about Sully." She gave him a mad look and continued "what, did you have a valet write you a note of excuse?"

Sully frowned and gave her the letter he received and said "it took me a minute to find the primer, but it's written in code sixteen." He looked down as she read the official SSO document.

Zoe read the document and the more she read the more furious the look on her face became. Sully left the couch quietly and got two little bottles of Dewar's out of the mini bar and poured them into a glass he took a big drink as Zoe finish reading. He got himself ready to duck.

Zoe looked at him with the nastiest look he had ever seen on her beautiful face. She crumpled the paper and threw it at him. Then she yelled "What a bunch of horse shit!! You have to be on a plane to La Paz, Bolivia in six hours." She had taken off her heels and Sully was ready to duck again.

She was pacing the room like a caged lion in a fabulous black dress, and then continued her rant with. "I am gonna call that fucking

Weathers and politely remind him of his god damned promise of a three week vacation. What the hell am I supposed to do in Hawaii for six days by myself?"

Sully timidly said "Zoe you can always get an earlier flight. You don't have to stay if you don't want to." He was hoping for the best.

Zoe's blood was boiling and she grabbed her shoes and purse and headed for the door, as she stormed out she said "fuck this, I'm going dancing. I don't give a shit if Weathers wants to send you to the moon, maybe you can dance with him." She slammed the door behind her and was gone.

Sully said aloud "well that went better than expected." He finished the Dewar's, took his phone out of his pocket, and called in.

Weathers took his sweet time taking his call, and Sully was getting irritated himself. When he finally picked up the phone ten minutes later he went straight to the logistics, he said "Mills, I have a boat at your resort's marina, in slip twenty seven, ready to take you to the Big Island. There a car will take you to a private airfield where your jet is waiting. Agent Joe Potter will be there with your dossier, and he will be your valet for this mission. All of the necessary equipment is onboard. We will have a conference call when you are in flight. Do you have any questions at this point Mills?"

Sully wanted to go off like Zoe had, but instead kept it all in and simply replied with a very cold "no Sir." He was hoping in his heart of hearts that Weathers was playing a cruel joke on him, but that wasn't his style, and this was obviously the real deal.

Weathers now said "agent Millstad will have to return on a commercial flight." His voice then became as cold as ice when he barked "your plane leaves in five hours, be on it Mills."

Sully heard the phone click and that, apparently, was that. He took several deep breaths and walked slowly over to a vase resting on a table next to the sofa. He inhaled the perfume of all the flowers, and gently turned the giant bird of paradise around and around. Sully grabbed the vase and threw it into the wall over the sofa turning what was a beautiful bouquet into a terribly ugly mess.

By his best estimate Sully had less than an hour before he had to meet the boat. He changed into black Dockers, a black Loren polo, black socks, and black Stanley Blacker loafers. The outfit was a direct reflection of his mood. He packed his pistols and some underwear into a small black leather duffel that Zoe had picked out for him. He thought about it for a second and realized that everything he was wearing had been picked out by Zoe.

He was packed, changed, and ready to go in less than fifteen minutes. He poured himself another double Dewar's and grabbed a swisher sweet tip cigarillo out of the pack Zoe had bought him yesterday. Sully took his drink and the cigar out onto the lanai. He sat in a deck chair and lit the cheroot.

He was contemplating whether or not to call Zoe, when his cell phone rang. His hopes of making amends with Zoe were dashed after he said "hello" and a male voice came back and said "agent Mills, this is Joe Potter. Sir, you have less than thirty minutes to meet your boat at slip twenty seven."

Sully said one word to Potter "understood" and ended the call. He finished his drink in one gulp and stubbed out the cigar.

Sully went back into the suite and went to the small desk and wrote a note to Zoe. He wrote "I love you" and laid it on her pillow with the now mangled Bird of Paradise on top of it. He grabbed his bag and left picking up the small box of cigars on his way out.

Sully walked to the slip with his mood getting darker by the second. By the time he found his boat it was as if he didn't even know who Zoe was. Now he was in the mood to kill, and luckily it was his job.

The boat was a cigarette style racing boat with two men aboard. Sully walked up to it and the driver of the boat looked at him. Sully said "the tomatoes are ready to be picked." That was the code phrase given to him in the letter shoved under his door.

The driver jumped up and said "good evening sir, why don't you hand me your bag and climb aboard."

Sully did just that.

The boat was very fast and the ride was very rough. The ride to the Big Island of Hawaii took more than two hours and by the time they arrived he was freezing, but he had pretended to sleep through the entire trip. As the boat slowed he opened his eyes to see they were heading for a commercial harbor filled with mostly large fishing trawlers.

They docked at a pier between two large fishing vessels that dwarfed their small boat. Sully had to climb a four rung rope ladder to get to the deck of the pier. Joe Potter was standing there smiling at him and offering him a hand. Sully crawled onto the pier himself scowled at Potter and said "get my bag."

Sully walked down the pier toward the agent mobile he saw parked at the start. He never looked back but heard Potter "oof" when he caught the bag of guns that was thrown at him. On any other day this would have amused Sully but his mood continued to get blacker and blacker. Especially with every minute that went by that Zoe didn't called him.

Sully thought that Potter must have hustled because he got to the car seconds after he did. Sully got in the back as soon as Potter unlocked the doors. He looked at his cell phone to see if he had missed any calls while he was on the loud boat only to find that he hadn't.

When Potter had cleared the docks and was on a small two lane highway he said "boy that was a cool boat agent Mills, I bet that thing is fast."

Sully said nastily "Potter, just shut the fuck up and drive." He was curbing the urge to beat the shit out of someone, and Potter was closest.

The car got to the plane in fifteen minutes. When Sully got onboard the Lear he went directly to the gear locker and went through his gear for the mission. Potter came onboard and brought his bag to him and gently put it at his feet. Sully said to him now robot like and devoid of emotion "put my dossier on the table in the conference room, and get me a triple scotch rocks. I will be there shortly.

Looking through the clothes for this mission he found that it was mostly military issue and mostly black. For right now he grabbed a black flight jacket and set it aside. He went into his bag and took out the silenced nine millimeter Berretta and slipped into the shoulder holster. He secured the weapon into the holster and put on the black jacket.

Sully felt better now that he had his favorite weapon with him and went back to the conference room. Potter was there laying out his dossier in order, and his scotch had been poured. He handed Potter his cell phone and said "unless it's Weathers I'm unavailable, take a message, and make sure that thing is fully charged.

Sully sat down and methodically poured over the dossier. The target was the chief of the Bolivian secret Police, Francisco Mendez. The set up was very public at the swearing in of the new Bolivian President, Orlando Ramirez.

Sully was immediately pissed off. This had set up written all over it. One and one half days to prepare for a public assassination. If "no" was an option he would have called it off right now. But they had him and this was going to be a large test for him. If the SSO had wanted him dead he would be already. Why the impossible mission so soon after he had completed a perfect assignment.

The dossier contained old pictures of the plaza where the inauguration would be held, but with only one day to plan the hit and subsequent escape it was virtually impossible. The entire Bolivian army, and Secret Police force would be there would be there for protection, and unlike Butch and Sundance he did not want to go out in a hail of Bolivian gunfire.

An hour into the flight while Sully was looking over satellite photos trying to find an escape route Potter sheepishly stuck his head into the conference room and said "do you have a minute sir?"

Sully didn't even look at him and said "if you can find me a Dos Equis dark I will talk to you briefly when you bring it in."

Potter said "yes Sir." Then he closed the door.

Sully leaned back and rubbed his eyes, he was wondering what he had done to deserve a suicide mission. His thoughts started to wander toward Zoe and he quickly shoved them away with thoughts about this mission and anger.

Potter came in with his beer and a glass. Sully finally looked at the man and took him in. Potter was at least a dozen years older than him, pudgy and had a slack, meaty face. He looked like a Butcher Sully once met. Sully said "sit down Potter."

Potter spoke quickly and said "you've had four calls from agent Millstad and she seems to be quite annoyed at you not taking her calls. Secondly, the conference call with Mr. Weathers is scheduled for five minutes from now.

Sully coldly said "fine, patch Weathers call in when it comes through, and put a block on my cell phone of the number that agent

Millstad has been calling from. After you patch Weathers call, I want you in here to know what's really going on.

Weathers' call came in on time and Potter came in with a notepad. Weathers' started the call with saying without emotion "sorry to cut your vacation short Mills, but this is a situation of utmost importance to the SOD. I take it you've had time to look over the dossier, any questions Mills?"

Sully was in no mood to pull punches and was as sarcastic as possible when he replied "just make sure my mother gets the money from my bank accounts, and any death benefits there might be."

Weathers said "now just what in the hell is that supposed to mean?" His tone was not happy.

Sully said "nothing Boss, been nice working with you, I'll do my best." He reached to the disconnect button on the conference call device and instead decide to be dramatic and picked it up and threw it at the wall. He walked out of the conference room and said to Potter when he was at the door "write this down. If anyone calls for me tell them to fuck off." He went to the small bedroom next to the conference room and sat down on the small bed.

Sully thought about the mission for the duration of the flight and came up with no good outcome.

He had decided when he left the resort that it would be much easier for Zoe if she thought he was mad at her or leaving her in case he didn't make it back from this mission. Sully was pretty sure that there was a ninety nine percent chance that two days from now he would be dead or wish he was.

Sully had no intent of being tortured in a Bolivian prison for the rest of his life. His plan was to go in armed heavy and make a good stand before they killed him.

When they landed Potter and he met in the conference room to go over the few assets Sully would have for this mission. Potter would drive him and be on the other end of his ear wig. He had a full complement of weaponry, and that was it.

The day he had to scout was wasting away rapidly, but from the satellite images he had there were only two possible places he had as a sniper's nest that gave him any reasonable chance of escape.

Sully was dressed in blue jeans, a Red Sox tee shirt, Ray Ban Frogskins sunglasses, and a crumpled straw cowboy hat to disguise his appearance as much as possible. Potter had dropped him off near the town square and he casually walked past the exact spot his target would be standing.

Sully stopped and took what looked like a camera out of his pocket, and pretended to take a picture of the town square. What he actually did was lock a waypoint into the memory of the highly sophisticated GPS unit he was holding. When, and if, he found a suitable sniper's nest he would use these coordinates to get a distance to his target within, plus or minus, ten feet.

He was looking past the GPS unit as he pretended to take the picture at both of his possible positions. Both provided a clear shot of over eight hundred yards, and reasonable concealment. He walked through the square like a tourist pretending to take pictures. But in reality he was locking in the coordinates of several key positions. Sully checked possibility B first so he could make a large circle and end up back at Potter.

Position B was a burned out old church that appeared to have a standing bell tower on the satellite photos. When Sully got to the church and assessed the situation it was bleak. It would be a very difficult climb, especially with the fourteen pound sniper rifle and other gear. There was no room for a proper rest for the rifle, and the shot would be well over nine hundred yards. There was not much hope for position B.

Sully slowly scouted for any possible positions along his way to position A, and found none. It wasn't like he could climb a tree and make an eight hundred yard shot.

Long range sniping took careful calculation for all conditions. The rifle had to be firmly rested. Wind, exact range to target, and even humidity affected the trajectory of the bullet. Sniping was usually done in teams of two with a spotter telling the shooter where to aim in increments of clicks of the scope field of view, but as usual Sully was on his own. It definitely wasn't like shooting jackrabbits back home.

Sully had spent a full eight months of his training perfecting this art, and was considered one of the best ever by his instructors. It was his favorite part of training. He absolutely loved it when he was concealed in camouflage so perfectly that members of the search team would walk right by him. He even got caught once when a searcher stepped on his back. He loved the shocked and dejected look on the trainer's, and search group's faces every time he made the metal target "ting" to their utter surprise.

This assassination provided no ground shot because of the enormous crowd expected to attend. A high window would be ideal, but all of the long-standing adobe structures surrounding the square were single story and way to close too provide any possible escape. The only two story building in town and it was the courthouse Mendez would be standing in front of.

The time frame and limited intel given to him offered no other opportunity than a long range sniper shot, and so far this one provided no opportunity of escape. It was a suicide mission, but it was never allowed to refuse a sanction at the SSO unless you wanted to be sanctioned yourself. It was obvious to Sully that Weathers, Spyes, or the SOD, McMillan, wanted him dead. Sully was going to do his best to disappoint whoever it was.

He had the option of just running into the jungles of South America, and live his rest of the life on the run, constantly waiting for the bullet to strike. SSO assassins had a tracking device implanted into their hip bone right next to the femoral artery the first week of training. It was mandatory, and almost impossible to remove. So it was fairly certain that life on the run would be very short.

Position A was an old schoolhouse that was still in use, so his scouting was going to be limited. He smiled like an idiot walking around the school house looking for roof access, there was none. Sully said aloud softly "this just keeps getting better and better." Sully approached the front parapet of the schoolhouse and pretended to take another picture.

Now he had both ends of the coordinates that he needed to estimate the length of the shot. According to the GPS, it was nine hundred and fifty yards. Sully could do the math when he got back to the Lear and narrow that number down considerably.

That information would allow him to set his scope for distance, but he would have to compensate quickly, and do all of the calculations that a spotter would normally do, for all of the other variables in his sniper's nest before he could take the shot. Shooting with pin point accuracy at over nine hundred yards required precise calculation.

Sully walked back through the town square running every escape option through his mind and none of them worked. Sully thought that without a hell of a lot of luck, he was a dead man walking.

When Potter got him back to the Lear he knew he had little to no time to strategize and prepare. When he walked aboard agent Rady was there to confront him. Ron Rady was another field operative / assassin, and Sully had trained with him a couple of times and considered him competent. He was acting as co-pilot on this mission for some unknown reason.

Rady was taller and heavier than Sully, but today Sully was not afraid of any man. Rady stood squarely in front of him and said "Weathers wants you to call in immediately, and that skirt you're banging keeps calling too."

Sully wanted nothing more than to beat the shit out of Rady right there on the spot, but he simply snarled "Ron we could tear the shit out of one another right now, but I've got work to do." He walked through him throwing his left shoulder into Ron's right to make a point.

Rady said nothing and sat down at one of the three small tables in the plane, with a scowl on his face.

Sully said with no emotion to Potter "let's get in the conference room and talk." Then he turned to Rady and said nastily "Ron, one more thing, if you ever utter another derogatory word about agent Millstad, I will beat your ass so bad your mother won't recognize you." Sully stood his ground glaring at him but Rady never said a word and just took a sip of his diet cola.

When they got into the conference room Sully said "Potter the first thing I need you to do is pack for me, I will need a retractor grapple, both desert and jungle camouflage, dumb ass street clothes like I am wearing now, and MRE's (military issued Meals Ready to Eat) for four days.

Potter said "Yes sir, what about weaponry?" Confused.

Sully said in an irritated tone "just get the clothing packed for now and leave the desert camo out for me to dress in, see if there is a ghilie suit onboard, and give me at least a half hour in here to make some calls. Give me my cell phone."

Potter was excited at being part of a mission and it showed when he said "you can count on me agent Mills." He handed Sully his cell phone, and left in a hurry.

Sully knew he had to make two very difficult calls before he could concentrate on the mission.

Sully decided to make the easy call first, Weathers. Sully pressed the two on his cell phone, and was connected to the SSO. He gave his code and the dispatcher connected him without saying a word. Weathers answered immediately and said calmly "agent Mills how nice of you to call in. Is it possible for us to talk this time, or are you going to shout at me and hang up again?" Oh yeah he was pissed off, Sully thought.

Sully decided to play along and said, with a happy lilt to his deep voice "you just caught me at a bad time Sir, I had a cake in the oven and I didn't want it to get overdone." Sully laid it on thicker and heavier as he said "I hope you can forgive me for my rude behavior Mister Weathers." Sully was trying to make him explode with anger.

Weathers replied in a voice with no tone "are you willing to talk to me seriously Mills, or do you just want to play games?"

Sully noted the subtle tones in his voice, and knew he had gotten him really mad. Sully replied in a tough military tone "Sir, the agent is ready to talk about anything the Master wants, Sir." Sully was on a death assignment and was not in the mood to fuck around.

Weathers said angrily "is there any chance of getting this done, or should I bring in another agent?"

Sully simply said "Why kill two agents instead of just me." He was not in the mood to play games.

Weathers said very seriously "do you want to refuse this mission agent Mills."

Sully scowled, as if it would be seen on the other end of the phone, and said coldheartedly "not on my life, Sir."

The phone clicked off on the other end and Sully suddenly felt his own mortality slipping away.

The next call was to Zoe, and he had no idea how to handle it. Sully took several deep breaths with his eyes closed and pushed and held the five on his phone to speed dial Zoe. He was praying to get her voice mail, but as luck would hold on this mission she picked up.

When Zoe had seen the flower and note on the pillow, and read the note she got more upset with herself than she had ever been. Zoe fought back tears as she was cleaning up the mess of broken glass and mangled flowers.

She was already at the house they had rented together. She left Hawaii the minute she returned to their resort suite to find Sullivan gone. She hadn't shed a tear, because she knew she had reacted the wrong way. They were SSO assassins, and could be recalled at any moment.

Zoe had been unpacking and organizing things in the small house to try to keep her mind off of why she ran away from the best thing that ever happened to her. She had read the coded document that required him to leave in less than an hour, and rather than spend the time with him she had chosen to run away.

She tried several times to call and apologize, but on the tenth try she got a recorded message that her number had been blocked by him. She had said aloud "fuck him, I hope he dies on this so important mission." She immediately regretted what she had said, and for the first time in her life she had prayed. She prayed to God to protect Sully and keep him safe.

When Zoe had landed and retrieved the Ford that Sully had bought, she grabbed the keys from on top of the passenger side front tire and drove it to their rented home. She smiled when she looked at the odometer and knew that Sully had been teasing her. With the mileage on this car, granny's church must have been three thousand miles away.

Zoe was in the house puttering around, because she had to focus on something. When she had returned to the empty house with another week of vacation she felt something that she had never felt before in her life, loneliness. She longed for Sully, and it made her heart ache.

Zoe was sitting on the sofa folding clothes when her cell phone rang for the first time in three days. She grabbed it, connected the call and urgently said "hello, agent Millstad." There was a long pause, then her heart leapt when she hear Sully's deep, beautiful voice.

Sully simply said "hello Zoe." He had no idea what to say next.

Zoe tried her best to be calm and said cheerily "hi Sully thank you for calling, I've tried to call you but I guess you have been too busy to talk to me." Her best attempt to be nice came out salty and mean.

Sully said with no emotion "sorry about that, I have a public sanction to perform and I needed the little time I had to research and plan."

There was a long pause as Zoe tried to let the situation sink in. She was horrified, sanctions like this required weeks of planning, not hours. She said "well I assume with that time frame you have a great team under you, and good Intel." She was afraid to hear the answer.

Sully tried to keep it as light hearted as he could manage when he replied "yep, the best three guys you could ever meet, me, myself, and I. The Intel is great though, I have three satellite photos, and the four hours of Intel I was able to do today. The sanction is at ten hundred tomorrow. This thing is a piece of cake." He tried not to, but got more and more sarcastic as he spoke.

Zoe replied "you're kidding me, right. Those circumstances equal up to a suicide mission." Zoe waited several seconds for a reply.

Sully said "it's a piece of cake Zoe. Please don't worry, I will see you in a few days. While you are there if you get a chance try to contact my mother, she is the only Donna Mills in Mirage Arizona. See you soon Zoe, I'll love you till death."

Before she could say I love you back the line went dead. And Zoe cried harder than she ever had.

Zoe immediately tried to call Weathers, but was told he was unavailable. When she hung up she said aloud "fine if that's the way they want to play, I've got a play of my own."

Zoe called the local airport and asked to speak to the private terminal. When she was connected she said "I need a private jet to La Paz, Bolivia as soon as possible." When the phone clicked for the third time a man came on and said through a yawn "On-time corporate services, what can I do for you."

Zoe said in a firm and efficient tone "how long would it take you to get me to La Paz, Bolivia?"

The man on the other end of the line perked up and said "hang on a minute." He put the phone down, but not on hold and Zoe didn't even have to strain to hear him yell "Chuck we got some broad on the phone that sounds serious about getting to Bolivia as soon as possible, how much and how fast should I tell her?"

Zoe heard nothing for several seconds until the phone was picked up, apparently by "Chuck".

Chuck Russo was a Vietnam Veteran in his late fifties, and a man who did not take well to being fucked with. He picked up the phone and nearly shouted "you had better not be wasting my time lady."

Zoe was stern and firm when she said "just give me your best time for a takeoff, and a price, or I can call someone else."

Chuck was immediately interested because he could almost feel the seriousness in the lady's voice. Chuck softened a bit and said "it's gonna take me at least two hours to file a flight plan and get clearance. The price depends on the cargo."

Zoe had no time to be coy, so she said "The cargo is me, and a whole bunch of gear and weapons that are registered to me personally." The registered part was a lie, but Zoe new she could get around that with some cash, and she planned on running to the bank as soon as she had a flight scheduled to get a whole bunch of it.

Russo said "as long as you got a passport, and papers on the guns, its seven grand each way." He was thinking that if this lady went for it, it would go a long way toward paying off his debts.

Zoe said coldly "how about twenty grand in cash, no more questions asked." She knew she had a flight.

Russo said "be at hangar twenty eight within two hours with the cash, and we have a deal."

Zoe said "fine, just make sure the flight plan is filed, and the plane is ready to go." Zoe hung up.

When the lady whose name he had forgotten to get hung up, Chuck yelled "Terry, get your ass over here and prep the jet. I gotta try to remember how to file an international flight plan."

Zoe took granny's car to the bank to withdraw the cash she needed, then to her apartment and grabbed all the gear and weapons she thought she might need and threw them into two large duffel bags. She was wishing that she had gotten the codes to Sully's cache of weapons in his gun safes, but what she had would have to do, hopefully.

The bags were so heavy she had to take two trips, one for each bag. While she was in the apartment she changed into black jeans, black socks, black tennis shoes, and a black Army issued sweater. She wore her shoulder holster with the silenced nine millimeter Berretta that she had worn on the Dallman sanction. She covered it with a light weight black windbreaker.

On the ride to the airport she tried desperately to formulate a plan, but had no luck. Zoe hoped her mind would clear and she would have a plan by the time she reached Bolivia.

Zoe reached the airport with twenty minutes to spare and found the only private hangar with a jet being fueled and was sure that it was her ride. The jet was a ten year old Odyssey, that at best could carry eight passengers, and this plane had seen its better days long ago. She parked the car alongside of the hangar and walked out to meet Chuck and Terry.

Chuck was a bald black man in his early sixties just under six feet tall with a husky build. He came up to her and stuck his huge hand out as an invitation to shake. He warily said "you must be the lady I spoke to about a flight to Bolivia." Chuck's voice matched his build, and reminded her a little of Michael Clarke Duncan.

Zoe slapped a package that contained five thousand dollars into his greasy hand, instead of shaking it. Zoe said "that's five, another five when we land in La Paz, five when we get airborne heading back, and five when we land here again." Zoe opened her coat to show the silenced weapon and said "if you're thinking of anything other than being my pilot, Chuck, think again. Now tell your lackey over there to get my bags out of the trunk of my car."

Chuck opened his mouth to tell her off, but the five grand he was holding made his mouth close. He yelled "Terry get the lady's bags out of her trunk and close it." Chuck continued "Then get ready, we taxi out in ten minutes." He turned to Zoe and said "by the way I never got your name."

Zoe used the name on the passport she had brought and looked Chuck squarely in the eye and said as intimidating as she could "As far as you know, my name is Kathy Jackson, and on a no questions asked deal that is strike one Chuck, for your sake don't get to three because I can fly this crate as well as you can, and probably better."

Terry got Zoe's bags as she watched and came over to her, he said "damn lady what you got in here, dead bodies?" Terry was a punk kid.

He opened the rear cargo compartment and scratched his head on how to get the heavy bags in by himself.

Zoe solved his problem by saying "Both of those bags go into the cabin with me." Zoe said it with an "*I'm the boss*" attitude, and Terry closed the rear cargo hatch and carried the lighter bag to her.

Terry was a small angry man with an attitude, and just as he was going to let Zoe have it when Chuck showed up and said in a loud voice "Terry until I tell you different, you will do exactly what this lady says, and not say a word about it, got it!"

Terry glared at Zoe as he answered his boss with a surly "whatever you say Boss."

They were airborne quickly and the Cessna Citation 500 made pretty good time. When the jet was on auto pilot Chuck came back and said to Zoe "listen Kathy, I was a green beret and did twelve covert ops in Nam, so if there is any way you think I can help you with whatever it is you are doing, all you need to do is let me know."

When Zoe said nothing he nodded and turned to walk away.

Zoe stopped him just before he reached the cockpit and said "there might be a way you could help me Chuck, but it's more than just a little dangerous." She waited for his reaction.

Chuck said "Kathy, I don't want to leave this earth as a broke pilot, you just tell me what you need me to do. I've got gear and weapons onboard that just might help." Chuck smiled at her and continued with "and by the way ""danger"" is my middle name."

Zoe smiled at him genuinely and said "thank you Chuck, I will keep it in mind, but if you don't mind I would rather not have Terry involved if I do take you up on your offer."

Chuck laughed and said "Zoe, I wouldn't trust that blowhard bastard to tie my shoelace, much less be involved in something that involved a weapon."

Zoe replied "thank you Chuck, he just doesn't seem trustworthy to me." She gave him a small smile, and started strategizing of what the hell she was going to do on this "wing it" mission.

Chuck replied with a large smile "I knew you were a smart cookie the first time we spoke on the phone."

Zoe tried to sleep on the flight, but failed. She went through her gear and put the weapons she wanted in one bag, and left out two ACP forty five caliber pistols for Chuck with six loaded clips. The flight was scheduled to land in La Paz at five hundred hours, and that didn't give her much time to strategize.

Sully had been up for thirty six hours and it showed. He had finalized his plan with Potter and had picked out four different pick-up points. They had plugged all of the points into both Sully's and Potter's GPS units and Sully had given Potter specific times for pick up.

When Sully was satisfied that the little preparation he was able to do was done to his best, he started getting dressed and ready. The only piece of luck on this doomed mission was that behind the school was thick South American jungle crept up within forty yards of the schoolhouse he had chosen as his sniper point.

The route he had planned was an hour plus drive well around the town square to his drop off point. With the vehicle they were given for the mission, a Jeep Cherokee, Sully would get the privilege of riding in the back with all of his weapons and gear, covered with a tarp. Then he had a five mile hike to the spot where he would drop his sixty plus pound backpack full of weapons and extra gear.

They left at oh four thirty. The ride in the back of the Jeep was bad at best, and between the lack of sleep and the bumpy ride in the back, Sully felt that he was in no condition to pull this off. He was hoping that the five mile hike would clear his mind.

Potter had dropped him off with no incident, other than a slight headache. Sully jumped out of the confined back end, shook his head vigorously to clear it, and said seriously to Potter, "are you sure you are clear on the pick-up points and times?"

Potter looked at Sully like he was mad, and said "we went over it six times, do you think I'm stupid?"

Sully wanted to reply "*hell yeah, I think you're a dumb fuck*", but instead said nicely "not at all, Joe, I just have to make sure we are on the same page."

Potter was still hurt, but less so than a minute ago, when he replied "Agent Mills I will do my best to make sure I am at our scheduled rendezvous on time."

Sully wanted grab him by the throat, but instead said calmly "that's all I can ask for Joe, and I'm sure you will be there when I need you."

Potter just got into the car and left without saying a word. Sully did not take this as a good sign. He tore through the jungle as fast as he could. Sully wasn't moving very fast because of the sixty plus pounds of gear he was carrying.

Sully had plugged in coordinates from "the" map of the area that he was supplied with. He had picked a spot about a mile from the schoolhouse that he could use as a staging area. Sully looked at his GPS in the dark, and just the backlit LCD Screen lit up the pitch dark jungle in a twenty yard radius. He quickly doused the light that had already given his position away, and shed his heavy pack to find his goggles. As much as he disliked wearing them, Sully put them on.

Wearing the night vision goggles would allow him to avoid trees and heavy brush, along with him being able to read the GPS without the backlight. Other than being uncomfortable, the night vision gathered so much ambient light that when he took them off Sully was virtually blind for a good two minutes.

Sully looked around with his pistol drawn for thirty seconds and saw nothing in the eerie green glow provided by the goggles. He took a reading from the GPS and let out a heavy sigh. He was only five degrees off course, but his destination was still over two miles away. Sully put the pack that was getting heavier with every step back on and pushed himself to continue on. He knew he had to try to move faster because it was already oh five thirty, and sunrise here was oh six fifteen.

Sully reached his destination at oh six twenty five, and immediately turned off and took off the night vision goggles, and crouched behind a tree. He sat with his eyes closed and then wide open in thirty second intervals until his vision normalized.

There was a pre-dawn glow in the thick jungle, and Sully saw a tree with heavy brush around it. He picked up his pack in his left hand and covered the fifty feet to the spot quickly. He carefully hid the pack in the thick jungle undergrowth and ran forward toward the schoolhouse and picked some brush for concealment.

The undergrowth that Sully couldn't pull up by the roots he broke off as close to the ground as possible. He hid the broken stems by turning them back into the dirt. When he was satisfied that he had covered his tracks well enough he headed back to his pack.

Sully unbuckled the long barrel from the side of his pack, dug out the action, scope, and stocks, and began to assemble his sniper rifle. The weapon he chose was by far his favorite. The sniper rifle was a Marine M-40, in a caliber of .338 Lapua Magnum, with an S and B 30x70 micro adjust scope, and a Meyers silencer. It took him one full minute less than the five required in training to have the weapon assembled, loaded and ready to go. Next he pulled out the ghilie tarp given to him and began to cover it with all of the native vegetation he had picked.

When Sully was satisfied with his concealment he carried the rifle, his pack, and the tarp with him and carefully crawled under the tree, brushing the grass he had disturbed behind him back into a standing position, and making sure that every small plant he bent along the way was righted.

After Sully carefully covered himself and all of his gear with the tarp he dug into the pack and pulled out his favorite MRE, Turkey a' la' king. He carefully and quietly ate his first meal in Bolivia. He was confident that unless the under equipped local Army had infra-red detection devices he couldn't be found.

The sanction was not for another two and a half hours, so after he ate Sully allowed himself a half an hour nap, it was oh seven thirty.

Chuck came back into the passenger compartment two steps and saw Zoe nodding off. He Yelled "Kathy, I need you in the cockpit right now!"

Zoe's head stood upright and her eyes popped open, and she headed for the door to the cockpit. As Zoe covered the fifteen or so feet she reflected on her own thoughts. She thought "I bet they named it the ""cock"" pit because, before Amelia Ehrhardt, women weren't typically allowed to fly planes". All of the pilots she had ever met had reinforced her viewpoint.

When she opened the cockpit door her heart leapt into her throat when she saw both Chuck and Terry, whom Zoe had dubbed "*Useless*", fighting the plane's controls with all of their might. She tried her best to remain calm when she said "is there a problem up here boys?"

Terry yelled back "does this look normal to you lady?" Before Zoe could say a word Chuck jumped in and said "our left engine has flamed out, and I can't seem to get it to re-start. Right now we are running on one leg, and as you can see, it isn't that easy. I just wanted you to know that at this pace we won't get there until nine thirty or ten."

Zoe said to Chuck "did you pull the fire extinguisher on the left engine and then try a re-start?"

Chuck would have laughed if he wasn't so worried about their situation instead he said to Zoe "Kathy, I have changed the date on both extinguishers every year, myself, when this bucket has its annual inspection. They didn't even work four years ago when I won this bucket in a poker game."

Zoe's mind was racing for a solution to the problem and finally said to Chuck "what if we climbed to forty thousand and did a steep dive to try to re-start it?" Zoe was grasping at straws to not be late for Sully.

Chuck said to Zoe nastily "Kathy you might want to crash into the jungles of South America, but I don't. Terry get in the back and secure everything you can. Kathy, get your ass in the co-pilot seat and help me keep this thing in the air.

Zoe jumped into the co-pilot seat and asked a question that she knew the answer to "are there any parachutes aboard?" She asked very seriously.

Chuck chuckled and said "take three guesses, but the first two don't count. We do have a really cool inflatable raft, if that helps."

Zoe didn't even bother to respond, but she had a small smile on her face at the joke. The controls were heavy and jumping wildly, making it a chore to be in the co-pilot's seat. Zoe wanted Terry to relive her as soon as possible. She had a bigger job ahead of her now that they were going to be late. These circumstances changed everything, and she had a lot more planning to do.

Terry returned to the cockpit five minutes later, and loudly cleared his throat as if to say "get out of my chair lady." Zoe turned to Chuck and said "push as hard as you can to make up time, my best friend's life depends on it." She tried not to but there was a weak pleading tone in her voice.

Chuck had caught the tone in her voice, and said "I will do the best I can, but I can't promise much with what I've got to work with."

Zoe left her seat and pushed Terry aside to leave the cock-pit.

Before Terry could utter a retort, Chuck said "God dammit Terry sit the fuck down and help me steer."

Zoe went back and sat down exasperated. She had no idea what to do if she was late. It occurred to her that she was going to lose the only man she had ever loved, and her plan to help him was falling apart.

Zoe continued to pour over the map book that she had bought at Walmart on her way to the airport. It was the best she could find, and wasn't much help. She tried to call Weathers again, but her phone kept losing signal. Sully was in a no win situation, and Zoe was going to be too late to help him.

Sully awoke from his half hour nap an hour and fifteen minutes later. His internal clock had woken him up in a half hour, but he had hit his internal snooze button several times. He had dreamed of Zoe, and a life together with her in the mountains of Arizona. Sully had kept "snoozing" to try to get the dream to continue, but had no luck. Nevertheless, he awoke refreshed and ready to do the impossible.

Sully had planned as well as he could and was determined to beat the unbeatable odds. He crawled as slowly as a snail toward the edge of his "hidey hole" and took out his powerful binoculars. The schoolhouse was still too far away to see, so Sully said to himself "time to move".

Sully was wearing jungle camouflage over light desert camouflage and the bulk had made him sweat profusely. The high humidity, that he guessed was at least eighty percent, was oppressive. He had already calculated for seventy percent upwards in the jet to adjust for the heavy air that would make his bullet drop a lot more than just the distance, which he had already adjusted his high powered scope for. Being on the floor of the thick jungle there was no wind, and the town square was surrounded by buildings, so wind adjustment wouldn't be much of a problem. But it still had to be done.

Sully was also wearing two pistols, they were carried under each arm in black tactical nylon shoulder holsters that also held two extra magazines for each. With the pistols alone Sully had over one hundred rounds of ammunition on him. The pistols were both nine millimeter in caliber. One was the silenced Berretta, the other was a Glock seven without a silencer.

Sully stood into a crouch and moved silently toward the schoolhouse carrying the heavy sniper rifle in his left hand. When he had covered eight hundred yards he crouched in a patch of thick jungle undergrowth.

The smell of the jungle was palpable, and Sully enjoyed the unfamiliar smell. Loud birds were continually screaming their mating calls, and there was the occasional yell of a primate in the distance.

Sully hid in a bush and raised his binoculars again and could see the rear of the schoolhouse well. There was one large jeep and two Bolivian soldiers milling around the back. He was pretty sure that at least two more were at the front.

Sully looked at his watch and it was oh eight fifty five. His plan was to move at oh nine forty, quickly dispatch the guards, and then get set up on the roof. The sanction was the easy part, the getting away part was nearly impossible.

Sully watched intently through the binoculars and eventually the two Bolivian soldiers from the front came around to switch with the two in the back. Good, Sully thought, only four to deal with. For the big event school had been canceled for the day, which he had been counting on. The plan was to quickly eradicate the rear guards, run through the schoolhouse and dispatch with the front guards, quickly drag them inside to hide them.

Then Sully planned to look for a roof access in the schoolhouse, otherwise it was back outside to the rear to use the automatic grapple. He was watching the change of guard, and it happened every half hour. This worked in his favor because he was going to hit them ten minutes after a switch.

Sully double checked all of his gear, then checked it again. He prayed for the first time in his life. He asked God to give Zoe a good life. Then it was "go time".

Zoe was startled awake by Chuck when he rushed out of the cockpit and said loudly "Kathy, you might want to get up here." Zoe shook her head twice to clear the cobwebs from her sleepy mind. She had been dreaming of a life together with Sully in a cabin in the mountains somewhere. Zoe had never had happy dreams before Sully, and now she was unable to help him.

She opened the door to the cockpit and it was immediately apparent that something was drastically wrong. In the pre-dawn glow she could see tree tops not too far below the plane, she didn't take it as a good sign.

Zoe gasped and said “what is our altitude Chuck?” Her tone was more than a little concerned.

Chuck looked quickly at the altimeter and shakily replied “sixty five hundred feet right now and falling rapidly.”

Zoe pulled no punches and said to Terry “you have two options right now Terry, get the hell out of that chair or I will drag you out.” She had closed the distance to Terry and was standing right beside him when she finished the threat that she was fully prepared to carry out.

Terry turned toward Zoe with no apparent move to get out of the co-pilot’s seat. Terry was able to utter “fu” before Zoe smashed his nose across his face. She unbelted him and threw him on the floor of the cockpit. Zoe sat down in the seat as Chuck said “damn lady, I guess he should have listened to you.”

Zoe buckled herself in and grabbed the controls. She turned to Chuck and said “now what? Did you think flying on one engine wasn’t challenging enough?”

Chuck said with all the urgency he could muster “stop fucking around, pull up as hard as you can, and listen to me. Our only engine keeps losing power, and I don’t know why. We are about four hundred miles from La Paz, and we are dropping like a stone.”

Zoe was pulling up with all of her strength, as she surveyed the gauges to try to find the problem. Chuck had already pushed the power levers to the max and the engine was sluggish at best. A light bulb came on in Zoe’s mind and she turned the steering control wheel to the right.

Chuck was fighting her bank maneuver and said “have you gone nuts Kathy? If you want to crash this crate let’s just do a nose dive!”

Zoe said quickly “Chuck, I think all of our fuel is stuck in the left wing. If we do a hard bank right we can hopefully get enough fuel into the right wing to keep us from crashing. So help me save our asses and bank right with me.”

Chuck figuratively picked his jaw up off of the floor and said graciously “man, I never would have thought of that. Kathy, if this works you might get a discount.”

They both had to fight to turn the jet steeply enough to move the fuel. When the fuel starved engine received its transfusion, it returned to full power and they were able to level off and climb. There was a collective sigh between them and Chuck sincerely said "thank you Kathy, I was looking for a good place to crash, but now I'm pretty sure we'll make it. I owe you a big one."

Zoe was ready to reply to Chuck when there was a groan from Terry. Zoe unbuckled, jumped up, and stood over him and snarled "ready for round two Terry?"

Terry slowly got to his feet and the last thing he remembered for quite some time was trying to throw a punch at a lady.

Chuck laughed, then said "remind me not to piss you off."

Zoe smiled and said "Chuck, don't piss me off."

They both laughed heartily, mostly from the relief they felt at being somewhat safe once again. Zoe sat back down in the copilot seat and said "we need to get some good altitude and do that bank maneuver at least two more times to be sure."

They climbed to twenty thousand feet and did the bank maneuver once more when the radio started barking. Zoe and Chuck put their headphones on simultaneously. Before Chuck could speak Zoe said "how far off course are we?" The La Paz tower was telling them that they were drifting into the flight path of a seven ten.

Chuck said "right now way of course would be a lie." They knew they could not bank to the left, because of the engine and fuel problem so Chuck called the tower and told them their status. They were going to reroute other air traffic around them, but they still had to do a slow left turn to get back on course before they reached La Paz. Their current E.T.A. was eleven hundred hours.

Zoe's heart sank. They were going to be way too late.

Sully ran out of the jungle looking like a crazed ghost with a gun. Neither of the rear guards new that their time on Earth was up when Sully's silenced pistol coughed twice and put a bullet in each of their skulls.

The back door of the school hose was unlocked, saving Sully some time. He entered and closed the door silently behind him. He left the sniper rifle just inside the door and low crawled rapidly to the front of the schoolhouse. Sully had a quick change of heart and hid standing against the wall on the hinged side of the door. His only hope was that the Bolivian language was close enough to all of the Spanish he had learned in southern Arizona.

Sully banged on the door with the butt of his weapon a loudly said "ese's, nessisito tu aqui rapido!" Loosely translated, Sully had said "friends, I need you here quickly!" It apparently worked because the two front guards came bursting through the door together. Two more coughs from the silenced Berretta and the front guards were ironically shot in the back of their heads.

Sully closed the front door and looked out the window toward his target area. There had been no alert sounded and the festivities were progressing nicely. It was time to get up on the roof.

Sully scanned the small school and saw no roof access possibility. He hustled toward the back door casually stepping over the bodies of the two men whose lives he had just stolen as if he were in expensive shoes, and they were puddles. If there were such a thing, Sully thought that the smell of death was in the stale air of the schoolroom.

Sully picked up his sniper rifle, hurried out the back door, and ran into the jungle. Five yards in he quickly shed his outer layer of jungle camo. Now in his light desert camo he ran back to the schoolhouse and deployed the auto grapple. He threw the hook, yanked on the rope to anchor the hook, and pushed and held the up button. The device simply fed the rope through itself at a rapid rate, the more you helped it along the faster you climbed.

Sully reached the roof easily and low crawled to the front parapet wall to get set up for his shot. The parapet wall was a good height for a kneeling shot, and Sully focused his scope on the target zone. He looked up at the Bolivian flag on top of the courthouse, and it was limp, fluttering slightly to the left. Sully estimated less than three miles per hour of wind, so wind adjustment calculations were easy.

The shot was set, and Sully had three minutes to spare. He laid down on the roof and tried to visualize his escape routes. Instead his thoughts turned to Zoe, and how much he loved her. Sully was confused about where their relationship was going, and why she had left him the way she did in Hawaii.

A loud cheer from the crowd snapped his thoughts back to the sanction. Sully looked through the scope and saw Ramirez speaking at the podium. The enthusiastic crowd cheered at the lying leader's every promise to better their lives. He could not hear the amplified speech from his position, but he saw Ramirez make a grand gesture to his right and Francisco Mendez made the fatal error of stepping into view of Sully's scope.

Mendez was apparently a good speaker because the last five words he ever spoke had whipped the crowd into a frenzy. Sully took a deep breath, held it, found his aim spot, and squeezed the trigger. After the recoil Sully worked the bolt action of the weapon to put a fresh cartridge into the chamber. He looked through the scope to see Mendez lying on the ground with a large portion of his head missing. All Sully could think was "time to run".

Sully slung the large rifle over his right shoulder and low crawled to the back of the schoolhouse. He quickly slithered down the rope and was literally running for his life. He covered the open ground to the jungle in seconds, picked up his jungle camo, and sprinted to his hidey hole. Sully put on his jungle camo, hid his sniper rifle under the ghilie tarp, grabbed his pack, and headed south.

Sully knew that it was a three hour run to his first extraction point, and with the heavy pack it would be a chore. He had plotted each point on his GPS, and ran like hell for the first one hoping Potter would be there. Sully stopped for a long drink from his canteen, and to check the GPS to see if he was on course. He was off by a few degrees, but at his current pace he should be there early.

The jungle was much rougher than he had planned for, and every exposed part of his body was covered with bleeding scratches. Several of the cuts required suturing. Sully had a machete attached to his pack, but had no time to use it. He simply bullied his way through the unforgiving Jungle with brute force. He was pushing himself to his very limit to get back to Zoe.

Chuck landed the jet in La Paz, Bolivia. Both he and Zoe breathed a sigh of relief when the wheels touched the landing strip. The arduous flight was over. When the plane finally taxied to their spot and stopped Chuck and Zoe unbuckled and embraced. Chuck said "I think I might owe you my life lady." He had a bigger smile on his face than Zoe had ever remembered seeing. It was at that moment that Zoe knew that she liked the old pilot, and more importantly, she knew she could trust him because he owed her.

Zoe got on her tiptoes and kissed Chuck on the right cheek. She smiled genuinely at him and said "thanks ace, I couldn't have done it without you."

They both laughed to shed some tension. Then Zoe looked at the cockpit floor, pointed to Terry, and said "what are we gonna do about him?"

Chuck chortled and said "leave him right there. That's the most useful I have seen him since I hired him."

Zoe smiled and said "can you watch my gear for a while? I've got to go see someone."

Chuck said "Kathy right now I would do just about anything for you, if I lost this piece of crap plane I would be screwed."

Zoe did not give him a reply as she opened the door/stairs of the passenger compartment. She had to find another jet that was sure to be close by, Sully's.

She exited the Citation, and immediately started looking for a Lear jet from the SSO stable. It took Zoe only seconds to find the only Lear parked at the private terminal, and she walked/jogged to it.

The small third world Airport was teeming with action. Bolivian military vehicles and personnel were moving seemingly everywhere. Zoe saw two military helicopters in the air, and heard others in the distance. She climbed the stairs of the Lear and agent Ron Rady was there to greet her. Zoe had never met him during training, but his reputation had preceded him. Looking at him she knew what she was told was correct, he looked like a first class jerk.

Rady slowly looked her up and down, smiled suggestively, and then said "sorry cutie, but this is a private jet."

His creepy come on smile made her flesh crawl. She gave him an icy stare, and pushed threw him. She said "I'm agent Millstad, who is the valet for Agent Mills. Not one of the three men on the plane uttered a word, but the older man sitting at the back had given himself away by quickly hiding behind a newspaper.

Zoe walked over to Potter and said to him in a vicious tone "are you gonna give me a situation report on Agent Mills, or am I gonna get physical with you?"

Before Potter could even open his mouth Zoe had done an incredibly fast turn on her left heel, pulling her silenced pistol at the same time and pointed it at Rady. She saw him coming up from behind her in Potter's eyeglasses. She snarled "sit down Rady, this doesn't concern you."

Rady had stopped in his tracks and sat down in the nearest seat with a shocked look on his face.

Zoe never turned back to Potter but instead kept her weapon trained on Rady's crotch. Zoe addressed him loudly, saying "what's it gonna be do I get the situation report, or do we go the other way?"

Potter sheepishly said "I can't tell you anything without authorization."

Again Zoe spoke to him, without turning around, and said "Well, I think for ole Rady's sake you might want to do that."

Rady angrily said "just call Weathers so this bitch quits pointing her fucking gun at me Potter."

Zoe sneered at Rady and said "now we are making some progress." Then to Potter "why don't you place that call on the conference room speaker phone, and Ron and I will join you."

When she heard Potter enter the conference room she said to Rady "what's the pilot's name?"

Rady was getting really mad now but simply said "Steve" giving her an icy stare.

Zoe loudly said "Steve why don't you go check the landing gear for a while." Zoe's stare never left Rady.

Steve was smart enough not to say a word and swiftly left the jet. Zoe walked to the door/stairs, and pushed the button to close up the jet, never letting her stare leave Rady. She said "let's go make that phone call Ron."

Zoe had Rady lead them to the back of the plane, needing only to gesture with the muzzle of the silenced Berretta. Potter announced them saying into the Telstra device that was duct taped together "they are here Sir."

Zoe wagged the muzzle of her pistol at a chair, then back to Rady. She said forcefully, yet emotionlessly "sit Ron." Rady begrudgingly sat down with a scowl firmly affixed toward his kidnapper. Zoe remained standing, and let the gun hang to her side.

Weathers voice was distorted by the broken Telstra device which made him sound like he was pinching his nose. In another situation this might have been amusing, but not today. He sounded more than just a little irritated when he barked "what in the hell is going on Millstad?"

Zoe felt silly talking to what sounded like a Weathers' impression of Kermit the Frog, but her resolve did not waiver at all as she said "well hello Jim, it's surprising the length an agent has to go to get you on the phone these days." Zoe had been wondering how she was going to deal with Weathers, but in addressing him now her sarcasm and newfound hatred for the man flowed freely. Her contempt for Weathers was blatantly obvious to everyone in the Lear jet with every syllable she pronounced.

Weathers voice came back "agent Millstad, you need to think about your answer to my next question long and hard. What are you doing in Bolivia?" He was as serious as a man could be while being heard through the inadvertently invented "Muppet" voice scrambler.

Zoe was still not in the mood for taking any shit, and replied "well Sir, I still have a week of vacation left, and I heard La Paz was beautiful this time of year. Besides, agent Mills asked me to meet him here for dinner." Zoe smiled slightly as if Weathers could see her through the phone.

Weathers said "I see, but that fails to explain why you are on one of my jets holding two of my agents hostage at gunpoint."

Zoe continued playing the game and quipped "it just so happens that my charter ended up parking right next to your jet, so I came over to say hello. Mr. Rady was a little rude to me so I decided that the gunpoint thing might be a good way to get in touch with you."

Weathers was done playing and quite angrily said "fine you got me, now what do you want."

Zoe was not done messing with Weathers and replied "well like I said, I have a dinner date with agent Mills and was hoping these boys could help me find him."

Weathers finally relented and snarled "fine Zoe, if we can stop fucking around, I guess I can let you help with this mission. But you, I, and Sully need to have a long talk when this is over. That is if you can extract him before the Bolivians find him."

Zoe simply said "thank you Chief."

Weathers said "Rady, Potter, consider agent Millstad in charge for the rest of this mission, but make sure she knows the rules." The broken speaker phone mercifully clicked off.

Zoe holstered her weapon, smiled at the two men and said "well now that we have that cleared up, what did he mean about rules?"

Sully reached the first extraction point twenty minutes early the last couple of miles the jungle had thinned out a little and was slightly easier to get through. He found a spot that offered great concealment but also gave him a sliver of a view of the road.

The plan was that he would wait here until twenty minutes past thirteen hundred hours, then move to the next point for a meet at sixteen hundred hours. He took his extra time to review his course to extraction point two. Sully hoped he wouldn't need it but he activated the waypoint in his GPS. He also took the time to eat two energy bars and finish the water he had left in his canteen he thought hopefully, the four small bottles of water he had in his pack would be enough.

The Bolivians were most definitely after him, but had not gotten close yet. Sully heard helicopters passing overhead, but they were useless because he was hidden under the thick jungle canopy. His only hope was in Potter, and that wasn't much.

He vowed to himself that somehow, someway he would get back to Zoe to figure out what went wrong and how to fix it.

Zoe was quickly briefed on the extraction plans, and the rules. The rules were mostly common black ops rules. No dog tags, no identification, no traceable weapons or gear, and no radio contact. The exception for Sully on this mission was that extraction was limited to ten hours after the sanction. After the time limit was up the Lear was instructed to leave, and any agents not on board were to be left on their own.

Zoe took in the extremity of this final rule, looked at her watch, and barked at Rady and Potter "get it into a higher gear boys, I will be right back and I expect you to be ready to go."

Zoe went back to Chuck and his jet. She found him talking animatedly to a mechanic by the plane. He saw Zoe walking quickly toward him and told the mechanic to wait there as he came to her.

Chuck said "we got problems Kathy, this local bastard won't even look at the plane without a ten thousand dollar retainer, and I ain't got it."

Zoe said "yes you do Chuck. Tell him you will give it to him in five minutes, we need to talk inside." Zoe turned and went to get into the small jet, and Chuck went back to talk to the mechanic.

Terry was sitting in a passenger seat, with an ice pack on his face when Zoe walked in. She said "Terry, the times for games is over. I could use your help, but it's up to you.

Terry's voice was reminiscent of Weathers', very nasal in tone when he answered her saying "I think you broke my nose." He had a hurt child's look on his face.

Zoe turned away from him and went to the small refrigerator in the back stifling a laugh. She grabbed three beers and went to the small table in the front and set two down. She took the third to Terry and offered it halfway toward him and said "it's your choice Terry you want to come up front and drink this with me, or I can hit you with it?" she had a small disarming smile on her face.

Terry smiled and said "I ain't fuckin' with you no more lady." His sincerity was palpable.

They laughed a second and moved to the front table as Chuck came in and said with a shocked look on his face and said "I would have bet against seeing this when I came in here. I was expecting Terry to be out cold again."

He and Terry laughed but Zoe was all business.

Zoe handed Chuck a beer and he sat down as she said "My best friend on Earth is out there in the jungle running for his life. I'm going to bring him back here safely. I need your help and will pay you well for it. Right now I want Terry to take all my gear to the Lear jet next to us, and Chuck I want you to talk to that mechanic about getting this bird ready to fly A.S.A.P. It's entirely up to you guys, I will pay you in full and you can take off as soon as you can, or you can help me."

Chuck said "I'm definitely in, like I told you, I owe you a big one.

Terry was not quite as enthusiastic when he replied "I'm in too, as long as nobody hits me in the face no more."

They all touched their beer bottles together as a confirmation toast, and then got to work.

Zoe went to her small day pack, took out three bulky envelopes, handed them to Chuck, and said smiling "that's fifteen grand, see if you can get them to put in a fuel cross-over valve while they're at it."

Chuck laughed and said "you bet your ass I will, but we're gonna have to have a serious talk later."

Terry had already left with one of her bags and Zoe rushed to pass him and helped him get the heavy bag into the cabin of the Lear.

As they walked in Rady came over and said "who is this." He was very skeptical of Terry.

Zoe replied "This is Terry, he is the copilot of the jet that brought me here, and a friend. Terry is going to oversee the preparation of that jet in the event that we miss our deadline, and need a ride home." She tried to make it sound official so that Terry could feel better about staying behind.

Terry left to retrieve Zoe's other bag and Chuck came up the stairs.

Before Rady could have said a word Zoe said "This is Chuck my pilot and he is going to help us, so let's all get into the conference room and get this deployment briefing started."

The all left for the miniscule conference room, and Zoe waited for Terry. She helped him in with the bag, and said to him "I really need you Terry, we all do." She handed him a fat manila envelope with five thousand dollars in it.

She spoke only to Terry, making sure she had his undivided attention, saying "We need you to make sure that plane is ready to go when we get back, this Lear is out of here in about eight hours. That's your deadline to be ready. That money is for bribing the mechanics if you have to, but you also need to stock the plane with a bunch of food, water, and medical supplies for when we get back. I provided you with a list of priorities and necessary provisions inside the envelope with the money."

Terry said "I got it, and trust me I'll be ready and waiting. Besides, without you or Chuck, I ain't got no ride home."

Zoe nodded at him and he left with an urgency that gave Zoe hope. Terry was most definitely the weak link. That was the easy part. Now she had to deal with the boys in the back.

When she got to the conference room Rady was grilling Chuck. He stopped when Zoe walked in and said "let's go over our assets quickly and go over my plan. It is eleven forty five, and we need to be on our way by twelve fifteen." Zoe's time frame was unrealistic, and she knew it, but she had to push hard to get to Sully before the Bolivians did.

Zoe said "agent Rady I want you and Chuck to get our gear together. Do we have vehicles ready?"

Rady replied "we have two Jeep Cherokee's, but one needs fuel." He seemed to be happy to be in on the action, and had lost some of his bad attitude.

Zoe said "good take Chuck and get them fueled up. Potter and I will go over the extraction plan quickly and start getting gear ready. Do you think Steve will help us load up?" She knew she could simply order Steve to help them but to procure Rady's support she knew it would be necessary to stroke the jerk's ego.

Rady almost sounded cordial when he said "yeah Steve is a good guy, you want me to ask him for you?"

Zoe said "no, as long as I know he's alright, I'll handle it. I need those vehicles back here pronto, and park them right by the door when you get back Ron, okay?" The "Ron" was way over the top, but she needed him on her side.

As soon as they left she turned to Potter and said "set us up with two sets of maps, and two GPS units programmed with the extraction coordinates, I will meet you back in the conference room in a couple of minutes. I need to talk to Steve."

Potter uttered a meek "of course agent Millstad." He scurried away to complete his tasks. Zoe was sure he was still more than a little freaked out by her with the pistol earlier.

Zoe walked quickly to the cockpit and entered without knocking. She gave Steve a hard stare as she said "Rady said you would help us, is that true." Zoe didn't have time for playing around, and was purposely intimidating him to save time.

Steve said "Anything you need, as long as you realize that I can't leave the plane."

Zoe did not change her demeanor at all when she replied "I am fully aware of that Steve. All I need is for you to gather supplies for us. I need two small coolers packed with food, bottled water, and a few beers. I also need you to put together two medical supply kits. Can you do that quickly Steve?"

Steve said "that's all, not a problem."

Zoe let her demeanor soften and said "thank you Steve." Then she left to go back to Potter.

Potter had the maps out and ready when she returned to the conference room. Zoe interrupted his work on a GPS, and startled him by saying “how long until we are ready to brief everyone?”

Potter said “I need about five minutes to finish the GPS waypoints, then I just need to brief you agent Millstad.” Potter barely made eye contact when she spoke to her.

Zoe was a little softer now to help Potter calm down, but still firm when she said “alright Potter, put that down and go over what Mills had planned.”

Potter immediately put the GPS unit down, stood meekly over her shoulder and pointed as he said “this is the route Mills designed. Extraction point one is nine miles from the schoolhouse where he performed the sanction. As you can see it follows almost directly south paralleling the town, rather than running away from it. Recent satellite imagery shows that point one is already out of the search zone that was concentrated to the west, and point two is six miles farther from that and, if we get there on time, should be totally in the clear.”

Zoe smiled the first genuine smile she had in days. She was impressed with Sully’s tactical planning, he was running away from the search zone. Zoe’s confidence rose a notch, and she finally let herself be optimistic. Her heart leapt at the thought of finding Sully safe, and soon.

She looked at the map and decided to send Rady and Chuck the long way around. Team A, as they would be called in her briefing, would travel the highway south forty miles and then circle back on the main road, then circle back north toward the extraction points on unmaintained jungle roads.

Team B, Zoe and Potter, would take the direct route through the jungle to both extraction points one and two, then meet in the middle if they needed to. Hopefully they would have Sully by then, but if not they could re-strategize when the met.

Zoe turned to Potter and said “Mills did well in planning his escape, I’ve got what I need for my briefing, let’s get ready.

Zoe went through her pack and took out a fresh set of clothing. She pulled out a pair of khaki Dockers, and a black silk Lands’ End blouse, fresh black socks, and the green bikini. She was hoping to find Sully, and give him a treat when they were alone.

Zoe disrobed fully right in front of Potter and Steve, who was putting the medical supply kits together. There was no time for modesty. Poor Potter almost had a stroke watching her undress, then dress. Steve's mouth was wide open, and Zoe thought she saw a trickle of drool in the right corner of his mouth.

She totally ignored them both and went back to packing her gear and weapons.

Zoe was fully packed, armed, and ready when the Jeeps arrived. She had packed civilian clothing for Sully as well, so when they found him, not if, he could change and look less like an assassin.

Zoe had no "if" they found him plan in her head. She was prepared to spend the rest of her life in Bolivia searching for him if need be.

The briefing was short but effective, when Zoe had helped them load the two vehicles, she told them to return to the conference room on the Lear.

When they were all seated, including Terry, she addressed them in a very strong military voice. Zoe said "gentlemen give me one minute to get Steve."

Zoe walked toward the cockpit, but Steve had been listening in and met her halfway. Zoe grabbed him by the elbow and guided him back to the conference room. Along the way she said nicely "thank you for your help." Zoe was playing to the egos of all the males on this mission.

When they were all in the conference room Zoe started her briefing. She steeled herself against the passel of men she was commanding.

Zoe was very strait forward, nice, yet assertive when she addressed the team. She started with "I want all of you to get one thing straight. Failure is not an option on this mission. We will get agent Mills back alive, do all of you understand?"

There was no response from the men other than Rady emitting a small groan.

Zoe continued the briefing with "now that we all understand the objective of our mission we can get to work." Zoe gave a hard stare to the men one by one before she continued with "we have good maps, but limited recon, so this will not be easy."

She then said "if any of you want to refuse this mission now is the time." Zoe waited for a response and there was none. She then said

"Rady, you and Chuck will be the A team." Zoe was further stroking his ego to get his help. Zoe continued with "the A team is going long, and they will probably reach extraction point two before Potter and myself, who will be the B team." Zoe was lying to them but it was necessary. She needed Rady fully onboard and confident, that is why she made his team the A team.

Zoe gave Rady a large envelope containing a CD, and a cassette tape. She said "the plan is to play this CD ten minutes before and ten minutes after the pick-up points with your stereo at full volume and all of your windows down. That was the signal agent Mills planned with Potter."

Zoe said "Rady I need to go over your route with you, the rest of you need to get those Jeeps totally squared away, Steve has packed us coolers and med kits, dismissed."

They left at thirteen hundred hours and the plan was finalized. Extraction point one was out, but they had plenty of time to get to point number two.

Rady and Chuck were already gone, and Zoe and Potter were ready. When they were well on their way Zoe put the CD into the player and laughed harder than she had in a long time. The song was Ricky Martin singing "living la vida loca", and she laughed because right now that is exactly what they were doing, "living the crazy life."

They a leisurely drive to extraction point number two, because it was the safest option.

Zoe pulled over and let Potter drive. They had three hours to go twelve miles, and she needed some personal time. Zoe sat in the back and wrote a letter to Sully to explain her feelings, and actions. She wrote:

Dear Sully,

I have no way to apologize for my actions. When I left I was mad at you for choosing our job over our love, but now I have come to understand our situation. You had the same choice I would have, none. I reacted like an ass and I hope you can forgive me.

Sully, my heart was a cold stone when I met You, and you have given me the world. I can now hear birds singing, and children laughing. I can smell flowers for the first time in my life. I have felt love for a man for the first time ever, and it is, and will always be you Sullivan.

Please forgive me for leaving you, and let me back into your heart.

Forever and ever yours,
Zoe.

Zoe folded the letter and put it the pocket of the pants she had brought for Sully.

Zoe cleared the tears out of her throat and said "pull over Potter, I will drive from here."

Potter pulled over and quickly got into the passenger seat. Zoe took over the driver's seat and said "how far are we from point two?"

He was still leery of Zoe, but said "we passed point one twenty five minutes ago, and our current ETA is fifteen hundred hours, so we are on time, and then some."

Zoe barked at him "what if we hit a spot in the road we can't cross, or run into a Bolivian patrol? Don't ever relax Potter, that's a good way to get us killed."

Potter didn't even reply for fear of saying the wrong thing.

Sully waited until just after the cutoff time for extraction point number one, and hustled to point number two. He had two and one half hours to cover six miles of thinning jungle, so knew he would be there on time for sure. He had not seen any signs of the Bolivians since the sanction, and thought that his evasion training had come into play when he decided to head South, instead of West.

Sully was at extraction point number two thirty five minutes early, and barely had time to dig a bottle of water out of his pack, when he thought he heard a song in the distance. He scrambled under the nearest bush with his pistol drawn. As the music grew closer and louder Sully knew he had made it, it was his stupid song. He crawled out of the bush and walked to the road. He could see Potter driving, but got immediately concerned when he made out the silhouette of a passenger in the back.

He raised his gun and ran toward the car, then he smiled the biggest smile of his life. It was Zoe in the driver's seat.

The Jeep skidded to a stop, and Zoe barely exited the vehicle before Sully almost tackled her with a hug. Sully finally broke the embrace and said with extreme surprise "Zoe, what the hell are you doing here?" he was smiling.

Zoe simply said "throw your gear in the car, and get in. Then I can explain how I saved your sorry ass." She hugged him tightly and whispered "I don't know what I would do if I lost you Sullivan Mills."

Sully whispered back "I feel exactly the same Zoe, but let's talk in the car before a Bolivian patrol shows up."

Zoe said "good idea" and they got in the Jeep.

Sully said "hey Potter thanks for coming to get me, where did you pick up the hitchhiker?"

Potter said "Sir that is agent Millstad and she is most definitely in charge."

Sully said "well then I should probably ask before I kiss her." Anything else he had to say was interrupted by Zoe grabbing him and giving him a big kiss.

Zoe finally broke the kiss and said "strip Mills." Sully was taken aback and did not know how to answer. Zoe crawled in the back for one of her packs, and came back with the civilian clothes she had brought for him.

Sully said "oh." Then he started to take off his camo clothing. He was barely re-dressed and he was just finishing putting his shoulder holster back on when they saw lights heading toward them down the road.

Potter stopped the Jeep, and they were all ready to scurry into the jungle when they hear faint music growing louder, and sure enough it was Ricky Martin, and they all laughed.

Zoe smiled, and said to Sully "Ricky Martin? I never knew you were into salsa dancing, are you gay?"

They were all still laughing when Rady came to the door. Rady saw Mills and smiled.

Mills said "Potter get us back to the jet as quick as you can, but on a different road. Rady follow us."

While they were still stopped Zoe went to the hatch back and found the cooler that Steve had packed. She grabbed four beers, two sandwiches, and the bag of first aid supplies.

By the time she got back to Sully, Potter had a road that led to the main high way plotted in the GPS and they were on their way. Zoe opened three beers and gave one to Potter and Sully, the third was for her. She said "to pulling-off the impossible mission."

They all raised there bottles, then took a long drink. Sully leaned over and held Zoe tightly for a long while. Then he said "thanks for coming to get me, I love you more than you will ever know."

Zoe said softly "I love you too Sully." Then she pushed him away and smiled, and then she said "I will love you even more after you take a shower, sorry Pal but you reek!"

They drove to the airport without incident, as Zoe cleaned up the wounds on Sully's face. Sully winced and pulled away from her nursing several times. When she was done he had three butterfly bandages on his face, but most of the scratches were superficial.

Zoe lightly kissed the bandages, and then gave him a big deep kiss. She whispered into Sully's ear "does the baby feel all better now?" Then she nibbled on his ear for a minute. Sully just kissed her without saying a word.

When they were close to the airport Zoe said "Joe, if you ever want to work in the field again, I suggest you keep our relationship to yourself."

Potter replied "of course agent Millstad."

They arrived at the private terminal and the Lear was gone. Only Chuck's beat up Citation was there. Zoe said aloud "that God damned Weathers recalled the Lear two hours early."

Sully said "I pissed him off by surviving, and you pissed him off further by being here, by the way, why are you here?"

Zoe said "I'm on vacation, and you owe me a night of dancing Ricky." She kissed him on the nose, then she whispered "you scared me Sully, I had to come see if I could help, and I wasn't kidding, you really do need a shower."

Sully laughed silently and held her for a second, just long enough to whisper "maybe you can shower with me."

Zoe whispered back "and maybe I could join you after you have a few minutes to wash stinky." She smiled a loving smile at him.

They parked the Jeeps by the door of the Citation, and they all got out. Sully looked at the old jet and said to Zoe "you came on that? You're braver than I thought."

Zoe elbowed him in the ribs as Chuck came over. Zoe gave Chuck a hug and said "Sully, this is Chuck, the pilot of the Citation, and a friend."

Sully shook Chuck's giant meaty hand and said "Thanks for all your help, and for bringing Zoe. Besides, it looks like we need a ride home."

Zoe had taken charge again and yelled "Rady start loading our gear in, and if you see Terry you tell him to see me right away."

Rady yelled back "you got it agent Millstad."

Sully smirked, shook his head at her, and said "how the hell did you get Rady on your side? He really doesn't like you very much."

Zoe gave Sully a suggestive smile, and said "after I slept with him he was putty in my hands."

Chuck started laughing and said "I think it has more to do with her left jab, or her right cross. That's how she got my copilot to cooperate."

Zoe said "not really Sully, I slept with him too." She said it with as straight a face as she could muster.

Sully was starting to look mad until Terry came running over with two big black eyes and a broken nose.

Terry stuck his hand out to Sully and said "you must be that Mills guy they were looking for, wow. I didn't think they had a chance in Hell of finding you."

Sully smiled big at him, shook his hand, and replied "yes I must be. What happened to your face?"

Terry leaned into sully and said quietly "no matter what you do don't fuck with that blonde lady."

Sully chuckled and said "I will keep that in mind Terry."

Chuck was over by the plane talking to what appeared to be a mechanic, and Zoe. Sully walked slowly over to them to see what was going on.

Chuck was shaking Terry's hand and the mechanic was leaving. The Odyssey looked its age, but Sully was pretty sure it would get them home.

Zoe had disappeared inside, so Sully went over to Chuck and said "how are we doing"

Chuck said "perfect, I guess Kathy must have knocked something straight in that boy. The flight plan is filed, the plane has been repaired, and we can taxi out right now if you are ready."

Sully put an arm around Chuck's shoulder and said "Chuck I'm more than ready." And they walked to the plane together.

They were in the air ten minutes later, and forty minutes after that they were over international waters. Sully finally felt safe. He went to the cockpit and said "Chuck is there a shower onboard?" He felt silly asking, but he could smell himself now that they were inside the small jet, and it embarrassed him.

Chuck said "I can fix you up in a minute." He yelled of his shoulder "Terry get in here!"

Terry, Zoe, Potter, and Rady had been toasting their success at the small front table. Sully had joined them for one beer, but then sat down in a seat to relax. Then he went up to talk to Chuck.

When Terry came up to the cockpit and said "yes Boss?" Chuck almost fainted, but instead said "Terry, it's on auto, but if anything changes get me right away." Terry said "yes Sir", and Chuck thought he was in the twilight zone.

Chuck led Sully to the miniscule back cabin, which was sadly also his home. It was very clean and well kept. Chuck said "there is a small bathroom with an even smaller shower in there." He pointed to the only door in the room. Chuck dug in a drawer and pulled out a long sleeved tee shirt. He said "sorry, that's the best I can do. Go on and shower and I will bring you a towel."

Sully said "thanks for everything Chuck, I mean it." Chuck just nodded at him and left. Sully stripped and took a quick military shower, he knew the jet couldn't have that large of a fresh water tank. He stepped out of the shower and there were no towels. He walked out of the miniature bathroom to see Zoe wrapped in a towel.

Zoe said in a sultry voice "is this what you're looking for?"

Sully simply said "all my life" and stood looking her in the eye, dripping. He said again softly "all my life."

Zoe said "can you ever forgive me for leaving you like I did in Hawaii? I was such a fool." Zoe could not bring herself to even look at him now, and looked at the floor.

Sully grabbed her and held her close. His voice cracked when he held her so tightly he thought he might hurt her and said "I didn't think I would ever see you again Zoe, so I really didn't care if I lived or died."

Sully started drying himself with the smelly shirt. Zoe stopped him and handed him the towel she had on. He took it without looking at her and dried himself. Sully said "I'm sorry Zoe I just thought I was done for, and before you I wouldn't have cared, but now I do, a lot." He finished drying off, and was looking through his dirty clothing for something to put on.

Zoe said "I brought you fresh clothes, and a surprise. All you have to do is look on the bed."

Sully turned to look at her and smiled through his melancholy mood. She had clothes laid out for him on Chuck's bed, and was lying in a sexy pose, wearing the awesome green bikini that she knew he loved seeing her in. Sully moved to her and they kissed long, hard, and lovingly. They both knew that making love was not an option right now. They dressed and went back to the crew.

They sat with Rady and Potter for one more beer. Sully went to a passenger chair and immediately fell asleep. Zoe went to make sure Chuck and Terry were alright in the cockpit, and then sat in the chair next to Sully. Zoe put her head on his shoulder and they slept that way until they landed in Virginia, safely.

When they taxied to the hangar there were four agent mobiles, with matching agents waiting for them. Zoe went to the cockpit and said to Chuck "they are going to have to take you and Terry in for debriefing. Just be honest and complete. I'm pretty sure they are gonna search the plane, but don't worry about that."

Chuck replied "I kinda figured that's what all the men in black were for. The hardest thing I'm gonna have to do is explain to Terry that debriefing doesn't mean they are gonna take his underwear." He continued through their laughter "but seriously Zoe, I'm giving all of your money back, it might take me the rest of my life, but I'm not sure I'd have a rest of my life without you."

Zoe said "I want you to keep all of it, and what you don't think you earned, consider a retainer. I'm pretty sure I will need you in the future."

When they stopped in the hangar Terry came up to Zoe and Sully. He handed Zoe back her envelope and said "I spent just over a grand." Then he turned to Sully and said "you better be nice to this lady, she can get mean quick, man."

Zoe handed Terry back the envelope, and kissed him on the cheek. Then she said "split that with Chuck for a job well done."

He stammered "gee, thanks Kathy." Then he ran to the cockpit to tell Chuck.

Sully had a pleasant, but puzzled look on his face and said "you're gonna have to tell me about everything I missed, and why you messed poor Terry up like that. Now when we get off this crate, you're gonna have to follow my lead. I'm not letting them take us in right now, so let's grab our personal stuff.

They both grabbed their packs and loaded them, mostly with guns. Sully put on his shoulder holster with the silenced Beretta, and slipped into a light brown windbreaker. Zoe wondered why they were going out armed, but followed suit, and put on her shoulder rig.

Rady had opened the door/stairs and they were all filing out of the plane. Chuck was last, and before he left he came over to Zoe and Sully and said "any time you need me, even if you don't need the plane, you call me. Your money is gonna go a long way toward me squaring my debts."

Zoe gave Chuck a kiss on the lips, and replied "I couldn't have done it without you Ace." Zoe handed him a small piece of paper with her cell phone number, and said "same goes for you, any time you need anything don't hesitate to call me." They hugged, and Chuck left.

Sully said "whatever happens going forward, I love you Zoe." They kissed and left the Citation.

When they left the jet everyone was in the cars and they were leaving. An agent came over to them and said "agents Mills and Millstad, I have been instructed to take you to operations for debriefing."

Sully gave the agent a cold mean stare, and said "that's not happening today." Sully had seen their car when they taxied in and was heading for it.

The pick-up agent said "Sir's this is an order from Director Weathers."

Zoe was walking shoulder to shoulder with Sully, and it was her turn. She icily said "tell Weathers to stick his order up his ass."

Sully followed up with "tell him we will call in tomorrow, and tell Weathers that if he wants a bunch of dead agents he should send them after us."

The agent was dumbfounded, and didn't say a word.

They walked as a pair to their car and Zoe grabbed the keys from on top of the passenger side rear tire and said "do you want to drive Sully?"

Sully said "not unless I have to, I'm still pretty tired Zoe." He was hypnotically staring at Zoe's perfect ass, as she walked around the car to unlock it. Sully still thought that this whole thing with Zoe might be a dream, but if it was he never wanted to wake up.

Sully threw his weapon laden pack into the back seat, and just before Zoe put the car in gear he leaned over and gave her a big kiss, then he said "take me home beautiful."

Zoe didn't reply, but instead started driving. She had a broad smile across her face because Sully had called it "home". She had never had a home and they had both been careful to call their rented house anything but home.

She looked over at Sully five minutes later and he was asleep in the passenger seat. Zoe lightly stroked his hair, and softly whispered "I'll take us home baby" she was happier than she had ever been. She had a wonderful friend and lover, and they were going "home" together.

When Zoe bumped the car into the gravel driveway and stopped. Sully woke up and said "where are we?"

Zoe leaned over, gave him a light kiss, and said "we are at our home Sully" then she kissed him deeply.

They went inside, and Sully grabbed her and kissed her gently, he whispered "we need to sweep this house, I'm sure they have been here."

Zoe whispered back "I'll do it, you go get comfy." Zoe went into her duffle bag, found the frequency detector, and started sweeping the house.

Sully stripped down to his boxer briefs and went to the bathroom. He relived himself, then brushed his teeth. He went into the closet and found a short sleeved Hawaiian shirt that Zoe had bought for him on vacation, and put it on without buttoning it.

When he returned to the kitchen he grabbed a Corona light out of the fridge, and looked in several drawers before he found an opener.

Sully opened the beer and sat at the kitchen table, silently waiting for Zoe to finish the sweep of their home.

Zoe came in five minutes later and said quietly "come here."

Sully took his beer with him to the kitchen sink and looked down at the nine bugs and three miniature cameras that Zoe had found in the sweep. He looked into one of the cameras and held one of the listening devices and said "you boys need to quit wasting your time and money, and pray I never catch one of you bastards planting this shit in my home. Bye bye for now." Sully tossed them all into the garbage disposal as Zoe turned on the water and hit the switch. It made an incredible racket for a few minutes, then the bugs were gone.

Zoe grabbed the beer from Sully and took a long drink, then she said "what do we do now that the house is clean.

Sully said "I was thinking we could take a nap, then make love, then shower, then cuddle some more. What do you think?"

Zoe wrapped her arms around his neck and said "I think that sounds absolutely wonderful."

Sully picked her up in his weary arms and carried her into the bedroom and laid her on the bed. They kissed for a minute, and Zoe said "let me get comfortable."

Zoe stripped provocatively into only her panties and came back to the bed. When she spooned against Sully, she felt something hard poking her in the back. Zoe turned to Sully and said "I think I want to change the order of our plan." She reached down and rubbed his erection as he kissed and licked her breasts. When she moved down to try to perform felattio on him her pulled her up to his face and kissed her.

Sully said softly "you don't get to do that unless I do too."

Zoe said breathlessly "at the same time? I've never done that."

Sully replied "there is a first time for everything, and trust me, you will enjoy it as much as I will."

Zoe moved on top of him, and they made oral love to one another. It made Zoe wild with passion and she had to stop several times to moan loudly and push herself harder into Sully's face. She had climaxed several times, and felt the dire need for penetration. Zoe climbed off Sully and then straddled him again. She bucked wildly with passion until they were both spent.

They fell together and slept the sleep of angels. They awoke three hours later and made love in the shower. Then they went to the kitchen and each had a frozen dinner. They went back to bed and slept again.

When their nap was finished two hours later, the sun was coming up. Sully went to the kitchen naked and made coffee. Zoe came in shortly after wearing a sheer Victoria's Secret robe, and slapped Sully lightly on the ass. She kissed him and said "I'll watch the coffee, you had better go put something on sexy man or I will have to drag you back into that bedroom."

Sully went and brushed his teeth then went to the dresser and found a pair of plaid pajama bottoms that clashed perfectly with the Hawaiian shirt he picked up from the floor. Sully was a little tense, because he knew what time it was, it was time to talk about the mission.

Sully went back to the kitchen, and Zoe was sitting at the table with a cup of coffee, and had one ready for him too. He sat down and took a drink of his coffee. Sully said "thanks for pouring me a cup, you look absolutely beautiful Zoe."

Zoe smiled and replied "you look pretty damn good yourself, if you can get past the outfit you're wearing cowboy. I think we need to tell each other about our side of the mission before we go in to debrief."

Zoe said "I'll start. When I got your last phone call, I thought I was going to lose you and I was not going to let that happen."

Zoe told him her whole story. She really only hit the high points. She told Sully about coming home, trying to call Weathers, meeting Chuck, beating up Terry, saving the Odyssey, telling off Weathers, and finding him. By the end of her telling of the story, she was emotionally exhausted.

Sully said "I can never thank you enough for everything you went through for me. I think I've had enough coffee." Sully took their mugs and put them in the sink, then he took Zoe's hand and led her to the sofa in the small living room.

They sat and kissed gently for a couple of minutes, then Sully said "sit back and I will tell you what happened to me." He told her about the limited recon he was able to do, killing the four guards, his perfect shot at eight hundred and ninety yards, his run through the jungle, and how he felt when he saw her at the pick-up point.

When he finished Zoe said "I know I am as well trained as you are, but I think I might have refused that mission and accepted the consequences."

Sully said "that thought never crossed my mind. I thought I had lost you, and a no win situation kind of appealed to me. I don't have words to describe how happy I was to see you pick me up. Then I found this."

Sully reached behind the sofa and showed her the back of a picture frame. He turned it around and Zoe saw her crumpled and folded note that Sully had placed over a wildlife scene print that had been hanging in the spare bedroom.

Zoe grabbed the now framed note and set it aside. She hugged Sully, kissed him deeply, and said "how was I lucky enough to find you?"

Sully replied "I guess you don't play the lottery much." He smiled at her, grabbed her quivering chin, and gently kissed only her lower lip.

Zoe pushed him away and crossed the small room to a small stereo that she had bought before she decided to go after him. She pushed play on the stereo's CD player and the introduction to Lionel Ritchie's "Hello" started playing. Zoe went back to the sofa and pulled him up. She said "you owe me at least one dance mister."

They held each other and swayed to a song that was perfect for both of them. When it ended Sully kissed her, and then the next song started.

Sully laughed heartily when it was his pick up song, "Living la Vida loca", which he had picked because it too was perfect for them, "living a crazy life".

Sully was now laughing so hard tears were coming to his eyes, as Zoe was dancing like a white guy, and moving all over the room. Sully decided to join the silliness, and danced in his white man style right along with her.

They fell on the floor in uncontainable stress relieving laughter for just a minute, then the fun was over.

Chapter 7

Four "agent-mobiles" screeched to a halt in front of the house, and the agents that got out were heavily armed. They all had long guns in their hands. Some had M-16's, the rest had tactical twelve gauge shotguns. There were nine agents in all, and Sully didn't like the odds.

Sully said "go get dressed quickly, no weapons. I guess Weathers wants to see us."

Zoe started to leave, then turned to Sully and said "are you going to change, you look ridiculous."

Sully replied "no, I'm comfortable, and I think ole' Jim will get a kick out of it." Sully thought, this is only the start of pissing off the man that tried to get him killed. He yelled back to Zoe "grab me some socks and my boots, that should finish off the look." Sully took the cheap cowboy hat that Zoe had bought for him at Walmart off of the post of one of the kitchen chairs, and put it on.

Zoe walked out carrying Sully's boots, and socks. She was dressed in black Calvin Klein pencil pants, and a yellow Beebe sweatshirt, accompanied by black Roper boots. She looked at Sully, who had buttoned his shirt and put his cowboy hat on, and laughed. She said "I wish we had a camera sweetie" then tossed his boots at him.

Zoe and the fashion challenged cowboy left their home from the side door and were immediately accosted by two of the underling agents. Sully tried to look tough in his silly outfit, and said to the agent closest to them "listen closely buddy, it may save your life. We are coming in easy, and we ride together no matter what your orders are, so talk into your watch, or cock, or whatever you have to and let the rest of these idiots know." He continued "and one more thing, let them know that if anyone lays a hand on me or the lady, your entire team will regret it."

The agent turned away and talked into thin air. A moment later he turned to them, with his gun at his side, and said "just follow me closely to my car, and don't make any sudden moves."

Zoe said "buddy, if we had any intention of making sudden moves you would already be dead." She had said it so coldly that even Sully felt a shiver run through him.

They encountered no resistance on the way to the agent's car, and they both climbed in the back without saying a word. The ride to Weathers' office was about ten minutes, and not a word was spoken by anyone for the entire trip.

When they arrived at Weathers' office building, several armed agents surrounded the car, and opened the back doors.

Sully and Zoe both exited their respective side, and Sully pushed the agent closest to him to the ground. He turned to the next and said "if you ain't gonna use a gun, never point it at someone who would." He ripped the shotgun from the agent's hands, and broke his nose across his face with the butt end. Sully pumped a shell into the chamber as Zoe got to his side and said quietly "don't do this Sully, please don't make me watch you die."

Sully threw the shotgun at agent broken nose, and they walked inside. As they did, not a single gun barrel was pointed anywhere but at the ground. The normally flirtatious Stephanie barely looked up and said "sit down, Mr. Weathers will see you in turn."

They sat on the waiting room couch, and Zoe said softly "what the hell was that scene outside all about?"

Sully replied softly "I guess I needed to flex my muscles, and I didn't like the way they were treating you."

Zoe smiled and said quietly "just try to keep your cool with Weathers."

Stephanie broke in and said "agent Mills Mr. Weathers will see you now,"

Sully stood and turned to Zoe. He held out his hand to Zoe and said "let's go, I am not into playing it his way, let's play it ours."

Zoe stood and they walked in together, hand in hand.

Weathers looked up as they walked in together, closed his eyes, and shook his head. When he opened his eyes they were both sitting across from him in the armchairs. He said "I could have sworn I asked Stephanie to only send you in Mills. But I guess you were just interested in saving my time by bringing agent Millstad in with you." He wasn't happy with them, and it showed.

Sully threw the first verbal punch when he said "sorry to disappoint you Boss, but here I am alive and unharmed. I guess you are just gonna have to put me back on your Christmas list."

Weathers tried to open the humidor on his desk but Sully leaned forward and slammed it shut. Sully said "I'm not in the mood to watch you play with a cigar for five fucking minutes, so let's get this over with."

Weathers was really pissed now, and said "let me tell you the facts right now so maybe you will calm down a little. We have given the Kumiega test to fourteen agents now including you. Twelve refused the mission and one has been lost in the jungles of Cambodia for six years."

Weather continued "You were supposed to refuse the assignment Mills, not pull it off. I have been on the phone with the SOD since you completed your sanction, and I am getting a little sick of it. At this point I have a pretty good idea of how you blew the head off of Mendez at over nine hundred yards, what I would like to know is why you did."

Sully replied "you recruited me, and trained me to be the best. I just didn't want your investment in me to go to waste." The tension from both sides of the desk was palpable.

Weathers said "fine I guess I will just have to accept that for now. That leads us to contestant number two. Why did you go to Bolivia agent Millstad, and please don't insult me with the vacation story again."

Zoe said "for some reason you knew we were a couple and tried to break us up by killing Sully. I decided not to let that happen. If you want to demote us, kill us, or kick us out, do it. Just don't hide behind some test if you don't like us being together."

Weathers didn't have a cigar to chew on so he got straight to the point by saying "the two of you having a romantic relationship violates several articles of the code of conduct for field agents. If you weren't my best active field agents you would both be dispatchers right now. I am going to let this go for now, but if your relationship affects even one assignment in the slightest, it's over, and so possibly are you."

Zoe said "alright, now it's my turn. Let's not forget who put us together Mr. Weathers, you did everything you could to make us a couple, and now your pissed that we are? I find it highly hypocritical of you to be calling us out for our actions at this point. And another thing, I will continue to sweep our rented house daily, and if I find anything from the SSO in there again I will personally return it to you rectally!"

Sully chimed in and said "so far I don't see how our relationship has negatively affected our work in the slightest. If anything it has given us motivation to perform well so we can get back to one another. Until this becomes a problem, don't make it one."

Weathers had been put in his place for the first time in a long time, and didn't like it one bit. He said "you will both go from here to Intelligence, and be formally debriefed, separately. From there consider yourselves on leave for a couple weeks, but remember you can be recalled at any time. Please try not to disappoint me again." When he finished he slid an envelope to Sully.

Sully didn't pick it up but instead said "I am assuming that is my sanction bonus, but why don't you keep it instead of playing this bullshit game with Zoe."

Weathers replied "take it Mills, the Kumiega test has been abolished by the SOD. He is still trying to explain to the President why the SSO sanctioned a high ranking Bolivian official without Presidential authorization."

Weathers opened his humidor then stopped and said "would it be alright with you if I had a cigar now Mills?"

Sully said "if you really feel you have to, but you do realize that smoking is bad for you, don't you?"

Weathers let a small grin invade his stern face as he started preparing a cigar. Then he said "get the hell out of here, and over to debriefing, and would the two of you stop intimidating my other agents. One more thing Mills, you look pretty stupid in that outfit."

Sully replied "Thanks Boss, it's the look I was going for."

Debriefing took most of the day, and when Sully was returned home it was almost dark. The car was gone and so was Zoe. There was a note on the table that said; "*Sully, I went to get us some groceries, be back soon. Love Zoe*"

Sully grabbed a beer and sat on the sofa with the radio on to wait for her. When he sat down he felt the crinkle of the envelope in his back pocket, and he pulled it out and opened it. The envelope contained a check for two hundred fifty thousand dollars.

Sully thought about it for a while. "*I guess that's what the SSO thinks my life is worth, and it's a hell of a lot more than the value I put on it.*" He figured he would wire fifty thousand to "D", and spend the rest on whatever Zoe wanted.

Sully walked around the small rented house looking at all of the little touches Zoe had put around to make it their home. He went out the back door and saw that Zoe had bought a small propane grill and he fiddled with it for a minute, and it lit well. Sully turned it off, and thought that they should grill up some steaks sometime.

He went back inside and put on a black sweatshirt and some blue jeans. He was just pulling on his boots when he heard a car pull into the gravel driveway.

Sully went out to see who it was, and helped Zoe bring in several bags of groceries.

They had greeted one another with a kiss, and while they were putting the groceries away Zoe said "you look much better than you did this morning, I think we need to ceremoniously burn that outfit."

Sully replied "I agree, maybe we'll have a fire tonight." The house had a small fireplace in the living room that they hadn't tried to use yet.

Zoe's eyes brightened, and she said "that would be wonderful. I saw a pile of wood behind the house." Zoe finished putting away the food, and left two big porterhouse steaks wrapped in butcher paper on the counter.

Zoe said "do you want a beer Sully?"

Sully said "not really, but I could really go for a scotch rocks, maybe I'll run out and get a bottle."

Zoe came over to him and said "I've got you covered cowboy." She kissed him, then went to a lower kitchen cabinet, and pulled out a bottle of Dewar's, and a bottle of Beringer Merlot. Then she said "if you open the wine, I will fix you a drink."

Sully smiled at her and said "you got a deal beautiful." He went over and got the corkscrew he had seen before when he was searching for a bottle opener. He opened the wine, found a wineglass and poured her a glass as she finished making his drink.

They exchanged glasses and Zoe raised hers and said "to better days"

Sully lightly clinked his glass against hers and said "I will definitely drink to that." He took a long drink, and so did Zoe. They sat at the table and Sully asked "how did your debriefing go?"

Zoe let out a heavy sigh and answered "long, invasive, and annoying. They seemed to be focused on our relationship more than the mission. I was uncomfortable the entire time, how about yours?"

Sully said "pretty much the same, but longer." He wanted to change the subject and said "do you want to go out for dinner or stay in?"

Zoe knew he was troubled about all that had happened today, just like she was, but tried to change it with the meal she had planned. She smiled and said "I would prefer to stay in, I got us two beautiful porterhouse steaks that have been seasoned and marinated, twice baked potatoes, and almandine asparagus. Or we can go out, your choice."

Sully smiled the best smile he could muster right now, and said "Zoe that sounds great, what can I do to help?" The booze was depressing his already blue mood, so he pushed it away.

Zoe said "well I've never heard of a cowboy that couldn't cook with fire, so you are in charge of grilling the steaks. Other than that I just want us to try to be happy on this shitty day, I will take care of the rest of the cooking."

Sully said "all you have to do is tell me how you want the meat, and when you want it done, I was already playing with the grill before you got home." He smiled and did a caveman voice and said "Me man cook fire good." He was trying to ease the tension between them and lighten his own mood at the same time.

It worked because Zoe came over to him and gave him a big kiss. She wrapped her arms around his neck and said "how did you get to be so wonderful Sullivan Mills. Wait I don't want to hear that answer again, but I still want names."

They both laughed, and the tension was gone.

After a wonderful dinner, they cleaned up together and were cordial, but not as loving as they were earlier. They smiled and laughed, but Sully was someplace else and Zoe was unable to bring him back to her.

In Sully's mind a switch had flipped and he realized that he was her only problem, and he was certain that she would be better off without him. He had decided to push her away slowly, and eventually become so unbearable that she would leave.

After they cleaned up Sully said "Zoe, I have a terrible headache, maybe from the wine. I'm gonna take some aspirin and go to sleep.

Zoe was shocked at the sudden change in him, and said "what's wrong Sully, I know it's not a headache. We were going to have a fire."

Sully came over and kissed her lightly. He said "I'm just tired, have your fire, I'll see you in the morning."

Sully left her in disbelief. He took a quick shower, put on fresh underwear and climbed on Zoe's side of the bed, with his face to the wall, and pretended to sleep.

Sully was scheming on how to distance her further when the lights came on in the small bedroom. He closed his eyes and breathed very deeply to feint sleeping.

Zoe was having none of it, and she was really pissed. She said loudly "Mills if you want me to leave just say so, but if you keep playing this stupid fucking game, I'm gonna kick your ass!" Zoe was seething and not in the mood for any of this shit. She continued by saying "if you want to go a few rounds, get your dumb ass out of that bed, and we can tear this place and each other apart."

Sully said "just let me sleep Zoe." It was obvious to her that he was upset when he said it.

She said "if that's what you want, you got it. Give me a couple of minutes to pack, and you will never see me again." Zoe went to the back room and grabbed the biggest suitcase they had, then it hit her. It was the biggest suitcase that "they" had.

She was about to fall to her knees and cry, when she heard a voice behind her. It was Sully who softly said "I think we should talk, before I break my promise to you."

Sully turned and walked to the living room and sat on the sofa, and Zoe was right on his heels.

Sully said "let me finish what I have to say, before you react or interrupt me. I have been thinking a lot about the events of the past week and especially today. I came to the realization that you wouldn't even be in any trouble with the SSO if it wasn't for me. I've thought long and hard, and the only solution to the problem is me being away from you. You know we can't run or hide, and you know we can't quit. All I have been for you is trouble, and I can't mess up your life by your being involved with me. I would never be able to forgive myself."

Sully had his head down and was rubbing his eyebrows with his right palm as he continued "Zoe, I do love you. Much more than I could ever love myself, that's why I think it's best for you to leave now. I don't want to drag you into the black hole that I am in. Please take a moment to absorb and understand what I have just said. You don't have to answer right now if you don't want to, I'm gonna go get a beer."

Sully was barely at the kitchen table with his opened beer bottle when Zoe walked in. Her face had softened slightly, and she didn't look quite as pissed any more, but it was obvious that she was still upset. She sat down at the table and said quietly and evenly "I understand your position, but now it's your turn to shut up and listen to me.

You know the story of my childhood, and you know why I jumped at the opportunity Weathers offered me. Now for the first time in my life I find love, and the man I truly love tries to push me away. Your life is a fucking rainbow compared to mine.

Zoe got up and got a bottle of water out of the fridge. She sat back down and took a long drink, then continued "you have opened my heart to love for the very first time in my life. You are the only man I have ever made love to. If you truly want me to leave, I will, but realize I will die inside without you. The ball is in your court Mills, I will do whatever you want. Be careful what you decide, because whichever you choose, it's final.

Sully stood, walked around the table and put his hand out to her. Zoe took it and they held one another closely and danced to no music. Sully gently pulled her chin up to look at him and he gave her a sweet gentle kiss. He said "are you absolutely sure about this?"

Zoe answered him with several deep kisses that lasted quite a while. The she said "what do you think?"

Sully just smiled and picked her up in a bear hug. Then he said "I think you're getting heavier is what I think." He let her go and chuckled until she hit him in the chest full force and knocked him backward.

Sully was truly upset, and ready to scream at her when she said "see you made the right decision not to fight me, and the wrong one joking about my weight."

Sully was rubbing his left pectoral with his right hand when he said seriously "if you keep hitting and pinching me so hard I'm gonna call the cops on you for spousal abuse."

Zoe laughed then pouted and said "aww come over here, Zoe will make it all better."

Sully was now acting serious, and mad when he replied "I ain't goin' anywhere near you lady, you're mean."

Zoe came to him and he put up a fake fighting stance. She walked through it and kissed his well-defined chest lightly right where she had punched him. She started to giggle and Sully backed away and said "what?"

Zoe laughed aloud and said "that's gonna be one hell of a painful bruise tomorrow."

Sully said "ha, ha, laugh it up fat girl." Then his eyes got wide at what he had said and he ran into the back yard with only his underwear on.

Zoe was right on his heels and tackled him in the grass skinning his right knee badly on the way down. He rolled over clutching his knee in pain, and Zoe was on top of him instantly. She grabbed his bruised nipple between her thumb and forefinger, and said "before you say uncle, I want you to promise to never comment on my weight again."

When he paused Zoe started to squeeze. Sully immediately yelled "I promise, I promise, now get off of me you sadistic bitch."

Instead of getting off, Zoe fell on top of him and he rolled her over into the dew soaked grass.

Her clothing was now soaked through, and she said "that was mean" as Sully limped back to the house.

He muttered under his breath "you're lucky I like your breasts so much, or your right would look like my left."

When Zoe came into the house Sully was wiping his bloody right knee with a wet paper towel by the kitchen sink. She said "thanks to you I need to change and shower." Zoe came toward him and Sully put up a hand and said "don't, not right now, I need a while to cool off."

Zoe sauntered off to the shower, and he heard her say "what a big baby."

He waited until he had heard the shower running for a couple of minutes, then snuck into the bedroom to grab his clothes. He took them, and the car keys and quietly went out the side door and got in the car. Three blocks away he stopped to dress himself, and then he went to Safeway and quickly grabbed a box of Franzia White Grenache wine, and a case of Duraflame logs. On his way to the checkout he passed by the floral department and picked up a pre-arranged dozen rose bouquet in a crystal vase.

When he got back twenty minutes later the shower was not running, but he could hear Zoe's hair dryer. He put the roses on the kitchen table, the wine on the counter, and lit a fire. He was sure to check that the flue was open before he lit the fake log, and he was set. He had just enough time to pour two glasses of wine and hurry back to the fire before Zoe came out in a light blue satin pull over that barely covered her bottom or top.

Zoe came over to him and kissed him. She said "do the flowers mean I am forgiven?"

Sully smiled and said "you look delectable, but you are not quite forgiven yet." He handed her a glass of wine and they each had a sip.

Zoe said "I like your fire, and I am sorry if I hurt you Sully."

Sully replied "me too, I'm sorry if I hurt you Zoe, you are the best thing that ever has, or will, happen to me. But you gotta quit beating on me, I'm fragile."

Zoe laughed and snuggled close to him. She was stroking his arm lightly and said "this is the best fire I have ever seen, maybe it's the company, or that it's the first fire in our home, but I've never seen a better fire."

Sully was rubbing her smooth thigh and said "thanks it's my first."

Zoe replied "don't be silly, you mean first here right?"

Sully said "no, it's the first fire I've ever sat in front of ever."

Zoe said "quit teasing me Sullivan you must have wooed plenty of women in front of a fire like this before we met."

Sully snuggled back tightly to her and said "honestly Zoe there were no other women before you, I've had sex with a few girls, but only as was seemed like a need, and never saw any of them again. You are the first woman I have ever made love to, and hopefully I will be able to go to my grave saying the same thing."

Sully continued "as for fires, sure I've seen plenty, but I had to ask the guy at Safeway how to even light one. Don't forget I'm from southern Arizona, and even on the coldest nights we never needed a fire. This is very special for me snuggling up to a nice fire with a wonderful woman who just beat me up for the fun of it."

Zoe kissed him and looked him in the eye when she said "I love you Sully. I'll be right back." She ran to the bedroom and came back with clothes in each hand. The clothes in her left she tossed at him. The clothes in her right she threw in the fire. She sat on the sofa with her legs under her and said "get comfy and come sit with me and watch your outfit from this morning burn."

Sully took off his boots and jeans, and put on the grey sweatpants she brought for him. Then he took off the sweatshirt and put on the black sleeveless tee shirt she had brought him. He laid down on the small sofa with his legs hanging over the arm and his head in Zoe's lap.

They sat like that for a long while, watching the fire die down, then Sully said "I can get another log if you want me to."

Zoe stroked his hair and said "no we can watch the embers for a while longer then go to bed."

Sully sat up and reached for his jeans, he pulled the sanction check out of his back pocket, and handed it to her. He laid back down in her lap, and said "this is for you, I'm pretty sure I wouldn't be here to even receive it if it wasn't for you."

Zoe didn't even open the envelope and said "no way Jose, you're the one who earned this money."

Sully said "let me lay it out for you so you are sure to understand. Was Potter or Rady ready to go when you got there, no. Was the Lear there to take us home when we got back, no. If you had not have come with Chuck and Terry, I would be dead somewhere in Bolivia right now, or wishing I was. I owe you my life, and that check is just a down payment."

Zoe was speechless. She had never thought of all the true things that Sully had just told her. All she could think to say is "it all worked out in the end Sully."

Sully said nothing but stood and went to the kitchen. He found his box of Swisher Sweets tip cigarillos, and matches. He went out the back door, sat on the last stair and lit his cigar.

Zoe came out and said "can we talk some more? I thought we had a lot of things about our relationship figured out, but you just brought up things about Bolivia that I had never thought about."

Sully replied devoid of emotion "you can never understand what it felt like out there in the jungle knowing there was no hope."

Zoe said "you are right I can't. But we are here now safe and together, and to me that is what counts."

Sully just smoked his cheap cigar and said nothing.

Zoe stood in the doorway for a while watching her troubled love, the she said "I am going to bed, please join me soon."

Sully said nothing, and when the lights went out in the house he started walking. He walked for two hours, assessing his life, and love, and options. He knew he loved Zoe with all of his heart, but he had committed himself to death in Bolivia, and had made peace with it. He was finding it very hard to live again. As much as a life with Zoe appealed to him, he didn't know how to live that life. Sully had let his heart turn black again in that jungle and he was afraid of letting it change back to red. He wondered what time it was, and where he had ended up.

Sully was tired from thinking and laid down under a large Elm tree to take a nap. He set his internal alarm clock for four hours from whatever time it was and finally let himself sleep.

Zoe did not know what to think when Sully was gone. She waited three hours for him to come back, but he didn't. She dressed in a matching pair of grey sweat pants, and a hooded sweatshirt. She put on a pair of Avia running shoes, grabbed her purse, and took the car keys off of a hook next to the kitchen door.

Zoe headed out to find him again, not having the slightest clue where to look. She drove slowly south, away from town in hopes that she could find him and bring him home.

Sully found it impossible to sleep, even though he was exhausted. He felt like he was taking his troubles out on Zoe and he knew that wasn't fair. He started walking back, trying to figure out what to tell her about his foolish behavior.

He had walked back for about forty minutes when he saw headlights coming toward him. His trained reaction was to bury himself in the ditch and hide until the vehicle passed, but he was on no mission, so he suppressed the urge. He thought it was probably a local farmer getting his day started, when his own day had yet to end.

Zoe saw a figure in the distance and hoped it was Sully. She continued slowly forward, and her hopes were rewarded when it was indeed Sully walking toward her. She stopped the car fifty feet from him, placed the transmission into park, and jumped out and ran to him. She almost knocked him over with her embrace. She said "I would have gone for a walk with you if you had asked."

Sully replied "I just needed to try to get some shit straight in my head. I'm sorry I didn't tell you, but I thought you were sleeping." He was trying his hardest to be pleasant.

Zoe asked "will you come home and talk with me?" She was hoping she wasn't pushing too hard.

Sully kissed her and said "that's where I was heading when this strange lady came and picked me up."

Zoe smiled at him and said "watch out about who you're calling strange Mr. Glass house." She kissed him on the neck.

He grabbed her hand and they silently walked back to the car. They got in and she drove him home. Not far into the drive with them illuminated only by the dashboard lights Sully said "I hope you don't mind that I was the one that started calling that little house our home."

Zoe continued driving and said "mind, my heart leapt the first time you called it our home. I had wanted to, but I wasn't sure how you would react. That's very special to me because living with you here is the first time in my life that I have truly felt that I have a home."

Sully said "I guess what I've been struggling with since I fell in love with you is how to let myself truly love someone. I have always hardened myself against my feelings, and you let me feel true love for the first time in my life. When I was alone in Bolivia I thought my life was over, and I had to let all those feelings about you die to allow me to focus on the mission. Now I am struggling with letting you back into my heart, because I'm afraid of feeling that loss again."

Zoe pulled the car over and hugged him. She understood how he felt and was eternally grateful that he had the guts to tell her. She whispered "I've got news for you buster you will never lose me unless you truly want to."

They shared their first true and honest kiss. It was only for a moment, but Zoe felt a sense of completeness.

When they got home it was almost five in the morning. They went to bed and held one another until the sun came up.

Sully woke first, brushed his teeth and went to the kitchen to make some coffee. He was sitting at the kitchen table reading the newspaper he bought yesterday when he thought it might needed to start their fire, but the manufactured log had lit on its own just fine.

Zoe came into the kitchen smiling and said "good morning Sullivan" she came over and kissed him. She looked at his bare chest and the huge bruise she had given him on his left pectoral muscle. She tried not to, but a small laugh escaped her as she was crossing the small room to get a cup of coffee. She came back and sat across from him picked up a piece of the newspaper to hide her face that was ready to burst into laughter.

Sully said "you want to let me in on what's so funny?" He had a good idea what she was trying not to laugh about, but wanted her to say it.

Zoe didn't even lower the paper when she burst into laughter for several seconds. Sully pushed on and was smiling at her laughter when he said "I'm looking at the comics, and I really doubt there is anything that funny in the business section that you are holding, so come on Zoe tell me what's so funny."

Now Zoe's laughter was uncontainable, and when she put the paper down for a second and looked at him she started roaring with laughter. She put the paper back up and Sully said "fine, don't tell me." He purposely limped to refill his coffee cup, and then exaggerated his limp as he walked past her out to the back stoop to drink his coffee.

He didn't think it was possible but her laughter got even louder when he limped by her. He sat on the back stairs and smiled as he laughed to himself. When her laughing died down Sully put his coffee cup down and pulled up the right leg of his sweat pants to expose his wounded knee. He was pretending to tend to the wound on his knee that was really nothing. He heard the screen door squeak open, then it quickly shut, and he heard laughter running away from him.

He went inside to take a shower, and locked the bathroom door. He showered quickly, but not fast enough. The shower curtain opened and Zoe stepped into the tub. She said "now you didn't think that little lock would stop a trained agent like me did you?"

She was soaping his back and rubbing her breasts on him as she said it. Sully replied "no I didn't, but I was thinking you might respect my privacy." He had turned to her and smiled as he said it. He wrapped his arms around her and kissed her deeply. Then he said "are you done laughing at me?"

Zoe was soaping his privates as she said in a very sexy voice "baby I don't have laughing on my mind right now."

They made love in the shower until the hot water was gone then moved to the bed. They kept going until they were exhausted, then they fell asleep in each other's arms.

When they woke up it was almost dusk, and they had caught up on their sleep. Sully went to the bathroom and urinated for an incredibly long time prompting Zoe to say "Jesus, when is the last time you peed, last week?"

Sully finished and said "it seems like it." Then he moved to the sink to wash up and shave. He looked all around for his razor and couldn't find it. He said to Zoe who was still lying on the bed watching him "have you seen my razor, I can't even find the shaving cream." He was looking at her in the mirror as he said it.

Zoe replied "yep, I saw them both when I hid them. I want you to grow a beard. I think it would look sexy on you." She was smiling at his reflection as she said it.

Sully smiled back and said "I don't know, If I get any sexier I'm gonna have to carry a big stick around to beat off the ladies."

Zoe let out one big laugh and said "I guess I will have to protect you." She left the bed and walked up behind him and kissed the back of his neck. She put her arms around him and grabbed his penis with one hand and whispered "besides, you already walk around with a big stick."

He turned and kissed her, and then he said "I think with that comment I can finally forgive you for beating me up."

Sully said "I'm gonna take you out to dinner, anywhere you want to go. I'll figure out what to wear when you decide."

Sully put on fresh underwear and a too tight white tee shirt that Zoe had bought for him, actually she had bought several of them. She had said they made him look "hot".

Sully grabbed a bottle of water out of the fridge, and he sat down with the yellow pages to see what their options might be other than Sizzler or Outback. There were a couple of pizza joints, several taverns that served food, and that was about it, other than about fifteen Italian places. Sully thought "whatever Zoe wants".

Zoe came out in one of Sully's tee shirts that was way too short to leave anything to the imagination.

Sully said "if you don't want to go out, keep dressing like that." He winked at her and she turned fully around in a slow provocative circle to show off the rest of what he had not seen. He said "wow is the only word that comes to my mind right now."

Zoe came over and kissed him, then she said "good answer cowboy." She sat at the table and looked at the open phone book for somewhere to go. When she was disappointed with the selections she said "I know I'll call Chuck and ask him, besides I wanted to talk to him to see how his debriefing went."

Sully said "great idea, but put it on speaker so I can talk to him too."

Zoe had not even thought about her cell phone for last couple of days and fished through her purse to find it. When she did she came back to the kitchen and searched the phones memory for Chuck's number. She dialed his number, and then set the phone on the table. The phone rang once and a strange voice answered professionally "on time corporate services how may I help you"

Zoe was confused by the new voice, and warily said "may I speak to Chuck please?"

The odd voice came back and asked "who should I tell him is calling?"

Zoe said "tell him Kathy Jackson would like to talk to him." Sully had the same confused look on his face and when Zoe looked at him with a furrowed brow all he could do was shrug his shoulders.

They only waited a few seconds when Chuck came on the line and said "boy have I been wanting to talk to you." He sounded happy and excited.

Zoe said "you're on speaker, Sully is with me. We wanted to know how your debriefing went." Sully added a "hey Chuck" when he was introduced.

Chuck said "well the debriefing part sucked. It was a whole day of different agents asking the same damn questions. Mostly they wanted to know about you Kathy, and then what I knew about you and Sully's relationship. The rest after that has been awesome."

Sully now had his brow furrowed and asked "what do you mean by the rest after that?"

Chuck's smile could be heard over the phone when he answered Sully by saying "well I'll tell you what you guys have totally change my life, and Terry's too. When we were done with all the questions they recruited Terry into some kind of valet (he pronounced it ""val-ett"") training program that takes like a year and a half."

Chuck continued "Then they did a new background check on me and made me an emergency pilot. You wouldn't believe it, but they are paying me twenty two hundred a month to sit on my ass, and they have had a team of eleven guys over here for the past couple days fixing up my old plane! They are gonna be done in a couple hours. They even gave me a furnished condo in town rent free"

Zoe said "that sounds really good for you Chuck. Sully and I will try to keep tabs on Terry and let you know how he is doing every so often." She tried to sound upbeat, but there was clear disappointment in her voice.

Sully continues with asking "What happens to your charter business now, and who was that answering your phone?"

Chuck said "oh yeah, I almost forgot about Luke. They gave me Luke as my copilot and helper, and I don't have to pay him. I still have the business, but any charter I take has to be cleared with them, who and where. But I'm telling you this for sure, you guys fly free anywhere, anytime, for the rest of my life."

Zoe shook her head at Sully while Chuck was talking to him. Then she finished the call by saying "that all sounds great Chuck, we couldn't be happier for you. We gotta go we have dinner plans."

Sully yelled from the fridge "see you later Chuck." He was grabbing a beer.

Chuck whispered "you should really try Vincent's on Third Street at eight o clock." Then he almost yelled "okay, bye guys." And the phone clicked off.

Sully laughed and said "I guess super spy Chuck was sending us unbreakable code to meet him at Vincent's tonight."

Zoe didn't smile but rather frowned and said "I just can't stand that those assholes got their hooks into him. By now it's too late for him to get out."

Sully replied "I agree, how the hell are we going to tell him what a mistake he made." Sully took a long drink of his beer.

Zoe looked up Vincent's in the phone book and was not surprised to see it listed under Italian. She picked up her phone and called them for a dress code, and reservation.

When the phone was picked up with a nasty "hello" Zoe knew she didn't need to ask but she did anyhow. Zoe said nicely "yes can I get a reservation for two at around eight fifteen tonight?"

The restaurant voice replied "lady we have never need to worry about reservations."

Zoe said "great, we are new in town and I wasn't sure. What is your dress code?"

Now he laughed and said "no shirt, no shoes, no service. You must be really new in town."

Zoe laid on her charm and said "would you be kind enough to give me directions?"

Sully watched as she scribbled down directions and was getting very aroused by her in that tee shirt.

Zoe said "the restaurant is only about ten minutes from here so we have about two hours, and there is no dress code. Any idea what we should do until then, other than the one I can see in your pants?"

Sully smiled and answered "well, I would never want to take that out as an option, but I want to run something by you. I have quite a bit of cash right now, and I think you should decide where we should go. But I think we should go somewhere, so we aren't so close to the SSO. Even if you want to go to the South Pole I think it's obvious now that we can't hire Chuck to fly us. I think we go out tomorrow and I will buy us our own plane.

Zoe was excited about the idea and said "you know I've got a lot of money too, we could buy it together."

Sully smiled at her and said "let's see if we can find one first. We can talk to Chuck tonight."

Zoe came over to him and said "I think this is a wonderful idea Sully." She wrapped her arms around his neck and gave him a big wet kiss. The she whispered "If we are going to own a plane I'm gonna need some stick time." She was rubbing him through his underwear. She ran into the bedroom pulling off her shirt as she went.

Sully smiled and walked into the bedroom taking his shirt off. Zoe was lying on her back with her knees up and legs spread wide. She said "I thought you might like an appetizer." Zoe was really enjoying oral sex after having found it for the first time in her young life, and Sully didn't mind a bit.

Zoe was frantic after the oral part of their lovemaking and was rougher than usual. They were very sexually compatible, and this time it was over quickly and they were both breathless and sweaty.

Zoe kissed him when they were done and said "either you are really good at that or I just really enjoy it."

Sully said "Like I've told you before, years of" and that was all he was able to say because she kissed him.

Sully went outside to have a cigar while Zoe was showering and getting ready. She had told him she would pick out clothes for him.

Sully was enjoying his cigar, and a Corona, but he was troubled. He was wondering how he could tell Zoe that shouldn't go together on a plane purchase. It was too big a commitment for him and he sure as hell couldn't just come out and say that. He had a plan, but it was far from foolproof.

He heard the hair dryer turn off, and tried to put all of this out of his mind as he walked to the bathroom to take a shower. When Sully walked in Zoe was naked doing that upside down hair brush thing that women do and he said "wow! Are you sure we have to go out, I could sit here and watch you do that all night."

Zoe stood up and stuck her tongue out at him. Sully smiled and said "I'm good with this view too." His eyes never left her ass.

She said "come on Sully take a shower, we have to meet Chuck."

Sully said "did you say something, I think I was hypnotized." He shook his head and blinked quickly. The he walked over and gently squeezed her butt. He winked at her in the mirror and said "wait until later, if you're good." As he got in the shower Zoe tried to snap him with a towel and missed.

Sully still found it hard to break his Marine training when it came to showering, at least showering alone. He was fully washed and toweled off in less than two minutes.

He quickly dressed, brushed his hair, and was ready to go in less than six minutes. Zoe had laid out brown Dockers, a red Tommy Hilfiger long sleeved polo, a brown western belt, and his boots.

He walked into the kitchen and stopped in his tracks to look at Zoe. She looked absolutely gorgeous. She only had on a red Gap jersey knit dress with a low neckline, red Fendi high heels, and pearls with matching earrings, but it was more than enough to make him stop and stare. Zoe turned around and saw the open mouthed look on his face and said "what's wrong Sully"

He crossed the room and gave her a light kiss. He said "I've never seen anything more beautiful in my life than you look right now."

Zoe said "you look pretty damn good yourself cowboy, and thank you, that was a wonderful compliment. We have a little while so I made you a drink." She handed him a double scotch rocks and she had a glass of wine. She said there are chairs on the front porch, why don't we go sit out there and you can have a cigar."

Sully said "that sounds good, but I'm out of cigars."

Zoe went to a drawer and pulled out a bag of cigars and a small box with a bow on it. She walked to him and handed him the cigars. He looked at the package of Backwoods Smokes and said "thank you Zoe."

She said "I bought this for you in Hawaii when you weren't looking." Zoe handed him the box.

He opened it and pulled out the Zippo lighter inside with a hula girl on it. He looked on the back and it said *"to the first man I ever loved"* Sully said "thank you that's very nice."

Zoe laughed and said "the guy at the pawn shop said it would be an extra two bucks to remove the engraving, so I left it. He had three more so I bought all of them just in case."

Sully laughed with her and said "let's just go sit on the porch wise ass." Sully headed for the porch, and Zoe followed grabbing his cowboy hat and her red Brighton purse on the way.

The sat on the porch and Sully tried his new brand of cigars. Zoe had brought him his hat, so he put it on. The cigars were the same size as his old brand, but they had no tip. They looked like cheroots from the old western times and he liked them immediately.

Zoe asked him "Sully would you do me a favor for me if I asked?"

He answered "of course Zoe, anything."

Zoe smiled and pulled a small digital camera out of her purse and said "good I want to get a picture of my sexy man, and from now on we take a picture a day, no matter what."

Sully said "you know the policy on pictures of field agents as well as I do, they are not allowed."

Zoe replied "yes but this is digital, and we can buy our own laptop and save them just for us."

Sully said "as long as you think it's all right I'm in." He was leery about the idea but he would let it go for now.

Zoe posed him leaning his back against the willow tree in the front yard with his hat pulled down, and a freshly lit cheroot in his mouth. She took the picture twice, with and then without the flash. It made her happy so he didn't mind much.

Sully finished his drink on the porch and said "let's go, I'm gonna sweep the place for agents before we decide to eat there."

Zoe said "good idea, let's go" she was almost giddy about the camera and Sully's agreement to her daily picture idea. Sully saw it as an opportunity to give her something to do tomorrow while he shopped for a plane.

On the way to the restaurant they talked about how to gently explain to Chuck how screwed he was.

The closer they got to Vincent's the more the neighborhood declined. Vincent's was a run-down place in a bad neighborhood. When they walked in it was apparent to Zoe why they didn't need reservations.

There were only eight people in the place including Zoe and Sully, an old couple eating spaghetti, two agents sitting in a corner booth, the bartender, and Chuck sitting at the bar.

They walked over to Chuck and said hello, then Zoe stayed with Chuck and ordered drinks, and Sully went to the corner booth that contained the agents.

Sully walked up to them and said as harshly as he could "hello boys, I am only going to say this once so listen closely. You need to disappear, and I mean right now. Then you need to go back to headquarters and call it a night. If you or any other agent follows me the recruiters will have a lot of work to do. For your sake I hope you understand me. I'm heading back to the bar, and I want to see that door close behind you before I sit down."

Sully turned and started heading toward the bar when he heard the agents scurrying to leave. By the time he got back to the bar they were gone. He sat down, took a long drink of his beer and said to both Zoe and Chuck "let's get out of here."

When they were outside Zoe said "Chuck is there somewhere close where we can talk?" Sully was sweeping him with a frequency detector as he answered her question.

Chuck answered "well there's Beano's down the street, but they don't serve food, it's just a bar."

Sully said "your clean, Beano's sounds great, how far away is it?"

Chuck said "it's about two blocks down the street, we can walk." He was looking more confused by the minute.

Zoe grabbed him by the arm and walked him to their car and said "get in Chuck we can explain everything in a minute." Now he not only looked confused, he looked a little scared.

Sully got into the driver's seat and Zoe handed him the keys. They started their ride around town and Chuck said "what's going on?"

Sully said "first thing we need to do is order some take-out food. I'm starving. Chuck what do you want to eat?"

Chuck answered "I know the best pizza place in town. It's called Za Palace, and their deluxe pie is the best I've ever had."

Zoe was on the phone almost immediately and, after calling information, she had two deluxe pizzas ordered within two minutes.

Sully was driving in circles around the sub-par part of town, to make sure they didn't have anyone following them. When he was confident they didn't have a tail he said "Chuck I know your happy now but we think it's important for you to know what you've gotten involved with."

Chuck shook his head and said "I knew this was too good to be true. Tell me straight, how fucked am I?" There was a sound of hopelessness in his voice when he said it.

Zoe really liked Chuck, so she tried to sound upbeat when she answered him by saying "I don't think fucked is the right way to put it, but you were lured in by some very persuasive people into a very serious organization. The biggest problem is that with the SSO once you are in, there is no getting out."

Chuck let out a heavy sigh and said "I knew you guys had bad news from the tone of your voices when we talked earlier."

Sully tried to lighten the mood for a moment and said "were gonna pick up those pizzas, go to a liquor store, get some booze, and then we are all going to get drunk at our house. What do you drink Chuck?"

Chuck was still shaking his head and said "right now just about anything. But I usually drink brandy if there is a choice."

Zoe said "then brandy it is Chuck. We can tell you a little bit more about the situation during dinner. For now let's try to be happy." Zoe was very sad because she had caused all of this.

Sully pulled into the first liquor store he saw. He went in. In the car Zoe said to Chuck "I am sorry I got you into this and I don't know how I can ever forgive myself." She wept, and when Chuck grabbed her shoulder she cried harder.

Chuck was trying to console her and said "Zoe it's alright, I'm getting on in years, and I can make the best of this."

Zoe said through tears "there is no best of this, the SSO only causes heartache and pain."

Sully went right to the counter and looked at the glass case behind it. He was the only one in the place, and the old man behind the counter looked at him skeptically. He saw what he wanted and went to the cash register where the old man was and said "give me two bottles of Napoleon brandy and three bottles of Christal champagne."

The old man went to the glass case and got the prices, but not the bottles. He rang up the order on the cash register and said "That'll be four hundred and eighty dollars, and for that I gotta see the payment before you see the booze."

Sully got his wallet out of his back pocket and counted out five one hundred dollar bills and laid them on the counter. He said nastily "keep the change."

The old man fumbled to get the keys out of his pocket and filled Sully's order. When he finished bagging each bottle individually and carefully placed them in a larger bag. He said "thanks mister, I might close early tonight."

When Zoe saw Sully walking out of the store she stopped crying, quickly grabbed a tissue from the glove box, and wiped her eyes in the rearview mirror. She said Chuck please don't tell Sully I was crying."

Chuck simply replied "not a problem."

Sully got to the car and put the clinking bag next to chuck in the back seat. He could feel the sullen mood in the car and tried to change it by saying "we are gonna drink the good stuff tonight." He grabbed his bag of little cigars off of the dashboard and offered one to Chuck as he pulled one out for himself. Chuck took one and he offered one to Zoe and she said "why the hell not." And she helped herself to one as well.

Sully lit his cigar with his new Zippo, and then held it out to Zoe, and then Chuck, so they could light theirs. He laughed aloud at Zoe puffing on what he expected was her first cigar and said "did you bring that little camera along, I would love to get a picture of you with that cheroot in your mouth."

Zoe was digging in her purse for the camera, and Sully reached in the back seat for his cowboy hat. When Zoe found the camera, he handed her the hat, and she put it on. Sully took several pictures of her in different poses with the little cigar. Chuck was laughing along with them, and when they were done taking pictures Zoe took of the hat and handed it to Sully. When he had put the hat on her Zoe said "you need a new hat, that one is starting to look kind of ratty."

Sully replied "not on your life, I'm gonna be buried in this hat."

They all laughed again, then Zoe handed him the cigar and he carefully put it out in the ashtray. Zoe said "I don't know how you guys can smoke those things, they taste like shit."

Sully said "they are an acquired taste, kind of like me." He really wasn't kidding, but they both laughed. The he said "Chuck, how do we get to the pizza joint?"

Chuck said "Go out of the parking lot to the right, and then you will go up about six blocks and take a left. I will tell you." Chuck's mood had lightened, and Sully was going to keep it that way.

The pizza was just ready when Zoe went in to pick it up. They just chatted and laughed on the way to Sully and Zoe's home. The pizza was as good as Chuck boasted it to be and they all ate their fill while drinking beer.

Over dinner they tried to remain upbeat while explaining to Chuck exactly what he had gotten involved with. He took it pretty well, and it seemed like he had resolved himself to the situation he was in.

After they cleaned up after dinner, Sully took a bottle of the champagne out of the refrigerator. And said "this is supposed to be the best there is, and I think we need to make a toast to our successful mission properly."

Zoe grabbed three wine glasses as Sully carefully opened the champagne. They raised their glasses and each made their own toast to surviving the mission. When they drank each of them agreed that Christal was worth the price. It took the three of them an hour of talking to finish of the bottle.

Then Zoe said "we have something that involves you that is very exciting. Since we all agree that it's not in our best interest to use you as a charter we were hoping that you would help us find a plane of our own!" Zoe was really excited about the idea.

Chuck seemed excited about the idea too he said "really, what are you thinking of?"

Sully came over to the table with three wine glasses filled a quarter full with the napoleon brandy. Chuck picked it up and sniffed it and said "hey, this smells great, what is it?"

Sully said "nothing but the best Chuck, Napoleon. I've never had it, and I'm not a brandy drinker, but you're right it smells great."

Zoe lifted her glass and said "to our new plane" they all took a drink and agreed that it was very good. It really wasn't Sully's thing so he pushed his glass to Chuck and went to the fridge and grabbed a bottle of beer. He had asked Zoe if she wanted anything, and she declined.

Sully said "why don't we sit in the living room, I will light a fire." Now that he had lit one he thought of himself as the "fire maker", as long as it was with a manufactured log.

They all moved to the living room. Zoe and Chuck sat on the sofa, and after Sully lit the log he sat on the floor next to Zoe's legs. They were all winding down, and it was already past eleven hundred hours.

Chuck was still jazzed about the plane shopping idea and said "so what kind of plane are you thinking about?"

Zoe's head was swimming from the drinks and she got up from the sofa and said "I'm gonna make some coffee, for once I will let the boys talk about shopping."

Sully laughed a little and said "she's right it is kind of role reversal. But I don't know when I will be recalled for another assignment so I would like to buy a plane soon, tomorrow if possible. Can you go out with me tomorrow to start looking?"

Chuck said "sure, all I do is sit on my ass and wait for phone calls anyhow. I'm pretty sure Luke could do that for a day without me. What kind of bird are you thinking about?"

Sully answered "I was thinking about a twin turboprop that maybe seats four, but I want to be sure that I can still fly instrument flight rules, and don't have to file flight plans.

Chuck said "well that leaves out anything with a jet engine, because then flight plans are mandatory. What you are talking about is gonna be pricy, I know of a couple right here in town that fit the bill, but one is around two hundred, and the other is closer to three."

Sully replied "we will start with those, and then maybe rent a piper cub or something like that and fly around to the nearby airports to look at others."

Chuck said "sounds great, I love plane shopping, and I watch a cub for a guy that never flies, so if we need it we only have to pay for fuel. The first one I want you to look at is a Piper Seneca that is in a hangar at a small airfield about ten miles from here, it's where I take care of the cub."

Zoe walked in with a cup of coffee and said "can I get anyone coffee?"

Chuck said "no thanks, but if it's alright I'm go get some more of that fancy brandy." He stood and headed toward the kitchen.

Zoe came over and sat next to Sully and kissed him deeply. She rubbed against him and whispered "I really want you right now, and I mean right now."

Sully smiled and whispered back "about a half hour and Chuck will be on the couch, why don't you leave for bed in about fifteen and get him some bedding and a pillow. Then we can play, as long as you can be quiet."

She moaned at him softly and nodded yes. She was snuggling with him when Chuck came back with his brandy. Chuck got the hint, and he said "I'm gonna have this brandy and call a cab."

Zoe said "nonsense, we don't have a spare bed yet, but that sofa is plenty comfy, and I want you to stay." She smiled at him as she said it, and as Sully knew, she was hard to resist.

Chuck said seriously "I ain't used to imposing on people, especially those I consider friends."

Sully said "it's no imposition, I would worry more if you went back to your condo before I can teach you how to search for listening devices. I'm gonna go out on the front porch and smoke a cigar, then I will get you squared away for sleeping."

Zoe sat and talked with Chuck for a while about living with the SSO, then she found the extra bedding, and made up the sofa for him.

Sully didn't have a chance tonight to start enacting his plan for tomorrow, but he continued scheming while he had his cigar.

Sully finished his cigar. When he came in and Chuck was already asleep on the couch, or pretending to be. Sully said softly "goodnight Chuck" then walked to the bedroom. Zoe was in bed curled up and appeared to be asleep. He quietly took his clothes off. He hung up the shirt, folded the jeans and laid them on a shelf in the walk in closet, and threw his socks and underwear in the hamper.

Sully brushed his teeth in the faint glow of one of the night lights that Zoe had put in the bedroom, kitchen, hallway, living room, and even the back room that no one ever went in. Sully had joked that they could never turn on a light and be just fine.

He washed his face, looked in the mirror at his two day beard, and smiled at what Zoe had said.

He snuck into bed as quietly as he could, but turned and saw Zoe lying with her head propped up on her bent arm smiling at him. She said "I will give you fifty bucks to go brush your teeth again. Your cute little ass wiggles when you do." She smiled bigger and winked at him.

Sully said "I thought you were sleeping. I was trying to be quiet." He was smiling back at her. He got out of bed, went to the sink, and brushed his teeth again. He was watching her in the mirror and she threw the sheet off of her, and was rubbing her breasts as he brushed. He finished brushing for the second time and went back to the bed, this time fully aroused.

Zoe grabbed him and kissed him. She whispered "I love you, thanks for being so wonderful. You did a great job making Chuck feel better about this situation, and I really appreciate it." She kissed him deeply over and over. She said I want just you and Chuck to go plane shopping tomorrow, I trust his judgment on aircraft, and I trust you. I think he will want to talk tomorrow, and he might be more open man to man" She had been rubbing herself on his leg as she spoke.

Sully was shocked that she had taken care of his plan for him. He finished the other end of the plan while caressing her breasts. He said "if you don't have plans tomorrow I have something you could do for us."

Zoe was writhing and rubbing his penis with both hands. She moaned, then said "whatever you want, as long you make love to me soon. I'm ready to explode."

Sully was rubbing her private part as he breathed to her "I want you to go out and get us a better vehicle. I think that we deserve a better car than the granny mobile."

Zoe moaned almost too loudly and said "I love the idea, now please make love to me." She tried to guide him into her but he rolled over and away from her.

Sully said "not tonight dear, I have a headache." He was smiling and waited for her reaction.

Zoe said "right now I wouldn't care if your hair was on fire." She rolled him on his back and straddled his face looking at the wall, and hanging on to the headboard. After Sully had made her climax several times, she was glistening with sweat. She moved down his body and slipped him inside of her.

She put her hands on his chest and started to make love with him wildly. She was consumed with passion and only slowed after squeezing his chest and feeling him wince in severe pain.

She had squeezed his chest where she had caused him the large bruise. She leaned over and kissed his chest lovingly several times. Zoe said "I'm so sorry baby."

Sully said "it's fine Zoe, as long as you don't hurt my chest I'm fine." He rolled her over and entered her from behind. He had never done this with her before, and it was very apparent that she liked it. She had buried her face in a pillow, and was screaming into it. When they were finally spent they slept in each other's arms.

Sully woke up before the sun, and he slipped out of the bed and silently found clothes to wear, and grabbed his wallet off of the top of the dresser. He snuck out of the bedroom and into the kitchen, he placed his clothes and wallet on the counter, and then looked through the refrigerator to see what they had for supplies, and found nothing fit for breakfast. He headed back to the bedroom to tell Zoe he was going out, and almost ran Chuck over. Sully jumped back and said loudly "Jesus Chuck, you scared the shit out of me."

Chuck replied "sorry buddy, I needed to use the latrine." He was laughing lightly at Sully in a naked fighting stance. Then his eyes opened more widely than Sully had ever seen anyone's ever before. Chuck saw Zoe come out in her birthday suit to see what all the commotion was about.

Zoe made no attempt to cover herself when she put her hands said "what the hell is going on?"

Sully, who was also naked, answered "I was checking our supplies to see what we had for breakfast when I almost ran Chuck over. I was coming to tell you I was going out, and Chuck was heading to use the head."

Zoe laughed and said "you might want to put some clothes on if you're going out." When she said it, it made her conscious of her own nudity, and quickly disappeared into the bedroom.

Sully simply said "good point" when Zoe had left.

Chuck laughed as he walked out of the kitchen, toward the bathroom, shaking his head. He muttered "I didn't know you guys were nudists, I feel way overdressed."

Sully dressed and grabbed the car keys off of the hook by the side door as he headed out. He drove the fifteen miles to the Super Walmart with visions of Zoe running through his mind.

One of his favorite memories from his bleak childhood was when his mother had made biscuits and gravy for them one Sunday morning. He raced through Walmart finding what he needed to try to duplicate the meal. Sully was throwing things into his cart rapidly, one after the other.

For the meal he bought a roll of sausage, Pillsbury biscuits, powdered country gravy mix, eggs, bacon, white bread, whole milk, Tabasco sauce, orange juice, and tomato juice.

He hustled through the house wares department and found a cookie sheet to bake the biscuits on, then he headed toward the electronics department. On his way he passed the ladies wear section of the humongous store and found two lace teddies for Zoe, one black and one white.

He found a bored employee who sold him the second most expensive laptop computer they carried, and three pre-paid cellular phones, each of a different style. He purchased one hundred minutes for each. The older woman who had been helping him in electronics checked out the entire contents of his cart. She continually raised her left eyebrow at the eclectic nature of his combined purchase.

When she had the total on the register Sully handed her a prepaid Visa card in the name of Ted Sextant.

Ted was the alias he had used to rent the house, and he had over eighty thousand dollars in the account of the Visa card. The Sextant alias was complete with passport, Social Security number, credit report, driver's license, birth certificate, and pilot's license. It was his primary alias, and he had used it to open three different bank accounts at the Wells Fargo bank in town.

Sully drove back to the house in a better mood than he had been in since before Bolivia. He attributed the mood to Zoe, and the true love he felt for her. He was a little troubled at his reluctance to trust her fully.

When he got home it was just starting to get light. He went through the bags in the trunk and put the bag containing the lingerie way in the back of the trunk out of sight. The rest of the bags he was able to carry into the house in one trip.

As soon as Sully entered the house with his bags he could tell that Zoe and Chuck were still asleep from the odd smell in the air. He knew there was no way to cook without waking them, so he didn't even try to be quiet. He emptied the contents of the bags, and he put the perishables in the refrigerator. The laptop he hid in an upper cabinet, and the cell phones he left on the counter.

Sully loudly opened and closed cabinet doors and drawers until he found all of the cookware and utensils he needed. He put the sausage in a large cast iron skillet to brown and carefully measured the water and milk he needed for the gravy according to the directions on the package.

When that was started he made a pot of coffee, and then he sat at the table to read the paper he had bought. Sully got up every couple of minutes to check the pot, and to stir the sausage.

In the "Around the World" section he found what he was looking for. It was reported that Bolivian rebels had assassinated Francisco Mendez with a sniper's bullet shot from over eleven hundred yards, in a failed attempt to kill President Orlando Ramirez. Sully didn't want the credit, but the suggestion that he had missed his target gave him the faint urge to call CNN to set the record straight.

He folded the section open to the section in a way that Zoe and Chuck were sure to see it, then focused on cooking. He whisked in three gravy mixes into the milk and turned up the heat on the stove to bring it to a boil. He turned off the burner under the almost over cooked sausage, and then pre-heated the oven to four hundred degrees, as per the directions on the roll. He popped open the biscuits and arranged them on the cookie sheet he bought.

When the gravy started to bubble he took it off the heat and spooned the sausage in. He stirred in probably too much pepper, and covered the pot with the cast iron skillet, because he was unable to find the lid that fit it.

Sully was fairly certain that he had made enough noise to wake Zoe and Chuck, but he didn't hear Zoe moving, and he could hear Chuck snoring.

He stirred and tasted the sausage gravy and was very satisfied with his work. When he went into their bedroom Zoe was curled up into a ball, and sleeping with a small smile on her face. Sully clicked on the bathroom light, and hummed loudly while he brushed his teeth. He was watching Zoe in the mirror and she hadn't even moved. He took off his jeans and put on a pair of grey sweat pants. Then he crawled into their bed and cuddled with his love.

Zoe stirred and then moved into him and gave him a big kiss. Her breath was minty fresh and he knew she had already been up to brush her teeth.

Sully said "you cute little faker, you weren't even asleep." He kissed her.

Zoe said "who in the hell could sleep with all of the racket you were making in the kitchen, other than Chuck, who I can hear snoring all the way in here." She was smiling as she said it, and her smile warmed Sully inside.

He said "you look absolutely beautiful in the morning Zoe. When is the last time I told you I love you?"

She answered with a kiss and said "as far as I can remember it was two or three weeks ago."

Sully said "well then I owe you a whole bunch of them. Zoe I never dreamed I could be as in love as I am with you."

She held him tightly and they snuggled for a while. When Sully almost drifted off to a happy sleep, Zoe squeezed him tightly, nibbled on his ear, and then whispered "I never thought our lovemaking could get any better than it was, but you hit a homer last night. That was incredible, and I will never forget it."

Sully said "I've got a few more tricks up my sleeve, but I agree, last night was wonderful. Now haul that beautiful ass out of bed and get dressed. We both have a big day ahead of us, and I bought you a present."

Zoe jumped on top of him and said excitedly "a present, what is it?" She was hopping up and down like a five year old child on Christmas morning.

Sully laughed at her excitement and said "go get dressed beautiful, I've got to go check on my gourmet breakfast."

Zoe leapt off of the bed and ran into the bathroom she said "man, I shouldn't have jumped up and down like that, I've had to pee for an hour. You're lucky I didn't pee on you."

He replied "it wouldn't have mattered if you did, every day with you I feel like the luckiest man in the world." He walked out of the bedroom before she could reply.

Breakfast was done other than the biscuits so he just turned on the gravy to very low. Then he hurried to the front porch to make a phone call. Sully looked through the memory of his phone and found the number he wanted. He pushed the send button, and the phone on the other end picked up after one ring.

The other end of the phone said "Hello agent Mills, what can I do for you?"

Sully answered "Julian, I need a favor. I need you to go to records and find out what agent Millstad's birth date is. Julian, there's a catch, you have to make sure no one knows about it, but you and me."

Julian said "I will do my best sir." Then the connection was lost.

Sully knew it was a gamble using his SSO issued phone, but it was a harmless request.

Sully walked back into the house slamming the front door almost off of its hinges, and Chuck continued to snore.

Sully walked over to the stove to stir the gravy. As he stirred Zoe came out of the bedroom dressed in her breakfast attire. She was wearing a light blue Victoria's Secret terry cloth robe that was just barely long enough.

Sully had never asked why, primarily because he liked it, but Zoe only owned three pairs of panties, and rarely wore any of the three. Zoe walked over to him and wrapped her arms around his waist. She said "who slammed the door?"

Sully answered "I did in apparently a vain attempt to wake up Chuck, he snored right through it."

Zoe said "let me try." She went to Chuck and whispered in his ear. He stirred, then started snoring even louder. Zoe came back to Sully in the kitchen and said "that man sleeps pretty soundly."

Sully smiled at her and asked "what did you say?" He had a pretty good idea, but he wanted her to say it.

She filled a glass with water and drank half of it. Then she answered Sully saying "I told him I was Halle Berry, I was naked, and I wanted him to make love to me. The jerk barely stopped snoring for a second."

Sully laughed as she walked over and dumped the rest of her water on Chuck's head. He was definitely awake now, and he was definitely pissed off now. Chuck jumped up off of the sofa and when he saw Zoe and heard Sully laughing he said angrily "the next time you want to invite me to stay over do me a favor and don't."

Zoe said "I'm sorry Chucky" in a little girl's voice.

Sully went to the bathroom and got Chuck a towel, and grabbed him one of his sweatshirts. He came back and handed them to him, then he said "if there was any way of stopping her I would have Chuck."

Chuck laughed and said "Sully, run. Run fast, and run far. Get away from this she-devil while you still have a chance."

Zoe went over to Sully and stood behind him, with her arms around his waist, and said "it's too late Chuck, he has already promised me his soul in exchange for ravaging my body."

Chuck replied "actually not a bad deal for Sully from what I saw earlier."

Sully laughed and said "you've got a lot to learn buddy, you say something like that around this house, you've gotta be ready to duck."

Chuck said "I thought you got that giant bruise on your chest, and the scabs on your knee from the mission, but now I think I know better."

Zoe said in an evil tone "would you like a cup of coffee?"

Chuck answered "not unless Sully made it and I can pour my own into a freshly washed mug."

They all shared a laugh. Zoe and Chuck sat at the table, and Sully put the biscuits in the oven. He stirred the gravy, then turned up the heat a touch. He said "I made biscuits and gravy, but I also bought some eggs and bacon if you guys would rather have that.

Chuck replied "I haven't had good B and G since I left Alabama seven years ago." He did look excited, and Sully could only hope about the good part.

Zoe said "I've never had it, but I'll try it once." She had wanted to say something to flatter Sully, but she didn't want to be too mushy around Chuck.

Sully looked at the biscuits in the oven, then he said "we've got about ten minutes before breakfast if you need to wash up Chuck."

He said "I'll take you up on that, just keep an eye on the she devil while I'm gone."

Sully said "I will. There are a couple of new toothbrushes and some paste in the medicine cabinet."

Chuck left for the back bathroom, and as soon as he was out of view Zoe stood and walked over to him and kissed him. She said "I can't believe you made us breakfast. That's the only thing that got you out of agreeing with the she devil thing. You said something about a prize earlier, where is it?"

Sully said "maybe later if you're really good. For now you get the first choice." He dumped the three cell phones out of the bag and onto the counter. He said these are pre-paid with no contracts. We can talk to one another when we are apart without much worry of the SSO listening in."

Zoe grabbed the one in the middle. Then she said "this was such a good idea. I'm guessing the third one is for Chuck, right?"

Sully smiled and answered "not really, I was supposed to hide the third one, it's for my other lady." He tried to run, but was too late. When Chuck came out of the bathroom Zoe had Sully in a headlock and was playfully beating the top of his head into the wall.

Chuck said "I'd help you Sully, but that broad scares the shit out of me." When Zoe heard Chuck she released Sully, and they all laughed.

Sully was rubbing his head as he took the biscuits out of the oven. He took them off of the cookie sheet with a spatula, and then wrapped them in a dish towel. He put a stick of butter on the table, then grabbed three plates and three place settings. Sully snatched a handful of napkins, and put the ceramic penguin salt and pepper shakers that came with the house on the table. He stirred the gravy one last time, and then he placed it in the center of the table on a hot pad with a ladle in it.

Zoe and Chuck had sat down and were laughing and chatting while Sully got everything ready. When everything was on the table Sully grabbed the orange juice and tomato juice from the fridge and placed three wine glasses on the table. Then he went back and took another bottle of Christal out of the refrigerator in case anyone might want a mimosa.

Chuck was the first to "dig in" and they all followed. Sully took a biscuit and looked at Zoe as he opened it with his fork. He placed it on his plate opened side up and put a thin pat of butter on each side, and then ladled some gravy over it. Zoe followed his lead and did the same.

Chuck was the first to speak at the table during breakfast. He complimented Sully saying "this is about the best I've ever had. You didn't mush up the sausage into crumbs like they usually do, and the gravy is good and thick, just like it's supposed to be."

Zoe had taken a few bites and made a yummy sound before she said "this is really good Sully, I can't believe you made this all by yourself."

Sully said "what can I say, I'm a renaissance man, I can do it all." He was happy that his idea had turned out and was being so well received. He wondered about Zoe calling him "Sully", but he let it go for now.

Chuck was filling his plate for the third time when he said "man I can't believe how good this is. If you were just a little better looking I would marry you."

Sully had taken a few bites, but was really not hungry. He was happy with the company, but he was regretting having made the meal. It was the first time he had ever felt even a twinge of homesickness, and he didn't like the feeling. He was thinking about "D" and hoping she was alright. He was shook back to reality when Chuck said "what's the plan."

Zoe grabbed the two boxes containing the other cell phones and simply said "pick one Chuck, Sully bought us pre-paid phones so we know big brother isn't listening in."

Chuck took one of the boxes and said "this was a really great idea Sully."

That was the last straw as far as Sully was concerned. He said with a surly edge to his voice "pick a phone and I will program all of our numbers into them while you two clean up. That's the golden rule, he or she who cooks does not clean, and by the way you can call me Sully, Sullivan, or Mills. I'm going to go get dressed." He didn't storm out of the room, but it was far from a cordial exit.

Sully got all of his clothes out and was starting to dress when Zoe walked in.

Zoe said "I'm sorry if I made you mad Sullivan, but I have been trying to come up with a pet name for you, and apparently I missed the mark."

Sully was still pissed and it showed when he said "I don't need a pet name or a nickname."

Zoe came over to him, held him tightly, and then said "I totally understand Sullivan, I had a nickname all through school and then in the reform school, and I hated it."

Sully was shocked when he softened and replied "so did I and cannot believe that anyone ever hated a nickname more than I hated mine. They used to call me "Milly". Please don't, ever."

Zoe had a look of horror on her face and put her right hand to her mouth. She moved past him and sat on the bed before she said "you have got to be kidding me. This is too weird. Your teasing me aren't you?"

Sully answered "sometimes I feel like going back to Mirage and shooting every person who ever called "Milly" in the forehead. Does that sound like teasing to you?" Sully had been pacing back and forth like a caged animal as they spoke.

Zoe said "Sully this is scary, my nickname was "Milly" too. I know you probably don't believe me, but I swear it bothered me as much as it did you. I promise never to call you that ever, and I will never try to call you anything other than Sully, sweetie, honeybunch, lover boy, cowboy, or sex machine ever again."

Sully took it all in and then said "God, I love you Zoe." He went over to the bed and laid down next to her, pulling her down next to him in a lying position and kissed her very lovingly.

Sully finished dressing in jeans, a khaki Eddie Bauer button down long sleeved shirt, and his boots. He went in the closet and grabbed an olive drab military surplus coat. When he went back to the kitchen Chuck was drying the dishes, and Zoe was programming the phones.

Chuck heard his boots clacking on the linoleum and turned from the sink and said "hey man, I didn't mean to piss you off."

Sully replied in a pleasant tone "It wasn't you at all Chuck, the nickname thing is a hot button for me, that's all." He walked over and slapped him on the shoulder then said "let me put that stuff away."

Zoe was sitting at the table and stopped fiddling with the phones long enough to say "geez guys, if you want some time alone right now just let me know." She was smiling at them as she said it.

Chuck said to Sully as if Zoe wasn't in the room "I don't know how you can live with that Lady Sully, she is mean as a snake."

Sully replied "I tried to run away the other day, why do you think I look all beat up. I can't run away even if I want to. Don't make it obvious, but see if she is looking at me like she heard that."

Chuck moved quickly to Zoe with his arms outstretched and said "run for it Sully, I will hold her off as long as I can!"

The guys were laughing there asses off, and then laughed even harder when Zoe said "well you guys are just fucking hilarious." Then she joined the laughter.

When everything was cleaned up and put away it was just after oh eight hundred hours. They sat at the table and Zoe gave them their phones. Then Sully laid out the plans for the day. He would take Chuck to his car then come back to the house and wait for him to go to his condo, shower, and change. Then they would leave Bealeton and drive to the first plane in Culpepper. From there they would fly to Sperryville to see the second plane on Chuck's list, then to the small airports in Madison and Elkton.

When Sully got back from dropping off Chuck, it was decided that Zoe would take the granny mobile and go car shopping in Manassas. All things considered they would spend the day covering most of North East Virginia. Zoe gave them their new phones, chargers, and instruction manuals to complete the network of three.

The guys were ready to leave and when they were out the door Sully said to Chuck "shit, I forgot my wallet." He tossed him the keys and said warm it up, I'll be right back."

Sully ran into the house and Zoe was right there waiting for him. He almost knocked her over when he ran to her and hugged her he said "I couldn't leave without telling you I love you, and giving you your prize." He went to the cabinet he had hidden the laptop in. Sully pulled it out and gave the large box to Zoe. He said "I thought you could set this up while you were waiting for me to come back."

Zoe gushed at him as she said "I would ask how you got to be so wonderful, but I don't like your joke anymore."

Sully said "ask me again, and I will give you a better answer."

Zoe set the computer down and kissed him then whispered in his ear "how did you get to be so wonderful Sullivan Mills?"

Sully nibbled her ear for the first time, and whispered "I never was until I met you Zoe. You make me be a better person than I could ever be without you."

Zoe felt weak in the knees as she kissed him deeply. She was speechless for the first time in her life. When she let him go she was crying.

Sully said softly "I'm sorry I broke my promise to you. But I will be back in about a half hour, then I will make it up to you. Right now I gotta go, Chuck is waiting."

He ran out the door and jumped in the car smiling even though he was trying not to. He said "sorry Chuck, I couldn't find the damn thing" as he backed out of the driveway.

Chuck replied "you had better get used to carrying that thing if you fly, because they will check your pilot's license every time you fuel up."

Sully said "thanks Dad, I would never have thought of that." He tried to be sarcastic but he was too happy to really pull it off.

The chatted as they drove and Sully told Chuck that it was a one hundred percent chance that his home, office, plane, and car were covered with listening devices, and video cameras. He explained how to search for them and told him he would lend him a device to detect them.

They reached Chuck's car in less than fifteen minutes and Chuck said "I'll see you in a while." He had gotten quite depressed after the talk with Sully.

When Sully was almost to Chuck's car he said "come hell or high water I'm gonna buy a plane today, so you better perk up and help me."

Chuck said sullenly "I will be back at your place in about an hour and a half, so make it a quickie."

Sully just said "see you soon Chuck." Then he did a quick u-turn and headed back home. He tried out the new phone and called Chuck right away. He answered on the third ring saying "hello".

Sully said quickly "don't say a word, just listen. I was just testing our new phones. I will see you soon Chuckles." Sully hung up and thought it was a good way to get back at him for copying Zoe's "Sully".

When Sully got home he parked on the street, opened the trunk, and took out the Walmart lingerie that he had bought for Zoe. He stopped ten feet from the door and called Zoe's new cell phone. He heard it ringing on the kitchen table, and after the fourth ring he saw one of the most majestic sights he had ever seen. It was Zoe running for the phone unclothed.

Zoe answered the phone saying "hello?" She looked at the caller I.D. and knew it should be Sully. She said "Sully is that you?" then there was a knock on the kitchen door. Zoe went to the door, crouched under the window, and said "who is it?" a voice came through the door saying "UPS" and there was no mistaking that it was Sully disguising his voice. She opened the door still nude and said "I've been expecting a special package."

Sully laughed and handed her the Walmart bag then he said "I don't know how special it is but here's your package."

Zoe didn't even look in the bag and jumped on him wrapping her legs around his waist the second he was inside and closed the door. She was kissing him passionately, and said "I love you" several times.

Sully walked to the bedroom carrying her. He laid her down on the bed and kissed her neck and breasts. When he stood to undress she opened the bag she still had clutched in her hand. She looked inside the bag and said "wow, I'll be right back!"

Sully disrobed and laid on the bed waiting for her. She came out of the closet wearing the black lace teddy, black Lauren riding boots, and his black felt Stetson five x cowboy hat.

Sully was barely able to choke out "looking good cowgirl. You don't have a whip, do you?"

Zoe raised her eyebrows and said "what a great idea, I'll stop at a leather shop today."

Sully replied "you seem to do just fine at beating me without tools, and I'm leaving if you get a whip."

Zoe put her right index finger on her lower lip and said "you paid for me Mister what do you want me to do for you?"

Sully said "turn around and let me see if I got my money's worth." Zoe turned slowly, and although the teddy he bought wasn't designed as a thong, Zoe was wearing it as one.

When she was done with her show she walked slowly and sexily over to Sully and said looking him up and down and asked "do you really think that thing will fit inside me?"

Sully played along and said "I guess we will never know until we try."

Zoe threw his hat across the room and then attacked him.

They were young and in love and seemingly never got tired of exploring their passion for one another. It was collectively the best time of their lives.

Chuck arrived just as Sully finished packing a lunch for them. He took a paper grocery bag and threw in a six pack of cola, and then he wrapped four pieces of the leftover pizza individually in tin foil. He placed the pizza in the bag and folded the top over.

He said loudly "Zoe Chuck's here" he went into the back room to get his frequency detector out of his mission bag. He and Zoe had decided to pack just about everything they would need into what they had called "mission bags" in the event that they were recalled suddenly. He put the small device into his back pocket and returned to the kitchen.

Chuck and Zoe were talking and drinking coffee at the kitchen table when Sully got back. He leaned on the counter and let them finish their talk. Then he said "Zoe can I borrow that digital camera of yours, that way I can take pictures of the planes I look at.

Zoe replied "that's a great idea." She hustled to the bedroom to get the camera from her purse. Zoe gave Sully the camera and said "take a lot of pictures, and make sure you pick out a good plane for us. I don't want one that a little old lady flew to church in Canada every Sunday."

With a puzzled look on his face Chuck asked "what does that mean?"

Zoe answered before Sully could "ask the genius about that beauty we drove around in until today." All Sully could do is shake his head and groan.

Zoe and Chuck laughed at Sully's expense, until he said "let's get out of here before I get verbally, or physically, assaulted further."

Chuck stood from the table and so did Zoe. Zoe came over to Sully and playfully cowered as if she were going to hit him. She said "ha, ha, I just wanted a kiss goodbye but now I've changed my mind." She turned and stood by the table.

Sully smiled and said "I just never know when you are going to get the urge to beat me up."

Zoe gave him an evil stare and said "If you keep up your little games it will be sooner than you think." Then she smiled at him.

Sully replied "you better not right now, I have a witness."

Zoe came back to him and he cowered again. She playfully punched him in his right shoulder and he lurched to the left as if she had hit him with a baseball bat. Zoe said angrily "you are such a shit." Then she stormed off into the back room.

Chuck, who had been roaring with laughter stopped when he knew that Zoe was now upset for real. He said to Sully "I guess that last bit was a little over the top."

As sully crossed the room toward the bedroom, he groaned, then said "Chuck, if I'm not back in five minutes call nine one one."

Zoe met him just inside the door of the bedroom and wrapped her arms around him and gave him a huge kiss, Then she said "I just wanted to get you alone so I could give you a kiss to remember, and didn't want to do it in front of Chuck."

Sully replied "I was hoping that is what was going on." Then he kissed her again. After they kissed for a short while Sully said "there is nickel Taurus three fifty seven under the driver's seat of the car, a 'just in case' weapon. While you are out, try to think of where you want to go for a few days. Be careful. I love you Zoe"

They kissed again and Sully squeezed her butt with both hands. He winked at her, then left the bedroom and headed for the door. As he was walking toward Chuck he said "hey Chuck your place has two bedrooms, right?" Before he even took one more step a red high heel hit him in the back.

As Sully and Chuck walked to Chuck's car Sully explained quickly how to sweep a car, room, or plane with the frequency detector. Chuck watched intently as Sully walked slowly around the outside of the car and on his second time around stopped by the trunk. He took a key out of his wallet and wiggled it in the lock for only a moment and then opened it.

Sully looked in the trunk for only a few seconds then put something in his pocket. Sweeping the inside of the car took Sully less than two minutes, and Chuck watched as he played with the rear view mirror then took something out and crushed it under his heel. Then he said "come on over Chuck it's clean now."

Chuck was fascinated by Sully's efficiency with the tool. He said "what did you find in the trunk?"

Sully pulled the small tracking device out of his pocket and showed it to Chuck. Then he answered "This is a tracking device and we need to get rid of it before we go anywhere. Give me the keys and I will find the team tracking you. Then all we have to do is lose them and place the tracker at your hangar, of someplace else."

Chuck was excited. He gave Sully his keys and hopped in the car and when Sully did a quick U-turn and went as fast as the old Buick would go he said "I know this is serious and all, but I feel like a kid playing spy games."

Sully replied "that's a dangerous attitude Chuck. It's important that you always remember that all of this is extremely dangerous, and very, very real. I might make the other agents look soft and weak, but believe me when I tell you that they are highly trained, and they are heavily armed.

Sully had wiped the smile off of Chuck's face. Chuck said "I guess I was trying to forget.

Sully got animated and pointed to a car on the side of the road. He said "there they are waiting to follow us." Sully pushed the accelerator to the floor and drove in the oncoming lane of traffic. When he was about five hundred yards away he steered onto the gravel heading straight toward the agent mobile at over ninety miles per hour.

Chuck was pushing on the dashboard in anticipation of a horrific crash when Sully hit the brakes and slid to a stop not three feet from hitting the other car. He was out of the car in a second, and was beside the passenger window in three more with a pistol in his hand that Chuck didn't expect him of having.

He was barking at them, and as Chuck stepped out of the car and slowly walked over he saw them handing their weapons out the window, by then he could hear Sully as he said "now your phones boys." The agents reluctantly game him their phones.

Now that Chuck was beside him he handed him one of the agent's weapons and said "rack a shell in the chamber and cover these assholes. If they make any kind of move you don't like kill them." As Chuck did as he was told Sully continued with "driver get out and walk to me."

When the driver came around the front of the car Sully grabbed him and threw him against the passenger fender. He tucked his weapon into his pants in the back, the he said in a mean voice "put your fucking hands on the hood as don't move if you know what is good for you. Sully frisked the agent and found another cell phone, handcuffs, and a spare Smith and Wesson three eighty semi auto in an ankle holster. He walked the agent to the ditch and said "eat dirt, and if you so much as twitch you're dead."

Sully repeated the procedure with agent number two, and found a silenced Glock and hand cuffs and threw them both on the hood. Once they were both on the ground he went to them and handcuffed them cross corner. That entailed right ankle of one to left wrist of the other, and vice versa. Then he went back to Chuck and whispered "is there a strip club in town?"

Chuck nodded and whispered back "yeah, why. I thought we were gonna go buy a plane, and I'm pretty sure the titty bar ain't open at nine o clock in the morning."

Sully Said softly "take your car there and I will follow you." He was gonna make these guys pay for following Chuck.

The reached "the hot spot" ten minutes later. Chuck walked over to the agent mobile and Sully put a finger to his lips. Chuck nodded his understanding of the gesture. Sully found the small tool kit in the glove box. They were standard issue for all SSO vehicles.

He pulled the three eighty out of his pocket and took the handgrips off. He peeled the tracking device off both grips and stuck them to the dashboard. Then he did the same with the Glock. When both were completely reassembled he placed the tracking device on the dash. He said loudly thanks Jim, and exited the vehicle.

Sully had completed this in less than five minutes. He put the two weapons he had worked on in Chuck's car. He said to Chuck "give me your SSO cell phone." Chuck did and Sully was surprised that, when he took the battery out there was no tracking device. He put the phone back together and handed it back to Chuck. Sully took the agents service weapon from Chuck and got the other out of the agent mobile.

He scared the hell out of Chuck when he emptied both weapons, one in each hand, into the front window of the club. Sully threw the empty weapons through the window followed by their cell phones, and car keys. He hurried over to Chuck's car and got in the passenger side. He put the three eighty in his coat pocket, and the Glock under his seat.

Sully looked at him and said "let's go buy a plane." Like the last half hour had never happened. They headed out of Bealeton on highway twenty eight headed for Culpepper. When they were close to the spot Chuck slowed down without being told, and they both sat up in their seats and saw the agents still hog cuffed to one another in the ditch and they both laughed.

Chuck said "damn man, remind me not to piss you off."

Sully said "Chuck don't piss me off."

They drove the twenty miles to the Culpepper airfield and Chuck was telling him about the plane the whole way. It was an eighty one Piper Seneca twin turbo prop, seated six very comfortably, ran great, had only seventeen hundred hours, was just inspected, and according to Chuck looked really cool.

Chuck was driving to the hangar when he said "Carl said he wants two hundred twenty for it, but he's going through a nasty divorce right now and I think you can get it for a lot less than that, if I were you I would start at one eighty."

Chuck drove past the hangar to see if it was open, and it was. He parked along-side of the metal building. Before they got out Sully said "Chuck for now I'm Ted Sextant, Real Estate investor out of Richmond, alright?"

Chuck said "whatever you say Ted." He thought 'Here we go playing spy games again'.

They walked into the hangar and Carl saw them. He had been rummaging through a box, but he jumped up quickly when he saw Chuck and came over to them. He slapped his hand into Chuck's and said "where have you been old man, I haven't seen you in a couple weeks."

Carl was in his late thirties, about six foot two, with a bushy mustache, a way over done fake tan, and one of the worst toupee's ever made. He was loud and obnoxious from the first words he uttered.

Chuck figured he had enough lies to keep straight so he said "I caught a honey of a charter to Rio then had to sit there for a week waiting for the couple to finish their honeymoon. I got a good tan though."

They all laughed then Chuck said "Carl this is friend of mine Ted. He wanted to see the Seneca because he is in the market for a twin turbo, and I told him he should look at yours first."

Carl said "looking is free, but it costs money to dance." Then he let out a laugh.

Sully thought to himself 'I would bet a thousand bucks that this douche bag is a salesman'. But he smiled at the comment and played along and said "well let's see if I'm gonna dance." Chuck was right, outside it looked great. The Seneca was polished white with a royal blue racing stripe from its sleek nose to the tail.

Ted said "come on aboard and I'll show you around." They all climbed the stairs and went inside. Ted said "isn't she a beauty, I hate getting rid of her, but the ex is bleeding me dry."

Sully looked around the passenger compartment that had four tan over-stuffed leather first class seats, light brown commercial carpeting, eight oval windows, and a privy in the back that was an imitation of a commercial airliner bathroom.

Ted said "come up here to the flight deck and check it out." He was selling his ass off and Sully made the decision that he did not like him. The cockpit was impressive. The windshield on this model was larger than most due to the Concord like design.

The instrument panel was normal but wrapped in a burled walnut frame to match the wainscoting in the passenger compartment. The main difference in the cockpit was that both the pilot and copilot seats matched those in the passenger compartment.

Sully cut right to the chase and said "It looks like something I might be interested in but I'd have to fly it first of course." He was trying to be nice but was afraid that he was coming off as cold.

Carl said "I have tons of boxes to go through here today, but if you go up with Chuck I guess that would be okay." He obviously wasn't comfortable with not going, but was willing to allow it.

Chuck said "that's great Carl and you just wait, once this baby gets up there she'll sell herself. Ted I'll set it up with the tower with Carl, I just need your license I'll be back in a couple minutes." Chuck and Carl left the plane to make the arrangements and Sully sat in the pilot's seat looking over the controls. He ran his flight training back through his mind, a quick refresher course if you will.

He saw a forklift coming out with a dolly arm on the back, and knew they were about to be pulled out to the runway. He looked in the drawer to his left and shuffled through the flight charts to find one that covered this area as Chuck entered the plane and closed the cabin door.

He came into the cockpit and buckled into the copilot's chair. Sully took his hat off and put his headphones on. Chuck did the same, and called the taxi wagon to take them out. Chuck said "so what do you think?"

Sully showed no emotion when he replied "well so far it rolls pretty good." He smiled at him and continued "You were right Chuck, I am impressed so far, but let's see how it flies."

The taxi wagon unhooked and thirty seconds later came over the radio telling them they were clear for startup and taxi to runway two. Sully called them back with their tail number and affirmed their directions.

He pushed the starter for engine one, then two and they both caught easily and smoothly. He checked his flap setting and pushed the throttles forward. The Seneca was easy to start and taxi, and when he was lined up for runway two he called the tower for takeoff clearance and thirty seconds later they were airborne.

Chuck said "this thing almost has as much takeoff thrust as my jet."

Sully was checking the gauges and leveled off at twenty three hundred feet. He handed Chuck the Virginia area flight chart and said "plot us a course toward Roanoke, then we'll head back to Sperryville to look at that Cessna."

Chuck said "well now what do you think Sully?"

Sully laughed and said "we haven't crashed yet. Chuck the plane is great, and you don't have to worry so much about it being your recommendation, I appreciate your guidance." Just then his SSO phone rang. He said I better get this in the back. You fly for a while. He exited the cockpit and closed the door behind him.

Sully pushed send on the phone and said "Sullivan Mills." There was no doubt who was on the other end of the phone, Weathers.

Weathers was not very emotional when he said "Mills, can you explain to me why last night you scare and threaten two of my agents, and today I hear that you hogtie two more with handcuffs, then steal their car and implicate them in vandalizing a strip club."

Sully said "They were harassing a good friend of mine. I was with him at the time, so they were harassing me, and I thought you had said you were done tailing me Boss."

Weathers let out a heavy sigh and replied "from now in if you feel threatened by the minor SSO agents please call me before you go to such drastic actions as this morning. Understand this Mills, you are skating on very thin ice with me, and I would hate to lose you. Play it clean from here on out, if you know what's good for you Sully." Then the phone clicked off.

Sully took the opportunity to take a few pictures in the passenger compartment, and then he returned to the cockpit. He sat down in the pilots chair, put his headphones back on, and said to Chuck "how's it going up here?"

Chuck replied "it's a hundred percent up here Sully. Was that phone call about our little detour this morning?"

Sully answered "Yes it was, I just got a good ass chewing from my boss, but don't sweat it Chuck, if he wasn't pissed off at me I wouldn't know how to act. Where are we now?"

Chuck said "we are just coming up to Buena Vista. I cut over to interstate eighty one and figured we could just follow that Southwest toward Roanoke."

Sully was impressed with the Seneca. At three quarter throttle their airspeed was one hundred ninety five, and when he was in the passenger cabin it was not nearly as loud as he had anticipated. He said to Chuck "I want to do a couple steep banks, a dive, a climb and a stall, and then we will head to Sperryville and look at the Cessna."

The plane out performed Sully's expectations, when he was done putting the Seneca through its paces, he did a steep banking turn to the right and put them on course for Sperryville. Chuck said to Sully "that was some pretty fancy flying kid. How long have you been flying?"

Sully had a wry grin on his face, because he knew when he told him it was likely to shock the shit out of him. He answered "I have a total of around a hundred hours of airtime in all types of aircraft, but I've never flown a twin turbo before this morning."

Chuck swallowed hard and opened his mouth to speak but nothing came out. On the third try he was able to stammer "you maybe could have told me that before right now."

Sully chuckled and said "you never asked, but it was definitely worth it to see a black man turn white right before my eyes."

Chuck simply said "Fuck you Mills." Then he laughed with him.

Sully said "as of right now, I'm sold, but when we land in Sperryville I want you to help me go over this bird with a fine toothed comb. I think we are going on a trip tomorrow or the next day, and I don't want any problems."

Chuck said "when we land there we can taxi right to the garage and have the mechanics look over the engines, and we can check out the rest. What about the Cessna?"

Sully answered him by saying "I can't imagine that it can be a hundred thousand better than this, and honestly it's a little out of my price range."

Chuck said "I guess that makes sense. The only thing different about the Cessna is its a bit bigger, and is plusher."

Sully and Chuck landed in Sperryville, and when Chuck was able to pry his hands from the armrests of the copilot's seat, he said shakily "nnice llanding SSully."

Chuck suppressed his urge to laugh at his friend and said in a fake cheery voice "why thank you Chuck, I believe it was an almost perfect landing."

Chuck relaxed at Sully's messing with him and said "you know you really are a son of a bitch."

Sully hardened and said "I take that as a compliment. Now where is the mechanics hangar?"

Chuck guided him to the hangar and they inspected the plane for over two hours. The mechanics printed Sully a full report on the engines and general specifications of the plane. He and Chuck had found no structural defects, only a few dings and scratches that were to be expected on an aircraft that was over fifteen years old.

Just before the inspection was completed, Sully gave Chuck five hundred bucks and said "pay the mechanics bill, and give them a good tip, then ask about renting a hangar for two weeks. If they will do it pay them for it, do you think five hundred will cover it?"

Chuck answered "it damn well better."

When Chuck went to deal with the mechanics Sully placed two mini cameras in the plane and one listening device. If anyone messed with the Seneca he would know.

Sully stepped off the plane and saw Chuck walking back to him. Chuck said "it's all handled, want to tell me why?" He was puzzled by Sully's actions.

Sully said "when we are airborne."

Sully handled the tower like an old pro, and they were in the air and headed back to Culpepper in ten minutes. Sully explained his plan to buy the plane, and give Carl two weeks to get out of the hangar in Culpepper. Then he would move the plane into that hangar, and take over the lease.

Chuck was amazed at the plan that Sully seemed to come up with on the fly. He had even told Chuck how to act and what to say when Sully negotiated with Carl.

They left the Seneca in the bullpen when they went back to see Carl, so they could get out quick if the deal was made. Before they left to see Carl, Sully gave Zoe's camera to Chuck, showed him how it worked, and said "take a couple of pictures of me with the plane." Chuck walked away from the plane and took several pictures.

When Sully and Chuck walked into the hangar Carl was rummaging through boxes full of paper work. They walked up to Carl and he said "hey Chuck, Ted where's my bird?"

Chuck was somber as instructed when he answered "it's in the bullpen, they said something about the tow tractor being in the shop, and it might be an hour or so."

Carl said "happens all the time in this place. So what did you think Ted?" He was back in salesman mode with a big fake smile on his face.

Sully said with very little emotion in his voice "I like the plane Carl, I like it a lot. But we kept having a problem with the left flap controller. It kept failing and every ten minutes or so we had to pull it up again. We had it inspected in Elkton, and they said it might be able to be fixed, and it might not."

Carl's demeanor changed immediately to sour after hearing about the problem with the plane. He said "I know I haven't flown in about two months, but the last time I did everything was fine."

Chuck jumped in and said "Carl would I lie to you about an aircraft? The mechanic said it could be as simple as a seal, when is the last time you changed your hydraulic fluid?"

Carl softened and said "well it has been a couple of years at least, maybe it's due. So Ted, other than that little problem what do you think?"

He was back into salesman mode and Sully wasn't in the mood to play with this jerk. He was cold and harsh when he said "Carl, I might be willing to deal with you but you've gotta be straight with me. You're not on the job now Carl and if you keep trying to sell me I'll walk, and quick. Chuck told me about your financial situation and I can help, but only if you shoot straight with me. Are we on the same page, or do I go buy a different plane?"

Carl put the salesman act in park and asked "What do you mean you can help me?"

He was curious, and Sully knew that was all he needed. Sully answered him even colder when he said "I have researched your plane extensively and the base value. I know you have made some upgrades and I have calculated, and adjusted for them. If you take you emotions for the plane out of the deal you will know that the offer I am going to make is fair and reasonable. Are we on the same page here Carl, or do I walk."

Carl was getting a little intimidated by Sully's demeanor and softened even further when he shyly said "what is your offer and how does it help me?"

Sully thought 'the deal is done' when he laid out his plan by saying "the base price and blue book value for your plane is one forty five. I am willing to offer you one sixty five, cash, and I will let you write out the bill of sale for one forty. That gives you twenty five grand of hidden cash to do with what you want, but keep in mind, this is a one-time offer. Take it or leave it."

Carl was shaking his head, but his eyes were bright with the opportunity of hidden cash. He said "I sure was hoping to get a lot more than that for the Seneca, but the way you structured the deal with the cash out is a great idea. You've got a deal, even though I wanted more, I gotta have that cash right now."

Sully was a little softer, but not much when he said "here is the other end of the deal. I will give you two weeks to get all of your things out of this hangar, then you will sign the lease over to me."

Carl was actually happy now and he said "Ted you've got a deal."

Sully was still matter of fact when he said "here is what we are going to do. For tonight I will let you hold this." He took his prepaid Visa gold card out of his wallet and handed it to Carl "then we will meet tomorrow at nine thirty and I will sign all the papers you need signed. I will bring you a cashier's check for one forty, and twenty five green."

Carl was happy, and went as far as giving Sully a hug. That's when Sully picked his pocket.

When Sully and Chuck walked to Chuck's car Sully said "meet me at the hangar in Sperryville, and we will go from there."

Chuck was incredibly impressed and said "Sully, remind me never to negotiate with you."

Sully said "Chuck, never negotiate with me."

Chuck drove Sully to the Seneca and said "I should be about twenty minutes behind you."

Sully replied "Chuck I can't thank you enough for all of your help today, but I promise you will like your end of it." Then he walked to the Seneca.

The trip to Sperryville was uneventful, and by the time he got towed and parked, Chuck was there. They drove back to Bealeton, and Chuck gushed the whole way about how Sully had played Carl perfectly. Chuck couldn't believe that Sully had got that plane for that price.

Sully said to Chuck "here's your end of it buddy. Any time you want that plane and I'm not using it it's yours. I don't even care if you want to use it for charters, as long as the SSO doesn't know about it."

Chuck was shocked and said "are you serious? That would be great. I always get corporate ass holes that need a flight, and I make shit with the Citation because that thing eats so much fuel.

Sully said "I'm totally serious, the only catch is that I need you to keep up on the maintenance, and make damned sure that it is always topped off with fuel."

Chuck frowned a little when he replied "Sully if we weren't stuck in this SSO mess we could make a lot of money together."

Sully said "Chuck, Zoe and I have talked about it, and we are going to do everything we can to get you out, so for now just bide your time."

Before Chuck could respond the bank was upon them. Sully told him to pull in and wait. It was less than ten minutes when he came out carrying a briefcase. Sully had gotten the cash and the check and for all intents and purposes it was his plane now.

He asked Chuck to take him to the SSO campus Operations center, and when Chuck asked why he showed him Carl's wallet.

Chuck said "where did you find that." His mind was spinning.

Sully answered "right out of Carl's pocket. I thought he would be a great alias."

Sully took out his SSO phone and called Ron Rady. When Ron picked up Sully said "Rady it's Mills, can you meet me at ops in ten minutes?"

Rady answered "I'm here Sully, what do you need?"

Sully said "meet me at the South entrance in five."

Rady said "I'm there."

They both hung up simultaneously. Sully said to Chuck "pull over, I'll drive."

Sully drove them no-where near operations but to a duplex on the edge of campus where Rady as waiting. Sully pulled up right next to him and he jumped in the back seat. Sully said "the car is clean if you are."

Rady said "one hundred percent Sully, what's going on man?"

Sully answered "Ron I need a favor." He handed him Carl's wallet. Then he continued "take what you need out of there and create me a complete alias package."

Rady said "shit Sully I thought it was something difficult."

Sully said "it's just a little harder than usual. The SSO can't know about it." Sully smiled as Rady's grin turned into a frown. Sully continued "and here's the really fun part, I need it in three hours."

Rady replied, with a cocky look on his face "now that is a challenge. Are you out of your mind?"

Sully played him like a fiddle saying "when I saved your life you promised me anything, anytime. But I guess that was just talk at the time."

Rady shook his head, then said "I'll do my best, but I don't know about three hours."

Sully said "just do your best Ron. Do you have a clean phone?"

Rady said "yeah, doesn't everybody?"

They exchanged numbers, and agreed that Rady would call him when he was done. They dropped off Rady where they found him, and Sully was driving for home.

They stopped at Safeway and bought what they wanted for dinner. Sully told Chuck he could have anything he wanted, and he picked up some sirloin steaks, crab legs, and all the fixings for a Cesar salad. They got back to Sully and Zoe's place at thirteen hundred and Chuck helped Sully carry the groceries in.

When that was done Chuck said he would call later when he had cleaned up and taken a nap. When he left Chuck, Sully called Zoe.

Zoe answered on the third ring saying "hello."

Sully said "well hello beautiful, where are you?" He couldn't believe how happy he was to hear her voice.

Zoe said "I missed you today Sully, and I had no luck finding a car. I should be home in about fifteen minutes."

Sully replied "you have no idea how good it feels to hear you say you are coming to our home." He truly felt it and meant it.

Zoe's voice was smiling when she said "I will be there soon." Then she hung up.

Sully went to the back room and unloaded the jacket he was wearing mostly into his mission bag. He was pissed when he grabbed the frequency detector out of his pocket. He had forgotten to give it to Chuck.

When he was finished in the back room he ran to take a shower. Ten minutes later he was freshly dressed in straight leg Levis, a black and grey striped Roper shirt, and his boots. As soon as he walked out of the bedroom he heard a car pulling into the driveway.

He looked out and it was Zoe walking toward the door, but it was not his old car. When Zoe walked in he grabbed her and kissed her several times. Then he stepped back and asked "why did you lie to me?"

She knew he was not mad, but she looked down and rubbed her right toe back and forth, and said as a bad child would "I uz juts foolin, please don't be mad at me."

Sully grabbed her tightly and said "Zoe I could not, and will never truly be mad at you."

She kissed him, smiled, and said "come on and look at our car." She grabbed his hand and led him out to the car. It was a ninety five gold Toyota land cruiser. Zoe said "what do you think?"

Sully squeezed her hand and said "it's perfect, and it looks really good."

Zoe went on and on for five minutes explaining all of the features and highlights of the vehicle. Sully truly liked it. It was not too big, and not too small at the same time. It featured four wheel drive, low mileage, a decent sized v eight engine, leather interior, and larger than stock new tires.

When Zoe finished her sales pitch she tentatively asked "what do you think of it Sully, do you like it?"

He answered "Zoe it's perfect, and just what we talked about. You did a great job."

Zoe almost knocked him over when she hugged him aggressively. She said come inside and I have something else to show you." She had winked at him when she said it.

They walked inside and Zoe attacked him kissing almost every exposed part of his body. She desperately tried to disrobe him and he fought her at every chance he could. He finally relented and let her drag him into the bedroom where they made slow and passionate love kissing and professing their love for one another time after time.

Halfway through, she dragged him into the shower, while making love they soaped and rinsed one another until they were dirty and clean at the same time.

After they had toweled each other dry they laid on the bed to recuperate, and they talked.

Zoe was so lost in Sully and their lovemaking that this was the first time she had even thought to ask about the plane shopping and how it went.

Sully gave her a quick synopsis of the whole day. He told her about hog tying the trail team, the strip club, and how the plane purchase went. She laughed several times when he told her about how he had scared Chuck, and how he had played Carl. He told her about picking Carl's pocket, and how he had Rady working on the alias.

Zoe said "why would you trust that jerk-off."

Sully said "Ron is a really nice guy. I picked him to go with me to Bolivia because I do trust him. I had told him all about you and how to act in the event you showed up. He was supposed to discourage you so you went home. Thankfully it didn't work."

Zoe asked "how do you know him?"

Sully answered in an odd monotone. It was like he was narrating a movie playing in his own mind. He took a deep breath before droning coldly "Rady was in my airborne training class and did great until we did our first non-static line jump. His chute tangled and he panicked and didn't cut away to his reserve. I didn't want to see him bounce, so I cut away my main and did a bullet dive toward him. I cut his main and pulled both of our reserves. We were at three hundred feet when the reserves deployed. I was lucky, I hit a tree and only broke a couple of ribs. Ron hit hard and shattered both ankles. His left tibia blew out the back of his leg shredding his Achilles' tendon."

Sully had been staring blankly at a wall up to this point, but he blinked his eyes twice, softened his facial expression, and turned to look Zoe in the eyes before saying "the SSO fixed him up and Ron busted his ass in P.T. They are keeping him on as a support agent, but he swore never to jump again. He will never advance beyond where he is now unless he can complete jump training, and it has given him a unique attitude. You might want to consider cutting the guy a little slack."

Zoe broke eye contact and looked at the floor before she said "I'm sorry, I had no idea. That is the most noble and brave thing I've ever hear of. I doubt that I would have the guts to risk my life for someone I barely knew." She was embarrassed at her earlier reaction, and although not knowing absolved her she still felt guilt in the pit of her stomach.

Sully gently lifted her chin to look her into her eyes. He winked his left eye, kissed her gently, and then said "don't be too impressed, I've run it over in my head a thousand times, and nine hundred ninety nine times, I've let him bounce."

He went to the fridge and grabbed a bottle of Dos Equis. He crossed the kitchen to the counter, found the opener, and after he opened it drank three quarters of it in one long swallow. His good mood went down like the beer.

Zoe came over to him and lightly kissed him on the cheek. She said "so now what?"

Sully rubbed his eyes at the bridge of his nose with his right index finger and thumb for a few seconds. He tried to seem cheery with a small smile on his face, even though his mood was almost completely the opposite, then said "tonight I want to do whatever you want to." Just saying it and looking at her made his mood lighten. He said "I just need to call Rady, and then Chuck." Zoe was preparing to leave the room when Sully lightly grabbed her arm and said "stay here with me I will put my phone on speaker."

He called Ron first and when he answered Sully said "Ron forget the deadline. I realize now how unrealistic three hours is. You remember Chuck, the pilot that brought us back from Bolivia, well he has been recruited and lives on campus. He is in those civilian condos by the park, number seven fourteen. I will have him call you with a meeting place, and if you can, dig up a frequency detector for him. Just try to get it done before dark tonight, okay Ron?"

Rady said "now that I can do, later man." He had hung up.

Zoe was hugging him around the waist when he called Chuck. Chuck answered and Sully said "Chuck, I'm sorry but dinner is going to have to be another time. Zoe broke down and got towed into Manassas. I've already arranged for a rental car to go meet her. I want you to call Rady about the papers." Sully gave Chuck Ron's number.

Chuck said "is Zoe alright, she didn't get hurt or anything, did she?"

Sully said "she's fine, sounds like a blown radiator or engine. Call me as soon as you get up tomorrow, and we will figure out how to meet Carl. I'll talk to you tomorrow." Sully clicked off.

Zoe said softly "how come you didn't tell Chuck about Rady?"

Sully kissed her and said "I want to see how they deal with each other one on one. So, everything is handled, what did you have in mind gorgeous?"

Zoe walked around the table and play fully said "well your car is parked at the Leaf Land Lodge just outside of Manassas in front of a suite with a hot tub, other than that, I have no idea what to do?"

He grabbed her and kissed her deeply. He said "just give me ten minutes to pack."

When he turned to leave Zoe grabbed him by the arm, kissed him again, and whispered "your bag is already in the room cowboy. How are we gonna get there?"

Sully said "did I mention that I bought a plane for us today?"

Zoe said "can we really? It's not paid for yet, couldn't we get in trouble?"

Sully answered "not a chance, I put over a fifty percent deposit on it, and I have a signed bill of sale,"

Zoe was extremely excited and said "when do you want to go?"

Sully answered "now is good for me, unless you want to wait for a while. It's up to you if you want to bring your laptop. I took a bunch of pictures.

I almost forgot, I got you a present today." He took the three eighty semi auto out of his back pocket, handed it to her and said "I'd feel better if you carried a gun in your purse."

Zoe looked at him sexily, licked her lips, and said "I really don't have pictures on my mind for later."

Sully smiled and said "let's go."

Sully drove the land cruiser the thirty five miles to Sperryville. Along the way the talked about the new car, the plane, but mostly they talked about the feelings they shared for one another.

When they left Sully called the airport and told them to get the Seneca out of the hangar and ready. He told them to leave the hangar doors open so they could park their car in it. Zoe called the Manassas airport and arranged for an overnight tie down.

Forty five minutes later they were at the Sperryville Airport. Sully drove the land cruiser to hangar six and backed it in as Zoe called the private terminal for a courtesy car.

The grabbed the few things they needed out of the land cruiser and Sully said "Zoe the truck is great, I couldn't have picked out anything better for us if I tried." He continued with "don't get your hopes up on this plane, it was available and checked out mechanically. It's a Piper Seneca, and Chuck tried to talk me out of buying it, but I kind of felt sorry for the old gal."

Zoe replied "I'm sure it will be fine honey." Her heart sank expecting another shitty vehicle.

The car showed up and they got inside. On the ride the driver / mechanic said "so you're the one that bought the Seneca."

Zoe was getting more and more apprehensive about the plane Sully bought. When they turned the corner, and Zoe saw the plane her jaw dropped she said "oh my god Sully, it's beautiful."

The courtesy car pulled up to the plane and Zoe ran out to the plane. Sully grabbed her things, and went to the plane. He opened the door/stairs, and went inside the plane. It was even nicer than he remembered. He barely turned around, and he was almost tackled by Zoe running to hug him.

Zoe hugged him and said "I can't believe how nice this is!" She toured the small plane taking everything in. She went into the cockpit, and Sully closed the cabin door.

Sully went to the cockpit and Zoe was standing there. She kissed him and said "this is just wonderful Sully."

Sully kissed her several times, and then he said "I love you. Do you want to drive?"

Zoe's eyes got so wide Sully was afraid they were going to pop out of her head. She answered "can I, really?"

Sully nodded his head as he said "why not, your trained as well as I am."

Zoe literally jumped into the pilot's seat and started running through her pre-flight check list in her mind. Thirty seconds later she started the engines. Carl had put two adhesive labels on the instrument panel in front of both pilot's seats that had the tail number and call sign written on them.

Zoe called the tower for clearance to taxi, and take off. Two minutes later they were in the air. Sully gave her the course, and bearing for Manassas, and they were on their way.

Zoe was beaming as she said "this is a great ride Sully, it practically flies itself." She had the biggest smile she could muster on her face.

Sully said "I'm glad you like it Zoe, I didn't want to have to take shit for this like I have for the car."

Zoe replied "I love it Sully, and I hope you know I was teasing about the car." She was busy flying, or she would have kissed him.

Sully said "of course I know, if I had thought you were serious I would have gotten you a new one a long time ago. Did you decide where we are going tomorrow?"

Zoe's smile faded, and she responded "I have thought long and hard about it, but I can't think of anywhere I would want to go. Anyplace will be fine with me, as long as I'm with you."

Sully said "well that's just great, we have a nice new plane, and nowhere to fly it to." He rummaged through the map drawer to his right and tried to come up with something. Sully thought about it for a little while, but he also came up with nothing.

He saw the airport beacon ahead and was going to tell Zoe, but before he could utter a word, she reached over and cut the throttle as she called the Manassas tower for landing clearance.

Zoe's proficiency at everything she did rivaled his, and he was constantly impressed and amazed by her. He played a game in his mind watching her. He pretended he was the pilot, and ran through what he would be doing during the landing procedure, and when he thought it, Zoe executed it virtually at the exact same time.

Zoe executed a perfect landing and Sully said "I watched you during the landing procedure, and you were absolutely perfect."

Zoe teased him and replied "well what did you expect, like the old song goes, anything you can do I can do better."

Sully smiled and chuckled as he said "really? Let's have a contest where we piss for distance standing up."

Zoe jabbed back "let's see who has better tits." She gave hers a little shake.

Sully said "you win, you've got the best I've ever seen, and believe me I've studied every pair I have ever looked at."

Zoe laughed and replied "if that was supposed to be a compliment Mills, it failed."

She smiled at him and then started talking to ground support. She said "I need an overnight tie down and a fueling." She listened for a couple of seconds, then said "roger that slip three."

When Zoe parked the Seneca and shut it down. They grabbed the few things they needed from the plane, and exited.

Zoe said "what's with the briefcase? Are you a business man now?"

Sully said almost coldly "I have the cash for the plane in here, and a few weapons."

Zoe didn't care for his sudden change in demeanor. She said nothing until the ground crew van arrived. Zoe gave them an imprint of her prepaid Visa card to cover the fees. Then she asked "can you call me a cab?"

The older man who had taken her card said "we have a courtesy shuttle if you're not going too far."

Zoe replied "it's not far at all, were going to the Leaf Land Lodge."

The ground attendant grabbed the radio off of his belt and said "Holly, we've got a couple here at three that need a lift to the Leaf." The radio crackled back "I'll be there in a minute Erv." Old Erv simply replied "ten four Holly."

Holly was there in less than two minutes in a Lincoln town car. She was a young cute girl of maybe seventeen. Holly said "hop in, I'll have you guys to the Leaf in no time."

Sully opened the door for Zoe, then went around to the passenger side and got in. Holly drove quickly and somewhat irresponsibly to the hotel.

During the ride Sully said softly, but coldly, to Zoe "how about Chinese food later?" He didn't know what had put him in a bad mood, but something had, and he was trying to get out of it.

Zoe smiled at him and said "that sounds great." She was wondering if she had done something wrong in the plane or at the airport to change his mood so dramatically.

Sully nodded at her and although he tried to be nice it came out with a hard edge when he said "Holly what is the best Chinese place in town that delivers?"

Holly snapped her gum, then answered "oh it's Chang's Palace for sure. It's on the way, I'll run in and get you a menu."

Three minutes later Holly skidded to a stop at the restaurant. She said "I'll be right back." She jumped out of the car, and ran inside.

As soon as she had left Zoe turned to Sully and asked "what's wrong Sully, we were both happy on the plane? Now you're acting like you want to rip someone's head off."

Sully answered "I honestly don't know. Sometimes these moods just come over me, and it's very hard for me to get out."

Zoe kissed him on the forehead and said "don't worry baby, when we get to our room I will make it all better." She had been kissing him all over his face and neck as she said it.

Holly ran back with the menu. When she got back in the Lincoln she thrust her right arm, holding the menu, into the backseat. Zoe took it and Holly said "you gotta try the moo goo, and the shrimp egg rolls."

Zoe answered her by saying "we definitely will Holly, thank you very much."

They rode in silence the rest of the way to the hotel. When they got there Zoe told her where the room was. When they got to Suite number two Sully gave the girl a twenty dollar tip and turned away from her without saying a word. Zoe went to the girl and said 'thank you" and gave her a hug.

Zoe opened the door and cheerily said "what do you think Sully?" She was trying like hell to get him out of this bad mood he had gotten into for some reason.

Sully put the briefcase down on the desk by the front window and went back to the door. As he left he said "what do I think? I think I need a walk." He closed the door behind him and ran around the back of the building so she wouldn't know which way he had went.

Zoe didn't even go to the door. She laid on the bed, fully clothed, and turned on the TV with the remote. Before she even found something to watch she went to the desk by the front window. She opened Sully's briefcase and looked inside. There was the cashier's check made out to Carl, three pistols, two cell phones, and a hell of a lot more cash than twenty five thousand, a hell of a lot more. Zoe said aloud "oh my God."

Zoe counted the money quickly, and there was well over two hundred thousand dollars. There was a note with a key. It was the key to his SSO apartment and detailed instructions on how to open every safe and what was inside each one.

It was all, and everything he had. Zoe almost broke down and cried, but rather steeled herself, she thought 'fuck it'. She went back to the bed and started channel surfing.

Sully crossed the small river behind the resort and headed north. His plan was to get to Warrenton and catch a bus to Canada. He had kept two thousand dollars for himself, and he hoped that in Montreal he could turn himself in and explain everything.

"*As usual*", Sully thought, his luck was bad. When he left there was a light mist that had turned into a steady rain, then into freezing rain. Sully sat under a large oak tree and unzipped the collar of his jacket to pull out the hood. Sully sat under the tree and wondered what he was doing and why in the world he was doing it.

On one hand he was truly in love with Zoe and wanted to be with her as much as possible, but the other hand had won. He realized that he was deathly afraid of commitment and things had gone too far too fast.

In the battle of fight or flight, flight had won, and flight was going to ruin his life or get him killed. He didn't know if he was bipolar, schizophrenic, or clinically insane. All he knew for sure was that he was an asshole.

Sully's mind was going in two directions at once. Side A wanted to sit here until dark before they moved out, and catch a bus in Warrenton. Side B wanted to return to the Leaf Land Lodge and be with Zoe. He fought with himself mentally until way past dark. When he stood and started for Warrenton he got about fifty yards and stopped. His feelings for Zoe had won, and he knew he couldn't leave her, not like this.

He had covered well over two miles in his run away from happiness, and his slow, thinking walk back was going to take quite some time. He was glad to have the time. He had to try to figure out what he was going to say to Zoe.

On his way back he was thinking more than he was looking where he was going, and he fell into a small, rocky trench. Sully had hit his forehead hard on a rock. Besides making him dizzy, the fall had given him a deep gash on his forehead that was bleeding profusely.

At this point Sully didn't care. He made no effort to tend to his wound. He walked trying to un-jumble his fragmented mind. He reached the highway two hours later. His dizziness combined with a lack of focus had put him far off course, but he recognized the area and took a right.

Sully walked on the side of the road toward the hotel. He had tried several times to figure out how to explain his actions to Zoe, and nothing made sense. He finally settled on the truth. He had no idea if it would work, but he had to try something. He was walking into the wind and the icy rain, that was starting to turn to snow, was stinging his face.

He could see the lights of town, and the hotel when a car came up behind him. He heard the rocky dirt beneath the tires of a car, and turned around to see a Manassas police cruiser behind him.

Sully shook his head and sighed. He thought 'the hits just keep coming'. The gung ho officer used the loudspeaker mounted on top of the car saying "walk to the front of the car and place your hands on the hood. Sully could have dove into the woods and ran, but he chose to face the cop and let the circumstances play out.

Sully walked to the police cruiser and placed his hands on the hood as instructed. The young officer continued barking orders at him as he exited the vehicle. He yelled spread your legs, and step back two feet. Sully did as he was instructed. The young officer frisked Sully and had thrown Sully's wallet on the hood of the cruiser.

The wallet was clean, the Ted Sextant alias and some cash were the only things in it. The officer cuffed him, then said "what's going on here tonight buddy?"

Sully said defiantly "I'm staying at the Leaf with my girlfriend, Suite number two, and I wanted to take a walk. I slipped, fell down, and cut my head."

The officer asked "you sure you weren't fighting with your lady?" He was looking at sully with disdain, having already made up his mind that he was the type that beat women.

Now Sully was pissed when he said "I ain't sure of much jag-off, but I'm pretty sure that if you keep giving me attitude, you'll regret it."

The officer stiffly said "just stay there while I run you're Identification."

Sully said nothing. He knew that if the SSO alias was run through any government database he would come up as a high level justice department official.

The policeman hadn't come back in three minutes, and Sully was getting bored at glaring at him through the windshield, so he stood up and left. He had hardly taken a dozen steps when he heard the officer yell "freeze!" Sully said aloud to himself "too late fuck head, I'm already freezing."

He kept walking until he heard the policeman running up behind him. He stopped and waited until he could feel him right behind him. He executed a spinning leg kick and caught the office directly in the ear with the toe of his boot. The officer went down in a heap, and after Sully smashed his nose across his face with the heel of his boot, he stopped moving.

Sully quickly slipped his hands from behind his back to in front of him. He unhooked the key ring from the officer's belt, and un-cuffed himself. Sully took off the unconscious officer's gun belt. He tucked the pistol in the waistband of his pants and put the radio in his jacket pocket.

Sully grabbed the officer by the arm, and dragged him back to the patrol car. He was about to pick the limp body of the policeman up, and put him in his patrol car, when the radio crackled "Officer Tobias be advised that suspect is a G fourteen military advisor and is to treated as a V.I.P." Sully took the radio out of his pocket, depressed the transmit button, and said "Tobias to base, ten four on V.I.P. status." If Sully had waited five more minutes he wouldn't have had to hurt this man.

Sully hefted Tobias into the driver's seat of the patrol car, and threw the gun belt and radio onto Tobias's lap. He took his wallet off of the dashboard and quickly reviewed the contents. Sully looked for and found Tobias's notebook on the passenger's seat. He paged through it to the last page, and there was no mention of Sextant at all.

Sully started the engine and turned the wheel hard to the left. He grabbed Tobias's head with both hands and turned it to the right, and then just before he was going to quickly and violently twist the man's head down and to the left, effectively snapping his neck, he stopped.

Leaving him alive was a big risk, but Sully felt no need to kill the man. The SSO gave field agents only one get out of jail free card, and Sully was sure he would need it in the future. After that card was played agents were sanctioned quickly if they wound up in jail, or prison.

Sully stuck the right hand of the unconscious officer's body through the steering wheel, found Tobias's night stick and wedged it between the seat and the accelerator. He moved the seat forward with the power seat lever until the engine was almost at full throttle.

Sully took a step back and reached across Tobias's body and pulled the shift lever into Drive, and then he quickly jumped back.

The patrol car spun in the gravel until it hit the pavement, then it raced across the road and crashed, with a horribly loud sound, into a heavily wooded area across the road.

Sully was running after the car as soon as it started moving. Not long after the crash he reached the vehicle. Sully pulled the night stick off of the accelerator, grabbed the gun belt and radio, and turned the ignition key off to stop the sputtering engine. Then he turned the ignition back to the run position. He grabbed the head of the Tobias by the back of the hair and smashed his face into the steering wheel once, to help sell the crash. Sully then leaned Tobias's head back gently against the headrest and returned the seat to its original position. When he left the man he was breathing well and had a strong pulse. Sully hoped he would be found soon.

Sully moved quickly to the front of the car and pulled up the twisted hood. He found the battery and twisted on the power cable until it broke, and then he closed the hood and ran back to the driver's door. He picked up the gun belt, and the radio. Sully turned the volume on the radio way down and put it in his pocket. Then he ran.

Sully ran five hundred yards in the opposite direction that he had been walking earlier. He threw the gun belt as far as he could into the trees. Then he crossed the road and started jogging back toward the hotel. When he was parallel to the crash he quickly rubbed the patrol car's tracks out with his feet. The freezing rain had turned to snow, and it was falling in fat wet flakes. It was the cost of living in northern Virginia in late October.

Sully jogged all the way back to the hotel ten yards deep in the forested area that bordered the road. He tripped and fell down three more times. He was soaked, freezing, confused, and emotionally exhausted. His stone cold mood lightened a bit when he saw the old car still parked by the room, and the lights on inside. He walked slowly the rest of the way. The police radio had crackled several times, but there was no mention of the crash, Sextant or Tobias.

Sully walked to the room, and sat on the ground next to the door with his back against the wall. It was certain to be his imagination, or the pre hypothermic state he was in, but he thought he could smell Zoe's essence through the door. Real or not it comforted him and was slowly lightening his dark mood.

Sully knew that if he fell asleep he would probably die of hypothermia, so he fought a losing fight against it as long as he could. He sat shivering ferociously. He was trying, in vain, to figure out what he was going to say that might come close to explaining his actions. When he finally succumbed to sleep he dreamed of Zoe.

It took Zoe about ten minutes to become annoyed by the television. She turned it off and went to bed. She left the door unlocked in hopes that Sully would return. Zoe had placed the three eighty that Sully had given her under her pillow. Zoe had no idea what she had done to drive him away, but she was certain that she must have done something.

Sleep would not come to her, and after rolling around for twenty minutes she got up and turned the lights back on. Zoe paced the floor running all of the events of the day through her mind. Trying as hard as she could, she was unable to find anything that she had done to drive away the best thing that had ever happened to her.

Whatever had troubled him she wanted to fix, however possible. Zoe was not religious, but she spent the hours yelling at God. She told him how she had endured the childhood rapes and beatings without ever asking for help. She asked him why he finally gave her true love, only to snatch it away. She cursed God for playing with lives like they were tinker toys.

In the end Zoe prayed. She asked the Lord to let Sullivan live a long life, and to let him be happy. She asked nothing for herself, only for Sully.

Zoe dressed and re-packed the few things she had unpacked. She sat at the desk and opened the curtains just far enough to see the entrance to the hotel. She decided to sit for an hour watching for him, willing him to walk down the road back to her, and then she was going to leave.

Zoe had decided to call a cab to take her to Sperryville, then pick up the Toyota and go to Sully's house. After tonight, she wasn't sure if she could ever call it a home again. She planned to pack the few things she wanted from there, and never return.

Zoe was smiling as she replayed, in her mind, their every encounter from the moment they met until today, the end. Now she was on the verge of tears.

Then Zoe saw him. She blinked hard twice to make sure it wasn't a mirage, or her hope, that she was seeing. As the dark figure got closer she was absolutely sure it was Sully coming back to her, and a tear rolled down her cheek. She involuntarily gasped, and her heart began racing. Zoe quickly picked up her bag and ran to the huge bathroom.

Zoe threw her bag onto a luggage stand and opened it. She disrobed like she was on fire, and then put on one of the terrycloth robes, and matching slippers that had been supplied by the hotel.

She ran back to the window, and saw nothing. She sat back down at the desk and waited for a knock on the door, or for him to enter. After an hour, she decided to open the door and look around. When she did she saw a bloody man sitting against the wall covered by a layer of snow.

She gasped, and put a hand over her mouth she knew immediately it was Sullivan. Zoe yelled "Sully, are you okay?" When he did not move she knelt in the snow next to him and shook him yelling his name. She felt for a pulse on his neck, and put her ear to his mouth to hear his breathing. While she was doing this the only thing running through her mind was '*no, please God no*' over and over.

Zoe felt a weak pulse through Sully's ice cold skin, and heard only faint shallow breaths coming from him. She opened the door to the hotel room, and then dragged him inside. She ran over to close the door, and then ran to the thermostat to turn it up to maximum heat.

Zoe ran back to him and stripped his soaking wet clothing off of him. She covered him with all of the bedding available. Her slippers had fallen off when she dragged his limp body into the room. There was a comprehensive medical supply kit in the trunk of the car. Zoe snatched the keys off of the desk and ran out barefooted into the accumulating snow to retrieve it. She shuffled through the trunk until she found it. She dashed back into the room without closing the lid of the trunk.

She dropped the med kit next to Sully on her way to the bathroom. Zoe grabbed two towels and two wash cloths. She wet one of each, and then ran back to Sully. She uncovered his chest to wash it, but checked his vital signs again first. They were the same if not worse.

She washed the blood off of his chest, and then covered him tightly. She washed his face carefully with the wet towel because the wet washcloth was already red with blood. When his face was somewhat clean she cleaned his forehead with extraordinary concern. The lump at his hairline was enormous and the two inch gash was very deep.

Zoe had him as clean as possible for right now. She had not washed the wound because it was not actively bleeding. The things she needed out of the med kit right now were a suturing kit, hydrogen peroxide, and lots of gauze pads. She retrieved all of the pillows from the bed. Zoe took the case off of one pillow and gently placed it under Sully's head. The rest she placed under his feet to combat shock.

Fear was running through Zoe as she prepared to clean and stitch the menacing wound on his forehead. She surrounded the wound area with gauze pads, and then poured some hydrogen peroxide directly onto the wound. She took a pair of gauze pads and wet them with the peroxide. Zoe carefully scrubbed wound clean. It took her twelve pads of scrubbing to feel that it was sufficiently sterilized.

Zoe had sewed hundreds of wounds closed during training, but they were all on cadavers. This wound was on the man who held her heart. She put on her gloves, and opened the suture kit. Zoe poured peroxide on the wound one more time.

She took more than thirty minutes to close a wound that would have taken her less than ten in training. Zoe put in twice as many sutures than were necessary, and each one was as perfect as she could manage.

Zoe carefully cleaned and dried the stitched area and covered it with a large band aid. There was a vial of penicillin in the med kit along with syringes. Zoe filled the syringe to the ten cc mark, and then gave him the shot in his left hip.

She should have iced the lump on his head, but right now ice was the last thing he needed. Zoe took off her robe and crawled under the blankets with him. She pressed her naked body against him, and he felt cold.

Zoe whispered in his ear "please don't leave me like this. I love you too much for you to die on me." Every half hour she went into the hot tub for ten minutes to warm herself up into a human hot water bottle. The first time she was in it she turned the heat of the hot tub up to maximum.

Every time she was next to him under the blankets she would talk to him about their life together. Zoe revisited all the things they had done together, and everything they would do in the future. Whenever she came back from the hot tub she would switch sides and check his vitals.

It wasn't until her sixth return trip, two and a half hours later that there was any change. Sully's pulse was stronger, and his breathing was a little stronger. Zoe smiled and said loudly "that's it Mills, fight you son of a bitch. You get your ass back to me now. You say you're a tough guy, well prove it. Don't think you can lie on your ass all day."

Then she softened and held him tightly. Five minutes later she said "please come back to me Sully."

Sully kept improving, and two hours later when Zoe came back from the hot tub he stirred and moved into her damp warm hug. Zoe yelled "yes! That's it, keep it up. Keep fighting baby!"

He slowly improved over the next two hours moving more and more, making small sounds in response to Zoe's constant talking, and he even blinked his eyes once. She was ecstatic about the positive progress, and she was pretty sure he was out of the woods.

After two more hot tub trips he was trying to speak, but was not quite ready. She took a little extra time and ordered from room service. She ordered three cups of beef broth ten pieces of white toast, two bottles of champagne, two buckets of ice, and three blankets from housekeeping.

Before she went back to the hot tub she took a minute to clean up the bloody towels, the med kit mess, and Sully's clothes. After her ten minute warm up she went back to Sully. He actually turned into her and tried to put an arm around her. She smiled, took his arm and put it around her, and kissed him lightly. He surprised her by kissing him back. She said "I love you Sully, more than you could ever imagine."

Sully slurred in response "wub…so." It was all he could manage, and he fell asleep. But it was more than enough.

Zoe whispered sweetly to him "don't try to talk yet sweetheart, just sleep and let me warm you up." She was stroking his dirty blood and peroxide soaked hair as she said it. Then it dawned on her. Sully's hair had been soaked with hydrogen peroxide for hours. He wondered how he would react when he woke up blonde. She laughed aloud and woke him up.

There was a knock on the door fifteen minutes later that woke Zoe up. She had fallen asleep with Sully's arm around her, and had forgotten all about room service. She scrambled to get up and find her robe. She yelled "just a second."

Zoe went to the door in the hotel robe to meet room service. She was stunned when there were two police men at the door. Zoe acted shocked because she truly was. She closed the door so that only her head was visible through the crack. She said "what can I do for you gentlemen?"

The taller officer said "we hate to bother you Miss, but there was an officer involved car accident about a mile up the road. We are checking all the rooms in the hotel to see if anyone saw or heard anything."

Zoe thought on the fly and said calmly "no sir, I've been here since four yesterday afternoon and have been sleeping mostly."

The short officer chimed in and nastily said "are you here alone Miss?" He was all of five four and had the typical short man complex. It seemed to her that any man under five eight constantly had to prove something, and nine times out of ten they were assholes, and this little prick had a badge and a gun.

Zoe answered with a sexy smile on her face "yes my fiancé has been with me the whole time, and it will be quite a while before he gets up again." She had raised her eyebrows when she said 'up', and placed extra emphasis on the word.

Shorty was about to say something when the taller officer who had been smiling said "thank you Miss, and here." He handed her a set of keys. He continued "you left your keys in the trunk lid, and left it open. We closed it for you, but I am afraid that everything in the trunk is pretty much soaked."

Zoe kept the sexy smile on her face and said "thank you, we were in a hurry to get into bed." She was still playing them and she thought Shorty was blushing.

The taller officer said "thank you for your time Miss." He grabbed the brim of his hat and nodded at her.

When they left Zoe threw the keys on the desk and turned around. She almost screamed when she saw Sully standing behind the door with a gun. He looked exactly like Sullivan Mills, if Sullivan Mills were a ghost. Zoe said "what in the hell are you doing up?" She grabbed his arm and put it around her shoulder and took him to the bed. Zoe noticed that he was still cold, but not like before.

She sat him on the bed and grabbed the blanket on top of the pile. She wrapped the blanket around his shoulders and rubbed his legs. Sully said in a slow measured speech "you did a great job with the cops." He continued slowly "I've been awake for two hours, but I couldn't stop pretending to be comatose because you kept rubbing you're hot body against me."

There was another knock on the door, and a voice called out "room service."

Zoe went to the door and it was indeed room service. She opened the door and he wheeled a cart into the room. The kid showed her everything she had ordered, including the blankets that were on the bottom shelf of the cart. Zoe signed for the service and wrote down a twenty dollar tip for him. He politely said "thank you" and left the room.

Zoe wheeled the cart over in front of Sully, and then picked up the bed spread off the floor and covered his lower body with it. She took the lids off of all of the food and put them on the desk. As Zoe moved the two bottles of champagne she had ordered to the desk she said "one is for later, if you feel better. The other is for christening the plane."

She went back to Sully and sat next to him. Zoe kissed him on the cheek and said "try to eat a little Sully, at least have some broth. You need to get your strength back. After you eat we will go sit in the hot tub together to finish warming you up."

Sully was still shaking badly and could not pick up the broth without spilling it. Zoe thought he would resent her feeding him so she said "just take a piece of bread and dip it in the broth." She desperately wanted to feed him, but let him try by himself.

Sully did as he was told and shakily took a piece of toast and dipped it into the broth. He barely made it to his mouth, and the one bite exhausted him. Sully said "Zoe would you help me? I'm starving, but I still don't have my muscle control."

His asking her to help filled her heart. She smiled warmly and said "I love you Sully, I wanted to help, but I didn't want to offend you."

Sully said "honey, I don't think there is anything you could ever do to offend me."

Sully probably didn't realize it but he had just given her the best gift possible, he was alive, and he had called her honey.

Zoe stopped him at five pieces of toast and one mug of broth. She helped him lay down on the bed, and covered him with the new blankets. She fixed an ice pack for the knot on his forehead, and went back to the hot tub.

When she came back ten minutes later Zoe she found Sully sleeping next to a pile of vomit. She tried to clean up the mess without waking him but failed.

Sully stirred and he said "would you come lay with me, I need your body heat."

Zoe replied "I guess I should have thought of that nine hours ago when I started doing it. Let me change the blanket first."

Sully was absolutely shocked when he heard her reply he said in amazement "you're kidding me. I was out nine hours?"

Zoe answered "you were fully out and ice cold for the first eight, then you started coming around. It's been about ten now, and you're getting better."

Sully was silent and shook his head lightly in wonderment at the fact that he didn't die. He said "thank you Zoe, apparently I wouldn't have made it without you, I owe you my life. I promise to never do anything like that again."

Zoe left the bed, went to the bathroom, and closed the door. She was trying to compose herself. She was tremendously thankful that he was going to be okay. The hours of nursing and incredible worry had caught up to her, and she was ready to collapse. She took several deep breaths, and then she returned to him.

He was sleeping again, and when she snuck into the bed this time, Sully didn't wake. She kissed his shoulder lightly and whispered "welcome back honey." Then she let herself finally rest.

They slept for six hours without moving. They would have kept sleeping but Zoe's cell phone rang. She looked at it and it was Chuck. She groggily said "hello Chuck, what can I do for you?

Chuck was upset and almost angry when he answered "you can tell me what the fuck is going on, Carl's ready to call the cops about a stolen plane. Where the hell are you?"

Zoe answered him with an edge to he voice that Chuck was sure to understand when she said "first of all Chuck if you ever speak to me that way again you will regret it. Second, Sully got hurt and almost died today. Finally, if Carl can't wait till tomorrow tell him I will personally see how far I can stick that plane up his ass."

There was a long pause before chuck meekly answered "I'm sorry, but I'm the go between on this deal and he's pretty serious about calling the cops."

Zoe said "tell him to go ahead and call them, but remind him that it works both ways, and I am more than willing to disclose the illegal terms of the deal for the Seneca, as well as call the IRS to see if all his other business dealings are on the up and up."

Chuck didn't even try to respond before Zoe said "you know what, forget it. Tell him to meet me at the Wachovia bank in Bealeton in forty five minutes, and you be there too with your own car."

When she hung up Sully was sitting up and said "Sorry, I forgot about the payoff."

Zoe smiled at him and said "I really don't think you have anything to be sorry for, besides I am pretty sure you weren't faking a near death experience."

Sully kissed her and said "do you want me to go with you for proof?" He tried a weak smile but just sitting up and talking had drained his energy and made his head pound.

Zoe looked at him lovingly, and said "I just need you to do one thing for me while I'm gone."

Sully said "anything you want Honey."

Zoe smiled at him and said "I want you to keep that cute little ass in that bed while I'm gone." She had gotten goose bumps when he called her "Honey" again, because this time he wasn't delirious.

Sully noticed and asked "are you cold Zoe?"

Zoe laughed and said "what do you think. I've been snuggling up to a human popsicle for the past sixteen hours."

Sully smiled and tried to laugh but his eyes were heavy. He had never felt this bad in his life, but he was still happy to be here with Zoe.

Zoe said "one other thing Sully, don't try to get in that hot tub until I get back. I'm not sure your strong enough yet and I think it could possibly put you into shock. I should only be gone an hour or so, so just try to sleep, please.

Sully said "I promise I will just wait here for you.

Zoe rummaged through the pile of his wet clothes and found his cell phone. She walked around the bed and put it on the nightstand next to him. She gave him a kiss and he was still cold. She said "I love you Sully."

He was drifting off to sleep again and weakly said "I love you too Zoe. Thanks again, and hurry back."

Zoe quickly got dressed, brushed her hair, and was ready to go seven minutes later. She was wearing black Gap pencil pants, a black Beebe sweater, and her riding boots. She had the three eighty in her black Coach purse.

She walked over to the desk and took the cashier's check and twenty five thousand dollars in cash and put them in her purse. Then she closed the briefcase and put it under the bed. She left the room as quietly as she could.

The storm had passed, and it was in the mid-fifties and sunny. Zoe drove way too fast and made it to Bealeton in twenty five minutes. She tried not to, but on the way she cried. The emotional roller coaster she had been on in the last day had finally fallen off of the tracks. Sully had wanted to be away from her so much he almost killed himself. They were going to have a long talk before she could ever let him get close enough to hurt her again, but he had to get better first.

She wiped her eyes as she pulled up to the bank and saw Chuck there standing next to Carl. She pulled the car into the parking lot and parked right next to them. She took a deep breath and got out of the car. She said to herself '*try not to hit him*'.

She walked up to Carl, who was holding a fat manila envelope and said "That had better be a clear title in that envelope or I'm leaving." She was coming across mean and cold just like she planned.

Carl was trying to match her demeanor as he said "I was told this morning, not mid-afternoon. I was beginning to think you and Ted were jerking me around."

Chuck jumped to save Carl's ass, and he asked "so it's a few hours late, can we get this done please?"

Carl said with venom "this is all of the planes inspection records, along with the title." Then he reached in his jacket pocket and said "here you might as well take this, it's useless." He handed her a visa card.

She took the card, but he hadn't handed her the documents. Zoe said icily "alright, enough of these games. I really don't think you want me handing you cash right here in your current situation, so why don't you get in my car." She turned and got back in her car, and Carl followed. She handed him the cashier's check, then the cash.

He put the envelope on the dashboard and started counting the money. He stopped when he noticed the pistol pointed at his face. Zoe said viciously "stop insulting me right now and get the fuck out of my car."

Carl looked ready to piss his pants as he scrambled to put the money in his pockets and jumped out of the car. Zoe put the pistol back in her purse and walked over to Chuck. Chuck laughed and said "I never saw someone get out of a car so fast until Carl just did."

Zoe wasn't in the mood to laugh she let her demeanor soften a little and said "Carl if you can help me I need a big favor."

Carl replied "anything for you Zoe, you know that."

Zoe said "just meet me at Sully's place and I will explain on the way to Manassas." She was trying to get back to Sully as soon as possible, and didn't have time to be polite.

She drove quickly back to the house wondering why she had called the house Sully's place. It could have been a slip of the tongue, but she felt it might be deeper than that.

She had Chuck park his car on the road, and when he got in her car, and they headed for Manassas, she said "thank you for your help Chuck I need you to fly Sully's Seneca from Manassas to Sperryville for me. My car is there and you can drive it back here to yours and just leave the keys under the floor mat."

She was being possessive about all of the vehicles, and still couldn't figure out why.

Chuck said "what happened to Sully? You said he was hurt real bad or something?" He was very curious about what was going on.

Zoe had been working on a lie most of the way after leaving Manassas, and had been unable to come up with anything remotely feasible. She told Chuck almost the truth when she said "Sully and I had a fight and he stormed off into the woods last night. He fell and hit his head on a rock. When he got back to the hotel he collapsed from exhaustion and hypothermia. I think he will fine in a while."

Chuck couldn't help prying when he asked "what were you guys fighting about?"

Zoe figured she could get the ball rolling by telling Chuck what she was thinking about. She answered him by saying "I told him I was moving out, and we started fighting about it." It was a lie, but it would be true enough in the near future. She stopped their conversation from going any further when she grabbed her cell phone to call the Manassas airport.

She called information for the number, and when she was connected she heard a young woman's voice on the line. She said "Holly is that you?"

Holly answered back cheerfully "sure is, who's this?"

Zoe answered "it's Kathy from yesterday. I was wondering if you could get Sully's plane ready to taxi?" She had said Sully's plane again, and now she was starting to think it was over between them.

Holly said "sure thing, hang on one minute." When she picked up the phone she said "the plane will be ready to rock in ten." Then she asked "how was that Chinese food?"

Zoe really liked the free spirited girl, and she lied when she answered "it was great Holly, thanks for the recommendation."

Holly said "cool, see ya in a bit."

The next call was to the Sperryville airport. Zoe talked to them and asked them to open hangar six, pull the truck out, and be ready for Chuck. She told them where the keys were, and that Chuck should be arriving in about an hour. By the time she finished her calls they were in Manassas, and very close to the airport.

She went in to the airport office and settled the bill with Holly. Then she said goodbye to Chuck, gave him the access card for the airport, thanked him for his help, and drove back to Sully.

About a mile from the hotel there was a two car traffic back up. She wondered, as everyone does, what the delay was all about. It only took five minutes or so to get through the area, and she was perplexed to see crime scene tape all over the place, and a patrol car smashed into a group of trees. The thought crossed her mind that Sully might have been involved in this, but dismissed the thought as soon as it had come to her.

When she got back to the room Sully was still sleeping. She had promised herself that she would not bring anything up until they got back to the house Sully had rented.

She undressed and sat in the hot tub warming herself for ten minutes like she had done a dozen times before, but this time with a heavy heart. There was obviously something wrong with her to make Sully empty his bank account long before this trip. She was determined to leave him so he wouldn't put his life in jeopardy again over her. She loved him too much for that to happen.

When she snuck under the covers and pressed her warm damp body against him he stirred but did not waken. She laid with him for the customary half hour thinking of how to leave him so that he would think it was his idea to cast her out.

Zoe went back to the tub to warm herself again, and she decided to let him get totally healthy again before she made any move. This would give her more time to strategize.

The next time she got up she called room service before she went to the tub from the phone in the bathroom. She ordered two club sandwiches, fries, and a bowl of chicken soup.

Then she got in the hot tub again. When she got back to the bed Sully was awake. She crawled in to warm him up and he hugged her and kissed her passionately. He whispered "I love you Zoe, more than you will ever know, please forgive me for being such an immature jerk."

Zoe was conflicted by his admission and plea for forgiveness. She said "you're forgiven, I'll go get you some clothes. Room service is on the way, and I think you need to try to eat." She left the bed and dressed in the clothes she had on earlier. She found a tee shirt and fresh underwear for Sully, and grabbed him the dry robe and slippers.

She came back to Sully and dropped the robe at the foot of the bed and handed him the shirt and underwear. She said "do you want me to help you get dressed?" Her tone was not quite cold, but close to it.

Sully was confused by the change in her, but right now he was living in the biggest glass house ever built, so he simply said "No, let me try." He struggled a little, but dressed himself.

Room service arrived just after he had dressed, and Sully was able to walk to the end of the bed and put the robe on while Zoe dealt with the attendant and brought the cart in.

Sully was ravenous and ate half of a club sandwich quickly. When he reached for the other half Zoe stopped him and said "eat the soup and slow down, I'm pretty sure you have a concussion, and if you eat too much you might throw-up again."

He smiled at her and said "whatever you say beautiful." He was trying to bring her back to him, but she was being polite, at best.

Zoe left without a word and started packing their things she left out jeans and a jacket for Sully. When she had the bags assembled by the door she packed the car, throwing his wet clothes and the med kit in the soaked trunk. The rest she put in the back seat.

When Sully finished eating she asked him "do you think you could make the half hour ride to your house?"

Sully hadn't missed the 'your house' in her question, and decided to give up for right now. Zoe was definitely not in the mood for his feeble attempts to soften her mood. Sully hardened himself and said "Whenever you're ready."

Zoe was getting colder to him with every response as she said "I'll go settle at the desk, and then we'll go. Your briefcase is under the bed if you want it." She walked out before he could reply.

When Zoe got back from settling the bill Sully was in the car. Zoe walked into the room and double checked that they hadn't forgotten anything. Her last stop was to look under the bed and the briefcase was still there. She was confused when she grabbed it and walked out to the car. She put it in the back seat and then got into the driver's seat.

They didn't speak to one another for the first ten minutes. Then Zoe said "I guess you didn't understand me when I told you that your briefcase was under the bed."

Sully softly replied "I knew it was there."

Zoe wasn't biting and she suppressed her urge to ask why he left over two hundred thousand dollars under the bed in a hotel room.

Nothing was said the rest of the trip. When they got there Zoe said "let me move my car." She left without a word from Sully. She ran up the driveway and moved the Toyota onto the road. She came back to the car and backed the car into the driveway. Sully got out and went inside leaving the bags to Zoe.

It took Zoe three trips to empty the car and a half hour to put everything away. Sully was lying on the couch, and Zoe brought him a bag of frozen peas and a bottle of water. She gently placed the peas on his forehead and handed him the water. She said "I'm going to the store to get you some things to eat. Do you want anything special?"

Sully said "yes, I would like you to talk to me for a while." His voice was weak and cracking.

Zoe replied coolly "I have a load of wash to get started, maybe after I get back from the store."

She turned to walk away and Sully almost yelled at her "don't I get a chance to defend myself before you shut me out of your life?"

Zoe was ready for this and spun on a heel and said loudly "just try Sully. Defend to me why you emptied your bank account. Defend why you ran away from me with no intention of coming back. Try to defend why you want me out of your life so much that you would rather die than be with me. You may not think I'm very smart, but I am, and obviously a lot fucking smarter than you are if you think I can't read the signals you're throwing at me." By the end she was yelling and was mad at herself for letting him bait her.

Zoe turned to leave and she heard Sully softly say "I'm afraid Zoe. For the first time in my life I'm afraid."

Zoe was still mad and let him know it by not turning around, and coldly saying "what Mills, what are you afraid of?"

Sully paused for a long moment then answered "mostly I'm afraid of losing you, but I am also afraid of keeping you. I know that doesn't make sense, I don't know if it does to me, but I have come to the realization over the last few days that fear is the only thing keeping me from giving you all of my heart. I love you Zoe, much more than I could ever love myself. I know I don't deserve you, and I want much better for you than I can give. I foolishly thought that I could run away from you, but your love brought me back, and your love saved my life. I wouldn't blame you for leaving, I probably would if I were you, but please leave knowing I will love you forever."

Zoe still didn't turn around, but now it was because she was on the verge of weeping. She waited until she was composed enough to respond, then she said "that's today Sullivan, what about tomorrow. I would rather go back to being lonely than to let you hurt me more." Zoe could feel him coming up behind her even though he didn't make a sound.

Sully whispered to her without touching her "please give me another chance, I won't let you down. From now on I will tell you my fears, rather than running from them. I love you Zoe."

Zoe turned and fell into his arms, and they embraced for a long while. She helped him back to the sofa to lie down. She went to the pantry and took a manufactured log out of the box. She took it to the living room and lit a fire. Zoe sat on the floor and Sully put his arm around her. She gently stroked his arm and they sat watching the fire not saying a word.

Sully thought '*this wonderful creature gave you another chance, so don't fuck it up*'.

Zoe thought '*one more chance Sullivan Mills, that's all you get*'.

The fire had gone out and they had never gone to bed. Sully was fast asleep, so Zoe snuck out from under his arm and went to the bedroom. She was still in her clothing from the hotel, and needed a shower. After she showered she climbed in the bed and tried to make sense of the last day and a half. She quickly fell asleep and didn't wake for hours.

Zoe awoke refreshed and happy. She had decided to put all of the negative aspects of the past few days behind her. She was going to give Sully one last chance to be the man she knew he could be.

She brushed her teeth and dressed in a tee shirt and sweat pants. Zoe started a load of laundry and then went to check on Sully. He was still sleeping on the sofa, so she went to see what they had for breakfast. There wasn't much to be had in the house, but they did have eggs, and the steaks that Sully and Chuck had bought. Zoe thought that steak and eggs sounded good.

It was nine in the morning, but she decided to call Chuck to see if he wanted to come over for breakfast, and she needed to thank him. She called his cell phone, but he didn't answer. She could have called his business, but decided not to.

Zoe went to the back yard and started the grill. When she went back to the kitchen Sully was standing there drinking a glass of milk. She walked to him and asked "how are you feeling Sully?"

He hugged her and answered "seeing you still here I feel great. I didn't know what to think when I woke up and you weren't there."

Zoe hugged him back and said "this is your last chance Mills, don't blow it. Would you please do me a favor right now?"

Sully answered "of course, anything." He was thrilled that she was willing to give him a chance, and was going to do his best not to screw up.

Zoe pushed him away and pinched her nose between her thumb and index finger. Then she said "go take a shower, you reek." She smiled at him as she said it.

When Sully left to shower she found a skillet for the eggs, and looked again for bread. There was no bread for toast, so she decided to make six eggs rather than four.

Zoe was walking in with the steak from the grill when she saw a freshly showered Sully standing by the stove playing with the eggs. Zoe said "hey cowboy, here's the meat."

Sully said "smells great. You can never go wrong with steak and eggs."

Zoe smiled at him and said "especially when that's all you have. We don't even have bread for toast."

Sully grabbed her and kissed her several times. He said "I don't care about toast as long as I have you."

Zoe kissed him deeply and replied "you have me as long as you want, don't screw it up."

Sully said "trust me, you won't have to worry about that ever again." Then he pointed to the cut on his forehead, that he had taken the band-aid off of, and continued "by the way, nice knitting."

Zoe looked at his forehead closely for a minute, and then she said "it looks good, the lump has gone down quite a bit, but I wouldn't wear a hat for a while if I were you. Even though you might want to Blondie."

Sully laughed and said "I don't plan on it. I already found out to be careful combing my beautiful blonde locks. I'm assuming that you used peroxide to clean the wound, and this wasn't a cruel joke."

Zoe said "I guess you'll never know the answer to that one."

They had a nice breakfast together. But they were awkward with one another, not at all as loving as they had been. Zoe was going to make sure that he earned her trust again, and Sully was trying too hard. It was going to take them some time.

When they were almost finished eating Sully asked "did you figure out where you want to go yet?"

Zoe answered "I don't have a clue, but I'm not sure you're ready to go anywhere. Remember you were close to death a day ago."

Sully said "the way I see it, it's all the more reason to live, especially since you've found it in your heart to give me a chance."

He continued "I only had one idea, and I want you to tell me what you think. My mother always talked about the only trip she had ever taken. It was to the White Mountains of Arizona. All I remember is the name of a town, Show Low. She had told me several times how beautiful the mountains were. What do you think?"

Zoe thought it sounded wonderful, but she wasn't sure Sully would be up to it. She replied "I don't know Sully, that's a long trip. I'm not sure if you're up to it so soon."

Sully said excitedly "I'm fine, by tomorrow morning I'll be one hundred percent. I'll call Chuck and have him plot out a course for us. Today we get to go shopping for gear, and pack!"

Zoe thought that a trip to the mountains did sound wonderful, but she was still a little concerned about Sully. She walked over to him and said "look at me. Look straight at my nose and follow my finger." She moved her finger back and forth twice, and determined that his ocular response was normal. If he did have a concussion it was mild.

Sully moved forward and kissed her on the nose. He asked "What do you think doc, am I gonna make it?"

Zoe tried to put a serious look on her face but failed when she said "I think you'll pull through, but I'm afraid that leg's gonna have to come off."

They both laughed and hugged one another.

Sully and Zoe drove to Charlottesville for a day of shopping in the big city. They gathered all of the things they thought they might need for a trip to the mountains, and several things they didn't. Zoe had insisted on buying him a World War two bomber style jacket, and he only relented with the condition that she get a matching one. They held hands, kissed quite often, and their relationship was getting better by the minute.

They had tried to call Chuck several times with no answer. They were getting concerned and vowed to check on him when they got back. Sully and Zoe went to the Charlottesville airport and bought a United States navigation map to plot their own course if need be.

It was a great day for them, a healing day, and a day to cherish.

They tried twice on the way back to Bealeton to reach Chuck to no avail. They didn't even stop at the house, but instead drove straight toward his private hangar. Zoe tried one last time to call him and he finally picked up.

After Chuck said hello Zoe was relieved when she said "are you alright Chuck we've been calling all day."

Chuck replied "I'm fine, I'm an idiot, but I'm fine. When I dropped your plane in Sperryville and got back here, I signed all the stuff Luke had ready for me, then I was gonna call you to see how Sully was. Then I realized I left my phone in your plane and had to drive all the way back. I never looked at the thing until about an hour ago, and that's when I plugged it in."

Zoe asked "how about dinner in a couple of hours?"

Chuck said "sounds great, I'll bring the wine."

Zoe relayed the conversation to Sully in its entirety, and then she said "well were this close to town we might as well go grocery shopping."

Sully smiled at her and said "sounds good to me Honey. I hope that you don't mind that I call you Honey every once in a while Zoe."

Zoe was thrilled. Sully recognized that he was calling her Honey, and it wasn't just an accident. She said "Sully I don't mind at all, in fact, I find it precious. I was thinking of calling you 'Binky', what do you think?"

Sully was smiling when he answered "I think if you ever want me to answer you, it would be best not to call me 'Binky'.

Sully pulled into the Safeway parking lot and parked the truck. They "made-out" like teenagers at the drive-in movies for ten minutes until the windows fogged up.

They were both more than ready to make love, but they had to shop first. They ran through the store getting only what they needed for dinner. They were in and out of the store in less than ten minutes. They were home in another ten and left everything in the car and chased one another to the bedroom.

They made mad passionate love to one another like it was the first time. When Sully was physically spent he said "I'm sorry Honey, I'm still not a hundred percent."

Zoe replied "don't worry, I'll take your eighty percent any day Binky."

Zoe jumped out of the bed before he could grab her. She was smiling and said "I kind of like you not being one hundred percent, you can't catch me."

They took showers separately, then dressed in casual clothes quickly and started getting dinner together. Sully had told her about the crab legs in the freezer when they were shopping, so the menu was salad, dinner rolls, sirloin steaks, and crab legs.

Zoe had asked the butcher in Safeway how to prepare the crab legs. He had told her that if they were thawed to place them on a hot grill for three minutes per side, so that was the plan.

While Zoe got the salad and rolls ready Sully sorted the bags in the truck. Those that needed to come in the house he took into the back room. The rest he tried to organize.

He had just got back into the house when Chucks headlights shone through the house as he entered the driveway.

Chuck walked in carrying two bottles of wine and almost dropped them when he saw Sully's hair. It took him a full two minutes to stop laughing, and after the first minute, Zoe had joined in on the laughter. Sully had finally had enough and said "Fuck you guys!" Then he walked out back to pretend to play with the grill.

They had a wonderful dinner, and they all pitched in on the clean-up. When they were done they sat around the table and it took them less than twenty minutes to route the trip together.

Sully started a 'fire' and they sat for a short while in the living room talking in front of it. When Chuck was ready to leave they loaded him up with all of the leftovers, and all the perishable food in the refrigerator.

When Chuck had one foot out the door he turned to Sully and asked "Sully, is it true?"

Sully bit hook line and sinker and answered "is what true Chuck?"

Chuck smiled a big toothy smile and said "are you having more fun?" He had said the last word as he was running down the driveway to his car.

Sully chuckled and shook his head until he turned around and saw Zoe with both hands clamped over her mouth trying to hold her laughter in. His smile turned into a wounded look and he said "et' tu' Brute'?"

Zoe burst into raucous laughter, and Sully joined her.

Sully went to sit by the fire, and Zoe turned off all the lights in the house. She joined him on the sofa and backed into him. Sully put his arms around her and they watched the fire together.

Sully said "remember the first fire we had together. I have a promise to fulfill to you."

Zoe said "I don't remember you promising anything to me. What are you talking about?"

Sully said "I guess it wasn't really a promise, but I had said I had a surprise for you that night. I couldn't give it to you because Chuck stayed over."

Zoe said "mmm' I remember that night as a fabulous night of lovemaking, what was the surprise supposed to be?"

Sully kissed her neck and answered in a whisper "I was going to make love to you in front of the fire."

Zoe wiggled tightly into him and whispered back "there's no time like the present."

They made love until the fire died. They fell asleep in each-other's arms naked and bathed in sweat. They each had happy contented smiles on their faces.

Zoe woke him a couple of hours later and they went to bed. They snuggled and closely and fell asleep quickly. Neither of them stirred until the bright light of a clear, new morning streamed through the bedroom window.

Sully went to the bathroom and urinated. Then he brushed his teeth and washed up. He went back to the bed to snuggle with Zoe. She was awake and put her arms around him and held him closely.

They stayed in bed for almost an hour just enjoying the feel and warmth of one another. Zoe finally kissed the back of his neck and said "I'm really excited about the trip. Get your lazy butt up, and let's get going."

Sully yawned and said "I'm happy right here." He snuggled his butt back into her and she pinched it lightly, and he quickly got out of the bed.

Zoe smiled and said "that's more like it, now I know how to make you move quickly."

Sully rubbed his butt, pouted, and replied "I don't think you realize how hard you can pinch."

Zoe put a sinister grin on her face and said "don't ever forget it either." Then she said "come here baby, I'll kiss it and make it all better."

Sully smiled and replied "I'm not falling for that one. I ain't getting anywhere near you lady!"

Zoe laughed and said "fine be a coward." She threw the covers off and pretended to sleep lying naked on her back.

Sully did what any red blooded male would do and fell right into her trap. He crawled onto the bed between her legs and she put him in a headlock with her legs. Zoe wasn't squeezing as hard as she could, but close, and after a minute of silent struggling Sully pretended to pass out. Zoe left him on the bed to go clean up in the bathroom and brush her teeth all the while telling him it wasn't funny anymore.

Zoe finally said "if I come over there and you're faking you're going to wish for a long time that you weren't"

Sully played dead until she went into the closet and grabbed one of his horsehair belts with a silver tip and started toward him. He jumped out of the bed a said "okay, okay I was teasing." He hid behind the bed, but was trapped.

Zoe looked him up and down and then dropped the belt. She climbed onto the bed and licked her lips. Then she said "why don't you come over here and accept your punishment. I promise not to hurt you, much."

Sully took careful steps toward the bed and when he cautiously got on the bed next to her she grabbed him and kissed him over and over. Sully reciprocated and kissed her breasts, nibbled lightly on her nipples, then moved downward kissing her belly button. As he tried to move farther down her body Zoe grabbed him lightly by the head.

She laid him down and rubbed against him as she whispered "this is your punishment, not a treat so just lay there and do as I say."

Sully was thankful that their nearest neighbor was more than a half mile away, or the police would have been there because of all of Zoe's screaming. They collapsed together kissing and professing their love for one another. Zoe said "your punishment is over for now" as she went to the shower.

Sully took out the clothes he wanted to wear and laid them on top of the dresser. He was glad that Zoe was in the shower, because he got so dizzy he fell to one knee. It took him three try's to stand up, and when he did he thought he was going down again. Five minutes later, his head cleared, and he felt fine.

When Zoe got out of the shower he kissed her and squeezed her bottom. She said "Sully that was absolutely wonderful."

Sully replied "the neighbors called and only gave it a nine, so I guess I will have to try harder."

Zoe said "mmm I can't wait." She kissed him and ordered "shower, now, I want to get going Sully."

Sully showered and got dressed wondering about the dizzy spell, but eventually dismissed it as an aftershock from the vigorous lovemaking. He wore wrangler blue jeans, a black Cabelas long sleeved Henley, and of course his boots. Ninety percent of the clothing was in the truck from their spending spree yesterday.

He grabbed some underwear and socks and went to the back room to grab their suitcases and mission bags. He took his suitcase out to the truck along with both mission bags. When he went back to the house he took Zoe's bag to the bed.

Then he went back to the truck and started going through the bags from yesterday. He put his things in his suitcase, and bagged Zoe's. The things they had bought for the plane he left in the truck.

He put on his bomber jacket, and took Zoe's inside along with the rest of her things. As he walked by the kitchen table he stopped to grab his straw hat, then took all of Zoe's things into the bedroom.

Zoe was ready to go dressed in Calvin Klein blue jeans, a hunter green Abercrombie and Fitch cowl neck sweater, and black ladies Tony Llama boots. Sully placed her things on the bed and commented "you look absolutely gorgeous Zoe."

Zoe smiled and replied "thank you Sully, I've got to try a little harder to keep up with you now that you're a blonde."

Sully growled "how long is my hair gonna stay like this, and how long are you gonna fuck with me about it?"

Zoe laughed, and then answered "as long as it takes to grow out, and as long as it takes to grow out."

Sully grumbled "great, if it wasn't against SSO policy, I'd shave it all off."

Zoe said "I'd color it for you, but the wound is too close to the hairline, and I don't want the colorant to get in it. I wish you would keep it covered with a band-aid."

Sully smiled and replied "no thanks. I happen to think I look dumb enough as it is."

Zoe said "okay, but if it gets infected and your head falls off don't come running to me."

They shared a small laugh, packed the truck, and were on there way. They reached the airport and were ready to take off less than an hour later.

They were in the air and headed west, and their lives had never been better. Two lost children that had grown up in difficult circumstances had somehow found one another and were experiencing a wonderful life. It was only for snippets at a time, but when they were exploring life together they were extremely happy.

They had plotted two routes. Route A had three lay-overs, and route B had only two. It was barely past fourteen hundred hours when they reached Lexington Kentucky, so they decided to push for Kansas City.

Zoe and Sully had agreed that if they got up early the next day they could make the trip with only one stop. They had a great night out in Kansas City. Taking the advice of the cab driver, they went to an out of the way spot for true Kansas City barbeque.

They decided that they could take their time on the return trip and stop at several different places. The excitement of flying on their own to points unknown overwhelmed them both. They were back at their hotel early, and after making love in the shower, they fell asleep in each-other's arms, talking about the joys of their day together.

They were up before dawn and ready to go. Sully laughed at her when she started chewing on the left over ribs for breakfast. She offered him some, but he politely declined. He told her that ribs without a beer was sacrilege.

They took a cab to the airport, and they were in the air before the sun. They took turns flying, and every time they were on auto pilot Sully had to rebuke Zoe's advances to join the mile high club. It made no difference to her that they were flying at thirty five hundred feet.

It was early afternoon when the Rocky Mountains rose to seemingly touch the sky in front of them. The plane was performing beautifully, and so was their relationship.

There was never a lull in their conversation as they flew. They told one another everything. They talked about hopes and dreams, and each came to the realization that together they had already surpassed what they had dared to dream.

They skirted the plane just South of Denver's outer marker and made a course correction for Northern Arizona. Sully took the plane down to nine hundred feet for the duration of their flight.

Once the Seneca was on its course to Show Low, and on auto pilot, Sully and Zoe were acting like the children life never allowed them to be.

They chased one another around the small cockpit looking at the beauty below them. They saw herds of deer, elk, and antelope. Each shouted at the other when they saw some new wonderment.

They continued this for quite a while, then Zoe took the controls and called in for an approach vector to the Show Low airport. When they were tied down, they asked the attendant to help them rent a car. The young man was nice, and when Sully asked him for a place to stay he recommended the Lake of the Woods Lodge that was on a private lake with cabins to rent.

When the blue Dodge Durango was driven to the plane they loaded in their bags and were off to their cabin. Zoe was thrilled with the cabin and the surroundings. They had hardly gotten their bags into the room when she had Sully light a fire for them. They went shopping for staples for the cabin at a small country market in a neighboring town named Pinetop.

They were picking out places to consider for dinner while they drove to and from the store. The sun had gone down, and so had the temperature. They were now at sixty five hundred feet elevation, and were both thankful to be wearing their new jackets.

The store was very quaint and they took their time soaking in the ambiance. Zoe told Sully that she was very happy with the choice of location. She insisted that tomorrow they find her an appropriate hat so that she could fit in. Zoe asked the overly friendly checker to recommend a place for dinner. The young plump girl didn't hesitate a second when she told them to dine at Charlie's.

When they got to the rental car Sully told Zoe that he had forgotten the receipt and ran back into the store to get it while she loaded the few things into the car.

Sully went in to talk to a different female employee, and Zoe watched through the glass storefront as he gave her a one hundred dollar bill for the hat she was wearing.

When Sully returned to the rental car he saw her watching him and knew that there was no hiding the hat. Before he could hand it to her she ran to him and embraced him tightly. Sully remarked that the hat looked a hell of a lot better on her than it had on the young checker in the store.

They unloaded the rented car at the cabin and set out for dinner. The dinner met all of their expectations. It was a cowboy bar that had a small dining room. The rowdy crowd that populated the small establishment consisted of deer and elk hunters straight from the woods, and the local boys that wished they had been hunting.

They crossed the room quietly and sat at the corner table farthest from the bar. They had been in the mood for a quiet dinner, but the yelling from the bar proved to be an interesting floor show. The food was outstanding despite the setting it was served in.

They went back to the cabin and fell asleep in front of the fire holding one another. When Zoe went to bed Sully said he would be right there. He didn't go with her because when he had tried to get up he had another dizzy spell and had to sit for a minute until it passed.

The bathroom in the small cabin was on the first floor, and the bedroom was a loft. Sully took his time preparing for bed, and told himself that the dizzy spells were due to pushing to hard after the Manassas experience.

They snuggled all night long. When he came to bed Zoe told him how happy she was, and how much she loved him. Sully kissed her and reciprocated the sentiment. Sully held her as she slept, although he never did sleep himself.

When the sun rose over the mountains they were there to greet it drinking coffee on the patio. They spent the day exploring the mountains. They went to the Sunrise ski resort and walked in the snow until their feet were cold. Sully was shocked and amazed that the state he grew up in contained such beauty. All he remembered was the ugly harshness of the southern deserts.

They drove all over the surrounding areas and towns. Each place was more fascinating to them than the last. They acted as young adults who had not seen much in their lives, because they were. It was the first true vacation either of them had been on and they were having the time of their lives.

They walked around a quaint little town called Snowflake, and Zoe had remarked that this was the kind of small town she would choose to live in if she had a choice.

They had four wonderful days together, and then Zoe was recalled.

Thankfully, it wasn't urgent, and Weathers had told her she could fly back with Sully. He had called her on what she had thought was her private phone.

On the flight back to SSO headquarters they made a list of rules regarding one another. The first, and most important, was that they not interfere with one another's assignments. Weathers had made it abundantly clear to them after Bolivia, that the SSO would not tolerate that again, under any circumstances.

Rule number two was that they could discuss, at their own discretion, only what they wanted to about a completed mission. Sully had insisted on this rule, because he tried his best to forget each sanction as soon as he was debriefed.

There was only one other rule. Always come back safe. The weight of the seriousness had turned both of their moods. Zoe had no idea what her upcoming mission would entail, and Sully was genuinely worried. The blissful mood they had been in was broken, and there was no getting it back.

Weathers had arranged for a military base for them to tie down, near Fort Smith, Arkansas. When they landed Weathers was waiting for them. They kissed and told one another to be safe. Weathers took Zoe in one of the organization's Gulf Stream's, and sent Rady back with Sully as a copilot.

Six days after returning to Bealeton Weathers called Sully in for a mission of his own. Zoe had not returned and he had not heard from her. Sully left her a note on the steering wheel of her truck that simply said "I love you, hope to see you soon."

That's the way life went for them for the next two years. They had the rare occasion that they would get a few days together, but the SSO had them apart much more than they were together. They tried extremely hard to recapture the magic they had once had, and most times when they got a few days together by the time the awkwardness ended it was time for one of them to leave again. Love wasn't easy for the two government assassins.

After a sanction in Barbados Zoe went to Weathers for a quick debriefing before being shipped to Intelligence for her formal debriefing.

Weathers was smiling when she came in and said cordially "another perfect sanction Zoe, I don't know what I would do without you." He motioned for her to sit in front of his desk.

Zoe sat down, but was far from cordial when she replied "I'm done Jim, it's over." She stared at him with a look so hot it could have melted steel, and he knew she wasn't kidding.

Weathers tried to match her stare as he said "Be reasonable agent Millstad, it has been made very clear to you several times before you agreed to this job that the SSO says when it's over, not their covert operatives."

Zoe matched his intensity, and said "you have a choice Jimmy and you need to think long and hard about your answer. You can lose one of your best agents, or two, your choice. I don't think that Sully would believe any scenario where I mysteriously disappear, and if you choose to simply erase my existence, you yourself had better hide fast, and far, because you can bet your ass that he will come after you first."

Weathers leaned back in his chair and lit a cigar. He spent several minutes mulling over what she had said and finally stated "I believe what you are saying is most likely true, but if I simply let you walk away I am still in the same position."

Zoe smiled at him and said "I have a plan to save your ass Jim, never underestimate the fairer sex, because when it comes down to it we're not fair at all."

Weathers smiled and replied "before I even listen to your plan I need to know one thing, why?"

Zoe answered him swiftly and directly saying "I'm pregnant."

Weathers shook his head and said "someone in medical is in deep shit over this, when you had your hip implant they were supposed to perform a tubule legation at the same time. It's standard protocol for all incoming female agents."

Zoe replied "well they obviously missed me. Do you want to hear my plan, or do you want to go it alone?"

Weathers took several puffs on his cigar before he answered "tell me what you have in mind."

Zoe laid out her plan in detail for him, and they discussed it for over an hour. Finally Weathers said "go to Intel and debrief, and then come back here for my answer. If you don't make it back here alive you'll know my answer was no."

Zoe accepted the terms and left the room, possibly for the last time in her young life.

Four hours later she was brought back to Weathers office. He had been hard at work finalizing the details of her death while she was being formally debriefed. He welcomed her in, and Zoe looked around for the shooter that might end her life. She saw no one and sat down across from Weathers.

Weathers started their conversation by saying "your status is still up in the air. The SOD's first reaction was to offer you the opportunity to terminate the pregnancy, and carry on. When I conveyed your intended plan to him he agreed to it with several conditions."

Zoe had always been rebellious when it came to being told what to do, and cautiously replied "and what if I don't accept the terms?"

Weathers didn't blink when he answered "then you don't walk out of here, you go out horizontally." He pulled out a pistol from his desk drawer and laid it on the desk in front of him, then he continued "my wife spent a lot of time and money picking out the rug under you, so please accept the terms."

Zoe tried to seem calm but she was obviously shaky when she softly replied "give me your terms and I will decide my fate. Just another great day as an SSO field agent, hey Jim?"

Weathers was not amused as he laid out the terms that were, most definitely, take it or leave it, and leave it would leave her on a slab in the morgue. The terms were very simple, the SSO would accommodate her to keep Sully, and make her "death" look like an accident. In return she would be given a new alias and as long as she never crossed the government's radar in any way shape or form, and still did occasional work for the SSO, she could live out her life as she chose.

Zoe accepted the offer, and was ordered to return the next day for a pre-mission briefing. Weathers made it abundantly clear that he was going to have to call in a lot of favors to make this happen.

Zoe was driven to her apartment on campus where she sat alone in the dark and cried. She was carrying the child of the best thing that had ever happened to her, and she had to shatter him in order to keep it. Sully had taught her to love and trust, and together they grew more than they ever could have apart.

To help her deal with the situation, Zoe wrote a ten page letter to Sully explaining everything that was going on and how to find her in the future. She wrote about her love for him, and how she swore never to leave him. Her letter went on, and on, about her feelings, her wants, and dreams. When she finished, she read it to herself, then burned it. She dropped it into the sink and symbolically washed the ashes down the drain.

When she met Weathers the next day she was emotionally exhausted. Weathers explained his plan, and told her that Sully would be back tomorrow. The mission was tentatively scheduled for four days from now, giving her three days with Sully. Her last three days with him ever, and she had no idea how to handle it.

Zoe was driven back to her apartment and took her truck back to Sully's house. She stopped to pick up groceries on the way. She shopped numbly, throwing everything she saw that Sully liked into the cart. She saw Chuck at the checkout, in the express lane, and quickly ducked into the Ladies room. She waited until she was sure he would be gone then finished her shopping and left.

She felt terrible for having ducked him, but the last thing she wanted to deal with now was Chuck. She drove to the small house and put the groceries away. It was silly of her to buy so much when she knew they were leaving in a few days, but it made her feel better in some small way.

She walked around the small house that was filled with so many memories and knew she couldn't stay there tonight. Her heart was so heavy that it ached. Sully had bought the house when the first lease was up, and they were continually upgrading the old place to suit them.

None of the original furniture was left, and they had contracted for a large deck on the back of the house. They had a large garage built that included an eight foot by eight foot walk in vault. Sully's collection of ordinance had continued to increase, and was threatening to outgrow even the vault. They had talked about adding on to south side of the house to expand the living room and master bedroom, but had not yet moved forward on the idea.

When they were home alone, they kept themselves busy by working on the house. Looking at the house now it truly was a home that reflected them in every corner.

Zoe had a meeting scheduled with an Operations agent, Janet Port, to finalize her new identity, and move most of her money into a private account. She made out a quick will that simply said "what was mine is now yours". The agent would take care of the rest.

Zoe went to her old apartment and sequestered herself for the rest of the time she had until Sully's return. She had to say goodbye to him now in her mind, so that she could be free to enjoy her last days with him.

She had asked Janet to call her when Sully was in formal debriefing, and the next morning she stared at her phone, dreading the call. When the call came in at ten hundred hours it startled her out of deep thought.

She drove to the house trying her best to lighten her mood. She was determined to make the best of their last days together as happy as she could.

Sully called her on the way home to see if she was there, and was happily surprised to find that she was there. He asked if she wanted him to stop at the store for anything, and when she said she had everything she needed, except him, Sully told her he loved her and hurried home. He had no idea that less than a week later his whole world would be shattered.

Chapter 8

When Sully walked in he looked at Zoe and cheerfully said "hello beautiful" as he put his bag down.

Zoe walked over to give him a welcome home kiss, and then she asked "where've you been cowboy?"

Sully answered "Mexico City, and I don't recommend it. But it's always worth it to come home to you." He hugged her tightly, and said "I missed you, Honey."

She kissed him deeply and rubbed his crotch. After a minute of fondling him she looked him in the eyes and said "I guess you did miss me."

Sully carried her into the bedroom and they made love in the shower, which had become their ritual when one or the other came back from a sanction. Zoe had started the practice saying that it "washed away the rest of the world".

They dressed casually in shorts and tee shirts and went to sit on the back porch. Sully smoked a cigar, and drank a beer while Zoe had a diet pop. Sully said "I couldn't help but notice some pretty dramatic tan lines, where did they come from?"

Zoe smiled and answered "I got back yesterday from a really rough one in Barbados. I tell ya, five days on the beach is rough duty."

Sully laughed and said "sounds like it. Do you have any plans for us while we are off?"

Zoe said "not a thing, I kind of thought we could just be lazy for a few days and hang around here." She was hoping he didn't have big plans for them.

Sully said "that sounds great to me. Answer me one question though. How is it you get more beautiful every time I come home?"

Zoe laughed and answered him with a question of her own. She asked "how many beers have you had?"

Sully just smiled at her and held up one finger.

Zoe said "then someone must have poked you in the eyes while you were away."

They went through this routine every time he hadn't seen her for a while. He would tell her how great she looked and she would call him blind. The normalcy of their relationship made them both extremely comfortable with one another. Today Zoe especially needed it, to try to forget the future.

They sat divulging what they chose to about their respective sanctions, and as was customary, it would never be discussed again.

Sully asked "what's the plan for dinner?"

Zoe answered "whatever you like, we can go out if you want to, but I went a little overboard at the grocery store. You name it and I probably bought it."

Sully said "I definitely vote for staying in, but if you would rather order in, I'm fine with that."

Zoe said "let me think about it. Maybe I can figure out something we can cook together." She was trying as hard as she could, but was still a little clumsy with him.

Sully replied "sounds fine, let me know what I can do to help." He stood and said "I've still got some things to get out of my truck."

Sully took two gear bags and a rifle case out of his truck. He had finally retired granny's car last year and bought a four door Ford pick-up. He took his gear to the garage and opened the vault. He quickly cleaned three pistols, and wiped down the sniper rifle that he hadn't fired on this sanction.

Zoe loudly said "hey you, I brought you a beer" as she walked through the door. She always made sure not to startle Sully when he was near his arsenal. Zoe walked over and kissed him, then handed him the beer. She said "how does salad, country ribs, corn on the cob, and rice sound?"

Sully answered "it sounds wonderful, I'll be done here in a little bit, and then I'll be in to help."

Zoe said "take your time, we won't start for at least an hour." She kissed him again and he squeezed her butt. Zoe smiled at him and said "watch it buddy, you don't get dessert unless you clean your plate."

Sully laughed and said "yes dear." He turned back to his pistols and carried them into the vault. He hung them in their appropriate places, and went through the rest of the gear and put it away. He took a purple felt ring box and put it on a shelf over his work bench and hid it behind a can of WD-40.

Sully washed up in the sink in the garage, then went in the house and emptied the bag he had brought in there directly into the washing machine. When the machine was running he went to find Zoe.

Sully found her reading a magazine on the back deck. He sat in the chair next to her, and when she put down the magazine, Sully asked "when is the last time I told you that I love you?"

Zoe put a quizzical look on her face the answered "you know I honestly can't remember" then she smiled.

Sully said "okay, I was just checking."

Zoe punched him playfully in the shoulder and stuck out her tongue at him. They shared a laugh, and then a kiss.

They had a wonderful dinner together, and after they cleaned up together they again went out onto the back deck to enjoy the cool night air.

Zoe had taken a bottle of red wine and emptied it into the sink and filled it with cranberry juice. She didn't want Sully to ask her why she wasn't having wine with her meal, which was her norm.

Sully had his usual scotch rocks and a cigar, and Zoe sat with him. He told her that he had made reservations for a nice place for dinner tomorrow, but refused to tell her where.

They both agreed that they were tired, and turned in early. They made slow passionate love for a short while, then fell asleep in each-other's arms. Zoe hoped that he had not sensed how troubled she was.

Sully could feel that Zoe was troubled, but that wasn't uncommon after she got back from a sanction. Usually it just took some time. If Sully had only known how little time they had, he would have done something different.

Sully woke up early the next morning, and Zoe was not next to him in the bed. He yawned scratched himself and brushed his teeth. He walked out in only his underwear and got a cup of coffee. Zoe was at the table reading a newspaper and he sat down with her.

She smiled at him and said "good morning sleepyhead. I was wondering if you were gonna sleep all day."

Sully yawned again and replied "I feel like I haven't slept in a week. I don't sleep as well in the field as I used to."

Zoe teased him saying "I had the same problem in Barbados, the bed in my Cabaña was way too soft, and the Cabaña boy talked in his sleep."

Sully glared at her and picked up a section of the paper without responding.

Zoe walked around the table and stood behind him. She put her arms his neck, and rested her chin on top of his head. She was rubbing his chest hair and said "you know you are the only man in my life."

Sully pretended that he didn't care and shrugged his shoulders as he turned a page of the paper he wasn't really reading.

Zoe continued "besides I don't think the Cabaña boy was even eighteen so he doesn't count."

Sully took a drink of his coffee and turned the page. He said "wow, cantaloupe is on sale for nineteen cents a pound."

Zoe took her hands off of him, stood and playfully pulled his hair. She rounded the table and quietly sat back down across from him.

Sully lowered the paper and showed her his smile. He winked at her then raised the paper again and said "as long as you had a good time Honey. Holy cow, russet potatoes, five pounds for a dollar ninety nine." They both laughed.

They talked all morning about things to do or places to go. No decision had been made until Sully's phone rang. They had given up on the private phones long ago, and decided to be careful when using their SSO phones. They even had a few simple code words to make the intelligence division work a little harder. Sully answered it and spoke just out of Zoe's earshot for a few seconds, then hung up.

The look on his face was pure fury, then he closed his eyes and rubbed the bridge of his nose between his thumb and forefinger. Sully took several deep breaths, and opened his mouth to speak, but no words came out. After several more breaths he breezed buy her and grabbed his keys and headed out the back door without saying a word.

Zoe turned and watched him open the garage door, and then heard loud heavy metal music. She knew that he was working out, probably taking out whatever frustration the phone call had caused him on the heavy bag. He had set up a small gym in the garage not long after it was completed. Nothing fancy, just a few different weight benches with literally tons of free weights, a tread mill, and his heavy bag.

Sully had told her that whenever he was alone at the house he took out his stress in the gym. Zoe gave him fifteen minutes to work off some of the aggression. While she waited she called Weathers, making sure to keep a close eye on the garage door.

Weathers picked up faster than usual and said in an irritated tone "what do you need now Zoe?"

Zoe answered "Sully didn't say anything to me before he went to our gym. I'm assuming that your face is on his heavy bag right now, and I was wondering why?"

Weathers was very stern when he said "I've done what you asked me to, and I told him that both of you are required at my office for a pre mission briefing at fifteen thirty." Then he added "I didn't realize that I had to clear my plans through you. Do you have more demands?"

Zoe was shaking, she had asked for this but now it seemed too soon. She meekly replied "see you at fifteen thirty." She hung up and tried to compose herself. Ten minutes later she felt calm enough to go talk to Sully.

She walked into the garage and turned the music way down. Sully was bathed in sweat and didn't even notice that the music had been turned down. He was practicing his martial arts training at a furious pace. Punch after punch landed on the bag as he circled it. He was performing side kicks, jump kicks, and spinning back kicks as if he were fighting a team of ninjas.

Zoe walked carefully into his field of vision and said firmly "Sullivan, stop for a minute."

Sully heard her and blinked twice. He doubled over shaking and gasping for air. He stayed that way for a full minute before his breathing slowed and he had gotten a hold of himself. He straightened up and walked over a bath towel that was hanging on a nail near the door. He angrily snatched the towel off of the nail and roughly wiped off his face and chest. Sully said "sorry, just had to get rid of some aggression."

Zoe replied "I called Weathers when you came out here, and I understand why you're upset. We just got home and we are going out again so soon." She was trying to calm him down with the tone in her voice as she continued by saying "at least we are going together, we haven't done that since our very first mission."

Sully was still very angry when he said "that doesn't make up for a god damned twenty hour turn around. I've barely sat down. You've only been here two days. This shit is getting old. I have half a mind to go rouge on the SSO and take my fucking chances." He had been pacing like a caged lion as he spoke, and the more he let his feelings out, the more enraged he became.

Zoe said "if and when you calm down, I'd like you to talk to me reasonably." She left the garage and went inside the house. Now Zoe was mad at herself for doing this to him. She tried not to think about what he would do when the SSO faked her death. She took a bottle of Gatorade out of the refrigerator and took it to Sully.

Sully was standing on the grass beside the garage rinsing himself off with the garden hose. Zoe stayed on the deck watching him intently. She was trying to commit everything about him to memory, especially scenes like this.

Sully saw her and walked toward the deck. Zoe tossed him the bottle. He stopped and drank almost all of it in one long drink. He walked to the side of the desk beneath Zoe, and said "sorry for the tantrum, I just had to get rid of that rage before I exploded."

Zoe replied "don't you think I am every bit as angry as you? In the last two and a half years I don't think we have gotten more than four days in a row together." Then she lied and said "if there was any way to get out of this, I would. I hope that you would too."

Sully answered her, looking at the ground, saying "let's not do this again. We've explored every option a hundred times, and there is only one way out, and I'm not ready to die yet."

Zoe walked down the stairs and out to him. She hugged him tightly from behind and said "just please remember that I will always love you, no matter what."

Sully was exhausted when he replied "let's just do this thing and move on." He was still mad, and he pulled away from her. Sully walked up the stairs, and to the house. As he opened the screen door he said with no emotion "I need a shower."

When Zoe followed him in she didn't hear the shower and was confused. Then she heard the clothes dryer start, and saw him walk out of the laundry room, naked. Sully didn't even look at her and went into the hall bathroom to shower.

One of the first things they had done to the old house was to have a new shower built in the master bathroom. It was a walk in shower with glass doors. It gave them much more room to make love in the shower than the original. The fact that Sully showered in the hall bath told Zoe that he wanted to be left alone. She had way to little time to let him shut her out, so she went into the small bathroom and asked if she could join him.

Sully turned the water off and grabbed a towel off of a hook outside the tub. He said "I'm done" and toweled himself behind the shower curtain until he heard her leave.

When he went to the bedroom to dress he didn't see her. He quickly dressed in jeans, a black tee shirt, and of course his boots. When he walked out of the bedroom, Sully saw her at the table, and walked to the garage without saying a word.

Zoe saw him walk out five minutes later with a large gear bag and two rifle cases. He went to his truck and put everything in the back seat of the truck. He got in to the driver's seat, slamming the door, and yelled at the house "I need some range time, see you at the briefing."

Zoe went to their bed and laid down. She cried harder than she ever had. She knew that leaving him would hurt him immensely, but now she was afraid that it would destroy him.

Zoe arrived at the pre-mission briefing ten minutes early in hopes of talking to Weathers before Sully showed up, but she was told to sit and wait.

Sully showed up ten minutes late, and sat next to her while they waited. They waited only ten minutes, but for Sully it was ten minutes too long. When they were told to go in Sully ignored the other two people in the room, both dressed in class A dress military uniforms, and said "thank you very much for the audience your eminence."

Weathers just shook his head and said "allow me to introduce agent's Mills and Millstad. Let's move into the conference room." He opened the door behind his desk that led to a large ornate conference room that neither Sully or Zoe knew was there.

Waiting in the room were both Fred Spyes, SSO Director of Operations, and Robert McMillan, the Secretary of Defense. They all walked in and took a seat around the large oak table.

McMillan started the meeting saying "I will make this short. The mission you about to embark on is of the utmost importance to national security, so much so that it is a total black operation. If any of you is compromised we will disavow your existence."

With that said, McMillan left the room. Weathers took over and started in on the particulars of the mission. He started with "do not take the SOD's commentary lightly."

Weathers went around the room and made introductions. The Army Officers that Sully and Zoe didn't know were both Majors, and both Army Rangers. The male was introduced as Scott Barnes, and the female as Jenna Carter.

Weathers continued the briefing by telling the group that the mission was to expose a United States Defense contractor that was selling weapons to Iran. Sully and Carter were to be back up, while Zoe and Barnes got the necessary evidence. The production facility was in Jonesport Maine, and they left in three days.

Weathers told them that until then they would have daily briefings, and in the mean while they were to learn everything they could about each other's capabilities. He sent Sully and Carter to ordinance to choose their weaponry, and Zoe and Barnes were to stay for a logistics briefing.

Spyes left with Sully and Carter, having not uttered a word for the entire briefing. When they left Weathers said "Zoe, this is actually Jamie Darko, he is an operative with the NSA. He knows your situation and is here to facilitate it."

Weathers continued by saying "Zoe has been working with Janet Port in our Operations department, and other than Spyes, is the only one besides us that knows the true nature of this mission. She will be here in ten minutes. I suggest you get to know and trust her quickly."

With that being said Weathers left them and returned to his office. Zoe and Darko were left alone to 'get to know one another'.

Darko broke the ice by saying "I was given your file a few days ago, and I have to say I'm impressed."

Zoe sneered at him and said "don't be, I have nothing to be proud of." She continued "do yourself a favor and, after this, don't ever get involved with the SSO."

Darko replied "I'll take it under advisement. Right now I need to know how you see this going down."

Zoe said "I guess we will have to wait until Janet gives us the layout of the installation, unless you already have it, do you?"

Darko answered "right now I know as much as you do, which aint a whole bunch."

Zoe was in much less than a good mood when she said "then shut up until Janet gets here, and know this right now Major, I am the lead on this. Your job is to follow along and back me up, get me?"

Janet walked in before Darko could answer. They introduced themselves, and got to work. Janet had brought aerial photos of the area, satellite thermographs, and a blueprint of the installation.

They spent three hours coming up with a tentative plan, agreed to meet at thirteen hundred the next day, and then they called it a night. Darko followed her out and asked "should we have dinner together or something like that?"

Zoe just glared at him as if to say 'get the fuck away from me right now'.

Darko left her without saying a word. Zoe thought about calling Sully, but decided to go to his house to see him instead. She was trying very hard not to refer to it as home anymore, because that only made it harder.

When she got there the house was dark, and Sully was asleep on the sofa. She did her best not to wake him as she got ready for bed.

Zoe undressed and brushed her teeth in the dark, and then quietly slipped under the covers. Sleep eluded her. Hanging on by a thread would have been and understatement for her mental state right now, and she could not help but let her thoughts run wildly.

At four hundred hours she gave up on sleep and went into the spare bathroom and filled the tub. Zoe rarely took baths, but she thought that soaking in the tub might relax her. She lay in the tub and tried desperately to let her mind go blank. The bath worked marginally, and she stayed there until the water got cool.

She went to check on Sully, and he wasn't on the couch. Zoe hurried back to the bedroom to snuggle with him, but he wasn't there either. She quickly looked through the rest of the small house and he wasn't anywhere to be found. She looked out of the kitchen window and saw a light on in the garage.

Zoe knew something must be troubling him as well because he hadn't come to bed and was in the garage at five hundred hours. She debated on whether to go to him, and normally she would not have, but she had so little time left with him that she had to. Zoe started a pot of coffee and went to the bedroom to dress. She put on a Victoria's Secret bustier that was a couple sizes too small, a black silk matching robe, and four inch black Anne Klein open toe heels.

Zoe walked into the garage with a large mug of coffee. Sully was working on preparing weapons, wearing only a pair of black sweat pants.

Sully smelled the coffee when it was brewing in the house, and as the smell got stronger he knew she was approaching. When she stepped her first step into the garage Sully said coldly "thanks, but I don't want any coffee." He had said it without looking up from the weapon he was cleaning.

When Sully heard Zoe continue to advance he tried to stop her by saying "look, if I am supposed to be your weapons boy on this assignment I have to be prepared for anything. Right now I have no idea what the mission even is, so I've got some mindless valet work to do." He said the last part with venom.

Zoe asked "why the hell are you mad at me Sully, It's not like I requested this mission. I didn't give you your orders." She had lied on purpose to throw him off of the trail to the truth.

Sully replied "I'm just pretty pissed in general. How the fuck am I supposed to plan ordinance for an unknown mission, and why the hell have I been demoted to valet?" He still hadn't even turned to look at her when he finished by saying in a meek, thickly sarcastic tone "you just tell me what you need boss, and I'll do my best."

Zoe threw the coffee mug at the wall next to him before she stormed out. Sully put both hands on the workbench, closed his eyes and thought *'why are you being such an asshole to her, Zoe's not the one messing with you'*.

He knew he should have gone to her to apologize, but he was not in the mood. He threw the weapons in the vault haphazardly, and locked the door. He had three pistols in a gear bag that he took with him to his truck. Sully started the engine and headed toward town. On the way he called Rady and said "be in front of your building in ten minutes." He hung up without waiting for a reply.

Rady was there when Sully arrived nine minutes later, and jumped into the truck. Sully had been paying Ron on the side to collect special gear for him that he didn't want the SSO to know about.

They drove to an old house about twenty miles from campus. Sully had bought the house and installed a vault right in the living room, other than a table outside the vault, the house was empty.

They hadn't said a word in the truck, and waited until they swept the house before they spoke. Rady laughed and said "this better be important, I was dreaming of twins."

Normally Sully would have laughed with him, but he was in no mood. He placed the gear bag on the table and took out the three pistols. Sully said "I need tracking devices in these, and a discreet way to view them."

Rady replied "that's why you pay me the big bucks chief." Ron opened the vault and brought out an old pistol box. He opened it and started working on the guns. His phone rang and he went outside before he answered it.

Sully looked at the caller I.D. and knew it was Zoe. He answered by softly saying "hi Honey." He had decided that he had been enough of a prick, and when he got back he vowed to try to make it up to her.

Zoe recognized the change in his tone, and asked "where are you Sully?"

He answered "I'm with Rady, I have a list of special ordinance for him, and I wanted to make sure that he could get it before our deployment. I'll be home soon."

Zoe asked "do you want breakfast? I've got food here I could make."

Sully answered "no thanks, I will see you soon."

He went back in to Rady, who was reassembling the last weapon. Rady said "come check this out Sully, I installed a ULF transmitter in the right pistol grip of each. You don't even know it's there unless you know exactly what to look for." He had disassembled the last weapon to show him while he spoke.

Sully was all business when he asked "what is the transmit range, and how do I track them?"

Rady was always excited about his new "toys" and he animatedly answered "this is the really cool part." He gave sully a large watch with an LCD display, then he continued "put it on and push the top right button."

Sully did and he saw three dots appear on the watches screen. One was red, one was yellow, and one was green. Rady picked up one of the pistols and walked across the room. Sully saw the red dot move with him. He nodded his approval of the system and asked "how do I tell range to target?"

Rady answered "It has a one thousand yard range, and the dots get smaller when the target gets farther away. The best part is that they are undetectable if the watch isn't in search mode."

Sully said "perfect Ron" he looked at the three weapons, picked up Zoe's nine millimeter Berretta and said "mark them all, and make this one red." He walked into the vault and grabbed two more gear bags. Sully filled one of them with more "toys" for the mission."

Sully thanked Rady, and then drove him back to his apartment. When he was on his way back home he called the SSO and requested a meeting with Weathers at eleven hundred. He told them not to call and confirm, just that he would be there.

He got back to the house and took all his bags to the garage. He opened the vault and put the weapons he had thrown in earlier carefully away. He put the gear bags safely on a shelf in the vault. When he left to go to the house he stopped abruptly, and his jaw dropped. Zoe was leaning against the wall by the door with her robe opened. She asked "see anything you might want?"

Zoe shrieked when Sully looked her up and down, and then chased her into the house. He was afraid he might have hurt her when he tackled her onto the bed. They kissed passionately for a minute, and then Sully stopped and looked her in the eyes and said "I'm sorry for being such a jerk to you, I love you, and you don't deserve it."

Zoe nibbled on his ear and whispered "make it up to me right now baby."

Sully was kissing the top of her breasts that were threatening to bust out of their containment when he felt something cold on his back. He arched his back away from the coldness, and started to speak, until Zoe showed him the can of aerosol whipped cream she had been holding against him.

By the time the can was empty they were both very sticky and very satisfied. They continued their playful lovemaking in the shower until the hot water ran out. Zoe said "we need a larger water heater." They both laughed as they dried one another off.

Sully carried her to the spare bedroom and said "if we are gonna wash one set of sheets we might as well do both." He carried her to the guest bedroom, dropped her onto the bed and they made love again.

Sully woke up with Zoe in his arms and kissed her on the neck. They didn't realize that they had napped until nine hundred forty five hours. When he tried to sneak his numb left arm out from under her she grabbed it and sleepily said "no leaving allowed, I'm way too comfy."

Sully kissed her neck again, and softly said "you're gonna be comfy and wet if you don't let me up to pee."

Zoe relented and rolled away. She whined "please come right back, I need more snuggle time."

Sully went to the master bath and urinated, then brushed his teeth. On his way back to Zoe he noticed the time on the microwave clock. It was nine hundred fifty five. He decided to allow himself twenty more minutes of 'snuggle time' with Zoe before he had to get ready to deal with Weathers.

Zoe was asleep when he crawled back into the small bed, but she woke up and pulled his arms around her and snuggled her bottom into him. They laid like that for fifteen minutes before he whispered "I have to get ready, I have a meeting with Weathers in an hour."

The statement snapped Zoe out of her contented sleep. She didn't move, but was worried when she said "why are you meeting with Weathers?"

Sully whispered in her ear "just snuggle with me for ten more minutes, and we will talk after that Honey."

Zoe pretended to enjoy the snuggling, but her mind was off to the races again.

Sully was dressed and ready to go at ten hundred fifteen. They sat on the deck enjoying coffee together when Zoe asked again "why are you meeting with Weathers two hours before our team meeting?"

Sully lied to her when he answered "I just want to ask him about some new gadgets that we might be able to use on this mission, and I'd better get going."

Zoe came to him when he stood and gave him a kiss. He seductively said "I'm going to make sure this is a quick meeting so we can be together again here soon."

Sully arrived at Weathers' office five minutes late, on purpose. When he walked in Stephanie said "he's been waiting for you, go right in."

Sully winked at her to tease her as he walked into the office. Weathers was chomping on a cigar and said "unless I forgot, I'm the one who calls the meetings around here, not you."

Sully was not in the mood to take any shit off of Weathers today when he replied "really sir, the last time I checked I was a full field agent, not a fucking ordinance valet." He continued before Weathers could reply, saying "if you want to demote me at least have the balls to tell me why, but don't play these stupid God damned games with me!" His voice had gotten louder as he spoke to the point that he was almost yelling at the end.

Weathers seemed confused when he said "your main mission briefing is in two hours. What would make you think you're not being included?"

Sully shook his head and answered with palatable sarcasm, saying "geez Boss, now that you put it that way, I feel foolish. I guess I should have expected to be the ordinance valet for a mission I have no fucking idea about."

Weathers said "Mills either lose the attitude or get out. Barnes is a real pain in my ass, and McMillan is behind him. He made the decision to start the initial planning without you and Carter, not me. My advice to you is to make damned sure that this mission goes as planned."

Sully wasn't ready to take Weathers word just yet. He asked "why couldn't you have told me this earlier?"

Weathers answered "Sully, I am out of the loop on this one, so watch your ass. You're the best agent we've got, even though you are an incredible pain in my ass."

Sully said "thanks Boss, I'll take that as the best compliment you've ever given me." He left not buying a word that Weathers was selling. He was going to go along with this mission and then get to the bottom of it.

Sully had some time to kill before the meeting, so he drove over to see Chuck. It had been over a month since he had seen Chuck, and he was curious to see how he was doing.

Sully still felt guilty about Chuck being dragged into the SSO, if he hadn't come to Bolivia with Zoe to save his ass, he would still be a free man. He owed Chuck more than he could ever repay, but Sully swore to do his best to keep him as safe as he could.

When Sully walked into the hangar he was shocked to see Terry sitting at the outer desk. When Terry saw him coming he jumped out of his chair, and snapped to attention. Sully walked over to him and smiled. He offered him his hand and said "take it easy Terry. When did you complete training?"

Terry vigorously shook his hand and answered in a way too military fashion "two weeks ago agent Mills, sir."

Sully heard Chucks laughter before he saw him walk around the back of the plane and over to them. He slapped Sully on the back and said "can you believe this is the same punk kid I was ready to fire two years ago?"

Sully answered "he can't be if he survived the SSO training program. That took a lot of heart and determination Terry, I'm proud of you."

Terry beamed like a child getting the best gift ever on Christmas morning. He said "thank you very much Sir."

Sully said "I don't care what your plans are, we are having dinner at my place tonight. Zoe's gonna shit when she sees you Terry."

Chuck smiled broadly and said "I'll bring the steaks, and Terry will bring the drinks." Then he asked "would it be alright if I brought Marie?"

Zoe had told Sully about Marie. She was a high level agent from the Operations department, and Zoe said she was very nice. Chuck had been dating her for about six months, and they were getting serious according to Zoe. Sully said "of course. Terry, feel free to bring a date too if you want."

Chuck laughed and said "not much chance of that, ole Terry got dumped last week." Terry blushed when Chuck told Sully the details of the loud, public break up.

Sully told Terry "don't sweat it kid, you're not an old broken down pilot, you are an agent of the SSO. You will find out soon that it's like being a chick magnet. Hell, look at how far over my head I scored."

They all laughed, and then Sully said "my place at six, we'll catch up then. I got a mission briefing to get to right now, see you guys later."

Sully left them, and his mood was a lot better than it had been. Dinner would be a nice way to take his mind off of everything for a night. He thought that it might be a good opportunity to give Zoe that little purple box.

The meeting went well. Zoe took charge, and welcomed everyone's input. Two hours later they all had working dossier's, and agreed to meet at ten hundred hours the next day, involving Janet Port from Operations.

When they walked out Sully looked at Zoe confused, and he asked "where is your truck?"

Zoe winked at him and said "I called in for a ride, so I could ride home with the man I love, if you don't mind agent Mills."

Sully smiled and replied "fine with me, but you better hurry if you're gonna catch Barnes, he is almost to his car."

Zoe gave him an icy look and said "you have no idea how lucky you are that we are on campus right now."

Sully reached into his pocket and handed her the keys to his truck, then he said "I'll stay here for a while. Call me when it's safe to come home."

Zoe smiled at him and said "get your sweet little ass in the truck, I will wait until later to punish you."

Zoe kept the keys and drove toward home when Sully told her about Terry being done with training, and the dinner party he had set up for tonight.

Zoe was truly excited and said "oh my God, that sounds wonderful!" Zoe was hoping to see Chuck before her final mission, and this would work out perfectly.

After telling her the menu they decided to stop at the grocery store for a few things. They walked through the store with happy smiles on their faces for the first time in a couple days. They bought asparagus, Hollandaise sauce, two cans of aerosol whipped cream, a chocolate cake, an apple pie, and six twice baked potatoes from the deli counter.

When they got home and unloaded the truck it was almost time to start cooking and getting things ready. Sully took care of putting the groceries away, and Zoe got their clothes ready. She came back to the kitchen having changed out of her meeting clothes. She was now wearing a tight tank top, without a brassier, and hot pink satin short shorts.

Sully heard her coming, and when he turned and saw her, he dropped the asparagus onto the floor. He stammered when he simply said "wow!" He hadn't even looked at the vegetables that had slipped from his grip.

Zoe walked over and picked up the asparagus. As she washed it in the sink Sully grabbed her from behind and kissed her on the back of the neck. Zoe said "stop right there buddy. This is the first part of you punishment for the Barnes comment. There will be much more after dinner. For now, no touching, and the snake stays in its cage."

Sully groaned and asked "wouldn't you rather just beat me up, please?"

Zoe let go with an evil laugh, and then answered "not today Mills, I plan on making this a punishment that you won't soon forget."

Sully said "I've always thought so, but now there is no doubt. You are truly evil and sadistic."

They both laughed, and then Zoe said "you have no idea. Now get your hands off me and go get the deck table and grill ready." She turned and whistled at him as he left. When he turned to look at her she licked her lips seductively and wiped her wet hands on her breasts.

Sully shook his head, and said "now you're being just plain sadistic." He stood and stared until Zoe turned back to the sink, then he stared some more. It was that very moment that he forgot his views about marriage, and decided that tonight would be the perfect opportunity to ask Zoe to marry him.

The guests arrived on time and they all had a great time catching up with one another. When Zoe ran to Terry to hug him he flinched and put his hands up to guard himself. They all laughed heartily, especially when Terry said "I wasn't sure if you were gonna hit me?"

As they all pitched in to get dinner ready Sully said "I'll go start the grill. Terry, why don't you come with me and see my garage. After the grill was lit, Sully took Terry to the garage.

Sully took out his wallet and handed him three hundred dollar bills, and the keys to his truck. He quickly said "listen to me closely. My truck is parked on the road. I need you to run to Safeway as fast as you can and buy three dozen red rose bouquets in vases, and three bottles of their best champagne." Then he added "when you leave the house and return, leave the truck's lights off."

Terry replied "yes Sir."

He didn't even ask why, and was out the door in a flash. Sully lit a cigar, and he tried to stop himself from shaking. He grabbed the ring from its hidden location, and looked at it one more time. It was a simple three carat diamond solitaire that he hoped would be enough. He put the box in his pocket and went back to the house.

Sully waked in and announced "the grill is ready whenever you are Zoe." He walked to the fridge and grabbed a beer.

Chuck said "just give me five minutes to finish seasoning, and marinating them. I'll grill them if you guys don't mind."

Zoe said "I wish you would, Sully usually ends up with one side black, and the other raw."

Sully laughed and said "it happened one time, and she won't stop bringing it up every time I light the grill. I told her it was Cajun style, but she didn't buy it."

They all laughed and Marie said "I'll get my pookie to teach you Sully, he is a wonderful cook on the grill." She walked over to Chuck and gave him a big kiss.

Sully frowned and said "if you two don't stop that I'm not going to be able to eat."

Zoe chimed in saying "I think it's wonderful, at least they are romantic, unlike another male in this room."

Sully replied "are you saying I'm not romantic?" He smiled knowing she was soon to eat those words. Then he said "come on grill master

Chuck, teach how to grill like a pro." Sully grabbed a couple of beers for them and they went out to the grill.

When the steaks were on, and the lid was closed, Terry came running up and nodded at Sully. Sully whispered "bring it all to the front door and then ring the bell three times." He turned the grill off and said "Chuck please go help him." Chuck shrugged and left with Terry.

Sully finished what was left of his beer, and then finished Chuck's. In the battle between his fight or flight responses, flight was screaming at him, but he was in too deep to turn back. He ran to the front door and Chuck was just about to ring the bell when he saw him and stopped.

Sully grabbed a vase and a bouquet and got in the back of the line. He took two deep breaths, nodded at Chuck, and said "let's do it." Chuck rang the bell three times, and when Marie answered they marched in single file and each set their flowers and champagne on the table.

Zoe walked over with a quizzical look on her face and asked Sully "what's this all about?"

Sully answered "I'm glad you asked. This is all about you Zoe. I thought this party needed a theme, and the theme is three. You have given me the best three years of my life, so I'm giving back to you in threes. Three dozen roses that pale in comparison to your beauty, three bottles of champagne that would not intoxicate me even closely to the way I feel when we are together, and three friends to share a moment with.

Sully moved close to her, took her hands, and said "last but not least, three questions for you. First, would you let me love you for the rest of my life? Second would you promise to tell me if I am ever being a jerk?" He pulled the ring box from his pocket, opened it, and knelt on one knee and said "and finally, would you make me the happiest man in the world by doing me the honor of marrying me?"

Zoe thrust herself into his arms and kissed him deeply. She moved back, wiped her eyes, and then she said "yes, without a doubt, I was beginning to think you might never ask me."

There was a cheer and applause from the group. Sully scooped Zoe up in his arms and turned to them, and said "allow me to introduce my fiancé. Zoe Millstad, soon to be Zoe Mills." They all clapped and cheered louder. Sully set her gently onto her feet and they shared a long deep kiss.

Chuck came over and grabbed a bottle of the champagne and opened it. He slapped Sully on the back and took the bottle to Marie. Marie had found the champagne flutes, and filled five.

Chuck passed them out and made a toast to them, saying "to Zoe and Sully, may they spend every day full of love." They all clinked there glasses together and had a drink.

Sully set his down and got a beer out of the fridge. He opened it and took a long drink, and then he said "now that's more like it." He walked out to the deck and lit the grill again.

Chuck came out, as Sully was shakily lighting a cigar, and said "that was about as smooth as that Napoleon brandy you gave me. I've never seen it done better than that Sully."

Sully replied "I'm just glad I got through it without passing out, and that she said yes."

Chuck laughed and said "with those moves there was never a doubt my man." He pushed Sully aside and asked "what do you think about Marie?"

Sully answered "I think she's great Chuck, and I suggest you don't wait as long as I did to pull the trigger. Last time I checked you weren't getting any younger."

Chuck smiled and said "fuck you punk. I was baggin' babes when you weren't even a tickle in your daddy's pants."

Sully laughed and walked into the house. As soon as he walked in Marie grabbed him, gave him a big hug, and said "that was the most beautiful thing I have ever seen."

Sully smiled and kissed her on the cheek. He said "thank you Marie, I'm glad you were here for it."

Marie kissed him on the mouth and said "I gotta get you to hang out with Chuck more to teach him some of those moves."

Zoe was suddenly there with her hands on her hips and said "we have been engaged for less than ten minutes, and I catch you kissing another woman!" She laughed and then kissed him herself. She said "I love you Sullivan, thank you for such a special moment."

He held her close and whispered "I never thought I would ever find someone that is perfect, and I don't ever want to lose you."

Zoe started to cry again, and broke their embrace. She walked quickly into the bedroom to hide her tears.

Sully shook his head, and said to Marie "now what did I do, I thought this would make her happy?"

Marie rubbed his arm, and replied "you're fine sweetie, she is just overwhelmed right now. I'm gonna go check on my meat man." She walked out onto the deck.

Terry was scribbling furiously on a legal pad at the kitchen table. Sully walked over to him and asked "what are you up to kid?"

Terry answered "trying to write down everything you did and said in case I ever get the opportunity to use it."

Sully laughed and advised Terry by saying "keep on the track you are on, and you'll get your chance. When you do, don't copy me or anyone else. Just do what your heart tells you to buddy. When you finish that give it to Chuck, but make sure Marie is with him."

Terry laughed and said "that will get him good. I'll do it right now."

Sully chuckled as Terry hurried out to the deck. He went to see what was wrong with Zoe. She was fixing her make-up that had run with her crying. She saw him in the mirror and smiled at him. She said "I'm fine Sully, it just hit me all at once. You are the most wonderful man in the world, when you want to be."

Sully replied "I'll try to be more often for my bride to be. You know you can change your mind once you've had time to think about it, and realize who you agreed to spend the rest of your life with."

Zoe turned and hugged him tightly. She said "not on your life buddy, you're stuck with me now Mills."

He kissed her sweetly and said "I've never been happier than I am when we're together."

She kissed him deeply and said "this is the happiest day of my life. Thank you sweetheart, let's go join the party."

They walked out onto the deck hand in hand and Chuck said "thanks a lot buddy, because of you I've gotta go ring shopping tomorrow."

Marie giggled and said "we are officially engaged! He wasn't nearly as suave as you, but he proposed five minutes ago and I said yes! Zoe let me have a good look at your ring again, I was promised a bigger rock than you got."

Zoe and Marie ran back into the house to talk, and Sully just shook his head at Chuck. Then he said "trying to steal my thunder old man. Where is Terry now?"

Chuck laughed and answered "errand boy is off to the store again, for me this time. I turned off the grill again, I'm afraid our steaks are gonna be like shoe leather by the time we eat."

Sully said "don't worry about me, I don't think I could keep anything down right now anyhow. I'm gonna get a beer, do you want one?"

Chuck answered "no thanks, but I'll take a brandy if you got any."

Sully nodded his head and said "coming right up." He turned and walked into the house the ladies were sitting at the table and Marie opened her mouth to speak, but before she could utter a word Sully said "three point two carats, white, flawless, and set in Platinum."

He took a beer for himself, and poured Chuck's brandy.

Marie smiled at him and asked "how did you know what I was going to ask?"

Sully laughed and said "that was easy. What the hell else would you two hens be cackling about, but I won't tell you where or how much, so don't bother asking."

They both laughed and Sully walked over and gave Zoe a kiss. He walked back and picked up the drinks as he walked out he said "Chuck and I are going to be consoling each other out back if you ladies would like to join us."

He walked back to Chuck and handed him his brandy. He heard the ladies voices growing louder and said "heads up buddy, we've got incoming."

Chuck was laughing as the girls walked out, and Marie asked "what's so funny pookie?"

Chuck answered "nothing dear, just guy talk. I'm sure you wouldn't be interested."

They all engaged in idle chit chat for another ten minutes until Terry returned carrying a bag, and a dozen lilies. He handed both to Chuck.

Chuck handed the flowers to Marie, she said thank you and put them on the deck table. Then Chuck reached into the large bag and pulled out a smaller one. He handed her the bag and got on a knee and said "Marie will you marry me?"

Marie said an emphatic yes, then reached into the bag and pulled out a candy 'ring pop' and put it on. They all laughed. She reached in the bag again, and took out a Charms blow pop. She said "I don't understand?"

Chuck smiled and answered "that's just a subtle hint for later on tonight."

Marie replied "tonight you just might get lucky pookie." They kissed, and everyone clapped and cheered. Chuck started the grill again and handed the bag to Marie.

She looked in the large bag and went to Chuck and kissed him.

The ladies went into the house to reheat dinner for the third time, and Terry followed them.

Sully asked Chuck "what was in the bag?"

Chuck answered "a pecan pie, her favorite." Then he said "I think Terry is hiding from us, so we don't send him out again"

Terry came out a couple minutes later with fresh drinks for them all. He said "man guys, this has been one hell of a night so far. I'm sure glad I didn't bring a date, or I'd be getting hitched too."

They all laughed and Sully lit another cigar. Then he said "do you want to see the garage for real this time?"

Terry said "hell yeah, what I saw for thirty seconds looked really cool."

They left Chuck at the grill and walked over to the garage. Terry was wandering through the gym area commenting on everything. Sully opened the vault, and Terry could barely speak because he was so enthralled with Sully's arsenal. Sully was having so much fun watching the kid's reaction that he hadn't seen Zoe come in.

Zoe said "hey baby, we are about three minutes from chow time. Why don't you boys come in and wash up."

Terry almost ran to the house, and Zoe said "I guess he's hungry." She grabbed him and kissed him. She nibbled his left ear lobe, then whispered "let's get these people out of here quickly, I need to thank you properly." She squeezed his butt with both hands and walked away swinging her hips wildly.

Sully hoped that every day could be one tenth as good as today. He walked into the house smiling from ear to ear.

As overcooked as dinner was, it remained tasty. Terry ate like a horse, as everyone else just nibbled. The conversation was lively and fun with everyone talking about wedding likes and dislikes. Terry was too busy eating to add much, but he had a good time with them nonetheless.

When the plates were cleared and the deserts brought out Sully ducked out for a beer, and a cigar. Zoe came out ten minutes later and wrapped her arms around his waist. She said "they are cleaning up, and I told them to take all the leftovers that they wanted, and I think Terry is going to take everything but the pecan pie, Marie had dibs on that."

Sully laughed and said "I am going to request him on my next solo to fully evaluate his capability. If I think he's good enough I can sponsor him through full agent training, if that's what he wants.

Zoe said "I can't believe the turn-around in him already, but make sure not to push him toward full field agent unless you're sure he understands fully, and is ready.

Sully replied "yes dear, boy engaged for three and a half hours and you're already bossing me around."

Zoe kissed him several times, and then she said "you better start getting used to it buddy. You're all mine now."

Sully looked at her seriously and replied "there is no place on Earth that I'd rather be."

Zoe grabbed his hand and dragged him into the house saying "come on and help me get rid of our guests so we can be alone."

It was almost twenty three hundred hours when they finished chatting and they left. Terry had taken a weeks' worth of food with him. Chuck and Marie took only their pie, a bottle of champagne, and the lilies. They promised to get together soon.

When they were gone and the lights were all turned off Zoe held him tightly and said "I honestly cannot think of words to express my thanks to you for what a wonderful day you have given me."

Sully replied "you only needed to say one word to make me happy, and thankfully you did."

Zoe smiled and said "I would have said yes to you three years ago if you would have asked. I've loved you from the moment we met Sullivan. It just took you this long to get over your fear of marriage."

Sully replied "you're right, I should have done this a long time ago."

They shared their most loving kiss and embrace ever. They went to bed and explored each other over and over. It was a perfect end to a perfect day, and Sully did not want it to end. When they were too tired to make love anymore they snuggled and talked about the life they had shared together, and the lives they had in front of them.

The morning sun brought them back to reality all too quickly. Sully got up first and brushed his teeth in the shower to save time. He was dressed and in the garage putting gear bags together for all four of the team members. Each was tagged by name and color.

While Sully was busy in the garage Zoe called Janet Port and told her about the meeting, and that she needed at least four days from today before the mission. Janet said she could do what she could, but would not commit to the four days. Zoe had asked for four days, while hoping for two. She knew there was no way to ask Weathers for anything else, he had already granted her life when he didn't have to.

For whatever reason Zoe thought that if they were married before the mission, it would help Sully cope.

Sully caught himself whistling for the third time this morning. It was something he hadn't done since he was a child, but somehow it fit his mood today. When the gear was ready and in his truck he snuck into the house and grabbed a rose from one of the vases. He opened Zoe's truck with his key and set the rose gently on her seat.

He locked the garage and called Rady. When Ron answered he said "hey it's me, what does your schedule look like?"

Ron answered "I'm not scheduled for two weeks, but you know how that can change. Why, what do you need?"

Sully said "I've got a one day job in the next two or three days, and I need someone along that I can trust. I couldn't find anyone that I trust, so I called you."

Rady chuckled and said "two days is short, what do you need?"

Sully answered "I've already handled the ordinance, I just need reliable back up."

Ron said "sounds like easy money if you did all of the work. I'm in, you clear it if you can."

Sully said "I have a meeting in about an hour, I will call you when it's over." He disconnected the call without letting Rady respond.

He went into the house and checked on Zoe. It was just about time for them to go. She was finishing loading her briefcase when he walked in. She said "hey there soon to be hubby, are you ready?"

Sully smiled at her and answered "ready, willing, and able. I just got off the phone with Rady, and I would like to have him ride along on this for backup."

Zoe looked at him oddly and asked "do you really think that's necessary?"

Sully answered "I don't think it would hurt anything. I don't like the idea of us being outnumbered by the military."

Zoe said "I guess it wouldn't hurt. I'll run it by Janet on the way over."

Sully said "I have us set to drive separately in case Rady is a go. I'll run over and brief him quickly." He looked at her left hand and she had the engagement ring on. He asked her "do you really think the ring is a good idea?"

Zoe sighed before she answered "I know it's not, but I love you, and it so much I never want to take it off. I'll put it in my purse before the meeting, okay?"

Sully said "fine, but don't forget or we might not live to our wedding day."

Zoe huffed out of the house saying "you remember that jerk thing from last night, well you're being one right now."

He locked the house and headed for his truck. Zoe was standing in his way with the rose from her seat. She kissed him and told him he was forgiven.

They drove to the Operations center and were set up in a conference room by Janet. As Sully set out the gear from the bags, Zoe left with Janet. He really hated being in the dark on this, but he had to swallow it and move on.

Zoe followed Janet to her office. Janet sat down and handed her a legal pad. Janet said "take your time reading that before you respond."

It was a hand written note that said: *respond only in writing, I was able to get you three days from today, it was the best I could do.*

Zoe went into her purse and took out the ring. She wrote *Sully proposed to me last night, I would love to marry him before I "die". Can you help me?*

Janet opened the ring box and put her hands over her heart. She wrote: *The ring is beautiful, can you meet me at Safeway at fifteen hundred?*

Zoe put the ring back in her purse, then she wrote: *Without a doubt. I can't thank you enough for all of your help!*

Janet ripped off the page and put it the shredder beneath her desk. Then she said "let's get to that meeting."

The meeting was very short this time with no one having any significant changes to the plan. It was quite simple insertion by cutting through a fence near the loading dock, take out any resistance along the way to the main computer data storage room. Download everything possible, and go out the same way.

The plan was to go in an hour after shift change at one hundred fifteen. Intel had a maximum of twelve guards, all Blackwell Security employees. Blackwell hired only ex-military mercenaries. These assholes took all the military training that the government paid for, then quit and were for sale to the highest bidder. They were scum.

Barnes and Carter were in charge of the downloading equipment, Sully was ordinance / security, and Zoe was the mission leader / security. Zoe finished going over the main plan, then she requested Rady as copilot / back-up. Janet immediately approved him, and then turned the meeting over to Sully.

Sully went through the weapons, and gear in their bags. Each team member was given a silenced Beretta nine millimeter pistol in a shoulder holster that held six extra fifteen round clips, a MAC ten compact machine gun with four extra fifty round magazines, three flash pucks, two grenades, and a throat mike with VOX.

Sully needed only a little time to explain. He said "your bags are color coded, and that will be your call sign. Millstad is red, Barnes green, Carter yellow, Mills black, and Rady will be pink. I am sure everyone is familiar with all of the ordinance, except maybe the flash pucks. These are new and simple, they are basically a flash bang grenade without the bang. Slid into, or thrown against, a hard surface with more than twenty pounds of force they create a blinding flash, but minimal sound. Shooting the puck will also activate it. Does anyone have any questions?"

Zoe took over again and said "our flight leaves here at twenty hundred on Saturday from hangar six. During the operation we do not break radio silence, or silent weapons protocol unless absolutely necessary. Read your dossiers completely before takeoff, and I will address any questions in flight."

Janet wrapped it up by saying "dress code is black, with full masks. There is a contact number in your dossiers if any of you need clothing. Extra weapons must be disclosed and approved by Millstad in flight. Mills will take care of briefing and equipping Rady."

Janet ended the meeting by saying "get in, get the Intel, and get your asses back here safe. We are done here, dismissed.

Not a word was said as they all left to go on their separate ways.

Zoe followed Janet and slipped here a note that said: *Can you meet me in twenty minutes?*

Janet nodded her head slightly, and they went their separate ways. Janet and Zoe had become close friends quickly after they met under Zoe's desperate circumstances.

Sully called Rady and told him to be out front in five minutes. When he got in they went directly to the safe house and swept it. When they were confident it was clean Sully opened the vault and said "you're in, we leave Saturday night, and I'll have a full dossier sent to you by courier later today. I'm going to give you a list right now of special ordinance. What we can't get here I will bring to you tomorrow. There is no pilot named yet, so I am assuming the pilot is not SSO. All kinds of things aren't adding up on this deal, so read the hell out of that file to help me find what I'm missing."

Janet pulled up right next to Zoe they walked into the store and pretended to shop together. Zoe told her the whole story of how Sully proposed.

Janet said "oh my god, that is the most romantic thing I have ever heard. Show me the ring again." Zoe obliged her because she was more than happy to show it off.

Zoe asked "what do you think we can set up for tomorrow or Friday?"

Janet answered "I have an uncle that runs a thirty foot charter boat out of Virginia Beach. All he has to do is motor out over five miles and he can officially marry you. I can get all of the paperwork online, and all you need is one other witness besides me, and you can be married tomorrow. All I need to do is make sure the boat is available."

Zoe said "Janet will you be my maid of honor?"

Janet was almost as excited as Zoe when she answered "you bet your boots I will. What do you need me to do?"

Zoe went into her wallet and gave her a pre-paid Visa gold card. She said "there is around thirty thousand on that card and the pin is three six three six. Blow it all, get us a limo from the Virginia Beach airport for two days. Find us the best rooms in the best hotel, get us reservations for a great dinner, and get yourself the best dress you can find. If you still have money left please keep it for all of your help. If you need more just ask."

Janet was beaming and said "I'm taking the rest of the day off! This is gonna be so much fun."

Zoe said "be at my house at eight thirty tomorrow, and we will be off to the wedding."

Janet asked "how are we getting to Virginia Beach? Do you need me to call the airlines?"

Zoe answered her by saying "I think we can just take Sully's airplane."

Janet's smile faded, and she said "I think it's only fair to tell you that after you're gone I am going after Sully."

Zoe lied when she said "Janet that would be fine with me, I wouldn't want him to be lonely. Just don't ever tell me about it."

Janet hugged her and started to weep. Zoe hugged her back and asked "what's the matter Janet?"

Janet sniffled and wiped her eyes and said "I finally find a true best friend, and you'll be gone forever in a couple days."

Zoe said "so we live it up for a couple of days Sis, besides, you will always know where I am. Maybe we can get together for a couple weeks every so often. Please don't be sad right now, it's taking all of my strength to live the next couple of days to their fullest."

Janet smiled and said "I've gotta get going, planning a wedding in half of a day is gonna be a lot of work."

Zoe smiled at her and said "thanks for everything Janet. I really mean it, I wouldn't be able to pull this off without you."

Zoe drove home hardly able to contain her emotions. She couldn't wait to surprise Sully with the wedding plans, but their time together was drawing to a close more quickly with every passing second. She felt like a manic depressive. One minute she couldn't contain her happiness, and the next she was ready to cry.

Sully wasn't home yet when she pulled into the driveway. Zoe went inside and started packing for her wedding. She had the perfect dress. It was an ivory Dior floor length evening gown that she had never worn. She matched it with a pair of ivory Gucci three inch heels. She found her triple strand pearl necklace, and pearl earrings.

She packed two dress casual outfits, some lingerie, comfortable lounge clothes, and a cranberry red Chanel suit. Zoe heard the truck pull in, and she went out to meet the groom to be.

She walked up to the truck, and embraced him as soon as he exited the vehicle. Sully kissed her and asked "do I know you?"

Zoe kissed him again and answered "better than anyone on this planet." She took his hand and pulled him along with her into the house. When they were inside Zoe asked "do you have any plans for tomorrow?"

He shook his head and said "only to be with you as much as possible."

Zoe kissed him deeply for a long minute, and then she said "good answer cowboy. I've started a ball rolling, and it's picking up speed as we speak." Then she asked him "if I made plans for us would you go along with them no matter what?"

Sully smiled a wary smile, and then answered "I will do whatever you want to Zoe, no matter what you have up your sleeve."

Zoe beamed at him, and then she asked "do you promise, anything, anything at all?"

Sully laughed, and then he answered "I promise Zoe, anything tomorrow, as long as we are together."

Zoe jumped onto him and wrapped her legs around his waist. She said "we are getting married tomorrow, so you can't change your mind." She told him the plan, watching his facial expression the whole time. Thankfully, his smile got wider as she spoke. When she finished she asked "what do you think?"

Sully kissed her and said "I think it sounds perfect, I will call Ron to be the second witness. I would prefer Chuck, but then our wedding would end up getting too big with both Marie, and Terry."

Zoe said "those were my thoughts exactly, besides, Janet and Ron might make a good couple, and thank you baby."

Sully asked "why are you thanking me Zoe, so far this is entirely your plan."

Zoe gave him a big hug and whispered "I'm thanking you for proposing, and for calling it 'our' wedding."

They sat for an hour and planned their strategy for getting what they needed. Sully would take care of Rady, the plane, and the wedding rings. Zoe was going to try to catch up with Janet to help with her work load. They both agreed that they would do their best to avoid any dinner guests tonight.

Sully called Rady and found out that he was already checking out the extra gear and weapons that he needed. Sully told him he would pick him up there in fifteen minutes.

Zoe called Janet and they were going to meet at her place in twenty five. Sully had time to give Zoe a smile and a kiss. It had gotten cool and looked like rain, so Sully grabbed a light jacket. He threw the jacket into the truck, and then went back inside.

Zoe laughed and said "now what did you forget?"

Sully went to her and gave her a big hug and a kiss. He said "I just forgot to tell you that I love you, and that by this time tomorrow, you will be my wife."

Zoe felt weak in the knees when she whispered "I love you more than you will ever know Sullivan."

Sully left whistling as he walked to the truck. He picked up Ron and the load of gear for the mission about two minutes late. They put all of the gear in the back seat of Sully's truck and covered it with a canvas tarp.

Ron got in and said "what's going on now?"

Sully said very seriously "Ron, we should be safe in the truck to talk. This is highly sensitive information I am going to give you, so treat it as such. Do you understand me agent Rady?"

Ron looked intrigued when he answered "of course agent Mills, you should know you can trust me by now."

Sully let a small grin creep on his face when he said "I need a big favor from you tomorrow, and until Friday afternoon. Do you have any conflicts on your schedule?"

Ron said "you already know I'm on your team through Sunday, now would you just tell me what the hell is going on."

Sully said "I have a one day mission that the SSO doesn't know about, and you are a key component to making it work. It could get you into hot water, and you need to know that going in."

Ron's eyes were as wide as possible when he seriously asked "you're not taking contracts from other agencies, are you?"

Sully shrugged his shoulders and answered by saying "I guess if you look at it the right way it is a contract independent of the SSO."

Ron said "wow, you know me man of course I'm in, but we had better make damned sure we don't get caught or we are screwed, blued and tattooed my man."

Sully was trying his best not to smile or laugh when he said "any way you look at it I am screwed whether I do this or not."

Ron said "are you absolutely certain that this truck is clean? When is the last time you swept it?"

Sully answered "I did a double sweep right before I called you, it's clean."

Rady said "man I hope you know what you're getting into. Me they will just demote, you'll be totally fucked. What's the job?"

Sully answered "I need you at my house at eight hundred tomorrow, and we will load what we need and take my plane to Virginia Beach. From there we board a boat to complete the mission."

Ron's brow was furrowed, and now he looked irritated. After a long couple of seconds he said "you still haven't told me what the 'job' is, or any kind of mission objective."

Sully pulled into a strip mall and parked in front of a store called 'The Well Dressed Man'. He shut the truck off and looked Ron squarely in the eyes, then he said "this is either going to be the best or worst thing I will ever do. When we are out to sea on that boat, I'm going to marry Zoe." He smiled and let out a chuckle.

Ron laughed and said "you are a shit head Mills. You really had me going, but you are right. With that hellcat you are screwed no matter what you do now."

Sully laughed with him and said "she is putty in my hands, but please don't ever tell her I said that. What do you say, will you be my best man?"

Ron said "hell yeah, I'd actually pay to see this go down."

Sully got out of the truck as he said "thanks buddy, let's go get you a tux."

They went in and Sully bought Ron a black Armani tuxedo to match his. He picked out three tuxedo shirts for each of them one white, one off white, and one black. He bought three bow ties for them in each color, and studs and cufflinks in all three colors as well.

He went back to where Ron was being fitted and said to the tailor "George, we don't have time for a custom fit. His girlfriend just went into labor and they want to be married before the baby comes. I'll be back in about an hour to pick it up, you can make it perfect some other time. If you have enough time, you can tailor my shirts."

Sully went to the register and paid for everything. By the time the transaction was complete Ron was dressed and ready to go. The got back into the truck and Ron started to laugh. He said "you are such an ass, nice touch with the baby on the way." Then he asked "did George ever ask you which way you dressed?"

Sully laughed and said "I thought he was coming on to me the first time I was there too."

Ron said "what the hell does it matter which side you wear your dick on. Are you a lefty or a righty?"

They were both laughing like teenagers, and Sully said "I'm a lefty, how about you big guy?"

Ron answered "lefty here too, must be the hip way to be."

Three miles down the road Sully pulled into 'Buck's Western Wear'. They went in and Sully bought Ron a five x hat to match his, and a pair of black ostrich skin Tony Llama boots. Then he picked out two matching silver studded hat bands.

They left and headed down the road about another mile and pulled into 'Maximum Jewelers'. Sully walked in first, and the young blonde rushed over to meet him in the empty store. She flirtingly said "hey Ted, how did it go?"

Sully said "bad for both of us Heidi, she said yes, so I'm gonna need the wedding bands."

Heidi said "damn, and here I thought you were coming to take me away from all of this."

Heidi went in the back to get Sully's order, and he walked over to Ron.

Ron said "don't even start to lie to me and tell me you tapped that, I aint that dumb."

Sully said "I'm less than a day before marriage, I ain't about to screw it up now. But I think if you showed her a wad of cash, even you might have a chance Ron.

Ron said "no thanks, something that young would probably kill me. Which one did you get for Zoe?"

Sully lied and said "hell, I don't remember, ask Heidi when she comes back."

Ron was shaking his head at the prices when Heidi came back with the wedding bands that she had sold him. Sully tried his on and said "why does that feel more like handcuffs than a ring?"

Heidi giggled, and Ron said "with your lady it probably feels more like a ball and chain." Then he said to Heidi "let me see what Ted picked out."

Heidi winked at him and said "I've gotta get the keys for that big guy."

Sully took the ring off and put it back in its box. He smiled and said to Ron "I told you man look at something expensive, and you can do what comes naturally, unless you would rather I take you back to George to have him check your swing again."

Ron didn't get a chance to respond before Heidi came back with a ring on a purple felt covered tray. She set it down gently in front of Ron. She said "this is the ring, but the stone in this setting is point six carats smaller than the one Ted bought." She offered Ron an eye loupe, and he looked at her like she was crazy.

Ron looked at the ring, and then he looked at the price tag. He set it down with both hands extremely carefully. He tried to sound cool when he said "that seems like a fair price for a ring of that quality and size." He blew his coolness when he swallowed so hard he coughed.

Sully said "sorry Heidi, but I guess Ron is smarter than I am after all. It doesn't seem like he is ready to buy today. Why don't you just ring me up for the balance on the bands."

Heidi winked at him and said "I got the owner to waive the balance for you Ted."

Sully took two hundred dollar bills out of his wallet and handed it to Heidi. He said "that's for all of your help Heidi, buy yourself something nice. Thanks again for all of your help."

They got back in the truck and Ron said "are you fucking goofy? The one I looked at was priced at thirty thousand, and the one you got was bigger." Then he said "how come these people who barely know you like you so much, you're a bigger jerk than I am."

Sully just shrugged his shoulders and said "I don't know Ron, maybe it's because I dress left better than you."

The next stop was at a seven eleven not far from the jeweler. Sully went in and bought five pre-paid cellular phones, and ten packs of his cigars. Ron had explained that the only way the SSO was getting the numbers from the pre-paid phones was if you used them more than three times in a ten hour period, they could pull the SID, and the number. Because Ron had washed out of field training they kept feeding him more and more technical training.

Ron started setting up the phones while Sully drove. Sully had asked him this same question dozens of times, but he asked him again. Sully said "Ron, if I make it through this wedding without bailing out and swimming to shore, will you go with me and finish airborne training?"

Ron actually thought about it this time without saying no immediately. He said "maybe if we could do a few private tandem jumps together. Let me think about it Sully, but I have to overcome this fear bullshit if I am ever gonna advance."

Sully said "Ron you could almost be as good a field agent as I am if we can just get over this one hurdle."

Ron was very sincere when he said "I really appreciate you always pushing me to do it, and I'm thinking it might be time. Give me a couple of weeks, and if we have down time together, maybe we will go off campus and do a couple static line jumps."

Sully grabbed the back of his neck and squeezed it. Then he said "that's all I can ask for Ron."

He handed him the first phone and said "the phones number is written on the back, and Zoe is speed dial number two.

Sully pushed and held the two button on the cell phone. When Zoe picked up he said quickly "hey it's me, meet me at 'The Hot Spot' in thirty minutes, and don't ever call this number back." He hung up before she could respond.

Sully drove to his bank before he went to the strip club. Ron waited as he ran in to the bank. Sully used the bank's courtesy phone and called Chuck's cell phone. When Chuck answered he said "hey it's me, meet me at 'The Hot Spot' in fifteen minutes."

Sully went through the teller line and withdrew twenty five thousand three hundred dollars in cash. The three hundred he requested in singles. He said thank you, and then he went back to his truck.

While he was in the bank Ron had finished setting up the cellular phones and they were ready to go. As they drove to the bar Ron asked "what kind of plane did you buy?"

Sully answered "I got a really good deal on a eighty one Piper Seneca turbo prop. The bird is in great shape and easy to fly."

Ron laughed and said "you're the one who bought Carl's plane for basically half price, I should have guessed it. I used to do ground maintenance on that plane when I was in training. That is one cool ride."

Sully said "Carl was a real asshole to me so I squeezed him a little. Now that asshole is running me down around the local fliers. I can't wait until I catch up with him again."

Ron said "I never got to like that guy either, he was always acting like he was 'big time', and better than everyone."

Sully replied "that's about Carl in a nutshell." That comment ended their trip. Sully parked on the side of the strip club, and he and Ron exited the truck. Sully had stashed the twenty five thousand in cash in a hidden, built in lock box underneath the drivers floor mat. The three hundred in singles he put in his jacket pocket.

They walked into the establishment and doubled the crowd. Sully said to Ron "see if you can get us a good table, you might have to wait for someone to leave." Sully went to the bar and talked to the bartender.

Ron watched Sully smooth out the bartender / manager. As soon as he left the bar, with a beer bottle in each hand, two mediocre girls came out of the back and danced in front of Ron. Sully sat with him at the table and handed him one of the bottles of beer.

Sully said "don't worry about these girls, I gave the manager my gold card and told him to call the prime talent. This is the only shot I have at a bachelor party, so I told him he could charge up to three grand so let's not hold back."

Sully handed him one of the three bundles of dollar bills and said "let's help these young ladies work their way through college. The first hundred is on me, then you have to spend your own cash on the ladies. I've got the drinks and food covered. When Chuck and the ladies arrive you need to take charge and explain the new cell phones."

Ron asked "if I am the best man shouldn't I be paying for this?"

Sully answered him by saying "yes you are supposed to, but I will waive the debt if you jump with me and make full agent."

Ron just nodded in his reply that he understood. Then he said "Sully, this is gonna be hard for me to do, but I think with your help I can do it."

Sully replied "Ron it's all in your head, from one bad jump, once you forget about that it's gonna be a piece of cake."

They hadn't even seen Chuck come in because of the serious nature of their talk, and both were startled when he was at the table. Chuck asked "what's the occasion?"

Sully was halfway through his first beer, but he felt drunk. He was inebriated with happiness. He smiled at Chuck and said "sit your ass down, this is my bachelor party." He gave Chuck the second bundle of dollar bills and continued by saying "the first hundred is on me, then it's out of your own pocket.

Ron shook Chuck's hand as a re-introduction, and after Chuck sat down he gave him a cell phone and quickly ran down the protocol for using it correctly."

Chuck looked at the girls that were dancing and said "if this is the top talent, I just made a hundred bucks for showing up."

They all laughed together, until Sully assured Chuck that the prime time dancers were on their way. Then Sully took out his wallet and gave each of the sub-prime girls a twenty by tucking them in their respective G-strings.

The dancers had left the stage just as Zoe and Janet walked into the rundown strip club.

Sully elbowed Ron in the ribs, and then he said "the one on the right is mine."

Ron laughed and said "the other one is much cuter, and most likely nicer, I'm in. How are you gonna explain meeting at a strip club?"

Sully said "watch me Ron, and you just might learn something. Don't take notes though, that's way too obvious."

As Zoe and Janet approached Sully stood and went to meet them. He grabbed Zoe and danced with her for a few seconds, then he dipped her and gave her a deep kiss. When he let her up they walked to the group holding hands.

When they had reached the table Sully made the introductions to everyone who had not met Janet, then moved Zoe in front of him holding her by her slim waist in his large strong hands. Sully continued by saying "and this lovely creature will be Mrs. Zoe Mills in less than twenty hours." He stood beside her as he made the announcement.

The group all clapped, then they sat at the table. Zoe looked around 'The Hot Spot' and said "wow, you guys picked a pretty swanky place for a party."

Sully put on a big toothy smile and answered her as he said "My best man Ron wanted to go to the Ritz Carlton in Richmond, but we are short on time. He found out that this place is having open try outs, and he thought it might be a perfect side job for you two beautiful women."

The ladies laughed for a moment, then Zoe placed a stern look on her face, and she said "nice try Mills, but please don't pile the bullshit that high, we are both wearing heels."

Ron tried to save himself by pointing at Sully, and then saying "I never even knew this place was here, Sully drove, and when we got here they treated him like a MVP."

Zoe glared at him, and Janet gave him a dirty look at the same time. Sully defended himself by saying "Chuck took me here about two and a half years ago and the food was great. Maybe I tipped a little too much, but they did welcome me today very nicely when I told them that Chuck was coming."

Chuck spoke up for himself quickly saying "hey, slow down there Mills, don't get me involved in your bullshit. I've never been inside this place before."

Sully said "Janet don't mind Chuck he's shy. Just ask his fiancé, Marie when you meet her, I've heard she comes here a lot with him." He smiled at Chuck as he said it.

Chuck jumped up out of his chair and was poised to yell at Sully when the ladies joined in on the laughter and sat down.

Chuck softened his demeanor, and sat back down when Zoe said "you've gotta learn to recognize Sully's bullshit quicker buddy. Then she asked nicely "why are we really here sweetie?"

Sully said "actually Ron and I are here bearing gifts for all of you. Ron figured out how we can use private cell phones without the SSO tracking us, and I use this place for field research."

Janet laughed, and then joined in by asking "really, what kind of field research are you doing in a titty bar?"

Sully laid it on thick and heavy as he answered by saying "Janet, I'm really glad that you asked. Not long after Zoe and I started dating I told her that she had the greatest breasts in the whole world. I've been doing field research ever since to make sure that what I told her wasn't a lie. I promised never to lie to her, so I have to make my best effort to be truthful."

They all laughed at Sully's defense, and then Zoe said "Mills, I don't know how you ever leave the bathroom being that full of shit."

Janet said "Zoe are you sure you want to marry someone who lies that well?"

Zoe responded by saying "if you are around him as much as I have been, you get to learn the smell."

Ron handed out the cell phones and explained about calls being under twenty seconds, and not more than three calls in a ten hour period. He finished by saying "I just want everyone to know that in a couple of weeks Sully is going to help me finish my airborne training so that I can finally get in the field for real."

Zoe went over to Ron and kissed him on the cheek, then she said "I am proud of you already Ron for committing to the attempt. It takes a lot of guts to get on the horse after it bucks you. I hate to be rude, but Sully and I need to discuss something with Chuck privately." The three of them left the table leaving Ron and Janet alone with one another.

They sat down three tables away and Sully tried to mend fences by saying "Chuck we really wanted to involve you in the wedding, but we wanted to keep it as small as possible. I wouldn't feel right inviting you without inviting Terry and Marie too. I hope you can understand and not be pissed at me."

Chuck laughed and said "I can't thank you enough for not inviting me. I thought I needed to apologize to you for getting engaged on your special night. That was foolish of me, but Marie had been hinting for the past three months." He continued saying "If we were invited, she would either ruin your day again, or mine."

Zoe said "look at me and please tell me that what you're saying is the truth."

Chuck did as she asked and said "Zoe I would be lying if I told you I didn't want to be there, but I can't go without offending Marie. I wish you both the best, and I will be there in spirit."

Sully and Zoe thanked him for his honesty and understanding. Then they all got up from the table to head back to the others, and they all stopped in their tracks simultaneously when they saw Ron and Janet kissing.

Sully said "well shit, it looks like it might be a double wedding after all."

They went back to the table and embarrassed the two of them terribly. When they sat down in different chairs the music got loud, and a cheesy announcer said "ladies and gentlemen please welcome Motion to the main stage."

Sully said loudly, to be heard over the music "watch this one closely, if they weren't fake, they are almost better."

Zoe slugged him playfully in the arm and said "I don't want to hear commentary on your 'research'. Then she said "Janet do you want to have an early dinner here?"

Janet answered "I forgot to tell you I've got plans for dinner." Then she looked at Ron.

Ron clumsily said "yeah, I do too. I totally forgot earlier, but I have dinner plans."

Chuck said "don't look at me I've been engaged for almost two days, and if I'm not home by seventeen thirty, she starts calling."

Sully said "Chuck, its past eighteen hundred already"

Chuck patted all of his pockets, then he quickly said "shit I left my phone in the car, Janet very nice to meet you, Sully and Zoe I wish you the best, and Ron it was nice seeing you again. I gotta go" Chuck jumped up from the table, put the bundle of dollar bills on the table, and left.

When he left they all laughed, and then Sully went to the bar and ordered one more round for them, and settled the tab.

Zoe had gone to the ladies room and when Sully went back to the table Ron and Janet were kissing again. He cleared his throat loudly when he was thirty feet from the table. When he got there he said "I settled the tab, and ordered one more round. I was thinking that I could take Zoe home with me, and we can shuffle the cars around when we get back on Friday afternoon."

Zoe came back to the table right before the topless waitress did. She asked "where did Chuck go?"

Ron smiled, and then said "he was out past curfew, and he had to go, or get grounded."

The waitress gave them their drinks, and Sully tipped her a ten dollar bill. After she left, Zoe gave Sully a nasty look.

Sully smiled at her and said "not even close."

The four of them chatted about the pending wedding as they finished their drinks. Zoe asked them to please not be late the next morning. They left the as couples, and went on their way. Zoe climbed into Sully's truck and they headed toward her truck at Janet's place.

On the way Sully stopped the truck on the side of the road so they could kiss one another. It was a happy day for them. It was a day that would take a hold of their souls for the rest of their lives.

When Sully and Zoe arrived at her truck, Sully apologized for the strip club joke, and all of his comments that were possibly hurtful to her.

Zoe said "don't ever stop being cute like that, I love it when you're playful."

They left one another to finish errands, and agreed to meet at home in no less than two hours.

On the way to pick up Ron's tuxedo, Sully stopped at the jewelry store to try to get Zoe a wedding gift. He had been wracking his brain for a great gift, but was coming up with nothing. Two doors away from the jewelers was a pawn shop. He went into the pawn shop browsing more for ideas than anything.

Nothing jumped out at him as a legitimate idea, so he kept thinking as he looked at the pistols in the glass case near the register. Sully left the pawn shop having purchased a snub nosed thirty eight special, a nylon ankle holster, and a used, dented waffle iron. The proprietor of the pawn shop had 'thrown in' the waffle iron with no charge. He put the pistol and holster in the truck, and then carried the waffle iron into the jewelry store.

Heidi was alone in the store, and immediately came on to him. Sully was flattered by the girl's suggestive advances, and if Zoe had not been his soul mate, he might have taught her a trick or two. Instead he used it to his advantage and flirted back.

Sully set the waffle iron down and said "Heidi, I need your help. What would a woman as beautiful as you are appreciate as a wedding gift? I'm torn between something useful for every day, and something dramatic."

Heidi answered him by walking around the counter to the customer side and got way too close to him when she said softly "everyday would probably be a watch, dramatic and fancy would be a bracelet or necklace."

Sully suggestively said "let's see what you have ….in a watch."

Heidi took him by the hand and took him to the case that held the watches. There must have been two hundred in the case. Heidi bent over, much farther than necessary, to unlock the case. She took out five watches and set them on the glass counter behind him, rubbing up against him as she set the watches down.

Sully looked at the watches she had picked out, and none of them seemed to express what he wanted. He shook his head, and turned back to the case to make his own selection. Sully pulled out four and put them on the counter to look at them. He said to Heidi "I'm pretty committed to a watch, can you call your engraver and have him here quickly? I am already close to being late for the rehearsal dinner."

Every time mentioned the wedding Heidi cooled off, and slowed down her sexual advances. She said "certainly, I can have Mike here in five minutes." She left him to call Mike the engraver.

Sully didn't want to settle on anything ordinary. He looked very carefully at the watches he had picked out and kept coming back to one. Heidi was back standing right next to him. Sully showed her the watch he liked, and then he said "show me more watches like this one." As Heidi searched through the case he took a note card from a box next to the register and wrote down what he wanted engraved.

Heidi took one watch from the case, and then looked in the drawer beneath the display. She took two more and handed them to Sully. Mike came in and yawned, then he said "what needs engraving?"

Sully answered him, before Heidi could speak, saying "a watch, and I am in an incredible rush." He handed Mike the card and said "here is the text, I will have the watch picked out in a minute. You can start setting the machine up."

Mike read the card, and then he said "what kind of font were you thinking of?"

Sully answered "you can pick one, but keep it simple. The watch is a gift for my soon to be wife, but don't pick out anything to flowery."

Mike said "I've got the perfect font in mind. It will only take me two minutes to set up the engraving machine, and another two when you pick a watch."

Sully nodded his approval to Mike. Sully turned back to selecting a watch, and Mike went to set up the engraving machine.

One of the watches Heidi picked out from the bottom drawer was perfect, exactly what he had been searching for. The watch was a Vacheron with a good sized, easy to read face, and it was all set into platinum with a platinum bangle instead of a band.

Sully picked up the watch and said "Heidi this is the one, it's not exactly what I want, but it will have to do for now." He was playing her for a better price than the twenty two thousand dollar sticker.

Heidi took the watch to Mike, and Sully went to the cash register carrying the watch box. He placed the waffle iron next to the watch box.

Heidi swayed her way toward him, and when she got there Sully said I would appreciate it if you could wrap this, and wrap the watch separately, but put them both in the same box.

Heidi had an odd look on her face when she saw the waffle iron and "That's a joke right?"

Sully answered "yes it is, I like to keep my bride to be on her toes."

Heidi smiled at him and said "are you absolutely sure about this marriage? I could treat you better than anyone else."

Sully smiled and said “Heidi I am flattered by your advances, but the woman I am going to marry is the only person I could ever see spending my life with. You will understand when you truly fall in love, and I'm sure you will someday.”

Heidi took the price sticker off of the watch box and went to find a box to fit it and the waffle iron. Mike came to Sully and showed him the engraving on the back of the watch.

Sully said “that's perfect Mike, I really like the font you chose.”

Mike put the watch carefully back in its box and took it to Heidi to have it wrapped. Five minutes later Heidi came back to him with a large, beautifully wrapped box. She said “here you go, I hate having to help the man I want to be super romantic with another woman.”

Sully said “Heidi I can't thank you enough for all of your help. I'm sorry to rush, but I am really late.”

The smile dropped from her face as she took his charge card. She ended up charging him seventeen thousand dollars, and some change.

Sully thanked her for all of her help, and headed toward the exit. When he reached the door Heidi said “Ted please remember I am here if things don't work out, and tell your bride how jealous I am.”

Sully replied “I will always remember you Heidi, and I will tell her.”

Sully drove to ‘The Well Dressed Man’, and picked up all of the clothing. Ron's tux had been ‘rough’ fitted, and all of the shirts had been pressed and tailored. He thanked them, took all of the clothing to the truck, and headed home.

Zoe wasn't home yet, so Sully backed the truck in, all the way to the garage door. He opened the overhead door and started unloading. All of the weapons went into the vault haphazardly, and then Sully closed the vault, and went into the house. He changed into shorts and a tank top.

Now comfortably in his flip flops he unloaded the other things in the truck. He hung Ron's tux and shirts in the hall closet, and then his own in the master closet. It took him almost an hour to unload everything, and Zoe still wasn't home.

Sully grabbed a beer, and he lit a cigar as he went to the garage to organize the vault. He carefully put all on Ron's mission gear in a corner, and then he put together a small bag to take with them. The ‘wedding’ bag contained two military forty five caliber pistols, eight loaded clips for the weapons, and five small FRS radios.

He carried the bag into the house, and put it in the master closet. Sully went to the back room and found a small black leather carry-on bag. He took it back to the master bedroom and packed what he thought he might need for the trip. He took a pair of jeans, a pair of khaki Dockers, socks, underwear, and his shaving kit. Zoe had a garment bag hanging in the closet, and he was going to wait to load it until they could do it together.

Sully took his tattered brown cowboy boots out on the back deck and put a heavy layer of mink oil on them. He buffed them for ten minutes, and the boots really showed no sign of improvement.

He had so much nervous energy running through him that he had to do something. Sully looked through the refrigerator for something to prepare for dinner. He ran several options through his head, and finally decided on the menu.

The first thing Sully did was to take out a package of boneless, skinless chicken breasts. He opened them, rinsed them, and put them in a zip lock bag. Sully added half a bottle of Italian dressing, sealed the bag, shook the bag to coat the meat, and then he put the bag back into the fridge.

Sully went to the pantry and took out a box of Uncle Ben's wild rice. He read the instructions as he walked back to the stove. Ten minutes later the rice was simmering nicely.

He looked in the freezer for a vegetable, and found an open bag of mixed vegetables. Sully found a small sauce pot and filled it halfway with water. He put it on the stove and added a couple tablespoons of butter. When the water was about to boil he added the frozen veggies.

With Zoe still not back Sully started to worry. He set the table. The roses were moved to one end, and the plates were set across from one another. Sully had to search for five minutes, but he finally found the candlesticks and candles.

He covered the pots, and turned the stove off. Sully went to the front porch to smoke a cigar. He wasn't kidding himself at all, he was getting very worried about Zoe, and he had chosen to sit on the front porch to watch for her.

Twelve minutes later, his cigar gone, Sully walked into the house to get his new cell phone off of his dresser. He grabbed a beer, and took the phone out to the front porch. He had decided to wait for one more set of headlights to come toward the house from town before he called. They weren't even married yet, and he didn't want to seem like an old worried husband, but he was the antithesis of that stereotype.

Sully was trying to get used to wearing the tracking watch Ron had given him for the upcoming mission, and had worn it ever since he got it. Sully had never worn jewelry of any kind, and even something as unobtrusive as a watch, made him uncomfortable.

He looked at the watch every minute while he paced back and forth across the front patio. Nine minutes and seventeen seconds later he saw headlights coming from town. Sully ran into the house and watched the lights through the kitchen window. When the lights slowed and turned into the driveway he ran to the sofa and pretended to be sleeping. His heart rate slowly returned to normal.

Zoe came in two minutes later with an armload of things and put them in the back bedroom. She came into the living room and kissed Sully to wake him up.

Sully stirred and opened his eyes. Still faking sleep he said groggily "you better watch it lady, I'm going to be a happily married man in about seventeen hours, and my wife could kick your butt."

Zoe smiled and said "I love you Mills, you are an incredible man."

Sully sat up and cleared his throat, then he said "oh, it's you Zoe, I thought it was one of the three hookers I brought over here."

Zoe laughed and said "if I thought you were capable of that I wouldn't be here. Thank you for cooking, or did the hookers?"

Sully leaned forward and hugged her. He kissed her and said "you smell great, I wish they could bottle your essence. Do you need help unloading?"

Zoe answered "yes, I had no idea how many stops I still had to make after leaving you. I'm really sorry, I'm almost two hours late."

They unloaded her car together and put everything in the back room. They decided to organize and pack everything after dinner.

Sully put on a long sleeved thermal Henley and socks before dinner because it was starting to get quiet cool outside. He turned the burners back on under the rice and veggies, and then went out to light the grill.

Zoe came up behind him and hugged him. She got on her tiptoes and kissed the back of his neck. She whispered "will you really marry me tomorrow?"

Sully turned around and grabbed her shoulders. He looked her in the eyes, and he very seriously said "Zoe, if you actually marry me, without coming to your senses and realizing how much better you could do, you will make me the happiest man in the world."

Zoe said "I bet you won't feel like that ten years from now. I just feel like we are living in a dream and someone will wake me up. Sully, please don't ever wake me from this dream."

Sully said "how about we live out the dream together."

Zoe went to the bedroom and put on comfy clothes herself right before dinner was ready.

They had dinner and chatted about how Ron and Janet had hit it off so quickly. Zoe commented that she thought they might be a good couple, but it was crazy that they had such an attraction to one another so quickly. She complimented Sully on finally convincing Ron to face his fears.

Sully had told her that he had been trying for years, and was very proud of him, especially for cementing his decision by voicing it aloud to all of them.

When they were finished with dinner Zoe told him how good it was, and thanked him for cooking. They cleaned everything up together. While washing the dishes Sully said "I couldn't help but notice a small gift wrapped box while we were unloading your truck. I wasn't supposed to get you a wedding gift, was I?"

Zoe flashed a sarcastic smile at him and said "did you really think I didn't notice that wrapped box behind the armchair in the living room?"

Sully new the game was over and asked "okay, I got you a wedding present, what did you get me?"

Zoe laughed and said "you can be such a little kid. I'm not telling, and I don't want to know what you got me either. We will open our gifts to one another at dinner tomorrow night. Promise me right now not to open yours and then try to re wrap it."

Sully looked at the floor like a scolded ten year old boy and sullenly said "okay, if you wanna be mean and make me wait, I guess I will have to."

Zoe laughed and said "hopefully you can wait until I can give you a gift as your wife, forever."

Sully hugged her, and put his wet, soapy hands, on her butt.

Zoe kissed him and hugged him back. She asked "do you really think that I'm going to take my pants off just because you got them a little damp?"

They both smiled uncontrollably as they finished the dishes. Then they went to the bedroom to finish the packing. Zoe showed him the dress she was going to wear. Sully told her it was perfect. He let her pick out the shirts and ties for the tuxedos, and she chose the off white shirts. She wanted Ron to wear a black tie and Sully to wear the off white. Zoe showed him the black evening gown that she had bought for Janet.

Zoe had bought the Dior dress, Prada high heels, and a small Prada clutch for Janet as an attendant's gift.

Sully showed her the boots and hat that he had bought for Ron. He carefully put the new hat bands on both hats as Zoe said "I didn't see the new boots that you bought for yourself, where are they?"

Sully didn't look up from what he was doing when he answered "I guess they are still at the store, because I didn't buy new boots for myself."

Zoe was very disappointed and it showed in her voice when she said "you're not planning on wearing those old ratty things you always do, are you?"

Sully had finished putting the hat bands on, and he put his on before he answered by asking "what do you think about the hat bands I picked out?"

Zoe crossed her arms across her chest and said, in less than a pleasant tone "they are nice, now where are your new boots?"

Sully walked by her and answered quietly, as he was walking into the kitchen "I don't need new boots."

Sully grabbed a beer from the fridge and went onto the back deck to have a cigar. Not long after he lit it with his hula lighter, Zoe came out and asked "why didn't you get new boots?"

Sully answered her with all the excuses at once, saying "the store was closed, they didn't have anything in my size, I forgot my wallet, I got a flat tire, and I was abducted by aliens, and spent the afternoon talking to Elvis."

Zoe tried her hardest not to smile, but she finally did, then she asked "how is Elvis these days?"

Sully smiled back at her and answered "you wouldn't believe it unless you saw it, but he is almost four hundred pounds, and still gets the best babes."

They both laughed and Zoe came over and hugged him. She said "I guess if it's important to you to wear those boots, I have to let you."

They held one another close, looking at the stars for a while. Sully finally interrupted the moment by softly asking "would you like to know why I want to wear those boots so often, and especially tomorrow?"

Zoe looked at him lovingly and said "if you want to tell me I would love to know sweetie."

Sully held her gently by the chin and kissed her lightly. Then he said "you probably don't remember, but those boots were brand new the night we met. They are very special to me, and they always remind me of how you took my breath away the first time I ever saw you."

Zoe said "no I didn't know that Sully. Please wear the boots, knowing their origin I wouldn't have you wear anything else." Then she continued by saying "do you actually know that you are the most charming and romantic man in the world?"

Sully smiled and answered "I never had a reason to be until I met you. You bring out the best in me Zoe."

Zoe almost knocked him over with an emphatic embrace. She said "right now I feel like the luckiest woman in the world."

They held one another for a minute, then they went back to their bedroom and finished the packing. Sully put all of the bags into Zoe's Land Cruiser, and they felt that they were as ready as they could be.

They were both tired when they went to bed, but not tired enough to preclude them from making love. They were both slow and passionate the first time, then they did all of their favorite things, and positions, at a furious pace.

It was just past midnight when Sully woke Zoe up. Zoe wasn't pleased, and she said "why did you wake me Sully, I was dreaming about us."

Sully said "it's just past midnight, and I wanted to be the first to wish you a happy wedding day, go back to sleep my love."

She was back asleep almost immediately, and she hadn't said a word. Sully quietly snuck out of the bed, put on a heavy robe, and went outside.

It was the first time in Sully's life that he felt truly happy. He wished the clock would slow down, he wanted this day to last forever.

Dawn found them awake, and at the kitchen table together. They were sharing one cup of coffee between the both of them. There was way too much nervous energy between both of them, so they decided to take a shower together.

They took their time washing one another. They made slow passionate love to one another. They took turns telling each other what they liked and disliked sexually. When the hot water ran out Sully and Zoe left the shower and snuggled under the covers for a short while. They were both dressed and overly ready to go at seven thirty.

Janet and Ron showed up ten minutes early. Sully was convinced that they had spent the night together, mostly due to the fact that Ron was still wearing the clothes that he had on yesterday.

Sully asked "did you guys get a good night's sleep?"

Janet blushed and said "we had an awesome night, but there wasn't much 'sleep' involved."

Zoe laughed at her comment, and then laid out the itinerary for the day. She said "we are all going to ride in my truck to Culpepper. Our plane is there and waiting. We will fly to Virginia Beach and then take a limo to the hotel. As soon as we are dressed and ready Janet and I will take the limo to pier sixteen. You two gentlemen will take a cab and meet us at slip thirty eight twenty five minutes later. Janet's Uncle will motor out to international waters, and then marry us. Does anyone have any questions?"

Ron carefully raised his hand and said "will any of us have time for a bathroom break?"

They all laughed, and then Zoe said "I'm sorry if I sound like a drill instructor, but I have planned this very carefully so that Sully can't run away."

When they had finished their coffee it was time to go. They all laughed together on the fifteen minute ride to the airport. Mostly they had talked about the blossoming relationship between Ron and Janet.

Ron and Janet found it impossible not to kiss and whisper to one another during the ride.

Sully drove right to the plane, and they unloaded everything onto the tarmac. Sully took Zoe's truck back to the hangar. He parked Zoe's truck inside the hangar, and then closed and locked the large sliding doors.

Sully jogged back to where the plane was tied down, and didn't see anyone. Zoe was giving a tour of the plane, and they were all inside looking around. Sully pulled the wheel chocks and carried them inside.

He stowed the chocks and went to his friends and Zoe. He said "well Janet what do you think?"

Janet answered "This is absolutely gorgeous, I can't wait until Ron and I can afford one."

Sully thought to himself 'one night together and she is talking about you guys as an old married couple? Look out Ron'.

Sully said "why don't we get going, Ron and I will drive, and the two of you can sit back and relax."

Sully sat in the captain's chair, and Ron in the co pilot's seat. Sully fired the engines, and they started to taxi. Ron took care of calling the tower for flight clearance, and six minutes later they were airborne.

Sully picked up the microphone that was wired to talk to the passenger compartment, and said, in a fake commercial pilot's voice "ladies and gentlemen welcome to Maybe Airlines flight sixty nine, nonstop service to Virginia Beach. We will be cruising at an altitude of thirty eight hundred feet, and our estimated flight time is thirty minutes. Please obey the seat belt sign at all times. Our stewardess will be through the cabin shortly with drink service. Thank you for flying Maybe Air, and remember our motto 'will we get you there alive and on time….maybe'.

There were claps, cheers, and whistles from the back. Sully took off his headphones, and turned to Ron. He quietly asked "How the hell did you and Janet hook up so quickly?"

Ron chuckled and quietly said "I think she liked the way that I dress left."

They landed and parked the plane in Virginia Beach. The limo was at their tie down area almost instantly. Sully handed the bags out of the plane and to the driver, and then he joined everyone inside the limo.

Zoe grabbed him and threw him onto the seat next to her. She gave him several deep kisses, and then she said "I thought this was all a dream until right now. You are really gonna marry me aren't you Sully."

Sully replied "I don't care if there is a hurricane warning. We are getting on that boat and getting married today."

Janet had made reservations for them at the beach Hilton and they all walked to the registration desk together.

Janet gave the name on the card she had used, Kathy Jackson and changed the accommodations from three suites to two. A bell hop arrived with their bags and led to the elevators. The suites were across the hall from each other, and Zoe directed the bell hop as to which bags went where.

Ron and Janet checked out both rooms while the bell hop moved the bags. Ron said to Zoe "it's a little less than I am accustomed to, but it should be alright for one night."

Zoe smiled at Sully and shook her head. When the bell hop was done Sully tipped him a twenty. They all congregated in the honeymoon suite. Zoe took the garment bag and opened it, she gave Sully and Ron their tuxedos and shirts. She said "the rest of your clothes are in the other room." She kissed Sully and said "please meet me at the boat."

Sully said "the entire Marine Corps wouldn't be able to stop me. I will see you soon."

Sully and Ron went to the other room and started to dress.

Zoe went into the garment bag and took out the dresses. As they were getting dressed Zoe asked "how did you and Ron get together so quickly?"

Janet answered "we just looked into each others eyes, and something clicked. That has never happened to me before, and the more I am around him the better I feel."

Zoe said "that's just wonderful Janet, I really hope it works out for both of you."

Janet said "me too. He is interesting, brave, handsome, sexy, and vulnerable all at the same time. Last night was the best sex I have ever had."

Zoe smiled and said "tell me all about it, I want details."

Ten minutes later Janet knocked on the door to the boy's room. Sully answered the door and said "do you need something Janet?"

She said "we're leaving now. Go down and get a cab in ten minutes, and we will see you on the boat. Isn't this exciting?"

Sully calmly answered "yes it is, we will be there, ten minutes behind, and Janet, you look absolutely wonderful.

Janet smiled at the compliment and said "thank you very much Sullivan."

Ron came out of the bathroom with the tie in his hand and said "it's no use, I can't tie this fuckin thing. Why didn't you get clip on ties?"

Sully stood behind him in front of the mirror and tied his bow tie for him. When he finished he turned him around to face him and made sure Ron's tie was straight. He finished and said "you look good buddy, are you ready?"

Ron answered "thanks Sully, and I can't thank you enough for all of your help. I'm gonna make my jumps, and become a full field agent, then we can work together as equals."

Sully said "you fuckin better, you promised me, remember?" He took a deep breath and continued "grab your hat, its go time."

They went down to the lobby and Sully guided Ron into the gift shop. He told Ron to look for a gift for Janet. He bought four pairs of Ray Ban club master sunglasses, and three packs of cigars. Ron came back to the counter with a cactus snow globe. Sully laughed and said "well, at the very least, it's a unique gift."

As they walked back to the lobby Sully handed Ron two pairs of the sunglasses, and a pack of the cigars. He said "make sure to fire one of those cigars up as soon as we get to the pier."

They went to the valet desk and asked the clerk get them a ride. They waited only a few seconds, and the clerk led them out to a courtesy car. Sully told the driver to go to the Marina, pier sixteen.

When they were dropped off at the pier a golf cart was waiting to take them to slip thirty eight. They both lit a cigar before getting on the little vehicle.

On the ride Ron noticed that Sully's hands were shaking. Ron said "Mills calm down, you are doing the right thing. Zoe is absolutely wonderful, and for whatever reason it seems like she truly loves you. Don't be stupid. If you don't marry her there are about a million other guys that will."

Sully said "thanks Ron, I probably would have run away if you weren't here."

Ron laughed and said "maybe that's why she chose a wedding five miles from shore, happy dog paddling pal."

Sully laughed a maniacal, nervous laugh, and asked the driver how far they were from the slip. The driver said nothing, and five seconds later, he stopped the golf cart and the pointed to his left.

Janet was standing on the stern deck waving at them. Ron walked over and boarded the boat giving Janet a big hug and telling her how great she looked.

Sully walked over and said "Janet, like I said before, you look absolutely gorgeous. Don't you know it's rude to look better that the bride?"

Janet laughed and said "thank you Sully, but don't take your boots off before you see Zoe, because she is gonna knock your socks off. Climb aboard cowboy."

Sully laughed, but made no move to get on the boat. He said "I was shocked that Ron cleans up so well."

Janet said "me too, you guys look so handsome I want to take both of you home with me."

Sully said "I think you probably have your hands full enough with the guy you're hugging."

Ron broke in and said "enough fucking around Mills, get your ass on this boat right now, or I'm gonna come over there and throw you on."

Sully still didn't move and seriously replied "if you think you can, go ahead and try it."

Janet seemed to sense the tension in the situation. She tried to diffuse it by asking nicely "Sully would you please get aboard so we can cast off?"

Sully took two deep breaths, and then stepped aboard the boat. A minute later the deck hand Raul had cast off the last line and they were slowly motoring out of the harbor. Sully threw his cigar in the ocean and turned a deck chair to face a rear corner of the boat and sat down without saying a word, his back to them.

Janet made a move toward him and Ron grabbed her by the arm. He shook his head and whispered to her "just let him be for a little bit. He is not used to being afraid of anything, and right now he is scared shitless."

Sully sat that way for five minutes, staring at the water and thinking. He finally wrestled his demons into a submission hold and stood quickly. Janet gasped loudly, because she thought he was going to dive off the back of the boat. He took his hat off and ran the fingers of his right hand through his hair. He put his hat back on tightly and turned to them smiling.

Janet let out an audible sigh, and Ron walked over to him. He slapped Sully on the shoulder and said "what do you say I go find us a couple of beers?"

Sully answered "that sounds good Ron, sorry about the dock buddy."

Ron said "believe me partner, I understand. I'll be right back." He left, and Sully walked over to Janet.

Janet smiled and said "are you okay Sully?"

Sully answered her by saying "sometimes life moves a little to fast for me. I just needed a few minutes to evaluate what was really important to me. Where is Zoe?"

Janet said "she is being old fashioned, and doesn't want you to see her before the ceremony."

Sully said "I understand, that's sweet. Would you do me a favor and give her these?" He handed Janet a pair of the sunglasses and a folded piece of notepaper.

Janet answered "I will right now. I am so happy for the two of you I can't stand it. I hope someday it will be my turn."

Sully said "I'm happy too Janet, and please don't ever tell him I said so, but you could do a lot worse than Ron. Deep down I know he is a really great guy."

She gave him a big hug just as Ron came back. Ron said "hey, hey don't think you're gonna have a last minute fling with my girl Mills."

They all laughed. Ron gave Sully a bottle of Dos Equis dark, and Janet kissed him, then she left. Sully smiled, and asked Ron "do you think it's too late to start swimming for shore?"

Ron answered by saying "I know you pretty well by now Sully, and I'm certain that if you didn't want to be here you wouldn't be here."

Sully divulged to Ron "I want nothing more than to spend the rest of my life with Zoe, but right now I am scared to death."

Ron smiled at him and said "that's normal man." Then he raised his bottle and made a toast, saying "to my best friend, may every day of your life be as good as this one."

Sully nodded his approval of the toast, and they both finished their beers in one long drink. He handed his empty bottle to Ron and said "that was good, let's do it again."

Ron went inside to get more beers, and the captain of the boat came out to meet him.

Shawn Port was a large man in his late forties. He was in good shape for his age, and had a stern face. He came over to Sully and asked "are you the groom, or the one sleeping with my niece?"

Sully stuck out his hand and answered "I am the groom sir, Sullivan Mills. I can't thank you enough for doing this on such short notice."

Shawn's big meaty hand engulfed Sully's, and he had a vise of a grip. Shawn let go of his hand and said "welcome aboard Mills, you're a lucky man. Your bride to be is a knockout."

Sully said "thank you sir, I think so too. You have a very nice vessel sir."

Shawn said "thank you Mills, I worked long and hard to get her, and now she pays my bills."

Sully said "I'm glad you brought that up sir." Sully handed him an envelope containing three thousand dollars. "Janet told me you were doing this as a favor to her, but that doesn't sit well with me. Please let me know if what I gave you is not fair."

Shawn softened his overbearing presence a bit, and he looked in the envelope. He nodded his head and said "this is more than fair, in fact it's about four times too much."

Sully said "that's good, I'd rather give you too much than not enough."

Ron walked up to them with a second round of beers and handed one to Sully. He looked at Shawn and said "want a beer skipper?"

Shawn was quite obviously not amused, and he let Ron know it when he said "no sonny I don't, and if you plan on addressing me it had better be as Captain or Sir. Call me anything else, and your going to have a long swim home." He turned to leave, then he stopped and turned back and stuck a finger in Ron's face. He yelled "one more thing, if I hear that you treat my niece in any other fashion than as a gentleman, I will find you and beat your young ass to a bloody pulp!" Then he stormed back to the bridge.

Ron's eyes were wide open as he looked at Sully and asked "what the hell did I do?"

Sully laughed and answered "I have no idea, he was a nice guy when I talked with him. What did you do to piss him off?"

Janet walked up as Ron answered "fuck if I know, that was the first time I ever met the guy, and I offered him a beer."

Janet looked confused after hearing Ron's last comment. She asked "what the hell is going on here, and who was yelling?"

Sully laughed and walked away saying "you are on your own Ron."

Zoe was in the main state room ready and waiting for the ceremony to start. All day she had been vacillating between elation and sorrow. She needed to be with Sully, and the longer they were apart the more morose she became. Janet had given her a note from Sully, but told her it would be bad luck to read it.

As soon as she left to go check on things, Zoe opened the note. It read:

> *My dearest Zoe,*
>
> *I am trying to write to you the things That I can't express in words. My love for you is so strong that it scares me. I am sad and lonely whenever we are apart. My heart is always full when I am with you. You make me a better person than I could ever be without you. Today will be the best day of my life. I will honor and cherish you until the day I die. All I am really trying to say is thank you for every moment you have given me. I can't wait for the moments yet to be. I LOVE YOU Zoe, thank you for agreeing to be my wife. I will do my best not to ever let you down.*
>
> *-Sully-*

Zoe was sobbing when she opened the note, but by the time she finished reading it she was smiling and happier than she had been in a long time. She planned on keeping the note forever, and reading it any time she felt down. Zoe carefully folded the note, and tucked it into her brassier next to her heart.

She was getting impatient, and could not wait for Janet to return and tell her it was time. She heard the engine slow and then stop. A huge smile covered her face, because she knew that the time had finally arrived.

Two minutes later Janet came bursting through the door. She asked "are you ready? We wait two minutes, and then go."

Zoe calmly answered "I'm more than ready. I've been waiting for this day for over two years."

Janet asked "what did the note I told you not to read say?"

Zoe took the note out of her bra and handed it to Janet. She read it and then clutched it to her chest and said "what a rare and wonderful man you have found. I need to make sure Ron hangs around with him a lot, maybe some of Sully will rub off on him."

Zoe laughed and said "I'm afraid you have tons of work ahead of you with Ron, but I think that he is worth the effort."

Janet handed the note back to Zoe. She folded it again, and put it back next to her heart. There was a knock on the door, and Janet giggled like a school girl. She said "It's time Zoe, let's go get you married to that wonderful man."

The ceremony was held on the front deck of the boat. When they walked out and Zoe saw Sully a tear of joy rolled down her cheek. She thought that the boys looked very handsome in their tuxedos accompanied by the hats and boots.

Zoe and Janet walked slowly to them, and when they were there Sully took both her hands in his after she handed her bouquet to Janet. Sully whispered "you look like an angel."

Zoe smiled and squeezed his hands. Neither of them had really heard a word of the ceremony. They were lost in each other's eyes. They said their respective 'I do's', exchanged rings, and the only thing they both truly heard was Shawn saying "I now pronounce you man and wife, you may kiss the bride."

It was a kiss to cherish, their first as husband and wife. They were both as happy as humanly possible. Zoe hugged everyone there, even Juan the deck hand. She thanked the Captain. And then grabbed

Sully and hugged him tightly. She smiled at him, and said "I love you Husband"

Sully kissed her passionately and said "I love you too, Wife"

They both heard the pop of champagne, and kissed again. As soon as they toasted their union the engine of the boat started and they were headed back as husband and wife.

They moved to the stern deck, and the four friends talked and laughed on the ride back. It was fifteen hundred hours, Janet told them that the dinner reservations were at nineteen hundred, so they all would have a chance to relax and change before dinner.

Zoe asked that everyone wear the same clothing that they were currently wearing for the wedding dinner. No one felt it was proper to deny a request from the bride.

By the time they got back to the hotel and in their rooms it was almost sixteen hundred. Sully had picked up Zoe and carried her from the moment they got out of the limo, until he laid her down gently on the bed in the honeymoon suite.

Zoe said "I love you Mister Mills, you are an incredible individual, and I feel blessed to have you as my husband."

Sully said "thank you Zoe, that was very nice of you to say, but we both know what a jerk I can be. But I promise you here and now that I will do my best to change that, because I love you misses Mills."

Zoe stood and slipped her shoulders out of the dress and let it fall to the floor.

Sully took off his hat and jacket, and Zoe helped him with the rest of his clothing. Sully sat on the bed while he took off his shirt, and Zoe tugged his boots off, unbuckled his belt, and then unbuttoned and unzipped his pants. Zoe ran into the bathroom and started to fill the large Jacuzzi tub. While in the bathroom she took off her bra and panties. She hid the note from Sully in a drawer by the sink.

She returned to Sully who was lying on the bed waiting for her. They kissed and fondled one another for a couple minutes, then Zoe took him by the hand and said "come take a bath with me hubby"

The tub was only half full when they climbed in. Zoe had adjusted the temperature perfectly. She looked through the wicker basket in the corner, and took out some herbal bubble bath, massage oil, and a washcloth. Sully was leaning back across the tub from her watching her every move. He had a big smile on his face and after she put half of the bottle of bubble bath in the tub, she looked at him smiling and said "what's the smile all about?"

Sully said "I'm just sitting here watching my incredible wife play with the bubble bath. I still can't believe it is really happening, and that you are my wife. If I am dreaming, I don't ever want to wake up."

Zoe sloshed over to him and kissed him. She said "Sullivan, you aren't dreaming, and I will be your wife for as long as I live." She reached behind, him rubbing all of her body on him. She pushed the pneumatic switch that turned the water jets on in the tub.

Sully had been kissing her stomach when she slid over him to turn on the jets, and as she slid back down slowly, she slipped him inside of her. They made intense passionate love in the tub.

They were so involved in their passion, they didn't notice, or even care, that Zoe had put way to much bubble bath into the water. The bubbles were sloshing out of the tub by the gallon. By the time they came to their senses the mound of suds that had spilled out of the tub was a layer six inches deep that covered the bathroom floor, and spilled out into the bedroom. When they finally noticed the mess Zoe turned off the jets and opened the tub drain. They walked, carefully shuffling through the slippery suds, to the shower. They were laughing at the mess they had made, then they rinsed off in the large shower stall together.

Their intention was to take a nap together before dinner, but the emotion of the day overcame them and they continued the consummation of their marriage in the shower. Unlike normal love making sessions in the shower, the hotel had a tank less hot water heater for every room, which meant that there was an infinite supply of hot water, and they would not be prompted to end their lovemaking by the water getting cold.

They collapsed together on the floor of the shower with the water still running. They laid like that for several minutes with the water still beating down on them.

They were interrupted by a knock on the door. They exited the shower and put on hotel robes. They held hands as they carefully crossed the bathroom floor. There was a second knock on the door, and a faint voice on the other side said "room service".

Zoe sat on the bed, and Sully went to the door. Sully looked through the peep in the door and saw a waiter with a cart. He stopped the waiter at the door and signed for the rolling cart, having no idea what it was, or who ordered it. Sully rolled the cart in, took off the hot robe he had put on, and quickly swept the cart with the frequency detector he had left on a sofa table near the door. This one was made to look like a calculator, and worked as one.

When Sully determined that the cart was clean he lifted the table cloth and looked at the bottom tray, and then he knelt down and looked at the underside of both trays. He said to Zoe "it's clean, but I have no idea who sent it, do you?"

Zoe was almost asleep on the bed and had watched him sweep the cart. She shook her head, and then replied "maybe Ron and Janet, other than that I wouldn't have a clue." She winked at him and licked her lips, then she said "maybe you should sweep it again, but bring it closer first."

Sully smiled at her, grabbed the frequency detector, and rolled the cart to the foot of the bed. He jumped onto the bed and said "your turn, without the robe."

Zoe laughed and kissed him, then she said "anything for my new hubby." She stood and seductively dropped her robe. Zoe put on quite a show for him as she moved around the cart scanning for listening, or video devices. She bent over, making sure that her ass was facing him, and slowly looked underneath both levels of the cart.

Sully didn't think it was remotely possible, but he was fully aroused again. He got off of the bed and went over to her. He lifted Zoe to her feet and kissed her. He said "thanks for sweeping the cart so thoroughly, I think we should see what we were given."

Zoe opened the note and read it aloud. It said:

Hey guys,

Congratulations on your marriage, we thought you might need these things. Don't forget dinner with us at nineteen hundred at "Comida del Sol". Thank you for making us a part of your special day. We both love you guys very much. See you soon.

- Janet - & - Ron -

p.s. – don't use too much bubble bath in the Jacuzzi tub.

There were three plates on the cart, each covered with a stainless steel dome. They were each marked with numbers. Zoe pulled the lid on number one. The plate contained one dozen Oysters on the half shell. There was a post it note that Zoe read aloud. The first note read: "*just in case you need help getting in the mood*".

Plate number two was uncovered to reveal a bowl of melted chocolate, aerosol whipped cream, and hand cuffs with no key. This note read: "*just in case you need a little motivation*".

The final plate was uncovered, and it revealed four cans of 'Red Bull' energy drink, and a bottle of vitamin supplement B – twelve. The final note said: "*just in case you need to recuperate*".

Sully and Zoe had laughed as each plate was revealed, and laughed harder when each note was read. Sully was hungry, and so was Zoe. They fed each other oysters with the miniscule forks provided. Zoe dipped the last one in chocolate, and sprayed a dollop of whipped cream on top. She scooped it up with her tiny fork, and offered it to Sully.

He pulled away and said "get that away from me, you weirdo."

Zoe ate it, and said "mmm, we should have tried this earlier."

Sully twisted his face like he himself had eaten the oyster parfait, then he said "you're gross."

Zoe jumped on him and wrapped her legs around his waist. She kissed him deeply, probing his mouth with her tongue.

Before he realized what she was doing he kissed her back just the same. Then he figured it out and pulled away and said "I didn't want to taste that in the first place, much less second hand Zoe."

Zoe laughed, and when he laughed with her, looking right at her she made a big 'O' with her lips and breathed right into his nose. She jumped off of him and ran back to the bed. On her way she asked "does it smell as good as it tasted?" Zoe dove onto the bed like she was sliding into second base, and hid under the covers.

Sully headed toward the bathroom, then stopped, saying "I'm going to brush my teeth, and then gargle kerosene to get that foul taste out of my mouth, and my mind. I suggest you do the same if you ever want me to kiss you again, wife." When he walked toward the bathroom smiling, he was looking back toward his wife filled with love.

Zoe had poked her head out from under the covers, to stick her tongue out. He had forgotten about the bubble overflow, and as soon as his first foot hit the soapy marble he fell straight onto his ass.

Zoe roared with laughter and said, breathlessly "watch out there are bubbles on the floor, and it might be slippery."

Sully carefully stood, and then rubbed his butt, with a hurt look on his face. His actions made Zoe laugh even harder, and roll around under the covers.

Sully ran over and jumped on the bed. He straddled her and tickled her ribs saying "if you want to laugh, I will give you a good reason to laugh."

Zoe got serious through her laughter, and said "Sully don't tickle me, I hate it. If you want me to laugh, go fall on your ass again." She tried to roll away from him, but his legs were way too strong. Zoe pleaded with him to stop, and finally was able to turn onto her belly.

Call it instinct, or accident, but when Sully continued to tickle her, she turned onto her back quickly. Her left elbow was up high and hit Sully right on the outside corner of his left eye.

Sully raised a fist, by instinct, but when he looked and saw that it was Zoe, he rolled off of her and held his eye, with his face in a pillow.

Zoe said "oh my God, are you okay Sully?" He was lifting his right, lower leg, and foot by bending it at the knee and repeatedly kicking the bed with it to try to dispel the pain.

Sully didn't respond, other than writhing around in pain. When he moved his head back and forth Zoe could see that the left side of the pillow was soaked with blood. She ran to the closet and grabbed the mission bag that Sully had brought. There was no med kit, and she started to panic.

She threw on her robe and ran back to him. He had stopped writhing, but he had clutched the left side of the pillow tightly to his face.

She said softly "Sullivan, I am sorry, please let me see your eye. I can't help you unless you let me see it honey. Will you please let me help you?"

Sully barely moved, but it was enough to free his mouth from the pillow. He said "just leave me alone, I will be fine. Go to dinner and fucking try to explain why I'm not there."

Zoe remained calm and said "fine, I will go to dinner without you if you let me see your wound, you are bleeding." She wanted to tell him he was bleeding badly, but that would have made him dig his heels in further.

Sully said "just get me a bath towel." When she left to get the towel, he took the case off of one of the other pillows. He walked across the room and looked in the mirror that was over the sofa table by the door. Blood was streaming out of the cut. It made a red river down his face, onto his chest, and onto the floor. The cut was over an inch long, starting at the corner of his eye, and heading toward his ear.

Sully took the pillow case, and wiped the blood off of the wound. He spread it apart with his right thumb and index finger to see how deep it was. When he spread it he knew without a doubt that it needed stitches, and with the amount of blood pouring out he was afraid that he might have a broken vein.

Zoe came back with the towel, and Sully wrapped it around his waist. Before either of them could speak a phone rang. It wasn't the hotel phone, but rather one of the four cell phones that they carried. He heard Zoe rummaging through the closet to find the ringing.

Sully took the opportunity to leave the room. He walked across the hall and knocked on the door across the hall. When Janet answered the door, wearing a hotel robe, she gasped said "oh God Mills what happened!"

Sully said "I slipped when I got out of the shower, and hit my eye on the corner of the tub deck."

Janet ushered him quickly into the room, closed the door, and yelled loudly "Ron I need you in here quickly!"

Ron walked in, wearing only a towel, and didn't even look at them. He said "sweetie I've told you three times that we can't make love again, we don't have time." He finally looked up and saw Janet holding a bloody rag against Sully's head.

Ron ran over to them and asked "what the hell happened?"

Janet answered "he slipped getting out of the shower, and hit his eye on the edge of the tub. It looks pretty bad."

There was a knock on the door, and Sully said "if it's Zoe, don't let her in, and don't tell her I'm here."

He heard the door slam against the wall, and suddenly Zoe was at his side. Sully said "hello wife, I just came over here to see if Ron or Janet brought a suture kit."

Zoe brushed Janet's hand aside to look at the wound again. The bleeding had slowed, and was no longer pumping out like a vascular wound would have. She said to Sully "I don't think there is any damage to the veins, and if I'm really careful of the eye, I think I can close it."

Ron brought the medical kit to Zoe. He said "I almost left this on the plane. I don't know why, but something told me to bring it."

Zoe said "well thank whatever told you to bring it. Ron help me move him into the bathroom where the light is better."

Sully winked his good eye at Zoe and said "just be careful, I don't want to slip and fall into the edge of the tub again."

Zoe smiled at him and winked in understanding of his cover story. She said "it would have been much more useful if you guys had sent that note two hours earlier, you gotta come over and see the mountain of suds in our bathroom."

As they picked him up to head for the bathroom his towel fell off. Sully was as exposed as on the day he was born. He said in a voice just a little louder than normal "Janet, come here once."

When Janet came over to him he said "take a good look, it's likely your only chance to see a real man if you are going to continue to hang out with Ron."

Janet laughed and said "you had better check him for a concussion Zoe, he is obviously delirious." She did look him up and down stopping for a long while on the look down.

Zoe had notice her ogling her husband and said "Janet find all the towels you can, and put them out on the vanity top in the bathroom."

It took Janet longer than it should have to reply. She shook her head to clear her mind of the fantasy she was having, then she ran to the bathroom to do as she had been told.

Ron and Zoe sat Sully down on the towels that Janet had placed on the bathroom countertop between the double sinks. Ron ran back to the main room and grabbed the medical supply kit, (a.k.a. med kit) and then ran back to Zoe.

Zoe acted like Ron was her nurse as she said "I need the Betadine first, and then give me twenty five ccs of Lydicane. After that we will open the suture kit. Have at least twenty four by fours opened and ready."

Janet was fascinated by the proficiency of the two agents as they worked together to fix Sully's eye. She finally asked "what else can I do to help?"

Zoe said "Janet you can find five or six hand towels, then get ten full buckets of ice and dump them in the sinks in here."

When Janet left Zoe went to the bed and grabbed the blanket. She ran back and threw the blanket around Sully's shoulders, and tucked it around him making sure to cover up his genitals, so that Janet could stop staring at them.

She washed the wound with water, then carefully scrubbed the area around it with the betadine. She said "Ron scrub your hands with the betadine." She did the same.

Ron handed her the syringe filled with lydicane and Zoe said "stand behind me and make sure that his head doesn't move."

Sully jumped in and said "hey, the patient has a name, and he is getting pretty fucking pissed off at being ignored."

Zoe was nice but firm when she said "Sully I need you to sit very still, and please be quiet. I love you baby, and I'm gonna fix this, but you have to cooperate."

Zoe carefully shot the lydicane around the gash. She administered three shots above the wound, and three below it. She irrigated the wound with what was left in the syringe.

Ron gave her the pre threaded suture needle, and Zoe began sewing. She started at the corner of Sully's eye. The first two sutures would be crucial, because they were so close to the tear duct. She completed sewing him up in about fifteen minutes. Having Ron there to help her tie off the knots, and cut the suture filament was a huge time saver. Ron cleaned the area again with hydrogen peroxide. Zoe cut six steri-strips to about an inch long, and then covered the wound with them.

Zoe let out a heavy sigh, and kissed Sully, then she very lightly kissed his wound, and finally she kissed Ron. Zoe started to clean up the mess, and Janet pitched in. Ron made an ice pack for Sully, and said "big bad field agent K-O-ed by bathtub. I think that's the headline they'll use."

Sully laughed and said "take your shots, I deserve it. Come on Zoe, make fun of me. Janet, you too.

Janet asked "did you happen to get the license plate number of the bathtub that hit you?"

Sully nodded and said "good one, obvious, but good. Alright Zoe, lay it on me. I saved the best for last."

Zoe gave him a nasty look and left the room.

Sully flashed a baffled look at Ron and Janet, shrugged his shoulders, and said "I have no idea what I did wrong, but I must have done something. Jesus, I just realized that this is how married couples act."

Sully walked to the door, stopped, and said "it's eighteen thirty now, is it a problem if we do nineteen thirty, or twenty hundred?"

Janet answered "I'm sure it will be just fine Sully, when Ron and I walked by the place earlier it was a morgue. So Black would be a fine color." Janet had never seen Sully when he wasn't wearing something black.

Sully said "I'll call you when we start dressing for dinner." Then he left the room.

He walked to their room and knocked on the door. There was no answer, so he knocked again. He knocked on the door every thirty seconds for five minutes. Every time he knocked, he knocked harder, and by the time he gave up he was pounding the door with both hands curled into fists. He sat with his back against the door and yelled "Zoe please let me in, I forgot my key card, because I don't have any fucking pockets." His voice grew louder and louder as he spoke.

Two doors opened after he had yelled in the hallway. A nosy older woman three doors down poked her head out and looked at him, and then the head disappeared. The other door was Ron's.

Ron opened the door, looked down at Sully, and then he asked "are you gonna nap there?"

Sully answered grumpily "pick this lock, or give me your kit. Get me some aspirin too."

Ron ducked into his room to get the items Sully had asked for. Sully was wondering what the hell was going on. Ron came back gave him a bottle of Tylenol and a beer. Sully got to his feet and washed down four of the pills with the beer.

Ron said "sorry buddy, the lock is disabled, but the door won't open. She must have the privacy lock engaged."

Sully dropped his shoulder and asked "you got any clothes that I could borrow?" He let his anger turn to confused sorrow.

Ron came out to the hallway with an armload of clothes and said "this is the best I can do." He handed the clothes to Sully, then said "why don't you come in for a while?"

Sully shook his head and said "no thanks." He dressed quickly in the hallway, and then he said "give me your pick kit, a weapon, a cell phone, and a few hundred bucks, if you can."

Janet had been on pins and needles replaying the event in her mind. She couldn't come up with any logical reason for Zoe to react the way she had, and lock him out.

Ron sighed and said "I know you Sully, and I have no idea what you are about to do, but I can be pretty sure it's gonna be something stupid. As a friend I'm gonna ask you, again, to just come inside my room and cool off."

Sully gave him a stern look, and in an unpleasant tone said "if you're done with the lecture, just go get what I need."

Ron replied "fine, but don't ever say I didn't try to stop you. At least come in and wash up, you still have blood all over your hands and face."

Sully went directly to the bathroom. He had brushed by Janet without saying a word. He was walking a little clumsy in Ron's Ostrich boots, because they were four sizes too big for him. He felt like a clown.

Sully looked at the bandaged gash on his face, sighed, and shook his head. He looked at his reflection as thought it was real, he talked to his reflection, in his mind, and said 'why were you such an asshole. She asked you to stop tickling her, but you didn't. You got what you deserved. Why did she run away? What did you do this time? You look like shit'.

Sully washed himself quickly, wetted his hair with two handfuls of water, dried himself with a towel, and combed his hair with his fingers.

By the time he left the bathroom his mood had turned to annoyed and morose. He walked out of the bathroom and Ron was right there with the items he had requested.

Sully was now in his robot mode, act don't think, and no emotions were allowed. He carefully inventoried the equipment. He un-tucked his shirt and put the pistol in the waistband of his pants, right in the small of his back. The lock pick kit was shaped like a wallet, and he slid into the right rear pocket of the jeans Ron had lent him, the cell phone went into the front right pocket.

He said to Ron "give me one of your key cards for this room." His voice was now cold hard and mean.

Ron said "there is one on the table by the door. Do you want me to go with you?"

Sully was seething, taking big, deep, audible breaths. He walked to the door and picked up the key card. When he was half way out the door he said "no" and slammed the door behind him.

Janet had a look of horror on her face, and said to Ron "I don't know who that was, but it wasn't Sully. He scared me Ron"

They moved to one another and Ron gave her a big soothing hug. He said in a comforting voice "even I don't know who he is when he's like that. I went through almost all of the same training that he did, and I wasn't trained to switch into killer mode. He is highly trained, and very, very good at what he does. Maybe now I know why."

I'm gonna knock on Zoe's door, maybe she will answer for me.

Sully went down to the lobby, crossed it, and got a cab from the pool of six that were waiting outside the hotel. The cab driver was in his early fifties, overweight, and wore a foot long white beard. When Sully sat down in the backseat, the Santa cabby said "where to buddy?"

Sully snarled "Virginia Beach Airport, private planes terminal." He was projecting his attitude through his voice, but Santa didn't get it, or maybe didn't care.

Santa smiled as he looked at Sully in the rear view mirror. He said "you got it buddy. Private plane terminal, pretty swanky, I've only ever been there one other time. Some rich prick lawyer had a Gulf Stream out there. Man, I would have given my left nut to see the inside of that thing, but the jerk just paid the fair and gave a shitty tip. Why is it that guys with loads of money are the tightest assholes around? I'll tell what I think it is...."

Sully stopped him right there by loudly saying "shut the fuck up and drive the car." The statement was straight to the point, and it worked. Santa didn't say another word for the rest of the cab ride.

On the way Sully took Ron's cell phone out of his pocket and called the hotel. He asked for room number eight thirty one, the honeymoon suite. The phone rang three times, and Ron answered the phone laughing as he said "honeymoon suite, how may I direct your call?" He could hear laughing in the background, and his blood started to boil.

Sully growled in a barely audible level "what the fuck is going on?"

Ron answered "hey Sully, come on back. It was all a big misunderstanding. Zoe felt really guilty about busting your eye open, but she is fine now." The laughing had stopped as soon as Ron said his name.

Sully was confused, and still very angry, when he said "put Zoe on the phone." He didn't know what to say to her, and was doing his best to calm down.

The smile had left Ron' voice when he said "just a minute Sully, Zoe's gonna pick up in the bedroom." Twenty seconds later he heard the click of Zoe picking up the phone. She softly said "I've got it Ron." Then there was the sound of Ron hanging up the other extension. Zoe softly said "Sully, are you okay?"

Sully was not ready to give in to happiness just yet and answered "yes, hold on for a minute." He told the cabby to pull over, and he got out. He went to the driver's window, and said to Santa "just wait here while I finish this call." He walked in front of the cab about twenty feet. He leaned against a streetlight pole and said "I'm here." There was still anger showing in his voice.

Zoe said in almost a pleading voice "please come back to me Sully, I will never be able to tell you how sorry I am for hurting you. When I realized how close you came to losing an eye because of me, I freaked out. I didn't let you in because I couldn't face you then."

Zoe waited for a response, but there was none. She continued trying to win back his love by saying "I love you Sully, please forgive me and love me back. Just tell me what to do to make this better, and I will do it, anything." By the end of her comment, she was pleading with him.

Sully softly said "I'll be back in twenty minutes or so, make sure that no one is in our room but you. Then we will talk, if you let me in." He snapped the phone shut ending the call.

Sully walked back to the cab in a slightly better mood. He got in and said "back to the hotel."

Santa did a u-turn and headed back to the hotel. On the way Sully did his best to change his mood. Lucy had a lot of 'splaining' to do when he got back.

The closer they got to the hotel, the better his mood got. When Santa stopped the cab in front of the hotel he meekly said "the fare is thirty seven fifty."

Sully handed him a hundred dollar bill and said "keep the change, take the Reindeer out for dinner." He left the cab and walked into the hotel.

He scanned the lobby, as he always did. He was trained to scan any room he entered, to identify possible threats. He saw Rady in a corner pretending to read a newspaper.

Sully walked nonchalantly to the bank of elevators. When he got in he pushed two, and seconds later he was exiting on the second floor. He ran down the hallway to the left until he found the set of stairs. He ran down the stairs to the lobby level.

Sully quickly circled the lobby around to the spot where Ron had been. Rady was gone from his lookout, so Sully made a bee line for the elevators. He caught up to Ron forty feet from the elevators.

Sully snuck up behind him and put him in a choke hold. He said in a disguised voice "give me your wallet." Then he let him go.

Rady spun around ready to fight. When he saw it was Sully he smiled and laughed. He said "you're a prick Mills, you scared the shit out of me."

Sully shook his head and said "did you really think I didn't see you sitting in the corner when I walked in? I'm gonna have to spend a lot of time with you, shaking that valet rust off of you."

As they got on the elevator together Ron said "I guess so, I had no idea you even saw me. I haven't had my guard up for a long time, and you just proved that it's time to."

Sully replied "you have to learn to spend each day as if you're being stalked. It's the only way you can say sharp. You only get one slip up in the field, and then you're taking a dirt nap."

Ron nodded his head in understanding. When the elevator stopped, and they got out on the eighth floor, they walked shoulder to shoulder down to their rooms. Sully stopped about four doors short of their target and Ron did too.

Ron said "now what's up?" He was wondering how Sully and Zoe were so in love, when their relationship was so tumultuous.

Sully reached behind his back and handed Ron his pistol. Then he unloaded his pockets giving him the rest of his things. He said "I owe you a hundred bucks, and when you get back to your room be ready to go to dinner in about thirty minutes if you can. One more question, what is going on with you and Janet?"

Ron answered "I don't know, but when we met it was like we had known each other forever. I really like her, and she's really pretty, don't you think?"

Sully smiled and replied "that's why I asked, she is very pretty, but she must need glasses or something to like your homely ass." They both laughed together, and then Sully leaned against the wall and took off Ron's boots. He handed them to him and said "take your clown shoes and give me a couple minutes alone before I go in to see Zoe."

Ron left and went into his room using the key card that Sully had just returned to him. Sully took a deep breath and went to see Zoe. He knocked lightly on the door, and it swung open immediately. Zoe wrapped her arms around him and hugged him like she hadn't seen him in years.

Sully hugged her back, but his hug was wary and somewhat platonic, kind of like a person would hug their grandmother.

Zoe held him for a full minute, and then took his hand and guided him into the suite. They sat down on the dark brown suede sofa. Zoe kissed him deeply and lovingly. Sully kissed her back, but his kiss was awkward, and detached.

Zoe looked him in the eyes and started to cry. His damaged eye sported a deep purple bruise, and was almost swollen shut. She said through tears "Oh my God your eye looks terrible. I could not be sorrier Sullivan. You could have lost your eye because of me, I feel terrible."

Sully softened his disposition, and replied "I've been thinking about what happened, and I need you to know that I am mostly at fault for what happened. When I was tickling you, you repeatedly asked me to stop and I didn't. When you turned over and hit me, it was an accident. I actually think that most of the blame should fall on me."

Zoe hugged him again and said "thank you Sully, but I can't blame you at all for what I did. I love you so much I feel empty when we are apart."

Sully then broached the larger issue by saying "I love you too Zoe, and I feel the same way when we are apart. What really made me mad was that you locked me out, I fail to see anything logical in your doing that."

Zoe looked at her lap said "right then I didn't think I could see you. I held myself together while I stitched your wound, but after I was done and you started joking about it I broke down for a while, I didn't know if I was feeling mad, sad, or remorseful, I just knew I couldn't see you right then. I finally went to Janet and Ron's room to find you, and they said you had just left."

Sully lifted her chin, looked her in the eyes and kissed her lightly. He said "Let's just put this behind us and move forward. We can never lock one another out, no matter what, and I'm not just talking about doors. Now let's get dressed and go to our wedding reception."

Zoe hugged him tightly and said "I promise Sully, never again." They kissed deeply and got ready for dinner, dressing in their wedding clothes.

As they walked to the door Zoe said "Janet told me you really scared her earlier, so maybe tread lightly around her tonight."

Sully replied "I keep forgetting that she is from ops, and doesn't truly understand our end of things. To her 'sanction' is just a word on a piece of paper. I will try to be nice Honey."

Zoe said "I know you will Sweetie." They both smiled and laughed at calling each other by pet names.

They crossed the hallway and knocked on their friend's door. Ron answered the door and ushered them in. He said "Janet is just about ready. Can I get either of you a drink while we wait?"

Zoe asked for a bottle of water, and Sully a beer. Ron brought the drinks and said "that is one hell of a shiner Sully. I bet that hurts like a son of a bitch."

Zoe replied "keep it up Ron, and you're gonna find out exactly what it feels like."

They all laughed, and then Ron stopped. While Zoe and Sully finished their laughter, Ron realized that Zoe wasn't kidding.

Janet came out to join them and walked immediately to Ron and sat on his knee. She asked "are you guys okay now?"

Zoe answerer "we are better than ever Janet, we both talked it out and realized we over reacted to the situation because of the extreme amount of emotion that we were experiencing."

Sully followed up by saying "besides, now I will have a really cool scar to remember our wedding day."

They all laughed and decided to head out for dinner. Ron went to the coat closet by the door and took the wedding presents. Sully called the limo driver and told him they were heading down.

They all climbed into the limo and the driver asked "where to?"

Sully said "We planned on going to Comida Del Sol, unless you have a suggestion Paul?"

Paul answered "Del Sol is okay, and it's the only choice if you're set on Mexican food, but you can do much better."

Sully turned to group and said "well what do we all think?"

They talked about it for a minute, and then Zoe answered for all of them saying "Paul take us to the best place in town that's not too crowded."

Paul said "yes ma'am I know the perfect place." He started the engine and drove to the outskirts of town. Twenty five minutes later, he pulled in the circular driveway of 'Nicko's Taste of Home' a quaint little Greek restaurant set on a hill overlooking the city. It was an older brick building with vines growing up all sides of it.

The ladies went up to the doors first while the men talked to the driver and got the gifts. Sully said to Paul "I would like you to join us for dinner."

Ron said "yeah, there is no sense of you sitting out here in the car, besides, if the place stinks, we can give you shit."

Paul said "it's against company policy, but you know what, why not. Thanks for the invite, I'll park the car and meet you inside."

Sully and Ron met the ladies at the door, where they were ogling the naked Grecian statues, and cracking jokes. As they walked up to them the girls started laughing harder. Sully just shook his head.

Ron took the bait and asked "what's so funny?"

Janet tried to stifle her laughter when she answered "Ron go stand by that statue and let me get a picture."

Ron turned and saw the statue and blushed. He smiled, turned back to her, and said "I'll show you all you want of that pose later, let's go eat."

They went in and walked up to the hostess counter. They place was busy, but not crowded. Sully started to talk but was cut off by a large robust woman in a blue blouse and white pleated floor length skirt. In a thick Greek accent saying loudly "hello, I am Maria Pattoules, you must be Mills wedding peoples, Pauly tell me you come to celebrate wedding with us, how nice. And here is now Paulos."

Paul walked up and Maria put him in a bear hug, then pinched his face and said to him "Paulos you such a nice boy, so handsome. Why you are not married, all the time you bring me married peoples, but you not bring me your wife."

When Maria walked away bellowing for a waitress Paul looked at Sully and said "now you know why I didn't want to come in."

They all laughed and Zoe said "thank you Paulos, I have a feeling that this is going to be a night to remember."

Paul replied "I guess that would be one way to look at it, the Pattoules' are certainly memorable." A pretty dark haired waitress came over to them and said "I am Iris, I will be one of your waitress'. Please follow me to the back room, we are setting up a wedding table for you." Then she went to Paul, and whispered something in his ear, then she gave him a suggestive look.

They all followed Iris to the back room where three of the kitchen staff were finishing the setup of a long narrow table with seven place settings. She sat Sully and Zoe at the head of the table, Ron to Sully's right, Janet to Zoe's, and Paul next to Ron. The table was adorned with candles, and a large arrangement of fresh flowers surrounded by seven pomegranates.

Iris left them and Sully said “wow, I would hate to have seen what they would have done if they knew were coming with more than twenty minutes notice.”

Zoe asked Paul “why are there seven place settings? There are only five of us.”

Paul answered “you are going to get exposed to a lot of Greek traditions and customs tonight, so don’t be afraid to ask me. The extra place settings are for Nicko and Maria. They will join us for each course to explain it, also the number of people at the bride’s table must an odd number. The odd number is a tribute to the newlyweds union, because the number cannot be divided.”

Janet said “awww that is so sweet.” She was gushing at Ron.

Ron said “where’s the menus, and that waitress didn’t even take our drink orders.”

Paul answered by saying “they are bringing a round of ouzo first, then we all drink and say hopa loudly. Then we can order our own drinks. They will bring nine separate courses, and feel free not to eat what you don’t like, it won’t insult them.”

Maria walked out of the door with a large, grey haired, portly man, in a black suit that had seen better days. He walked two steps ahead of her. He stopped at the table, and waited for her to catch up and stand next to him.

He spoke in a gentle voice that did not fit his size. His English was more broken than Maria’s when he said “hello, I am Nickolaos Pattoules, welcome here my new friends. I wish to you all happiness on wedding day of yours and bride. You all come with my nephew Paulos, so now you are family to me.”

Nickolaos took one of the pomegranates from the table and smashed it violently on the floor, then he said “please you all do, in Greek is very good luck.”

They all grabbed a pomegranate from the table and smashed it on the floor. Nickolaos yelled “hopa”, and when Paul waved a gesture for them to all join in there was chorus of uninspired “hopas” in return.

Nickolaos’ yell started a fury of motion from the kitchen. As he sat next to Paul, Maria moved around the table and sat next to Janet. Two bus boys came out and quickly cleaned up the mess they had made.

Three different waitresses came out carrying the drinks, the first had a serving platter holding seven stemmed shot glasses, and a bottle of ouzo, the second carried two large carafes of red wine, and the third carried the same carafes filled with white wine.

They all introduced themselves formally to Nickolaos, and Maria.

When the introductions were over, Nickolaos raised his glass of ouzo and said "to the happy couple, may the happiness today be forever." Then he drank the shot of ouzo and yelled and emphatic "hopa!" They all followed suit and drank and the shot and said "hopa", Zoe had only taken a small sip of her ouzo, hoping no one would notice.

They all commented on the black licorice flavor of the drink, and six waitresses, three waiters, and a cook came out and stood shoulder to shoulder at the foot of the table.

Nickolaos stood from the table, and then walked over to the lineup.

He introduced every one of them by saying "you must meet my family. This is my daughter Iris, who you already meet. This is Nicoleta, also my daughter."

At each introduction he stood behind the person and put his hand over that persons head. Next he put his hand over a woman roughly his age and said "now you see the sister of my wife, Barbara." He moved on and said "this is daughter of sister of my wife, and niece to me, Bethania. Now you meet Eva, who is also daughter of Barbara."

Nickolaos moved along and continued "this be Maria, sister to Paulos, and cousin to all of us." He moved on to the men and started with "This is my son Isaak, and this is Gabriel, also my son," This is Adam, husband to Bethania, and finally there is Artemus friend long time to me. My brother Markos will come later here to play music for you."

They all awkwardly said hello to the Greeks, and then they broke ranks and scurried off to their appointed duties. Zoe said to Maria "you have a wonderful family."

Maria replied "Thank you Zoe, soon you too will have a family to make you happy. I can see in your eyes this is true."

Moments later the first course came out. It was stuffed grape leaves, and everyone agreed they were delicious. Nickolaos and Maria described the origin and meaning of each dish as it came, and were truly gracious hosts.

After a mouthwatering baklava for dessert, the entire family came out of the kitchen. The men sat at the table while the women stood. Everyone was given a small, china plate with three candy coated almonds. Maria said "this is koufetta, sweet but bitter too like marriage will be, and you get odd number like the plates. This is for so Zoe and Sully cannot be divide." She put the three candies in her mouth and then smashed the plate on the floor. She explained "please do, is for good luck." They all smashed their plates to cheers from the family and shouts of "hopa!

Zoe kissed Sully and said "this is so wonderful, we have to give Paulos a big tip for bringing us here. I almost feel like part of a family."

Sully said "me too." Then he grabbed his large gift box from under the table and said loud enough to be heard by all "I would like to present a gift to my beautiful wife."

There were claps and cheers and the ladies all huddled around Zoe as she tore through the wrapping paper she folded back the tissue paper to expose the used, dented waffle iron everyone in the room that was smiling quickly frowned when she lifted it out of the box. There were murmurs circling the gathering. When Zoe gave Sully a confused look, and he smiled broadly, she knew it was a joke.

Sully said "you told me you like waffles. The guy at the pawn shop said it was the best he had."

Zoe laughed and found the other small wrapped box. Eva and Iris set the large box, and the waffle iron on a table nearby, and hurried back to watch Zoe open the other gift. After tearing off the paper and exposing the box, all the girls leaned in to see what was inside.

Zoe opened the lid to reveal the platinum Vacheron wristwatch. The girls that were able to get a good view oohed and awed, then Zoe held it up in its case for all to see. She took it out of the box and saw the inscription, it read:

> *Whenever you check the time, remember that my Love for you will last for all time.*

Tears came to her eyes and she reached over and hugged him. Then she kissed him and sniffled. She said "thank you for marrying me

Mister Mills." Before he could reply Zoe stood and read the inscription aloud to their 'family' for the evening. There were loud cheers of "hopa" and applause from the gathering.

She gave Sully a small box, and he opened it. Inside the box was hand carved and painted Christmas ornament of a house. If it was a joke Sully didn't get it. Zoe reached in her purse and handed him a note. Sully opened the note and it read:

Sully -

I have been working with the LaRoux brothers, and the plans are filed, the blue prints are approved, and they break ground on the addition in two weeks. I Love you Sullivan, thank you for making my life worth living.

Zoe

Sully stood and offered her his hand. She stood and he kissed her, maybe a little deeper than was appropriate, then turned to face the table and said "Zoe has arranged for an addition on our house." This was met again by cheers and applause.

Nickolaos stood to address the group, and everyone became silent. He said "Iris make for sure everyone have ouzo. I make toast, then we go to main room for dancing." All of the girls scurried to fill the glasses, and when they were filled, Iris nodded at Nickolaos.

Nickolaos raised his glass and said about twenty words in Greek, then translated saying "to the wonderful peoples that we have been honored to make for new members of Pattoules family, and for they sharing most important of days with us. May happiness finds you always, Hopa!"

There was the loudest 'hopa' of the evening, and everyone drank. The ladies, including Maria, mobbed Zoe wanting to see her watch and ring. Sully picked up his hat and moved swiftly toward Nickolaos who was walking toward the bar. He stopped him and said "Mr. Pattoules, thank you very much for sharing your family with Zoe and me, neither of us have one, and this was very special."

Nicko looked at him incredulously and said "what you mean you have no family? Everybody have family."

Sully didn't chose to pick a fight with him, so he changed the subject and said "about the bill for this evening..."

Nicko stopped him mid-sentence saying "tonight we drink and celebrate. Tomorrow Paulos will bring bill." Nicko was looking at Sully's hat and asked "where you get hat like this?"

Sully offered it to him and said "you would honor me by taking this from me as a small personal token of my thanks for this evening?"

Nicko took the hat and put it on. He grabbed Sully into a bear hug and said "you are good boy Sullivan." He turned and left for the bar. The comment made him smile, and then he turned to find Zoe.

Zoe was ten feet away from him and walking right to him. She smiled at him and said "hello Mr. Mills where have you been?"

Sully kissed her gently and said "hiding, I saw you disappear into that gaggle of Greeks, and I was afraid they were coming for me next."

She laughed and said "isn't this fun, it's almost like having a family for a night."

Sully replied "that's what I was just telling Nicko, but he refused to believe that we have no families, but I will always have all the family I need as long as I have you."

They kissed and hugged until Ron and Janet walked up Janet said "we had better get in there before we offend them, I can't believe how much fun this is."

Sully said "it's pretty rare nowadays to find a group of people as genuinely nice as the Pattoules family."

They followed the noise to where the family had reconvened. The men had already moved eight or ten tables to expose a large dance floor. Markos had showed up with his accordion, and when they walked around the corner the whole family laughed and cheered. They were seated at a center table again, and now were finally allowed to order their own drinks.

Zoe finally noticed and asked "where is your hat, did you leave it in the back room?"

Sully shook his head and pointed at Nicko. He said "hop along Pattoules expressed a liking to it, so I gave it to him."

Zoe scanned the room to look and when she saw him in Sully's hat she burst into laughter. Sully smiled at her and said "I actually think it looks better on him."

Those we about the only private words they got to say to one another until they left their wedding reception.

The reception was exhausting Sully and Zoe we required to dance with everyone at least once, there were group dances, individual dances, men only, women only, and any kind of dance you could think of.

If you liked Greek accordion music, Markos was the best, as far as Sully and Zoe were concerned. Of course neither had ever heard Greek accordion music before.

Ron and Janet ran off and hid several times, and Zoe was sure they were off somewhere necking. Sully's eye was a constant topic of conversation, and he stuck rigidly to the slipped and hit the tub lie, even though he was pretty sure no one believed it.

Marko bellowed for Iris and she took herself away from Paulos, and hustled to her father. She went to Nicoleta, and Eva, and they were soon passing out a final round of ouzo.

Nicko stood in the middle of the floor, still wearing his new hat, and loudly said "toast from Maria, then we do Kaslamantiano, we say goodbye to Mills, and they go."

Maria walked over to Nicko and raised her glass. She said "In life we come to meet many peoples, some are good, and some not so good. Today we luck to meet very good peoples, Zoe and Sullivan, and Ronald and Janet. They were good peoples to meet, and they let us to be with them on their most special of days. To Zoe and Sullivan, may they find days like this for all of life." She and Nicko drank their ouzo and said a loud "hopa".

Everyone else drank and loudly said "hopa." Then Markos picked up his large accordion and started playing again. They danced a final dance with Sully and Zoe in the middle of a circle of dancing Greeks, and Ron and Janet. The dance lasted more than five minutes, and everyone was throwing dollar bills at Markos' feet.

When the dance ended Sully threw a fifty dollar bill into the pile, not knowing why. Nicko's family formed a reception line toward the door, with Maria and Nicko at the end.

They filed out with Ron and Janet leading the way, and Sully bringing up the rear. Well wishes, kisses, handshakes, and hugs were given all way, and when they finally left and got into the limo they were all exhausted.

As they started the ride back to the hotel Paul said "I hope you didn't mind me taking you there."

Zoe laughed and said "are you kidding, that was great Paul, we can't thank you enough, you have a wonderful family."

Paul chuckled and replied "you got to see them at their best, trust me, they aren't always like that."

Sully said "well their best is definitely better than most. I have no idea how they can have so much energy, I'm in pretty good shape, and I'm exhausted right now."

Ron agreed saying "I'm glad you said it Sully, the Greeks wore my ass out."

They all laughed and chatted about their favorite parts of the reception. Janet said, in a not to subtle hint that she would love to go back there for a wedding reception, someday.

Ron faked being asleep, and got a hard kick in the shin from Janet. Their laughter finished the ride to the hotel, and before they stopped Sully chuckled and said "Paul, I'm pretty sure we won't be needing the car any more tonight. Pick us up for the airport at nine thirty tomorrow, and again, thanks for tonight Paul."

Paul told them they were more than welcome, and left. They all went up to their rooms, said sleepy goodnights to each other, and went inside.

As soon as Sully and Zoe entered the room. Sully stopped and raised a hand to Zoe in a stop gesture. He took two fingers and pointed to his eyes, and then his right ear. They quickly swept the honeymoon sweet and found six bugs, no cameras. Zoe flushed them down the toilet and asked "why the hell are they bugging us when we go away for a day?" But she knew the answer. They were tracking her through her hip implant to make sure she wasn't trying to run.

Sully said "I don't know, but I could smell it as soon as we walked in."

Zoe was impressed at his aptitude, and asked "how could you know?"

Sully answered "I smelled it as soon as we walked in the door. If you smell and concentrate, you will smell it too."

Sully dug his private cell phone out of his pocket and dialed Ron's. When Ron answered on the second ring Sully said "don't say a word, and bring Janet over here A.S.A.P." Then he snapped the phone shut.

He walked over to the door to watch the peep hole, and drew the thirty eight from his ankle holster.

Zoe said "I've tried Sully, what am I trying to smell for?"

Sully answered "Aqua Velva, or some cheap ass cologne. I can smell it every time I find a bug. I will let you sweep Ron and Janet's suite, and you will smell it, now that you know what you are sniffing for."

Zoe asked "how come I wasn't trained for this?"

Sully answered "I wasn't either, but I started picking it up even in training, sniff the bugs you find especially, that will give you a real sense of the smell you are looking for."

Zoe shook her head in amazement before saying "you are extremely good at this agent thing Mills, much better than any of the others I've worked, or trained with."

Sully saw them crossing the hall and opened the door before they could knock. He ushered them inside and closed the door. He said to both Ron and Janet together "give me your room key." Ron fished it out of his pocket and gave it to Sully. He held it up and nodded at Zoe. She quickly crossed the room and took the card. She scurried to the door and was off to check Ron and Janet's room for listening devices."

Sully walked through the dining room of the suite and opened the sliding glass door. He motioned for them to come over. They all went out onto the patio, and closed the door behind them. He whispered to both of them "we've been compromised, Zoe and I found six bugs in our room, and she is sweeping yours right now."

Sully turned and went to the balcony and called Paul. When Paul answered he said "don't say anything until I am done, we have an emergency, and have to leave tonight. How soon can you meet me back here?"

Paul answered "about thirty minutes."

Sully said "great, I owe you one." He slapped the phone shut and walked to Ron and Janet.

Sully whispered "as soon as Zoe gets back, pack as quickly as possible, saying as little as possible."

Sully knew that the rooms were pre-paid, but he still had to do the automated checkout on the television. Two minutes after he completed the checkout, Zoe returned and nodded at him. She held up four fingers indicating that she had found four bugs in the other suite.

Sully nodded at Ron, and he headed for the door. Zoe tossed him the key card as he passed her. Sully went to Zoe and whispered "I need your pre-paid cell." Zoe found it and handed it to him.

Sully called the front desk and asked for a courtesy car. He was told there was one waiting. He reserved it for twenty minutes from now, and went to pack.

He went into the bedroom, and grabbed Zoe by the arm. He kissed her, then whispered softly into her ear "I'm so sorry Honey, this is not at all the wedding night you deserve."

Zoe nibbled on his ear, then whispered "I don't care, as long as I'm with you. I love you Mr. Mills." She looked at her watch and smiled, then continued with "Besides its one hundred hours, the day after our wedding."

Sully kissed her and winked as his reply. They were packed, changed, and in the hallway in nine minutes.

Ron and Janet were waiting, but hadn't changed their clothes. The four of them walked quickly toward the elevator, but Zoe turned to the right and opened the door to the stairs. Sully nodded at her and pushed Janet and Ron to the open stairway door. Sully brought up the rear, and when Zoe reached the fourth floor landing Sully said "stop for a minute Zoe, let's get a plan together."

When they were all on the fourth floor landing Sully opened his duffel bag and was talking as he handed out weapons. He said "someone is tracking us, hopefully it is just the SSO checking up on us, Zoe and I will take a courtesy car and shake any tail, you guys wait five minutes, then take a cab to the airport. Ron watch for a tail on the cab and call me if there is one."

Zoe jumped in and asked Ron and Janet, very seriously "are you both clear on this?"

They both nodded their understanding, and Ron said "we got it, you two be careful."

Sully and Zoe had slipped on their shoulder rigs, and covered them with matching black Hilfiger golf jackets. The left the others and hurried down the stairs. The lobby was empty. They stopped at the front desk and signed for the car, the clerk called, and a black sedan pulled up to the door.

As they walked to the car Sully quietly said "I want you to sit in the passenger seat, and wait, I have to go pay Paul."

Sully dropped his bag by the car, and walked quickly over to the limo. Paul rolled the window down, and said "hey Sully what's up?"

Sully smiled at him and answered "We got an emergency at home, so we have to fly out right away, and I think you've done your duty for the day." Sully handed him two envelopes one for him, and one for Marko. Then he said "I wrote my cell phone number on the back of your envelope, if it's not enough, call me and I will wire more money to you. Thanks for everything Paul, and Iris, nice to see you again."

As Sully walked away Paul pushed the button that lowered the privacy screen, and Iris asked "how the hell did he know I was back here?"

Paul answered "I have no idea."

Sully hustled back to the courtesy car. Zoe was standing next to the open passenger door. Sully walked straight to her, and hugged her. He whispered coldly in her ear "when I say 'wheel' you grab it and slide into the driver's seat."

Zoe got a chill from the tone of his voice. She just nodded in understanding. They got in as planned and Zoe said harshly to the driver "take us to the airport, now."

The young driver noticed the tone and said "yes ma'am." Then he put the car in gear and started driving.

At one hundred thirty hours the roads of Virginia Beach were basically deserted, so at the first red light Sully said "Wheel."

Zoe reached over and threw the gear shift lever of the car into park, as Sully cut the seatbelt and yanked the driver into the backseat in one fluid motion. Zoe had slid over to the driver seat and put the car back into gear. They had executed the maneuver so quickly that they still had to wait for the light to turn green.

Sully was holding the driver by the windpipe, and squeezing just hard enough so that he could breathe, but not speak. He looked the terrified kid squarely in the eyes and said in a menacing voice "you have to choices here Kid, you can cooperate with us and nothing will happen to you, or you can be a pain in the ass, in which case I will kill you."

When Sully finished speaking, he opened his jacket to show his weapon. The Kid's eyes were already wide with terror, and when he saw the silenced Beretta, Sully thought they would pop out of his head.

Sully lightened his grip enough so that the kid could speak. He asked "so what's it gonna be Kid?"

The young driver croaked "anything you say mister. Eight fifty an hour ain't worth making any trouble, and its Kyle."

Sully softened the tone in his voice just slightly, and said "smart answer Kyle, now turn around and put your hands behind your back." Kyle did, and he cuffed him. Sully jumped into the front seat. He looked back at Kyle and said "lie down on your face." Kyle quickly did as he was told.

Zoe said "they are about a half mile back, and not trying to close. Do know a route to the airport other than the expressway?"

Sully answered "I sure don't, but I bet Kyle does, don't you Kyle." Then he harshly said "Sit up Kyle! You are going to route us to the airport on surface roads." Kyle mumbled something into the seat, and Sully reached back and grabbed the back of his shirt. He yanked Kyle into a sitting position.

Kyle said "I'd be happy to." He looked around to get his bearings, and then he said "two lights up make a left."

Sully said "after you make the turn go four hundred yards, then let me out. Take off slowly and watch for muzzle flashes, then hightail it back to me."

Zoe started to say something, but stopped. It was a tactic that she had been taught too, and it made the most sense in this situation. She made the turn, and three hundred fifty yards later slowed the car to almost a stop without hitting the brakes. Sully pulled a large knife from his shoulder holster, and disabled the dome light in the car with one swipe.

He opened the door and looked for ten seconds, then leapt from the vehicle onto the gravel shoulder. He did a near perfect dive roll, ending up two feet from the bush he was aiming for. He saw the headlights of the tail car make the turn, and when they saw how close they had gotten to the courtesy car, they slowed down to a crawl to let the gap between the cars increase.

Sully eased the Beretta from his holster and made sure that there was a round chambered. He clicked the safety off and, with two silent shots, took out both passenger side tires. Before the car even rolled to a stop, Sully took careful aim, and squeezed off one more shot to take out the passenger side, front window making sure not to hit the agent.

Sully was on them immediately and barked "don't move boys, or I'll let the air out of more than just your tires. Hands up, and give me your weapons, slowly, now passenger first. The first pistol was passed out the window, then the second. Sully threw them on the hood and continued with "now you're back up weapons, same way as before." Each of them handed out small pistols from their ankle holsters. Sully put the small pistols in his coat pockets, and continued "phones, wallets, and cuffs, same way boys." The other items were on the hood a minute later. Finally he asked for the car keys. These he threw on the hood of the car as well.

Sully saw Zoe almost there and he said "I'm gonna ask you a couple questions now, and if you're both honest with me, I will cuff you to the wheel. Play games with me and I will throw you in the ditch." He waited for a reaction, and then asked "which agency do you work for?"

There was a long pause, then the driver answered "we're with you Mills, SSO head to toe."

Sully said "can the fucking jokes, and tell me who sent you and why?"

The driver was serious now when he answered "Director Spyes sent us to keep tabs on that Port broad. He wanted to know why she suddenly took time off, and left town, to fuck that Rady asshole."

Sully thought '*two strikes, one; for calling Janet a broad, two; for calling Ron an asshole*'. He asked "what was your objective when she got to the airport?"

The driver answered "we placed a tracer on the plane she came in, and tapped the existing bugs on the plane. We have a company bird ready and waiting to follow."

Zoe walked toward them as Sully thought '*strike three, you fucked with my plane, these boys were going in the ditch*'. He said "last question, are you the only team?"

The driver answered "yeah Mills, this ain't exactly high priority, keeping tabs on one ops broad."

Sully said "if I find out you lied to me in any way, you better sleep with one eye open for the rest of what will be your short lives. You want to change any of your answers?"

His last comment had truly scared the driver, and he answered by meekly saying "no agent Mills, it's all the truth, man."

Zoe had her silenced Beretta drawn, and trained on the driver. Sully said okay boys, out of the car, slowly, hands in sight."

The agents got out, and Zoe and Sully took turns thoroughly frisking the agents, then hog tied them together in the ditch. Sully said "I'm going to lock most of your gear in the trunk. Snuggle together boys, it's kind of chilly out here."

Sully and Zoe walked back to the disabled car, and Sully grabbed her and kissed her, he whispered "I love you Mrs. Mills" into her ear. Then they searched the car together, all they found was a Taurus forty smith with two extra clips in the glove box, and a bug stuck behind the rear view mirror. Sully thought *'the paranoia of the SSO had no bounds'*, as he crushed the bug under his boot heel.

They locked their issue weapons in the trunk, but took all of the clips, and ammo. They left their wallets in the trunk as well, and closed the lid. They would be in enough hot water for losing their target and being hog tied in a ditch. Any agent that lost their issued weapon, or identification was in deep trouble.

Before they left them Sully said "I will leave your keys with your pilot, have a nice night boys."

They climbed back into the courtesy car and put all of the weaponry that they had taken from the other agents in Sully's duffel in the trunk.

They got back into the car with Zoe driving and headed for the airport on the expressway. Soon after they were back on the main road heading toward the highway they overtook a cab, and Sully saw Ron and Janet in the back. He called Ron on the cell phone, and the cab pulled over.

Ron and Janet put their bags in the car, and climbed in the back seat, with Kyle in between them. When they were back on the road Sully said "I want you guys to meet Kyle, he volunteered to let us use his car for our ride to the airport, say hello Kyle."

Kyle squeaked out a shaky "hello", and sunk back into the seat as far as he possibly could.

Ron laughed and said "take it easy kid, that guy in front is a big blowhard, his bark is less than his bite. You will be just fine."

They all laughed, and Kyle even smiled. The palpable tension had dissipated slightly, and the rest of the ride to the airport passed in comfortable silence.

When they pulled up to the Seneca, they were all shocked to find Chuck standing there.

They all got out of the car and Chuck walked over to them and said "imagine meeting you guys here. Where are my passengers, hog tied in a ditch somewhere?"

Sully had almost forgotten that Chuck was with him when he did the same thing to his tail, a couple of years ago. He laughed and said "you've got a pretty good memory for an older guy."

Chuck walked over to them and showed them a Ziploc bag full of broken surveillance devices and said "I swept your bird three times Sully, and I'm pretty confident it's clean. They had two tracers, one inside each engine cowling, they were the hardest to find."

Sully and Ron had started unloading the bags from the trunk, and Janet had walked over to Zoe and Chuck. Zoe said "nice work ace, you ended up being here for the wedding after all."

Chuck laughed and said "I actually called your hotel last night, but you were out. I thought about calling your cell, but I didn't want to bother you guys."

While the boys loaded the plane Zoe introduced Janet, and then regaled him with all of the details of the wedding, the Greeks, the gifts, and the circumstances that brought them together. Chuck laughed heartily when she told him about the reception, and said he was really sorry he missed it.

Sully and Ron came over to them with an un-cuffed Kyle. Chuck grabbed Sully gave him a quick hug, then he said "congratulations, it was even money on you showing up."

Zoe punched Chuck playfully in the shoulder and said "watch it buddy, I knew there was never a doubt. Besides, Sully had told me once that he couldn't swim that well, that's why I picked the ceremony to be on a boat."

They all laughed except Kyle who was still frightened, and confused. Sully said "Chuck this is Kyle, our driver. I want you to wait here an hour, and then go with him to un-cuff your passengers. He knows where they are, here are their keys." He handed Chuck the keys to the disabled agent's car.

Chuck nodded his understanding, and said "you guys better get out of here while you can, I'll call you when I get back."

They said their goodbyes and boarded the plane. Zoe took the pilot's seat, and Ron was in the cockpit as co-pilot so that Sully could brief Janet on the flight home.

Sully sat down in one of the plush chairs, and said to Janet "the agents that were chasing us were sent here by Spyes to keep tabs on you, not us."

Janet's reaction was what Sully expected, totally shocked. She was incredulous when she asked "why on earth would he send a team to follow me?"

Sully answered "Janet you are the lead agent on a mission that begins tomorrow evening, and you left town with all three of the SSO agents assigned to the mission. If you think about it from Spyes perspective, you would wonder what the hell was going on, wouldn't you?"

Janet mulled it over for a long moment then said "I guess I was too involved with the wedding and Ron to realize it, but you're absolutely right Sully."

Sully said "I just think you needed to know, what you do with the info is up to you. I'll go get Ron."

Janet quietly replied "thank you Sully."

Sully just winked at her and headed toward the cockpit. He went in and said "Ron, let me sit with my wife." Ron got up without saying a word, and left the cockpit, closing the door behind him.

Zoe smiled at him and said "hi hubby thanks for coming to see me." Then she asked "what did you have to brief Janet about?"

Sully answered "that team of agents wasn't on us, they were on Janet."

Zoe's eyes got wide and she stopped for a minute to think about it, then she said "I would never have thought of that, did you?"

Sully answered "not at all, I assumed they were after us as soon as I smelled them. When I asked who sent them and why, I was shocked when they told me about Janet, guess who sent them."

Because he had asked her to guess, she knew it wasn't Weathers. Zoe furrowed her brow and hoped it wasn't McMillan, so she guessed "was it Spyes?"

Sully smiled at her and said "very good, I guess her boss doesn't trust her very much. But, like I told Janet, running off two days before a mission, with both SSO field agents, definitely raises some red flags."

Zoe shook her head and said "I really hope we didn't get her into too much trouble."

Sully said "me too, I didn't know her much before this trip, but I really do like her, and enjoy her company."

Zoe sadly said "all we can do is hope for the best, let's have dinner with them at the house tonight and talk it over, what do you think?"

Sully shook his head and replied "I don't think that's such a good idea Zoe, if they have a team on her, we will just dig her in deeper."

Zoe said "you're right, let's just spend half an hour with them at the house when we get back."

Sully replied "I agree, but not too long, we are gonna have to sweep everything when we get home, and I mean everything. You can take the opportunity to train Janet. I have about three extra detectors in the vault. How much flight time do we have left?"

Zoe said "about twenty minutes, why don't you go get them."

Sully smiled and let out a little laugh and replied "I would rather you use the cabin intercom, I really don't want to walk in on anything."

Zoe laughed and said "they are kind of like rabbits in heat right now aren't they. I will call them." Zoe put her headphones back on and pushed the com button. She said "would you two come up here for a minute please."

Sully knew it was probably his imagination, but he thought he could hear scrambling for clothing.

It was twenty five feet from the back of the passenger compartment to the cockpit, and the longer it took them to get there the more Sully and Zoe smiled and snickered. A full two minutes later the cockpit door slid open with Ron and a blushing Janet standing there.

Ron said "what's up?"

Zoe apparently noticed the unintended sexual connotation of what Ron had said, and burst into laughter. It was infectious, and tension breaking, and suddenly they were all laughing along with her without Janet and Ron knowing why they were laughing, or what they were laughing about.

Sully quickly explained that when they landed he would sweep Zoe's truck and bring it back, they would leave the plane tied down for the time being, and they would go to the house and sweep everything.

Ron said "I can keep Janet with me and teach her how to use the frequency detector, starting with her car." Then he asked "Sully, do you have an extra detector at the house?"

Sully answered "I've got three in the vault, I will start in the garage, Zoe can get started in the house, and you and Janet can take your time with the vehicles." He continued planning saying "after everything is cleared, we can sit and talk some more."

Zoe said "we are about five minutes from final approach so go back and have a seat, and one more thing." Zoe waited for a couple of seconds, then continued "we were never above three thousand feet, so officially you are only in the half mile high club."

She put on her headset and called the tower.

Ron and Sully both chuckled as Janet turned red and left. Ron followed her shortly thereafter.

Sully put on his headphones, and when Zoe was done talking to the tower, he said "that was pretty ruthless Zoe, hilarious, but ruthless."

Zoe replied "I feel horrible, but I just couldn't help myself."

When they had landed and taxied to a tie down spot, Sully exited the plane and ran to his private hangar. He slid the left hangar door open, and unlocked Zoe's truck. It took him five minutes to thoroughly sweep the truck, and he was surprised to find that it was clean.

He drove quickly back to the plane where the others had completed the tie down and had the bags waiting to be loaded. They loaded Zoe's truck in silence, and then they started the drive to Sully's house.

Sully had given Ron his frequency detector so he could teach Janet the basics on the ride home. Sully put his right hand out to Zoe as he drove, and she put her left in it. He played with her wedding ring then squeezed her hand. Zoe leaned over and put her head on his shoulder for a few seconds.

They got to the house twenty minutes later, and they went to work. Sully unlocked his truck on his way to the garage, then entered the garage and went to the vault. He opened it and nothing seemed to have been disturbed.

He found one of his spare detectors, and took out one of the listening devices that he had bought for himself. He turned on the bug and checked the detector. Everything checked out, so he carefully swept the vault. He spent three minutes in the small space, and he considered the vault clean.

Sully searched all over the rest of the garage and still found nothing. The garage was clean too, and Sully was betting that the house and his truck would be clean as well. For some reason they were tracking Janet's movements. It could be as simple as he had surmised earlier, that it was too close to a mission to be running off, but for some reason Sully felt it was something deeper, much deeper.

Sully went back to the vault and took out a bug again and activated it. He stuck it to the side of a can of gun oil that was on his workbench. It would be easy to find for an agent, but a good test for Janet.

Sully went out to see the progress Ron and Janet were making on her car, and his truck. He walked up to Ron who was enjoying watching Janet squirm all around the cab of the truck, still in her black dress, and Sully had to poke him in the arm to get his attention.

Ron was startled, but quickly put his right index finger to his lips. He opened his left hand to show Sully what they had found in Janet's car. One bug and one old dirty tracer was all that they had found. Sully whispered in Ron's ear 'put them back where you found them'. Ron nodded his understanding, and left to replace the devices in Janet's car.

Sully headed toward the back deck of the house to find Zoe, and she was just coming out of the back door when he reached the steps. They smiled at one another and walked up to each other and embraced. Zoe whispered in his ear "I still can't believe we are married, you have made me so happy Sullivan. You will never know how much you have touched my soul."

Sully kissed her intensely and then replied in a whisper "Zoe, before you I didn't even know I had a soul. You taught me what love is Mrs.

Mills. Besides, I finally decided to marry you because we wouldn't have to buy new monogrammed towels.

Zoe pinched him on the arm, pouted, and then walked back into the house pretending to be mad, but he knew better. Sully quickly swept the deck for devices and when he found nothing he went into the house.

Zoe was in the kitchen finishing her sweep. Sully walked by her and pinched her butt on the way by. She swung to slap him, but he ducked and she missed. Sully went to the refrigerator and took out the carton of orange juice. He made sure she was watching, then took a drink straight from the carton, then put it back.

Zoe gave him a dirty look, and then looked away. Sully went over by her and watched as she swept the room for surveillance devices. Twice she turned to him as if to say 'what?' each time Sully just smiled at her. He followed her into the living room and sat in a leather recliner and watched her.

Five minutes later Zoe said "there is nothing in here Sully, the whole house is clean." She came over and sat in his lap, and then asked "why are you following me around and watching me baby?"

Sully answered "I still can't believe you are my wife, if I'm dreaming I don't want to wake up."

Zoe kissed him several times, and then she pinched his arm really hard. Sully winced and said "geez Zoe I know I'm awake now, you didn't have to pinch me that hard."

Zoe said "only half of the pinch was to let you know that you are awake and that we are most definitely married." She kissed him again, and then said "the other half was for drinking from the juice carton, you know I hate that."

Sully said softly "let's get Ron and Janet out of here so we can christen our home as husband and wife." He kissed her, and then she jumped up and grabbed his hand.

Zoe smiled and said "hurry up hubby. Let's get this done."

They walked out of the side door and found Janet and Ron kissing next to Sully's truck. Sully let the screen door slam and the bang brought them back from wherever they had been very quickly. Janet jumped back and would have fallen if Ron hadn't caught her.

Sully laughed and said "oops, door slipped out of my hand, sorry about that."

Zoe was not laughing. She shot him a dirty look and said "Ron why don't you take butter fingers and unload the Toyota, the house and garage are clean. Janet come on in the house, I will make some coffee."

The ladies went in the house and the men went to unload the Toyota. On the way down the Truck, Ron said "your truck is clean too Sully, why did you have me put those back in Janet's car?"

Sully answered "that tracer was covered with dirt, and the bug was an older model. I'm sure they were on that car for quite a while. It would have raised more suspicion on Janet if they were suddenly gone."

Ron nodded in agreement and said "good idea boss, I guess that rules out sex in the car."

Sully smiled and laughed, then he asked "did you two really do it on my plane?"

Ron answered "Just a little bit, then we got called to the cockpit. I can't explain it, but whenever we're alone, we are all over one another."

Sully said "well you better make sure her place is off limits until this mission is over, I'm still trying to figure out why they would have put a team on her."

They were able to get all of the gear out of Zoe's truck in one large trip. Gear and personal bags that were Ron's and Janet's got put in the trunk of Janet's car. Everything else was carried into the house. They dropped the bags in the back room. Sully went into his weapons bag and pulled out the two weapons that he had taken from the tail agents. Both were thirty eight snub nose revolvers. One was a Taurus, and the other was a Smith and Wesson. Sully put one in each of his jacket's pockets, and then they went to join the ladies in the kitchen.

Sully poured Ron a cup of coffee, and then he poured one for himself. He carried his mug to the table and sat down. Ron stayed by the coffee pot and leaned on the counter.

Zoe smiled and said "hi fellas, I was just calming Janet down. For once I had to agree with Sully, that the only reason they put a team on her was because she was with us two days before a high priority mission."

Sully jumped in and added "we all just have to act normally until this mission is over. Janet, I left a bug and a tracer on your car. It would raise too much suspicion to remove them right now. Same goes with your house, we are going to have to leave any devices in place for the time being. If you want to be with Ron tonight, I suggest you go to a hotel, using Ron's car."

He looked at Zoe as if to say 'do you have anything to add?'. Zoe said "When this is over I can talk to Weathers, to see if I can get Spyes off of your back Janet."

Sully reached into his pockets and pulled out the small frame pistols. He laid them on the table and said "I found you some belated wedding attendant's gifts. They are actually from the agents that were tailing Janet, but they preferred to remain anonymous."

Zoe laughed and injected "how nice of them. I find the generosity of stranger's heartwarming, especially when they have a pistol pointed in their face."

They all laughed, but Janet looked troubled about the weapon. She had gone through weapons training with the SSO, and was proficient in several types of weaponry. She asked Zoe "do you carry a purse gun?"

Zoe answered "Janet, I always have a weapon on me or in my purse. It wouldn't hurt for you to get used to carrying one, nowadays you never know whose lurking. You might end up running into an overzealous agent, or worse, someone like Ron."

Zoe and Sully were the only ones who laughed now. Ron said "It is a good idea Janet, and it would make me feel better knowing you were armed. As far as running into someone like me, there isn't much chance, I am one of a kind."

Sully almost spit coffee through his nose, and they were all laughing as he choked and coughed.

Ron and Janet left, leaving the newlyweds truly alone for the first time after their wedding. It was oh four thirty, and they were exhausted. They showered together, but agreed to get some sleep before they made love. It was just comfortable to soap one another and be close to one another.

When they were dried off they climbed into their bed, and held one another. Zoe had kissed his eye in the shower and told him again how sorry she was. She wasn't telling him she was sorry for the cut, and black eye, she was saying goodbye. Zoe kissed the back of Sully's neck, and a single tear rolled down her cheek.

They finally woke up at fourteen hundred hours, it was the best, and deepest sleep either of them had gotten in a week. Sully had woken up first, he put on a pair of dark green sweatpants and went to the bathroom to relieve himself, and then he brushed his teeth.

Sully went into the kitchen and thought about making a pot of coffee until he looked at the clock on the microwave. He shrugged his shoulders, and got a Dos Equis from the fridge. He went onto the back deck and lit a cigar. They had an extremely long day yesterday, filled with emotional highs and lows. He wanted Zoe to sleep as long as she needed to.

Sully smoked his cigar and ran the events of the past thirty hours through his head. He smiled, frowned, and laughed. While he was thinking he subconsciously rubbed the wound at the corner of his left eye. He stubbed out the cigar and went to the garage to work out.

He warmed up by hitting the heavy bag for five minutes, and then set up the weight bench, leg press, and several dumbbells. He did circuit training on five different exercises fifteen repetitions each, until his muscles fatigued. Then he would reduce the weight on each exercise and do it again.

Zoe walked in right as he finished his second circuit. She was wearing only a sheer silk Victoria's Secret black robe that left nothing to the imagination. Sully was shimmering with sweat in the well-lit garage, and the musky smell of his sweat was the only aphrodisiac she needed. She opened her robe and walked over to him.

Sully had seen her walk in and smiled at her suggestively. When she walked over toward him he grabbed a towel off of the wall wipe off some of the sweat he had generated. Zoe stopped him by wagging a finger and shaking her head. She walked over and rubber her bare chest against his.

They made wild frantic love in the gym. By the time they were spent, they were equally bathed in sweat. They laid right where they collapsed, and napped. They were sexually fulfilled, content, and deeply in love with one another.

It was just after sixteen hundred hours when Sully woke up alone on the rubber floor of the gym. He put his sweat pants back on and went into the house. He took a bottle of water out of the fridge, and took a long drink. Zoe was nowhere to be found, Sully looked in the driveway, and her truck was gone. Sully shrugged his shoulders and went into the master bedroom to take a shower.

He showered and put on jeans, a tee shirt, and, of course, his boots. Zoe still wasn't home and he was curious, but not worried. Usually she would leave a note if they were home together and she went out, but today she hadn't. He thought about calling her, but didn't want to play the role of worried husband on the first day of their marriage.

He waited for half an hour while drinking a beer, and when Zoe hadn't come back yet he decided to run into town. If he ran into her on the way, his pretense would be going to get her flowers, which he planned on doing.

Sully drove his truck slowly through the Safeway parking lot. Zoe's car was not there. He went in and bought a wedding card, and a bouquet of mixed flowers, he had the florist box them and add what she thought was appropriate. He got back in his truck and thought for a minute.

Sully finally decided he was being foolish, but since he was out, he drove to Culpepper to take care of the plane and pay the bill. The route he needed to take went right by the house, and his hopes were dashed when Zoe wasn't there.

Sully arrived at his hangar twenty minutes later, and having called ahead paid off. The tow taxi was ready to back the plane into the hangar as soon as he had slid open the doors. The Seneca was backed in easily, and he told the driver that he would be at the airport office in a few minutes.

Over the past two years he had moved into the small corner office in the hangar. Other than that, there was only a small bathroom in the corner of the cavernous space. Sully had taken two of his large gun safes from his SSO apartment, and had them delivered to the hangar office, the rest he had given to Ron. One contained a full complement of weaponry, just in case. The other contained his files.

Sully had started files on all of the SSO agents and operatives that he had come into contact with, including files on the hierarchy of the SSO. Most of the info contained in the files was just hand written notes. He went into the desk drawer and took out two new files. He wrote the names of the agents that he had hog tied outside of Virginia Beach on each of the new files, and wrote on the outside of each folder the details of their encounter.

He put the files in the file box corresponding with their last names alphabetically. Sully looked at the file box dedicated to Zoe, and decided not to open it today. He would always come here when he was off mission status, and Zoe was gone on a mission. He would spend hours reading and writing about their days together. Zoe's file contained all that he knew about her, but not everything.

He left and locked the hangar, and then Sully headed for home. His hopes were dashed when he pulled into the driveway at seventeen forty, and she was not there. He took the flowers and the card into the house, now he was getting a little upset. They had one day to be together before a mission, and she had spent it away from him.

Sully put the flowers in a vase, and wrote a quick note on the card. He leaned the card against the vase, he contemplated calling her, but now he was angry. He took a notepad and pen off of the refrigerator and wrote *'I'm out, call me if you feel like being courteous, Sully'*. He took off his wedding ring and placed it on top of the note. He sat for a long minute pondering whether he should, and finally he took the ring and put it in his pocket.

Sully put on a black Tommy Hilfiger oxford button down, and headed for the truck. On his way out he put his ring back on the note. He was boiling mad as he drove to the rundown part of Bealeton. He parked his truck at Vincent's, and walked the three blocks to Beano's.

It was Friday night at eighteen ten, and Beano's was doing good business. Sully quickly surveyed the room and sized up the eleven people there. The bartender was an old black man. The four at the bar were older regulars, and posed no threat. There was a younger couple at a table that were kissing. The four bikers shooting pool in the corner were already drunk and the only possible threat, any they were his target.

Sully went to the bar and ordered a double scotch rocks with a Corona chaser. When his drinks came and he paid for them with a twenty, he asked for three dollars in quarters. When the bartender came back with his change Sully had already drained the double scotch, and shoved the glass toward the bartender with a fifty dollar bill under it.

Sully said "do that with a Corona every half hour, and the fifty is yours." He took his beer, and walked toward the pool table.

Sully purposely bumped the shooter as he walked by. He placed two quarters in the number one slot, signifying that the next game was his. The shooter tried to intimidate him by saying "we start at twenty a rack around here punk."

Sully just squinted and nodded. He went over to the cue rack and carefully evaluated every stick. The game went on but all eyes were on him. He was not a great shooter, but good enough in his mind, and that's all it took. He was not interested in pool anyhow, he was there to start a fight.

Not long after he came over to the pool table, the game was over. Rather than play the winner, the biggest biker who had sitting in the corner said "sit down bones, I'll take care of the punk."

Sully was racking the balls into a nine ball rack because 9-ball was what the last game played had been.

The big biker that Sully had heard them call Buck said "money first, on the table. He pointed to the table where the other three were. Sully took his money clip out and went over to the table. He made sure that they all saw the large amount of cash he was sifting through to find a twenty.

Sully heard the balls break as his back was turned, which is poor etiquette in pool, but he didn't react as he turned back to the table to see Buck sinking the two ball. Sully stood stoically watching as Buck ran the table. He said with a surly edge "nice game, how about fifty?"

Buck snarled "put it up easy money, I got all night to whittle that wad of yours down."

Sully threw a fifty on the table and racked the balls. One of Buck's lackeys took the bill and went back to the table. Buck looked at Sully and said "spots are ten how many do you want?"

Sully nastily answered "how about I get a chance to hit a fucking ball before we talk about a spot." A spot was a free ball in sequence.

Buck laughed and said "you might as well sit down, it's gonna be a while, chump."

Sully was keeping track mentally, and so far he had been called punk, easy money, and chump. His rage was nearly uncontrollable, but on the exterior he remained cool. He stood, unmoving, staring at Buck while he broke the balls.

Buck ran three balls and set up a combo shot on the nine, when the nine ball wasn't touched Buck said "damn, your shot punk, and you better take advantage of it."

Sully walked over to the table and picked up his fifty dollar bill and started to walk away. The three soon to be wounded stood up from the table and followed him. Buck stood in his path and said "where the fuck you think you're going with my money?"

Sully sneered at him and said "you lost the game. The nine has to be struck on an attempted combination shot, you can forget the fifty you owe me and use it to buy a fucking rule book if you want to play for money, that is if your ugly fucking redneck ass can read."

Buck swung a looping right hook that seemed so slow, that it was as if it was thrown yesterday. Sully stepped into the punch and blocked it with the crook of his right arm, he spun and pushed all of his weight into his Buck's chest, and threw him onto his back. Before he could get up Sully yelled to the bartender "I'll take this outside right now, and if you don't call the cops you can keep that fifty." He was moving toward the back door as he spoke. The bartender nodded in his agreement to the deal.

Larry, Moe, and Curly were still stunned at how quickly Sully had put Buck on his back and just stood there with their mouths open.

Sully was standing with the back door open and whistled loudly with his thumb and index finger in his mouth, then he said loudly "hey ladies, feel free to bring some pool cues with you, it might give you a chance."

Buck scrambled to his feet and grabbed a pool cue and yelled at his gang "come on you assholes, let's kill that mother fucker. Buck rushed to the door and the trance was finally broken on the other three, and they followed.

Sully was standing fifteen feet from the door with a sneer crossing his face. He said "well, I was starting to think you chicken shits weren't gonna have the balls to come out here."

Buck spat on the ground and growled "this little prick is mine, you boys can wait for leftovers." He moved in on Sully wielding the pool cue in both hands. Buck was five feet from him when he raised the pool cue, not unlike he was wielding a Samurai sword.

Sully closed the gap in two quick steps and landed an overhand right to Buck's chin, and ripped the stick from him with his left when he was stunned by the punch. Sully jabbed Buck in the stomach with the butt end of the cue, and he doubled over with a loud "oof!"

Sully dropped the stick, grabbed the back of his head with both hands and brought his right knee up into his face as he pushed his head downward with his hands. Buck was functionally disabled when he stood upright, but that position didn't last long. Sully hit him with a left jab to his already broken nose, followed quickly by a vicious right cross that put him on his back, again.

Sully turned to Larry, Moe, and Curly and said "next, or you can all come at once, up to you gentlemen. He studied them quickly and assessed that Larry and Curly were on their heels and shocked at the efficiency that Buck had been dispatched, but Moe still had a bit of bravado left in him, and took two tentative steps forward.

When Moe moved forward Sully said "come on sweetie, you can take a nap right next to your buddy Buck." The back door to the bar opened and three of the four regulars came out as spectators.

Moe snapped the pool cue over his knee and marched forward swinging the sticks back and forth. Sully laughed and gestured him forward with his right hand.

Curly yelled "come on Deke, fuck that piece of shit up." The small group joined in to cheer Deke on.

Sully was timing Deke's advance, and when he was in range, Sully jumped and executed a spinning leg kick. His kick was marginally off target, but his shin impacted Deke with full force on the left side of his neck. Deke only had time to stagger to his right for a second before Sully swept his legs from under him. Sully had a ferocious look on his face as he knelt over Deke and punched him as hard as he could in the solar plexus.

He stood and was seething, before he could turn to Larry and Curly, he heard Zoe scream "Mills stop right now!"

Sully snapped out of the trance of violence that he was in when he heard her voice. He shook his head and saw her standing next to Larry.

His breathing and heart rate started to slow as he walked over to her and said "what are you doing here?"

Zoe replied "first I was just trying to find you, now it looks like I'm here to keep your immature ass out of jail." She had a sad look on her face.

Sully turned to Larry and Curly and barked "are you two good, or do you want to go?"

Both of the biker's backed up a step and Curly replied meekly "we got no beef with you man."

Sully snarled "smart answer, now go pick up what's left of those assholes and get the fuck out of here." His threat did not go unnoticed, and the biker's gave Sully a wide berth as they went over to tend to Deke and Buck.

Zoe was visibly upset when she softly asked "do you want to tell me why you are here, and why you decided to pick a fight?"

Sully was still quite angry with her. He walked past her back into Beano's as he answered "no." Sully walked up to the bartender who had his scotch and beer ready for him. He slugged down the scotch in one drink and pushed the glass toward him to signal the bartender to refill it. He took a long drink of the Corona, and then lit a cigar.

Zoe came over to him and softly said "do I get a chance to explain what happened?" She was trying to soften his mood with her voice to no avail.

Sully didn't even look at her when he answered with a nasty tone "not right now." He took a long drink of his scotch, and chased it with the rest of his beer. He pushed the empty bottle forward, and it was almost immediately replaced with a fresh one.

Zoe's ire was rising and her soft placating tone was replaced by a nasty one when she said "fine wait here until those bikers come back with guns, and shoot your fucking stubborn ass. You know they will, don't you? Do you remember that sweet promise that you made me? Well right now you are way past jerk, you are being a total asshole!" Zoe turned from the bar and walked away without saying another word.

Sully finished his scotch and put it forward and as the bartender filled it he said with an English accent "your lass is on it, that wanker Buck will be back here soon with more than one gun mate."

Sully said with his mood growing darker "I was counting on that" he had no idea what he was going to do until the barkeep spoke again.

The bartender simply said "if you want to go against four blokes with guns, you go ahead, but that lass that was here for you looks like a bloody good reason to live to me, mate."

Sully thought for a minute then nodded and said "thanks, I think you are probably right." He took the fifty dollar bill from the pool game out of his pocket and gave it to him. Then he said barely audibly "that's for the trouble, and the advice."

Sully left Beano's by the back door, and ran straight into Zoe. He was shocked when she grabbed him into a bear hug, almost lifting him off of the ground. She pushed her face into his chest and said "I love you Sullivan, let's go home so I can explain."

Sully had not even attempted to hug her back, and was still surly, when he replied "go ahead, my truck is three blocks from here and I need the walk to cool off."

Zoe released him from her grip and softly asked "will you just promise me that you will come home now?" Her eyes were wide and wet, and her lower lip was trembling.

Sully answered coldly "I will, just give me some time to cool off." He walked away from her and picked up one of the pool cues. Sully was using it as a walking stick as he slowly walked down the alley toward his truck. He derived some perverse pleasure in the blood on the ground as he walked by it.

Earlier, Zoe had driven to Sully's house formulating a plausible lie. She had spent the day at her SSO apartment trying to release all of her feelings for Sully. After they had made love, and he fell asleep, an incredible wave of emotion had washed over her. Her reaction was to run away from it.

Zoe steeled herself against her emotions, and vowed not to cry ever again. She had made this promise to herself several times. The only one to ever make her cry was Sully. Zoe tried to rationalize that he was no good for her, and she was going to be much better off without him. She knew she was lying to herself, but she had to try to believe it, or she would totally break down.

Her idea to deal with the next twenty hours with Sully, was to fake her menstrual cycle. It would explain her mood, and her not wanting any intimacy. How to hide her true feelings was something she did not have a clue how to do.

She drove to his house, and in the orange twilight of the sunset, the house was dark, as she expected his truck was gone. She walked in and turned on the kitchen light. She saw the flowers, card, and note but ignored them. She went to the back deck and called Ron.

When Ron answered the phone she quickly asked if he had seen Sully, and when he said no she abruptly hung up on him. She called Chuck and repeated the task again, with the same result.

She went to the bedroom and fixed her hair. She was wearing black Luck Brand jeans, a black Wrangler blouse, a light black Columbia windbreaker, and the black alligator Laredo boots that Sully had bought for her long ago in Arizona.

She went out and looked at the flowers and read the note. When she saw his wedding ring, she said aloud "fuck you Mills if you think that will hurt me you're wrong." She took off her rings and laid them beside his. She thought that saying what she had out loud would make her believe it, but she was only fooling herself. Her heart ached like it never had before.

Zoe walked out the side door and tried to decide what to do. First she drove to his hangar, and he wasn't there. She drove back to town and drove by the few restaurants they had been to, but did not find his truck. She cruised the Safeway parking lot and found nothing, then she decided to drive past the Hot Spot, though she doubted he would be there. Again, she had no luck.

Zoe drove to the seedy part of Bealeton, and finally found Sully's truck at Vincent's. She parked next to his truck and went inside, not knowing what she was going to say to him.

The bar at Vincent's was buzzing with activity, and Sully was not there, unless he was in the men's room. She walked to the bar, and her beauty drew the bartender to her immediately.

She said "give me a glass of white wine." Then she asked "what is all the excitement about?"

The bartender answered excitedly "some fool is down at Beano's challenging the whole Koeller gang to a fight."

Zoe put a five dollar bill on the bar and ran out. She knew without a doubt who the fool was.

She was at Beano's forty five seconds later and ran out of her truck without closing the door. Zoe was yelling as soon as she entered the sleazy establishment. She was running to the bar and had yelled only "where's the fight?"

The bartender pointed to the back door, and Zoe busted through it. She saw three men in the fight zone, and five people watching. The man alone was unconscious, and bleeding from his nose. The other man on the ground was also bleeding, but trying to escape the iron grip of Sully's left hand on his hair. His right fist was cocked and ready to explode the biker's face.

Zoe screamed at him louder than she ever had, and possibly saved the incapacitated man's life.

Sully walked slowly toward his truck, thinking the whole way. He finally decided to go back to Beano's and finish what he had started, that would keep him from thinking anyhow.

He picked up the pace to get to his truck and when he turned the back corner of Vincent's he saw Zoe's truck parked next to his. Sully tried to duck back behind the corner, but he knew she had seen him. He strode pointedly back toward his truck, determined to drive back to Beano's and kill all four of the bikers.

Zoe got out and met him halfway. She tried to stop him, but he sidestepped to get around her.

Zoe said loudly "if you are trying to hurt me you can stop, I don't know if you could hurt me anymore. Some ..." Zoe stopped herself because she did not want to fuel his rage any farther.

Sully was not in the mood for a confrontation with Zoe, because it was her that had caused him to act like a child. He got in his truck and drove toward Beano's. He kept looking in the rearview mirror, but Zoe wasn't following. He passed the bar without a glance, and took a side road heading toward Culpepper.

Sully drove through Culpepper to the Walmart on the edge of town. He parked his truck, walked into the store through the lube and tune center, and grabbed a cart.

He went immediately to the sporting goods department and bought a queen sized air mattress with a built in pump and pillows, three cloth sleeping bags with different comfort ratings by temperature, a propane heater, a propane lantern, ten small bottles of propane, a medium sized cooler, and two packages of beef jerky.

On the way to his hangar he stopped at a gas station / convenience store and bought the rest of his supplies. The "supplies" consisted of: a twelve pack of Dos Equis, two bags of Cheetos, one bag of Funions, a package of large red plastic cups, two packages of cigars, a bag of ice, and a fifth of Johnny Walker black. If anyone was ready for a campout, and a night of self-loathing, it was him.

He drove to the hangar, unlocked it, and unloaded the truck of its new found burden. All of the supplies were joined by two pistols and a sawed off, side by side, pistol gripped, twelve gauge shotgun. He parked the truck behind the hangar, and went in to set up camp.

Zoe had almost crashed on three different occasions trying to follow Sully at a sizeable distance with her lights off along the winding two lane highway to Culpepper. When he went into Walmart she was confused until she saw what he had purchased, and thrown into the back of his truck. She continued to follow him, unnoticed. When he stopped at the gas station, Zoe sped past, still with the lights off.

Zoe stopped quickly at the airport office and told them that they had just been married, and needed to get away from their families. Although it was strictly forbidden, the clerk said he would tell the night watchman to disregard them, but he made it clear that this was a one-time event.

Zoe drove past Sully's hangar and parked four hangars away. She called the airport office to let them know where she had left her truck, so they would not call the police. Zoe walked to the corner of the hangar and watched for Sully.

After he parked the truck Sully walked back to the hangar doors, and carried all he could in one trip. He set everything down outside the office door, and turned on the desk lamp just long enough to put the lantern together and light it. Although his hangar was equipped with a full complement of lighting, and electrical outlets, but Sully had decided to pseudo camp. His "campsite" was ready to go twenty minutes later, so he opened the cooler and filled one of the red plastic cups half full of ice, then covered the ice with the whiskey.

He opened a beer and sat on an old milk crate next to the inflated bed. Sully finally had a minute to think, and looked around the hangar in the hissing glow of the propane lantern. He rubbed his knuckles, feeling the pain of the punches he had thrown earlier. It was the very first time that he had let his rage dictate his actions, and Zoe had pushed him to it. Thinking deeper as to the cause of his actions only made him more ashamed of himself.

Sully took a swallow of beer, and was about to light a cigar when he stopped. He hadn't heard or seen anything, it was more like he sensed something. He turned the lantern to low, tucked one pistol in the front waistband of his jeans, and the other in the rear. Sully picked up the shotgun and moved toward the front sliding doors.

The only other point of egress to the hangar was a rear door, but he had parked his truck so close to the rear wall that a mouse would be lucky to get through the space that the outward opening door would permit.

When Sully reached the front sliding hangar doors, which he had barred from the inside, he sniffed the air and detected an aroma that was all too familiar. Zoe was right outside the doors, without a doubt in his mind. Sully let his shoulders slump, and took the bars off of the doors. He pulled the west door open just enough for her get through. He said "come on in Zoe." He walked back to his "campsite" and waited for Zoe to follow him.

Sully turned the lantern up to high, and lit the propane heater. He went to the office and put the shotgun, and the pistol he was wearing in his front waistband on the desk. He un-tucked his shirt to hide the Taurus three fifty seven magnum that was still tucked into his rear waistband. Sully rolled out the desk chair, and put it next to his milk crate.

Zoe walked ten steps in and asked "is it alright if I come over to sit by you Sully?" She appeared to be calm and collected when she was anything but.

Sully was staring straight ahead, and had not looked at her, when he answered softly "suit yourself." He had no idea how to deal with her absence on the first day of their marriage, but he was willing to listen.

Zoe came over and sat in the chair next to him and asked "where do we start?" Zoe was staring at the ground in front of her just like Sully was.

Sully didn't stop staring straight ahead, and softly said "I honestly don't know Zoe. There is virtually nothing you could say to me right now that could make me believe you care about me."

Zoe replied softly "after we made love and fell asleep, I heard a phone ringing in the house. I went in to check, and there was a voicemail on my SSO phone to check in immediately. When I did, dispatch told me Weathers wanted me in within a half hour, level one. I didn't want to wake you, so I got dressed and ran out the door so quickly, that I forgot to leave you a note."

Zoe was watching him for a reaction, but there was none. She continued her lie by saying "when I got to Weathers office McMillan and Spyes were there too. They grilled me for two and a half hours. It was all about the last two days. Where we were, who we talked to, where we ate, how often we used the bathroom, and just about anything else you could think of. Apparently tomorrow's mission is a lot more important than we were led to believe."

Again Zoe paused for quite a while, but there was no response from Sully. She said "I thought about calling you, but you probably would have crashed the meeting and got us in deeper trouble. When they finally dismissed me, you weren't home. When I saw your note and your ring, my heart almost broke and I knew I had to find you."

Sully was stoic and did not speak. As much he wanted to hold her and kiss her, he was unable to forgive her, not yet.

Zoe continued by rhetorically asking "did you think you were proving something to me by beating up those bikers? You were gonna beat one of them to death if I hadn't showed up weren't you?"

Sully got up and went to the cooler and grabbed a beer and opened it. He took a long drink and stood with his back to her, and then he calmly said "I don't know why you wouldn't at least have called on your way home. As far as the bikers, I was just blowing off steam."

Zoe was excited that Sully hadn't called the SSO campus and that so far her lie was intact. She continued by saying "I knew I was wrong not leaving a note, and not calling, but I didn't know what to say that wouldn't upset you."

Sully replied "nothing could have upset me more, or made me think that you really didn't care a damn about me, than what you did today, this is exactly why I never wanted to get married."

Zoe was truly shocked when she asked "are you serious? You are the one who proposed, why did you if you didn't want to marry me?"

Sully answered "I did want to marry you Zoe, more than anything, but I knew that this would happen. I committed that we would be together as one forever, and I knew that it would double the way I already cared for you. I can understand when we are on separate missions, but when we are supposed to be home together, and you leave with no explanation, I don't know any other way to feel than the way I felt today."

Sully walked out of the hangar and lit a cigar. He hadn't wanted to see Zoe tonight, much less explain himself to her. Zoe had always had a way of making him talk when he didn't want to, and today was no different.

Zoe came out a minute later having no idea what to say, so she said nothing. She stood behind him and wrapped her arms around his waist. When he didn't pull away, she held him tighter and stood on her toes to kiss the back of his neck. She whispered "Sully, I'm only going to tell you this once, because I will never have to, ever again. I'm incredibly sorry, and it will never happen again, I promise you."

Zoe could promise him anything she wanted to right now, after all she only had to keep any promise she made for about twenty hours.

Sully said "fine, but I'm staying here tonight. You might as well go home, I'll see you in the morning." He crushed the half smoked cigar under his boot heel, broke her embrace, and went back into the hangar. He went into one of his Walmart bags to get his dinner ready and, as he knew she would, Zoe walked back in.

Sully ripped open a bag of the beef jerky, and took a big bite out of a piece of the dried meat. He chewed without paying attention to Zoe. When she sat in the chair next to him he held the bag toward her.

Zoe smiled at him, even though he wasn't looking at her, and said "no thank you, I had a whole bag on the way over here. Sully would you please come home with me?"

He answered without looking, saying "No, I'll be just fine here. In fact it's getting late, I'm gonna have a smoke and turn in." He walked out to the front of the hangar, grabbing a beer on the way. He smoked his cigar waiting for Zoe to come out so he could say good night, but she didn't. He put his cigar out, finished his beer, and went inside.

One step inside the hangar he saw Zoe on the airbed with only her head, shoulders, and bare arms showing from underneath a sleeping bag. She said "lock the door hubby, I'm gonna camp with you."

Sully smiled for the first time in what seemed to him to be a long time. He said "if I had asked you to stay you would have left, right?"

Zoe didn't answer, she winked at him and motioned for him to come over to her with her index finger.

Sully turned and barred the door.

Sully woke on the airbed half expecting to be alone, but Zoe was there next to him. They had cuddled and talked for an hour before making love, then falling asleep. The hurt feelings of the previous day had antibiotic ointment and a band aids on them, but they would take some time to heal.

It was in the low forties outside and there was a deep chill invading the metal hangar. Sully had ignored the heater the second time it had gone out and was now wishing he hadn't. They were quite cozy under the medium weight sleeping bag, with the heavy weight bag underneath them, but Sully dreaded getting out to add a bottle of propane to the heater.

His stirring on the air bed had awoken Zoe, and she rolled over to spoon with him. The feel of her naked body against his, and her warmth was very comforting. Sully relished these moments that, as of late, were few and far between.

Sully tried to pull away to fill and light the heater, but Zoe was having none of it. She held him there tightly with her arms and sleepily said "don't you dare try to leave, I'm comfy and warm right now. You can fix the heater later, stay here and snooze with me sweetie."

Sully relented and snuggled more tightly into her embrace. She kissed his neck and whispered for him to sleep, but it was no use. Once Sully was awake, he usually jumped out of the bed to start his day, no matter what time it was. He waited until her breathing became deep and regular, and when he knew she was asleep he slipped carefully from her embrace and left the bed.

Sully slipped his jeans and tee shirt, and then filled and lit the heater. His feet were freezing on the concrete floor, and his socks were nowhere to be found. He put on his boots without socks and went to the bathroom to brush his teeth. The clomping sound of his boot heels woke Zoe. She groaned, and knew he was up for the day.

Sully had kept a shaving kit on the plane since he had purchased it, but this was the first time he had ever used it. He went into the small bathroom shaved, brushed his teeth, and washed up in the small sink. Zoe was not asleep, but definitely not ready to get out of bed yet. When Sully put his shaving kit on the plane he grabbed two bottles of water out of the cabinet in the back.

He closed up the plane and went over to the bed. He handed Zoe a bottle of water, and she said thank you, then he handed her one of the convenience store bags and said “this was supposed to be dinner last night, but you are more than welcome to it for breakfast.”

Zoe opened the bag and laughed. It was the bag containing the Funions and Cheetos. She said “just like the Ritz Carlton in New York, I had this once for breakfast in bed there, only it was on a silver platter.”

Sully brought her over a galvanized garbage can lid and said “this will have to do, I don’t want you getting spoiled.” They shared a laugh, then Sully said “I’m gonna pull my truck around to load everything up. Tell me where your keys are, and I will pull yours up too.”

Zoe whined “awe, Sully please come back to bed with me, I’m so cozy and warm.” Then she stopped whining and changed her tone to sultry when she continued “I’ll make it worth your while big boy, I’ve got Funions.”

Twenty five minutes later Sully had everything packed up, and in his truck except the bed and the sleeping bags. He had grabbed his bomber jacket out of the back seat and was nice and warm, except for his feet. He had looked three times around the hangar, but could not find his socks. Zoe was still in the bed snuggled up tightly.

When Sully had found Zoe’s truck and pulled it up to the hangar behind his, everything was ready to go except Zoe. Sully went over to her and sat gently on the bed next to her. She rolled over and asked "are you gonna come snuggle with me now?"

Sully sighed and then answered "I'll make you a deal, if you get that fabulous ass out of bed, I'll order us some breakfast on the way home and go pick it up. After I get something to eat we can snuggle all day. What do you think?"

Zoe laughed and said "Cheetos and beef jerky aren't good enough for you for breakfast?"

Sully shook his head and answered "the last meal I had was Greek food. Cheetos just aren't quite cutting it any more. My stomach is trying to remember what real food is like at this point."

Zoe finally relented and pouted as she said "I guess I don't have the appeal to you that I used to. Grab me my clothes and we will get going."

Sully sighed and said "move over brat, I don't know if I have the energy to satisfy you, but I will try." He took off his jacket and was pulling off his boots when Zoe stopped him.

She said "I'm not in the mood anymore, I shouldn't have to goad you into wanting to make love to me. Give me my clothes, and we can get out of here." By the time she finished her statement her tone was much less than pleasant.

Sully was exasperated and had no idea what to do. He finished taking off his boots, then slipped off his pants and crawled under the covers. He tried to snuggle up to her, but she scooted away. Despite her attitude, Sully was aroused by the thought of making love to her.

Zoe was on the far edge of the bed, with nowhere to go. Sully moved closer yet and spooned into her. He made it apparent to her that he was aroused as he rubbed himself against her and kissed her shoulders. Sully whispered "food can wait baby, I want an appetizer. As far as you not appealing to me, don't ever say that. If I could, I would never be away from you."

Zoe snuggled into him as he spoke and let out a small moan before she said "you appetizer is ready baby."

The metal hanger amplified and echoed Zoe's loud moaning and screaming as Sully had his 'appetizer'. He was worried about someone walking by the open hanger door, but was lost in the moment when Zoe moaned "I need you inside me right now Sully, please now, please!"

Sully roughly flipped her over, and she was more than accommodating to slide up onto her knees to allow him to enter her. They were both lost in each other's passion, and made wild and satisfying love for the first time as husband and wife, without injury.

Zoe finally broke their embrace of passion, and said "and you didn't want to, such a silly boy, that was absolutely wonderful! I want eggs over my hammy, French toast, and hash browns."

Sully smiled and said "Zoe you are the perfect woman. I have no idea why you decided to be my wife, but I have no words to thank you for saying yes."

Zoe practically knocked him off the bed jumping into his arms. She replied, with her voice cracking "Mr. Mills, I told you before that I would have said yes the day we met if you had asked, and that is the honest truth. I have never known love before you, and you fill my soul with it."

Zoe was hugging him so tightly it was hard for him to reply, but he breathlessly said "I couldn't have said it better myself. I feel the same way Zoe."

The hugged and kissed for a short while, letting their love for one another fill them with a warmth that was unexplainable.

Sully said "I kinda noticed that you have two pairs of socks on. Did you happen to borrow mine?"

Zoe put her right index finger to her mouth, playing with her bottom lip. She put the most innocent look possible on her beautiful face and answered, in a baby voice "I dunno, maybe they just landed there cause they knowed my feets was cold."

Sully played along and asked "could I maybe have them jump back onto my freezing feets?"

Zoe started taking the socks off, then stopped and said "you promised me breakfast, right?"

Sully answered "moons over your hammy, French toast, and hash browns, right?"

Zoe smiled and kissed lightly him on the gruesome eye she had given him and said "get me that for breakfast and I will be your slave."

They dressed and left the hanger. Sully decided to leave the air bed and sleeping bags just as they were. They embraced and kissed long and lovingly before leaving in their separate vehicles. Zoe reached into her pocket and pulled out his ring. When she handed it back to him she asked that he never use it as a weapon against her again. He put it on and promised, then they parted after a long deep kiss.

Zoe had a very long drive to Sully's house, not in actual time, but rather in reality. It was ten hundred hours and less than fifteen hours from now she would cease to exist. The wheels had been set in motion, and there was no stopping them. All Zoe had to hang onto was her forming baby.

In Zoe's mind the child she was carrying would set everything right. She could raise Sully's son or daughter in a normal, loving, and supportive environment. She thought that by raising a well-adjusted happy child she could right the wrongs done to her in her horrible childhood. She didn't know it now, but raising Sully's child would be a daily reminder of losing the only man she would ever love.

After their night and morning together, Sully could hardly remember why he had been so angry with her. He called Denny's as he exited the airport and ordered the left side of the menu, then he ordered some from the right. He was starving, and munched on Cheetos as he sped to town.

He brought the two large to go bags into the house and set them on the table. Zoe came running out and started digging through the bags. She looked at everything and started to pout. She whined "you didn't get the eggs over my hammy. Did you forget?"

Sully smiled and gave her the foam container he had hidden in the sink. Zoe opened it and her eyes lit up. She said "I knew you wouldn't forget sweetie!"

They ate their breakfast talking and laughing like an old married couple. Zoe put on a good show, but inside she was getting more sorrowful with every tick of the clock.

After they had cleaned everything up from the table Zoe said "wait right here. She ran into the back room. While Sully had gone to town for breakfast she had changed into sweatpants and a long sleeved tee shirt. Sully got up from the table to get a cup of coffee, and Zoe came back carrying a roll of blueprints with a red bow tied around them.

They sat for an hour and a half doodling on the blueprints, and redesigning the layout. Zoe told him that the LaRoux brothers were ready to start anytime. Then she lied and said "when we get back from this mission I will call them to get them started before we are called out again.

They showered together and then took a short nap. When they woke it was fourteen hundred hours. Sully was meticulous about his mission preparation, and spent almost three hours checking and re-checking his gear and Zoe's.

For this type of black op Sully preferred his black tactical vest. It had over thirty pockets for gear, and three pockets to accommodate pistols. When fully loaded the vest weighed over twenty pounds, but the weight was evenly distributed and hardly noticeable.

Sully carried the vests, and gear bags into the house. Sully went to the back room and took great time and care preparing their clothing. Both of the outfits were the same, they consisted of; black military cargo pants, black tee shirts, black turtleneck Marino sweaters, black socks, black high top Avia cross-training shoes, lightweight black gloves, and black nylon head stockings that had a large single hole to expose only the eyes.

Zoe had used the time to review the plan over and over. She was confident that in flight she could brief the team efficiently. After she finished preparing for the mission she went to the small computer desk they had put in the corner of the small dining room.

She booted up her laptop and downloaded over two hundred pictures from her digital camera, then another seventy five from Sully's. She went through all of the photographs and put them in categorized folders on her desktop. The ones she liked she sent to the color laser printer that was loaded with photo paper.

By the time she had sifted through all of the photos she had printed sixty two, and it was seventeen forty hours. Sully was finally done with his mission prep, and they sat on the sofa shoulder to shoulder looking at the eight by ten photos that Zoe had printed.

They smiled and laughed at all of the great memories they had together, and were never emotionally closer than they were in that half hour in time. The memory of that day would end up haunting Sully for a long time.

They were dressed and ready to go, and at eighteen thirty an agent mobile pulled up in front of the house. Zoe grabbed Sully as tightly as she could and kissed him, first deeply, then soft and sweet.

Zoe couldn't bear to look him in the eyes, so instead put her head against his chest as she said "I love you Sullivan, with all of my heart and soul. I never allowed myself to hope for a man to love me, but you taught me that love is possible for anyone. Try to be safe and take care of yourself." A single tear rolled down her cheek as she picked up her gear and headed for the door.

Sully raced after and caught her at the door. He held her by the shoulders, and looked her straight in the eyes when he said "Zoe, I feel the same, let's just do this job and get back safely. I love you honey, now and forever."

They kissed lovingly, and Zoe left. Sully knew his ride was scheduled for a half hour later, so he went to the garage and triple checked that everything was locked. He checked the security of the cars, and the house, and while he was waiting for the last ten minutes he paged through the pictures again, and then put them neatly face down on the computer desk.

Sully slipped into the heavy tactical vest and picked up his bag. He walked out the front door, locked it, and walked to the end of the driveway to wait for his ride. Twenty minutes later he was at the hanger. He had a scowl on his face and fire in his eyes. Sully was in full 'mission mode' and God help anyone who was his target.

At nineteen thirty Sully boarded a black Gulf Stream that was not part of the SSO fleet. It was loaded with ten people he didn't know, and their team. Sully went straight to the back where Zoe, Ron, Barnes, and Carter were. He sat down without saying a word or acknowledging anyone.

Zoe took the lead and reviewed the exact details of the mission with assertiveness and smugness. She instructed Sully to check Barnes and Carter's gear. He did as he was told and after ten minutes was satisfied. Zoe had left them to start kicking all of the non-essential personnel off of the jet. Ron had gone to the cockpit to assume the copilot's duties, and suddenly there were only seven people left on the jet, and the cabin door was closed.

Barnes and Carter had been whispering to one another the whole time, as Sully stared straight ahead. He looked like a pissed off statue, but Sully had been taking everything in. Carter had called Barnes Darko twice and Jamie once. He had suspected at the start that something was afoul with a mission conjoined with NSA, but now he knew for certain that his suspicions were warranted.

They took off and headed for Jonesport, Maine at precisely twenty thirty hours. Zoe came back to brief the crew on the extras onboard. She told them that the pilot was Rick LaGrange, and the other person aboard was Teri Russell, data specialist. They were both NSA, and even with Ron along, they were again outnumbered.

The Gulf Stream landed at an uncharted airstrip with no tower at twenty two fifty. Two mate black Suburban's raced up to the plane as it came to a stop. They were ushered into the vehicles with their gear almost immediately. They were split into the designated teams, and driven by what Sully assumed to be NSA agents. Nothing smelled right to Sully when this mission was proposed, and now his bull shit detector was working overtime.

Carter tried to start a dialogue by saying "this should be easy if you do your job. I will only need about seven minutes when we get to the data center."

Sully hadn't even looked at Carter, and now was no different. He didn't even acknowledge that she had spoken. He intensely asked the driver "how long until we reach the insertion point?" They were the first words he had spoken since arriving to the hanger.

The driver was a young, overweight, bald, black man who might as well had "AGENT" tattooed on his forehead. He almost disregarded Sully's question, but instead arrogantly answered by saying "twenty five minutes, give or take."

Sully was in the second vehicle and knew that, if his drivers estimate was correct, they were going to be much too early for the shift change. He resisted the urge to call Zoe and tell her to pull over for ten minutes.

Sully pulled out each of his pistols, one at a time, and pulled the slide to place a live round in the chamber of each. Jenna Carter followed his lead and did the same. The first words he had ever spoken to her were "when we get inside follow my lead, and don't hesitate. I don't care if it's a maid with a baby in her arms, everyone in that complex is a target. Kill them all and leave it to God to sort them out, that's the only way we can pull this off."

Carter nodded her understanding, but it was obvious that she was bothered by his statement. The cold, unfeeling tone that Sully had used when speaking to her sent a shiver through her. Sully pulled his mask on, and now looked as ominous as he presented himself.

Ten minutes later the driver turned off the headlights and all of the other interior and exterior lights. Both drivers were guiding via night vision. When the trucks came to an abrupt halt Sully practically dove out of the vehicle and was prone, and invisible next to the chain link fence before any of the other doors had opened.

The team was next to him within a minute, and Sully pulled what looked like a small flashlight out of one of the pockets on his vest. The device was actually an aerosol sprayer that emitted an extremely potent acid. Sully made a hole in the fence just larger than they needed to crawl through.

Sully carefully guided them all through the opening making sure they did not touch the fence. The Intel that they had alleged that the fence might be electrified, and or pressure sensitive. He was the last to go through, and they split into two teams.

The plan was simple, Mills and Carter would take a longer route through the complex, clearing the mercenaries along the way. Millstad and Barnes would take a more direct route, doing the same. Zoe had wished for at least a loving look with Sully, but it was not to be.

Sully led Carter all the way around the large warehouse type building. They had only encountered one guard, and had snuck by him unnoticed. Sully put a silenced nine millimeter round through his ear and yanked the body into some nearby bushes.

He stopped for only a second and activated the tracking function on his watch. Three colored dots glowed, and showed as they should. A yellow dot showed in the center of the grid on the display, and red and green dots were in the upper right quadrant, moving down the display. Sully turned the tracer function off, and hurried to the building.

They reached the North side service entrance, and Sully beat the lock in fifteen seconds. They entered the building and hurried toward the computer room. There was light spilling into the dark hallway ahead and voices coming from an open door. Sully hugged the wall and stopped two feet from door. He pulled a small round mirror with a telescopic handle from one of the pockets on his vest, and expanded the handle to its full length. He used the mirror to peek into what he assumed was the break room. The shift change was in progress. Sully counted at least five mercenary soldiers who were chatting and laughing in the room.

Sully grabbed Carter by the shoulder and whispered "I'm gonna slide a flash puck in there, then we mop up. You start on the right, and we will meet in the middle, Got it?"

Carter simply nodded her head in agreement to Sully's plan. She pulled her silenced nine millimeter Berretta out, and waited for Sully to make his move.

Sully had his silenced pistol out as well, and slid the flash puck with authority into the small room. He squinted as the puck hit the far wall and exploded into two seconds of blinding white light. Sully moved immediately and started acquiring targets. His pistol coughed four times, and four bullets hit four security agents, they all fell to the floor. Carter had fired three times to drop the other two. Sully ran into the room and took no chances, putting a round of ammunition into the head of all six men in rapid succession.

Carter's eyes were as wide open as they could possibly be watching Sully's cold brutality. She watched as he dropped the clip from his weapon and slapped in another in one smooth motion.

Her eyes never left him as he took the radio and bloody earpiece from the nearest dead body.

As he pulled up his mask to put the earpiece in Sully whispered "go watch the hallway." Carter moved to the doorway to do as she was told, and wondered why she had gotten goose bumps when Sully whispered to her, and why she was so sexually aroused by this brutal assassin.

Sully had the radio fitted and clipped to his vest, and then searched the body that he had taken the radio from. He finally found what he was looking for in the rear pants pocket of the corpse. The key card should allow them access to the computer room, and that would allow them to remain silent in the mission, rather than blowing the lock.

Sully moved quickly to Carter standing in the door frame. He pressed up against her and whispered in her ear "let's go find that computer room." He felt her shiver with excitement, and smiled underneath his mask.

They moved through the dimly lit corridors of the complex like ghosts. There were no more encounters on their way to the data storage center. Sully suddenly stopped when the stolen radio crackled in his ear. He held up a fist to signal Carter to stop, and she did, inches from him. A voice came over the radio saying "this is Jenkins, east entrance. It's twenty minutes past shift change, where the hell is my relief?"

While Sully monitored the radio for a response he turned on the tracer watch and saw that the red and green dots were very close to them, ahead and to their left. He waited for a response for two full minutes, and could feel Carter's hot breath on the back of his neck while he waited.

They moved out and three minutes later met the other team at the door to the data storage center. Zoe was working on the electronic lock, and Barnes was standing guard. He wasn't doing very well, because Sully had walked within ten feet of him before he was noticed. Sully nodded at Barnes, then went to Zoe to try the key card on the lock.

Sully put his hand gently on her shoulder and her eyes smiled as she looked up at him. He swiped the key card through the magnetic reader and heard the lock disengage. He pulled the door open, and shoved his half spent clip into the hinged crack between the door and the frame to prop it open.

Carter and Barnes hustled into the room, shed their backpacks, and got to work. Zoe came over to Sully and gave him a big hug. Sully halfheartedly hugged back because he was in mission mode, and Jenkins was on the radio again asking for his replacement.

Sully whispered to her "I've got one of their radios and there has only been chatter from the east entrance guard. I'll check the way we came, you cover to the east."

Zoe pulled off her head stocking, and whispered "kiss me first, cowboy." Sully rolled up his mask just over his eyes and kissed her.

Zoe stared him in the eyes and whispered "I love you Sullivan." She put her mask back on and turned to leave him forever.

Sully grabbed her arm and spun her back to facing him. He whispered "I love you too Mrs. Mills." He winked at her, and let her go.

Zoe disappeared around the corner, and Sully went to watch the corridor he and Carter had come down to meet them. There was no action for over five minutes, and Sully had an odd feeling running through him. He thought 'why would Zoe break mission protocol and act as loving as she did to him? Why did he feel that she was leaving him?' He hated being in the dark, and now he felt as if he were in a black hole.

Sully checked on Barnes and Carter, and they were frantically downloading everything they could into portable hard drives. When they completed the downloads they needed, the plan was to blow the computer banks to kingdom come. They each carried seven pounds of C-4 and the remote detonators needed to complete the job.

Sully hadn't seen Zoe check around the corner, so he activated his watch to find her location. He had expected to see the red dot close to the apex of the grid on the watch, but instead the dot was almost out of range heading east.

Sully did not hesitate to race after the red dot, and flew down the hallway Zoe had been watching. As soon as the red dot was straight ahead of him and within what he estimated to be two hundred yards, Sully's life changed forever.

Sully woke up in a hospital bed three weeks later, and he ached all over. He tried to put thoughts together but was unable to. He fought and fought, but consciousness eluded him.

For three days there was a haze running through his mind. He was finally able to put thoughts together, and tried to recall all of the faces that he had seen or dreamed. Sully recalled the faces of people who had stood over him. There was Ron, Janet, Chuck, Terry, Marie, and Jenna Carter. Nowhere in his fragmented memory had he recalled Zoe standing over him, or even her voice. He was very confused and let himself sleep.

On the fifth day he was awake but very tired and still confused. Sully angrily pulled the oxygen out of his nose, and ripped the intravenous line out of his left arm. He tried to sit up, but failed. Sully took inventory of his body and tried to assess his injuries. It was difficult to move his left leg, and could not move his right arm without excruciating pain. He tried to take a deep breath and realized that he had several broken ribs.

Sully was sweating profusely from the small amount of activity he had done, but he struggled to use his right leg and left arm to prop himself up on the hospital bed to find out what the hell was going on with his body.

He looked down to see that his left leg was in a splint, his right arm in a full cast, and most of the right side of his body was covered in bloody dressings. Sully used his left hand to remove the bandages on his right abdomen and was shocked to see how badly burned he was.

Sully tried to sit up again, but the pain almost made him black out. He laid back for several minutes and rolled to his left side out of the bed onto the floor. The next morning he was told what happened.

Weathers stood five feet from the foot of his bed and debriefed him of the events of the mission. He said "first of all, the mission was a huge success. NSA got more Intel than they had ever anticipated. Someone on your team tripped an infra-red beam that set off a self-destruct for the entire facility, and you were caught in the blast."

Sully took a minute to take it all in, and then asked the question he was afraid to hear the answer to. He said "where is Zoe?"

Weathers was as hard and unfeeling as a rock when he answered Sully by saying "agent Millstad is dead Sullivan, we did all we could, but she was gone when we got to her, we were lucky to save you. Rady assumed you were dead when he found you, but here we are. Personally I think you are too fucking stubborn to die.

He paused for a long moment, then said softly "I am truly sorry about Zoe son, I knew you two were close, and she was the best female agent we ever had." With that said Weathers turned and left the room.

Sully didn't say a word. He closed his eyes and pretended to sleep until the nurse left. When he was sure he was alone he wept for the first time in his life. He allowed himself one minute to grieve, then steeled himself against his emotions. Sully rocketed from grief straight to denial. He felt in his heart that Zoe was alive, and he was bound and determined to find her.

He used his pain as a motivator, and sat up in the hospital bed. He got a little light headed but pushed through it. Sully undid the Velcro ties on the brace on his left leg and took it off. He again pulled his intravenous line out and used the tape that had been holding it in to stem the bleeding.

Sully was amazed at the degree to which he had been burned, and when he bent his left knee the pain was the most intense he had ever felt.

He was close to passing out, but did his best to turn the pain into anger, and he knew how to use anger, he had done it virtually all of his life.

He scowled and stood on his feet. The pain was extreme, but it fueled his anger, and strengthened his resolve. Sully had no clue as to where he was and it was imperative that he obtained that information. He used a rolling I.V. stand as a crutch, and limped over to the wall locker in the room. It was empty, so Sully decided to check another room. It took him over five minutes to cross the hallway. By the time he entered the room across from his he was bathed in sweat.

Sully entered the room and assessed the situation. There was an elderly man in the bed hooked up to a respirator and more life prolonging equipment than Sully could comprehend. He took the chart off of the footboard of the bed and found what he was looking for. He was in the SSO campus medical center.

He was disappointed, getting out of here would be a lot harder than if he had been in a civilian hospital. Sully looked through the wall locker of the comatose man and found a dark blue Reebok jogging suit, matching ball cap, socks, and shoes that were two sizes too small. He looked through all of the drawers in the room. The only useful things he found were a scissors and a scalpel.

Sully used the scalpel to carefully cut through the cast around the elbow. It took him ten minutes to break through the cast enough to wedge the scissors in to start cutting down the inside of his arm, and another five to cut with the scissors down to his wrist. He pulled the cast down and off and saw a four inch, stitched, incision on the outside of his elbow. It hurt to bend his arm, but in the current grand scheme of things, it was a minor inconvenience.

Sully took his time dressing, not because he wanted to, but because he had to. By the time he was dressed he was exhausted. He went slowly to the bathroom to splash water on his face, and when he looked up he didn't recognized the face reflected back at him in the mirror. He had a grey tone to his skin, and it was loose and slack on his face. He looked like a caricature of death. The advantage was that nobody would know it was him.

Sully shuffled down the hallway with his head down. His head was down to hide his identity from any of the staff that might have seen him in his current condition. The shuffle was because it was all he could manage.

Ten minutes later he had covered the one hundred yards to the nearest exit. He pushed on the door and shuffled out into the cool night air. Sully looked around and saw his target, a pay phone about fifty yards away near the parking lot. He took a deep breath of the cool night air and immediately regretted it. He had forgotten about his broken ribs.

Sully made his way down the five stairs, and slowly to the pay phone. He was breathing hard when he got there, and waited a minute before he picked up the handset. He pushed the zero and waited for the operator to pick up. When she did he asked to call Ron's number collect. She came back and told him that they could not call a cellular phone collect, and suggested that he hang up and put a quarter in. Sully wanted to suggest a few things for her to do, but saved his energy instead.

He looked through all the pockets of the jogging suit for change, but found none. He shook his head in disgust, and tried to think of what to do next. Sully was contemplating breaking into the nearest car and hotwiring it, but he doubted he had the strength. He was about to head back inside, when a couple in their mid-thirties stopped next to him and the lady asked "are you alright sir?"

Sully looked at them and squeaked "I don't have any change for the phone." The man reached into his pocket and gave Sully three quarters and a dime.

He said "there you go pops." Then they walked into the medical center holding hands. Sully would normally have been angry, but right now he didn't have the energy. He put a quarter into the phone and dialed Ron's number.

Rady didn't pick up until the fifth ring and sounded annoyed when he answered by saying "hello, this better be good."

Sully cleared his throat and said in a weak gravelly voice "Ron its Sully, I need to pick me up at the campus med center as soon as possible."

Ron was stunned to hear Sully's voice, even though it barely recognizable. He replied "what do you mean Sully, you were in a coma the last time I saw you, how can I pick you up, they are never gonna let you leave."

Sully was now speaking between labored breaths when he said "I'm at the … west entrance by the pay … phone. Bring some aspirin … and a med kit, hurry." He hung up the phone and stood there catching his breath for the next two minutes. He limped to a row of nearby bushes and awkwardly laid down on his left side to wait for Ron.

Sully's breathing had slowed, and his mind was getting clearer every minute. He tried to replay the end of the mission in his mind, and couldn't get any farther than opening the electronic lock on the data storage center.

Ron arrived fifteen minutes later and parked in the handicapped space right in front of the pay phone Sully had called him from. It took almost all of Sully's remaining energy, but he finally sat up. He tried to yell, but it came out as a hoarse whisper. He said "Ron, over here."

Luckily it was almost silent in the parking lot and Ron heard him. He ran over and said "What the fuck are you doing Mills, you gotta go back in and get healed up buddy."

Sully shook his head and replied "not until I check a few things first. Help me to your truck."

Ron took Sully's outstretched left arm and helped him up. Sully put his good arm around Ron's shoulders and allowed him to drag him to his car. When he was seated in the passenger seat, Ron ran around the front of the car and jumped in the passenger seat.

Ron was very concerned about Sully having left the med center, but he was a good friend, and Ron owed him his life. When he started driving out of the parking lot he asked Sully without looking at him "where are we going Sully?"

Sully was exhausted from being put in the car, and it took a few seconds before he could answer "my house, then my hangar."

Ron put his new Subaru Outback in gear and started driving toward Sully's house. He reached into the back seat and grabbed a paper bag. He placed the bag gently in Sully's lap. The bag contained a bottle of aspirin, a half full bottle of Vicodin, and four cans of Tecate.

Sully took four Vicodin from the bottle, and washed them down with half of one of the Mexican beers in one long swallow. He said to Ron "tell me what you know about the aftermath of the mission."

Ron was almost to the house, and said "let's get you inside and settled before we get into that."

Three minutes later they were at the house, and Ron pulled the small SUV into the driveway, Janet came running out and helped Ron get Sully into the house. They took him in and helped him to the sofa.

Sully closed his eyes and caught his breath. A minute later Ron brought him a beer, and pulled the armchair closer to him. Janet stood in the doorway to the living room with a shocked and concerned look on her face. Sully didn't even open his eyes when he again asked Ron "what happened at the end of the mission?"

Ron took a deep breath and answered "when the four of you took off I was ready to follow, but some NSA assholes stopped me. It took me ten minutes to get past them and get a car, by that time you guys were already in the complex. I found your hole in the fence and hurried through it, Sully I'm sorry. You hired me for back-up, and I got there right when the explosions started. Barnes and Carter ran past me as I ran in to find you.

It finally all flooded back into Sully's memory, and he said "Zoe was right ahead of me did you see her?" He finally opened his eyes, sat up and looked Ron straight in his eyes to assess his answer.

Ron simply told him the truth, he simply had to tell him what he had found. He broke Sully's stare and took a deep breath. Ron again looked Sully right in the eyes when he said "Sully, all we found were dismembered burnt body parts, and this. He opened his hand to show Sully Zoe's bent and misshaped engagement ring.

Sully took it from him and calmly said "what agency confirmed her supposed death?"

Janet jumped in and answered "we did Sully, there was more than enough DNA, and we even got some partial prints. I'm so sorry Sully, but there is no reason to doubt that Zoe is gone."

Sully laid back again and closed his eyes. He said to no one "I need to inventory this house, and the hanger before I can believe anything anyone says. Right now I need to be left alone for a while."

Janet brought him some chicken broth twenty minutes later and whispered "Zoe is gone Sully, it hurts me too, but the sooner we get past this the sooner we can move on with our lives."

She left without any response from Sully, and twenty minutes later he saw two SSO cars and an ambulance pull up in front of his house.

Ron came into the living room and said "Sully there here, what do you want me to do?"

Sully weakly answered "find out who the lead is, and tell him I will only talk to him, or Weathers. Give me your weapon Ron, right now." He was a weak, fragile, former shell of himself, but he wasn't going back without a fight.

Ron reached for the Glock nine tucked in his waistband in the small of his back, and handed it to Sully butt end first. Sully reached out, but the weight of the weapon was too much for him. He had dropped it onto the floor and Ron picked it up and set it in his lap. Ron went out the rarely used front door to meet the SSO agents outside.

Sully saw Janet standing by the archway that led from the kitchen to the living room and motioned for her to come over to him. When she knelt next to him Sully asked "are you absolutely certain that Zoe is dead?"

Janet hesitated for a second, then answered Sully's question by saying "I'm certain Sullivan, and I honestly couldn't be sorrier, I loved her too."

The second that Janet had hesitated spoke volumes to Sully, and he dismissed what she had said entirely. He simply nodded his head and she walked away from him and back into the kitchen.

Ron came back in through the front door with an agent behind him. They both walked over to Sully and the agent introduced himself by saying "agent Mills I am Steve Phillips, sub head of agent relations, and a liaison between operations and field services. I am here to take you back to the medical center sir."

Sully croaked "that's not gonna happen Steve, but I will make you a deal. You get the fuck out of my house right now and nobody has to get hurt." He pointed the pistol at Phillips who swallowed hard and left.

Ron came over to him and said "I'm not sure if this is the fight you want right now Sully, why not just go back to the med center for a few days?"

Sully closed his eyes for a few seconds, and took several deep breaths. He snapped his eyes open and said "come over here Ron." Rady walked over and sat in the armchair that he had been in before. Sully whispered the combination to the garage vault to him and whispered a list of munitions and supplies he wanted brought into the house. Ron shook his head and left for the garage. Sully called Janet over and said "I'm not going back to the med center Janet, if you wouldn't mind I want you to order a hospital bed for here in the living room and arrange a private medical staff for me, I will pay for it. Would you do this for me?"

Janet answered "of course Sullivan, but you know they will all have to be SSO personnel. At your level they would never permit private health care."

Sully nodded and replied "just find me people that you think can be trusted." He was cold with her because he thought she was lying to him about Zoe.

Janet immediately got on the phone and started making arrangements. The rush of activity had exhausted Sully, and as soon as Ron came back from the garage with a bag filled with weaponry, he allowed himself to sleep.

Sully had no idea how long he slept, but he woke up in a hospital bed in his living room with a new I.V. line inserted. There was a young nurse taking his blood pressure, and as far as he could tell she was the only one in the house.

The nurse introduced herself as Haley Jaegerton and explained that she was his full time care specialist. Haley explained that she was staying in Sully's house in the back room, at Janet Port's request. She went on to explain that a SSO Doctor was scheduled to come by five times a day.

Sully could feel a pistol against his leg, so he assumed that Ron had done what he had asked. He saw a large manila envelope on the rolling table that he would eat on, and reached over and rolled it over his lap. The envelope contained several ID's and ten thousand dollars in cash. Ron had promised to get the contents of his and Zoe's SSO field lock boxes, but obviously had not yet.

When Sully had finally finished his inventory he asked Haley "where are Ron and Janet now?"

Haley answered "they slept in the master bedroom, then they went home to change and pack some things. They should be back soon with food to re-stock the refrigerator, almost everything in it was rotten."

Sully was confused and said "rotten, Zoe went shopping right before the mission, how could everything be rotten?"

Haley said “I'm sorry sir, apparently no one told you that you were in a coma for over three weeks.”

Sully hadn't been told, and couldn't believe it. Sully thought ‘three weeks, no way, I can't have lost a month of finding Zoe, no way!’ He said “Haley are you sure about that?”

Haley answered “I'm sorry to have to be the one to tell you agent Mills, but I was on the team monitoring you. You were definitely comatose for twenty six days, but even if you hadn't been we probably would have induced coma to deal with the burns you have.”

Sully took a long pause to take it all in, then said “Haley thank you for your help and honesty. If you are going to be staying here you are welcome to bring a friend to stay with you.”

Haley's eyes lit up and she said “are you sure? My boyfriend Chris would love that!”

Sully was already tired again when he answered “I'm certain, and that's the last time I want you to call me agent Mills, call me Sully.” He continued by saying “I've been meaning to get furniture for that room, I will talk to Janet about getting some.”

Haley said thanks and ran to call Chris. Sully let his eyes close and quickly drifted off to sleep, dreams of Zoe ran through his exhausted synapses and in his fragmented mind everything was going to be just fine as soon as he found Zoe.

Chapter 9

Sully awoke to a flurry of activity in the house. Ron was loading the refrigerator with food, Janet had brought in two large bags of luggage and was busy putting things away in his bedroom, Haley was cooking something, and a young man he could only assume to be Chris was helping her.

A man in his early fifties walked through the front door and directly over to Sully. He put down an overstuffed briefcase and said "good afternoon agent Mills, I am Doctor Maxwell. I will be your primary physician while you recuperate." As he introduced himself Haley came over from the kitchen, followed by everyone else. They all seemed as eager as Sully to hear what the Doctor had to say.

Maxwell started by saying "mister Weathers has consented for you to receive your care here because he doesn't want you escaping from the medical center again, and causing further harm to yourself. I'm not sure what you know, so I'm going to list all of your injuries and tell you how we are treating them."

Sully said "lay it on me doc, I just found out about the coma this morning, and I am pretty curious about all of the rest."

Maxwell said "the coma was caused by severe head trauma, and it was necessary to drill two holes in your skull to relieve the intracranial pressure, we don't think there was any significant brain damage, but now that you are awake we will have to do some cognitive testing to be sure."

Ron jumped in and said "you're in for a challenge there doc, any brain tests on Mills are bound to come up negative."

Everyone laughed with the exception of Sully and the Doctor. Maxwell shot a look at Ron that told him to shut up or get out of the room.

The Doctor continued "Mills your left leg has a fracture of the tibia, and your knee was severely dislocated tearing the medial collateral ligament. The tibia has been pinned, and the MCL has been surgically repaired.

Your right arm sustained a fracture to the ulna just below the elbow which has been surgically repaired with a nylon plate and screws." Sully rubbed the incision on his right arm unconsciously with his left hand as the Doctor spoke.

Maxwell then said "the explosive device that you were exposed to was white phosphorus based, and quite a bit of the corrosive chemical contacted your right side from the outside of your thigh up to the middle of your torso. The burns have been sanitized and five days ago were grafted with shark skin. If you have compromised the grafts, I might have to take you back to the operating room and perform the grafting procedure again. Now would be an appropriate time for you to ask any questions you might have."

Sully asked "what would you estimate to be a reasonable time frame for a full recovery?"

Doctor Maxwell was very serious when he answered "that will depend on your level of cooperation agent Mills. If you don't pull any more stunts like you did yesterday, I should expect that you will be fully healed in three months. You will also require four to six months of intensive physical therapy."

Sully nodded and said "thank you Doctor Maxwell, I will do my best to cooperate."

Maxwell spent an hour giving Sully a thorough check up, gave Haley a list of instructions, and left. Soon after he left Ron and Janet came over to his bedside. Janet had a sorrowful look on her face after having heard the list of his injuries, Ron on the other hand was smiling and chuckled before he said "way to go ace, you fucked yourself up good."

Sully's eyes were getting heavy, but he put a small smile on his face when he replied to Ron "you know me bud, I always do my best." He and Ron laughed for a second, then Sully said "Janet, I need you to go shopping for a complete bedroom set for the back room. See how fast you can have it delivered, take a bunch of cash out of that envelope on the rolling table."

The front door opened again and James Weathers strolled through it without having knocked. He looked skeptically at Janet and Ron as he stood five feet from the foot of Sully's bed. He said "I need to talk to Mills alone right now, get the others out of the house too."

Weathers waited until everyone was out of the house before saying "I don't want you to think this means that I approve of your actions Mills, but if being here will help you get healed and back to duty I will let it slide for now."

He walked over to him and put a large envelope on the table next to the other. Weathers stated "I've had your identifications recreated, and there is a replacement cell phone in there for you. Operations will be done processing your lock box tomorrow, and I will have it delivered."

Sully sat up straight, and before he could leave said "Jim I hope you're not messing with me about Zoe, I would hate to have to kill you."

Weathers stopped when Sully spoke, but never turned around. When Sully finished his threat Weathers strolled out the door without saying a word.

Janet came back and grabbed some cash to go shopping for the furniture, and Ron left with her. Haley brought him a small piece of a toasted cheese sandwich and a bowl of tomato soup. Chris was sitting at the kitchen table eating the same lunch.

When lunch was finished Haley told Sully that she had to clean his burns and change the dressings.

Sully said "fine Haley but I've got an errand for Chris to do for me if that's okay?"

Haley said "that would be great, he is out of work right now and would love to help." She turned and said "Chris come over here, agent Mills has an errand he needs you to do."

Chris was maybe twenty two, six foot two, athletic, and good looking. He hurried over to the hospital bed and asked "what can I do for you sir?"

Sully answered "first of all you can start by calling me Sully, then I want you to run to Walmart for me and pick up a television for this room. My thought is a medium sized flat screen with a wall mount. Then I want you to do the same for both bedrooms. Your budget will be three thousand dollars for all of them, do you think you can do this for me?"

Chris was chomping at the bit and said "without a doubt sir, I mean Sully. It sounds like fun."

Sully nodded and told him to take the three thousand dollars out of the opened envelope. He and Zoe had never watched much television, because when they were home together it always seemed like a waste of valuable time with one another. With the prospect of months of healing ahead of him he decided that now would be a good time to install some.

Sully watched Haley walk with Chris to the driveway and talk to him for a minute. They kissed and she came back in as he left for the store.

Haley came back to Sully who said "I need your help. In the future when you are going to change the dressings make sure no one is around. I know how painful this is going to be, and I don't need an audience, do you understand?"

Haley nodded her understanding to him and gave him a shot of morphine through his I.V. line. She went to the fridge and opened a bottle of beer for him and brought it to him. She also knew how painful scrubbing the burns would be.

The procedure took a full twenty minutes, and although he had never flinched or uttered a sound, when she was done Sully was soaked with sweat and breathing rapidly. When his breathing finally slowed, and she was sure he was asleep, Haley changed the bed linens and gave him a sponge bath. With no one in the house Haley took the opportunity to snoop a little bit.

She went into the master closet first to stare at Zoe's wardrobe and shoe collection. Haley was a simple SSO nurse, and had grown up poor. The only way she had made it to the level of nurse was by signing up with the SSO after her Air Force training.

Haley was satisfied with her work, but had expected more than what she was getting out of life with the SSO. She was fascinated by Sully and Zoe, and thought that just the idea of assassins in love was incredibly romantic. She felt guilty about snooping so she went to the back room to finish unpacking.

Chris was her fiancé and he had washed out of initial training with the SSO because he was too immature and hard headed to take orders. He had bounced around construction jobs for the past year, but always ended up quitting or being fired because of his attitude. Haley was sure she loved him, but was hoping for a better future than what was currently on her horizon.

Haley was looking through the refrigerator to see what she could make for dinner for four, and something simple for Sully. He needed to stay on mostly liquids for a while, until he was moving his bowels regularly.

She sat at the table planning menus when she heard a horrible scream come from the living room. It had scared her so terribly that she almost peed her pants. She knew it was Sully, and ran to see what was wrong. Sully was writhing in the bed yelling and screaming incoherently.

Haley ran back to the kitchen and ran water over a tea towel. She wrung most of the water out into the sink, then ran back to put the towel on Sully's forehead. She held his hand and whispered in a soft pleasant voice "it's okay Sully, everything is alright." She whispered this over and over until he calmed down. She had no idea what was tormenting him, but it took her several minutes to calm him.

Janet and Ron got back to Sully's house about a half hour later. Janet immediately saw the concern on Haley's face and asked "what happened? Is everything alright?"

Haley tried to manage a weak smile, but was not able to when she answered "it's okay now, Sully was having a nightmare and it took me a while to calm him down. Right now he is resting comfortably."

Janet dropped her purse and hurried over to Sully's bedside. She looked down upon his battered body and gaunt face and began to sob uncontrollably. She could not get over the tremendous guilt she felt for his condition.

Ron came over and held her, and she buried her face into his chest and sobbed even harder. Ron tried to comfort her by saying "don't worry about Sully baby he is as hard as they come. Knowing him he will be back to his old pain in the ass self in no time."

The commotion had woken Sully, and he said weakly "why is it that every time I see you with Janet she is crying? You gotta quit being such a prick one of these days Ron."

Ron chuckled at the jab from his friend and said "see Janet, he is getting better already."

Janet's crying subsided, and when she turned to respond to Sully, Ron's shirt was wet with her tears. Janet's voice was overflowing with remorse when she asked Sully "please tell what I can do to make you feel better?"

Sully was still under the effects of a strong dose of morphine when he drowsily answered "find Zoe for me." With those four words expressed, he drifted back into a disturbed sleep.

Zoe landed in New Mexico ten hours after the mission was completed. She had flown there with her heart empty and cold, and she was determined to remain that way. She had recounted her life with Sully from the time of the explosion backward to the day they had met.

She knew what she was doing was for the best, but could not come to grips with how her actions had effected Sullivan. The plan had worked perfectly with the exception of Sully running straight into the explosive device that she had dropped to cover her escape.

She was in the arms of two other SSO field agents, and hustled into a black Suburban before the explosion. They had driven about four hundred yards when the vehicle suddenly screeched to an abrupt halt.

The agents and the driver were talking to one another, and on their radios anxiously. The driver made a quick U-turn and headed back to the now smoldering complex as fast as the truck would move.

They were back at the facility and out of the truck ten seconds later. One of the junior field agents, Derek Hatter, stopped, turned around, and drew his weapon. He pointed it at Zoe's chest and said "Stop right there Millstad. Take the tack vest off and lay it down, then take two steps back."

Zoe was stunned by the turn of events, and did as she was told. She knew that the young agent had been ordered to kill her if she made any false move. Hatter moved toward the back of the truck as Zoe took the heavy tactical vest off.

Hatter opened the rear hatch of the vehicle and ordered Zoe to walk toward him slowly. When Zoe was eight feet from him he threw her a set of shackles and ordered her to put them on.

When Zoe was shackled and cuffed to the passenger side rear door. They left the complex. On their way out, on the only road, they passed an identical Suburban, and an ambulance heading to the munitions manufacturing facility at 'break neck' speed. Zoe's heart sank as she realized that something had gone wrong, possibly tragically wrong.

During the flight Zoe was briefed by Jill Ling, from operations. The SSO had arranged an entire new life for her.

Zoe now assumed the identity of Kathy Jackson for the rest of the lonely life ahead of her. The SSO had accessed her sizeable bank account and procured for Zoe a small house and vehicle in Madrid, New Mexico.

Madrid was a small eclectic community between Santa Fe and Albuquerque. It was a combination of the art community of Santa Fe, the people who worked in Albuquerque but preferred to live thirty miles from the city, and high country cattle ranches. It was a place that was easy to blend into, and remote enough to be obscure. These were the exact reasons it was picked for Zoe.

She was given the credentials to back up the job she was given as a second grade teacher at the small school in Madrid. Ling gave Zoe a file that explained her entire back story, and they went quickly over it on the flight.

Zoe changed on the jet, and was given jeans, tennis shoes, a western shirt, and a black leather jacket. Ling assured her that a full wardrobe was waiting for her, along with all of the resources she would need to do her new job.

They arrived at the Madrid house thirty minutes after landing at the Santa Fe airport. As far as Zoe was concerned it might as well be an igloo in Antarctica. She was in no mood to look around the diminutive two bedroom house, and Ling seemed disappointed in her attitude.

Zoe sat at the kitchen table with her and went through the motions of the briefing. She had a month before her teaching job started, which was more than enough time for Zoe to learn how to teach. Ling told her that she was staying with Zoe for the first two weeks, and was required to spend four days a month for the first year to make sure Zoe adjusted to her situation.

Zoe said "if you are staying, I'm going to bed. Which bedroom is Kathy's?" She stood from the table and put her hands on her hips.

Jill answered "down the hall to your right. Sleep well Kathy." Jill was disappointed at Zoe for resenting her. All she was doing was exactly what Zoe had asked for.

Zoe shed her clothing and threw it on the floor with utter disregard. She had done her best to prepare herself emotionally, but it wasn't enough. Now she was all alone and for all she knew Sully was badly injured or dead. There was no going back for her, ever.

Her mood was as cold and bleak as the high desert night she found herself surrounded by, and she could see no light through the blackness that was enveloping her soul.

The first week at home was the hardest for Sully. The pain from his injuries was intense, but the emptiness in his heart was pure agony. He vacillated between wanting to get out of the bed to start searching for Zoe, and needing more concrete proof to believe she was gone.

He tried to be a good patient and friend, but mostly he had become silent and withdrawn. He snapped at Haley every time she tried to get him to do the little bit of physical therapy that she deemed him able to.

He had Ron install a curtain rod on the archway to the living room, and asked Janet to find him dark draperies to segregate the room from the rest of the house. Once they were hung he insisted that they be kept closed at all times.

Chris had done well buying and installing the televisions, and Sully had put him in charge of arranging for satellite service. Everything was installed and working, and after the technician explained to Sully how it operated, the television in the living room was never turned on again.

Sully had called the LaRoux brothers and arranged for Chris to start working for them, but he made it clear that he was to be given no special treatment. He also called Terry and told him about the problems Chris was having, and asked him to spend some time with Chris to give him his own unique perspective.

Almost every time Sully slept he would have screaming fits of anger. Janet and Haley took turns comforting him as he got through them, but it was affecting the entire household.

On the sixth day he asked Ron to go buy him some crutches and a walker. It was a giant blow to Sully's pride to ask for the devices, but it would beat the hell out suffering the humiliation of using the bed pan.

While Ron was out he called him and said "when you get back don't bring that stuff in, I'm gonna try to get rid of everybody first."

Ron replied "whatever you say boss" and hung up the phone. It was more than Sully had spoken in three days. Ron was getting afraid that he was going to lose his best friend to a bottomless pit of despair.

Janet and Chris were both at work, leaving only Haley to get rid of. Sully called to her, and when she came into his room he said "I'm getting real sick of soup and sandwiches Haley, what I was thinking about was a pork roast for dinner, if you left now you could have it ready for tonight. What do you think?"

Haley smiled broadly at him thinking he might have turned a corner. She said "that sounds great Sully. As soon as Ron gets back I will run to the store, what would you like with it?"

Sully answered "whatever you think, if you talk to Dan at the butcher counter he always has great suggestions."

Haley said "if you don't need anything I'm going to freshen up." Sully shook his head and she left him to prepare to leave.

Ron got back twenty minutes later, and walked into the living room to talk to Sully. Sully was sitting up staring out the window when Ron got back. Ron said "the stuff is in the back of my car, what is the plan?"

Sully answered "Haley is running to the store to get a pork roast for dinner, when she leaves you can bring the stuff in. I have got to take a shower and put on something other than this fucking hospital gown."

Ron frowned and quietly said "you don't expect me to help you shower, do you? I mean I consider you a friend and all, but that seems a little above and beyond the call of duty. Why don't you let Haley help you, she has been washing parts of you I never want to come in contact with, she is used to your grotesque body."

Sully scowled at him and said "calm down dummy, the whole point of this exercise is to start doing things for myself. Besides, showering with you is against my personal Geneva convention."

Haley came in and said "hi Ron, I'm glad you're back. Sully wants pork roast for dinner, do you have any side dish requests?"

Ron answered "you know what, I could really go for some of that green bean stuff with the fried onion things on top, you know the beans you only seem to get at Thanksgiving."

Haley laughed and said "you got it that sounds good. Sully do you need anything before I go?"

Sully answered "I can't think of anything, unless you have a shopping list. You might as well get what we need while you're there." Sully wanted her gone as long as possible, he was sick and tired of being taken care of.

Haley left five minutes later, and Ron brought the walker and crutches in shortly thereafter. Sully used the adjustable hospital bed to raise himself into a sitting position and swung his legs over the side of the bed. He said "Ron just bring the walker over here and you can go. After I shower and change I was planning to sit on the back deck. Why don't you run to the "Stop 'n' Go" and get me some cigars, and pick up a twelve pack of Dos Equis too."

Ron said "sounds good to me Sully, I hate to be the one to have to tell you, but you've been a real asshole the last few days. It's nice to see you back to your old prick self."

Sully showed no emotion when he said "spoken like a true friend. You almost made me forget what a jag off you really are Rady."

Ron waited until Sully was on his feet and steady before he left. Sully had disconnected he I.V. at the connection points in the line, and crimped them off, rather than ripping it out again. Ron watched Sully use the walker like an old pro to walk through the kitchen and into the master bedroom.

Ron was satisfied that Sully would be alright, so he yelled "I'm going Sully, I should be back in twenty minutes or so." Sully hadn't answered him, but he was sure he had bellowed loud enough to be heard.

Sully looked through the triple dresser that held Zoe's folding clothes. Nothing was out of place. When he looked in the drawer that held her jewelry he was lucky to be hanging on to the walker.

Sully saw her watch lying face down, with the inscription staring at him, and his knees went weak. He got a lump in his throat so big it was hard for him to breathe. His eyes welled up, and if he hadn't looked in the mirror above the dresser he would have burst into tears.

He saw a shell of what he had once been, and it made him sick. A plan started formulating in his fragmented mind, and he slammed the drawer shut. He spat on the reflection in the mirror and said aloud "no way, this ends now!"

Sully threw the walker across the room and strode into the bathroom and to the shower. On the way he grabbed his old fashioned straight razor from a drawer and took it with him to the shower.

Zoe woke the next day to a cold rainy day in northern New Mexico. The weather was appropriate for her mood, and she went into the bathroom to brush her teeth and freshen up. She found a thick terry cloth robe and slippers in the closet, and put them on.

She went to the small kitchen and found Jill sitting at the table. Jill had made a pot of tea and when Zoe sat down she said "would you like some tea? It's all that was here, I will go shopping later. You can make me a list of anything you want." Jill was purposely being cold and distant to her because of Zoe's attitude from the night before.

It was impossible not to sense Jill's cynical way of behaving, and Zoe knew it was all her doing. She tried to be nice, but it still came out bitter when she said "tea will have to do if it is all we have."

Jill poured her a cup from the pot, then she said "I'm sorry to have to be here, but my orders are to stay with you for the next two weeks. It would go a lot easier for both of us if we try to get along."

Zoe replied "I am truly sorry about last night, but everything went so terribly wrong I got very upset. Would it be possible for us to start over?" Zoe was trying to gain her confidence before she asked her a very important question.

Jill smiled warily and answered "I would love to start over, but I can't help but feeling that I am being manipulated a little bit right now Kathy."

Zoe smiled a genuine smile and said "alright no games. I was hoping you could call in and at least find out the condition of agent Mills. If you do that for me I will try to assimilate into this life the best I can."

Jill smiled back and said "as long as you promise to be honest with me I will make the call." Zoe nodded her agreement and Jill went to her purse to get her cell phone. Her purse was on a small table by the front door, and she made the call from there.

Zoe closed her eyes while Jill made the call hoping for the best. Jill came back to the table less than three minutes later and sat down across from her. She looked her in the eyes and said "I'm terribly sorry Zoe, they did all they could for him, but he was damaged by the blast too much for them to save him. Sully is dead."

Zoe's reaction was the last thing in the world Jill would have expected. She said "well that's much more efficient than a divorce, at least I don't have to worry about him anymore."

Zoe stood from the table and said "I'm going to go get ready, then we can explore the town and do some shopping." She left Jill in the kitchen with her mouth wide open.

When Zoe got to her room and closed the door she shook her head. She knew it was a lie, and it really didn't matter what they had decided to tell her, her future was set in stone. For the time being she just had to grin and bear it. Janet had promised her that she would contact her when the coast was clear, and she just had to bide her time until then.

She spent the day with Jill and they toured the small town of Madrid. Jill took Zoe to a local Doctor for her first pre-natal check up. Then they went out to lunch at a very good Mexican restaurant. They finished their day by grocery shopping, then went back to the small house.

Zoe was determined to make the best of a terrible situation and the events of the day had made her realize that she had one precious thing to keep her going. Sully's child would be born in less than six months.

Ron had just checked out at the "Stop 'n' Go" when his phone rang. He set his bags on the hood of his car and fished the small phone from his pocket. He looked at the caller I.D. display on the phone and saw is was Janet. He flipped open the phone and said "hey baby, how are you today?"

Janet answered "I'd be better if I was with you cutie, but I will be back to Sully's in a couple of hours, how is old gloomy Gus today?"

Ron laughed and answered "I don't know what happened, but he actually got out of his chamber. He sent me out this morning to get him a walker and some crutches. He even sent Haley out to get something special for dinner."

Janet smiled, and it was apparent in her voice when she said "that's great news, maybe he is finally starting to come out of it. Can I talk to him?"

Ron answered her by saying "maybe when I get back, he sent me out for beer and cigars. He told me he wanted to sit on the deck for a while when I got back."

Janet's voice suddenly changed from happy to concerned when she said "Haley was there when you left right? You didn't leave him all by himself did you?"

Ron said "well he had the walker and was able to use it just fine, I sure as hell wasn't gonna help him take a shower."

Janet was frantic and said "oh my God Ron, I can't believe you would leave him alone, please get back there as fast as you can, and call me the minute you get there."

Ron said "don't worry about Sully, he would never do something like that Janet."

Janet was very upset now and said "you don't know him right now, nobody does. Now please just hurry back Ron."

Ron said "I'll call you soon, don't worry." He got in his car and hurried back to Sully's house shaking his head the whole way. Ron thought to himself 'there's no way, not Sully, no way'.

Ron pulled into the driveway and hurried into the house carrying the bags. He put the bags down on the kitchen counter and yelled for Sully. When there was no answer he got a little concerned. Ron looked in the living room, then the master bedroom, and finally the back bedroom. Sully was not in the house.

The final place for Ron to look was the garage. The side door was open and he was dreading what he might find. He walked in slowly and let out a heavy sigh when he saw Sully trying to work out. He said "hey man you are gonna get me in big trouble if you aren't back in that bed when Haley gets back."

Sully replied "I just had to get out of the house and do something. I think I lost twenty pounds of muscle in the last month."

Ron said "well lets go sit on the deck and work on gaining some of that weight back by drinking a bunch of beers."

Sully replied "go on, I'll be there in a minute." He found that there weren't a whole lot of exercises he could do effectively, and his plan was to get Haley out here tomorrow to help him get started.

Ron called Janet on the way back to the house and said "everything is just fine Janet, when I got back he was in the garage trying to work out. I told you not to worry baby."

Janet sighed and said "I'm sorry Ron, it's just that I worry about him right now, he has been very despondent about losing Zoe. No matter what ended up happening today, I still don't think he is ready to be left alone."

Ron was a little irked at Janet for scolding him like a child. He said "fine, I will see you later." With that he ended the call without saying goodbye.

Ron grabbed a plastic bucket from under the sink and filled half full with ice from the freezer. He shoved eight bottles of Dos Equis dark beer into the ice and carried it out onto the deck.

He set the bucket of beers on the table and lit a cigar as he waited for Sully. Ron opened two beers as Sully slowly made his way from the garage to the deck. It was obviously quite painful for him to climb the three stairs, but he managed it just fine.

Sully sat down across from Ron and took a long drink of the beer that was handed to him. He looked Ron straight in the eyes, and very seriously said "I want you to schedule your jump training for three weeks from now, by then I'll be ready to go with you."

Ron replied "that seems pretty ambitious Sully, for Christ's sake today is the first time you got out of bed. Why don't we wait and see what the doc has to say?"

Sully got angry and let it show when he answered "because I don't give a flying fuck what the doc has to say, and you have waited long enough to fulfill your promise to me."

Ron said "I will schedule it tomorrow, now can we just have a few beers together?"

Sully finished his beer and lit a cigar. He grabbed a fresh beer and opened it as he said "tomorrow I want you to do me a favor, take all of Zoe's things to my apartment on campus, and after dinner I want to talk to you and Janet about something."

Ron looked puzzled, but said nothing. Haley's car pulled into the driveway and he chuckled and said "I hope you are ready for an ass chewing from your nurse, because I bet she is gonna be pretty pissed to find us out here."

Sully shrugged his shoulders as Haley walked out the back door with fire in her eyes. She said "just what the hell do you think you're doing Ronald, he isn't ready to be out here sucking beers with you, and why did you take his gown off?"

Ron put his hands up in self-defense as Haley stormed toward him. Sully stopped her by saying "don't blame him Haley, I'm responsible for myself, and Ron had no idea what I was going to do when I sent him out for cigars."

Haley was still looking at Ron when she said "you left him alone too?"

Sully stepped in and said "Haley calm down, there are going to be some big changes around here, and you can go along, or leave. I hate to be cliché, but from now on it's gonna be my way or the highway."

Haley's jaw dropped and she pleaded "Sully believe me, if you start doing too much right now you will regret it. Your burns need a lot more attention, and your bones have just started to mend, start pushing too hard and you are going to end up back in the hospital, or worse."

Sully just shrugged and finished his second beer, then he replied through a large puff of cigar smoke "are you going to cook dinner, or do you want me to do it?"

Haley spun around on her right heel and stormed back into the house, slamming the door behind her. The sound of pots and pans being slammed around emanated from the house soon after.

Sully didn't react to Haley's tantrum, and turned calmly to Ron and asked him for his cell phone. He dialed Jack LaRoux's number from memory and asked him how soon he could come over to discuss the remodel, and how soon he could start the job.

Jack said he was swamped, and that tomorrow afternoon would be the soonest he could get to the house, but he told Sully that as soon as he wanted to start, he was ready to go. They decide on meeting at fourteen hundred hours the next day.

Sully left the table without saying a word to Ron, and although he had gotten quite stiff from all of his activity, he walked into the house with only a slight limp. About as far as his pride would carry him was back to the hospital bed, and when he laid down in it he collapsed into sleep.

Half an hour later Haley parted the dark drapes of Sully's lair and saw him sleeping. She quietly snuck in and carefully reconnected his intravenous line. Sully stirred and pulled away from her a little, and she knew he was awake, but he didn't stop her, and pretended to remain sleeping.

When Sully woke five hours later the world outside of his cave was buzzing with activity. He could hear the voices of all of the people that he had invited to be in the house. At that time he had not wanted to be alone, that time had passed.

He sat up in the bed and realized how much he was paying for the morning's activity. The clothing he had put on was drenched with a combination of sweat and blood. The skin grafts over his burns had cracked open. Sully carefully slid his legs over the side of the hospital bed, and stood next to the bed.

His bad knee gave out a little, and if he hadn't been hanging on to the side of the bed he would have fallen. Sully steeled himself against the nauseating pain and walked out between the heavy drapes and disregarded the gasps, and looks of horror that had replaced the lively banter that had been going on in the kitchen.

He went slowly to the master bedroom holding onto the wall as he went, looking at the floor. When Sully had entered the room and closed the door behind him he sat on the bed. It took him quite a bit of effort to strip off the soiled clothing, and when that task was completed, he was almost too exhausted to stand again.

Haley knocked on the door before opening it just enough to peek her head in, then she pleadingly asked "will you please let me help you Sully, that's what I'm here for."

Sully defiantly answered her by saying "not anymore Haley. The game has changed to my rules. You are here to do what I tell you to and nothing more. If you don't like the new rules you can get the fuck out."

Sully got a burst of adrenaline from yelling at Haley and stood up before he continued by saying "right now I'm going to take a shower. When I am done I want clothes laid out on the hospital bed, and when I go back to the living room you can treat the burns before I dress." With that said he turned and walked naked to the shower.

Sully took one of his 'Marine' showers, and it took only marginally longer than usual because of the burns that he spent extra time washing. After he carefully toweled off, making a white towel pink with blood and water, he put on a robe that he assumed to be Ron's and slowly walked out of the master bedroom.

Sully looked straight ahead with a scowl on his face as the soft spoken conversations in the house stopped. He thought 'let them talk all they want right now there are gonna be big changes tomorrow'.

After Haley had treated and dressed his wounds he ordered her to take out the I.V. line. Sully dressed and sat on the sofa, then he ordered Haley curtly to leave.

Sully was too self-absorbed to join the group for dinner. For the past several days he had been assessing his life and the current situation. First he was analytical and dealt with the facts. Then he was emotional and dealt with his deepest feelings. Finally he was realistic and dealt with his perceived truths.

Sully had finally decide that his initial feeling was accurate, and that Zoe had not been killed in the blast at the munitions plant. He knew for a fact that she was alive somewhere, but she had gone to enormous lengths to simulate a scenario that would make him believe she was dead.

Sully's final decision was that if Zoe wanted that badly to be rid of him, he would move on with his life as if she were dead to him. After that fatal realization Sully was ready to move on with his bleak existence. Sully made a promise to himself, which he almost never did. The promise was to never let anyone close enough to him ever again to make him grieve the way he had for Zoe.

Chapter 10

When the group had finished the dinner he had planned, and he heard the familiar sounds of clean-up, he harshly bellowed for Haley.

When Haley entered his sanctuary Sully spoke to her with no emotion, saying "I want everyone here assembled on the deck in five minutes."

Six minutes later Sully stood from the couch and slowly headed to the back deck. Someone had turned the outside lights on, and he turned them off before he departed the house.

The absence of light preceded Sully's appearance onto the rear deck. The four had sat at the table with drinks in front of them in anticipation of Sully's lecture. Sully crossed the deck and sat on the railing across from them.

Sully looked at no one and everyone at the same time when he said "we are going to make some big changes around here tomorrow, and I thought you all should know what is going to happen before it does."

Sully had grabbed a pack of his cigars off of the table by the back door before he went out onto the deck, and he lit one before he continued.

Sully's voice was almost monotone when he said "the hospital bed will be moved to my apartment on campus, and when everything there is situated that is where I will be staying. Haley and Chris will have this evening and tomorrow morning to pack their things and move out. Haley, I will discuss a schedule with you later, you and Chris are dismissed."

When they had left Sully moved to the table and sat down with Janet and Ron. He asked Ron to go get him a beer, and he quickly obliged him.

After Ron returned with a full bucket of beers and handed an open one to Sully, he asked "are you okay Sully, why would you want to go back to campus housing?"

Sully let out a heavy breath of cigar smoke and answered "I can't stay here anymore, I need to focus on my recovery, and this place holds too many memories for me to concentrate on that or anything else."

Sully paused for a long moment before he continued by saying "I want both of you to do a favor for me with no questions asked, can you guys do that?"

Ron and Janet both nodded but only Janet spoke. She said "you should know that we would do anything for you Sullivan, consider anything you need already done."

Sully finished his beer in one long drink and grabbed another before he said "I want you to accept this house as a gift. That seems to make more sense to me than burning it down."

Neither of them could comprehend what he was offering to them, and Sully continued by saying "Jack LaRoux is going to be here for a meeting tomorrow to discuss a remodel that was planned months ago. You both need to be here for that meeting to discuss the proposed changes to your house. I have a set of blueprints in the house that you two can go over with him when he gets here."

Sully gave them no time to respond before he said "before he starts on your house I am going to have Jack install a bathroom and a small kitchenette in the garage and, until I have fully healed, I will live there for a while. If you two would prefer a different deal, now is the time to let me know."

Ron and Janet were stunned by Sully's offer and it was over a full minute of silence before Janet said "as long as you are absolutely sure that this is what you want, I can't think of a better gift that you could ever give us."

Ron looked annoyed and said "I think you are fucking nuts, why would you give us your house, do you think I couldn't buy one if I wanted to? I don't think you really want to do this, and this place will always be yours."

Sully matched Ron's attitude and raised it a notch by saying "if you think I was kidding about burning this place down, try me Rady. You should know me enough by now to not test my resolve!"

Janet jumped in and said "don't be such an ass Ron, if you would take time to think before you spoke you would understand Sully's reason for doing this."

Sully stood and left the table shaking his head. When he reached the door he turned to them and said "let me know what you decide, I don't give a shit one way or the other."

When Sully entered the house Chris was standing in his way to confront him. He said "how dare you invite us to live here and then kick us out when you see fit, you are a total asshole Mills, just like everybody says."

Sully looked him squarely in the eyes and sneered "take your best shot kid, better than you have tried."

Chris threw a right cross toward Sully's jaw, and that action would be the last action he remembered for several days. Sully slipped the punch, and threw his battered body into Chris and let the boy's forward momentum carry him over his shoulder and through the screen door onto the deck.

Sully pounced on him like a crazed jungle cat, despite his wounded body. Before Ron could pull him off of the boy, Sully had broken Chris's nose, left cheek bone, right eye socket, larynx, and enough of his right ribs to collapse his lung.

Weathers had shown up shortly after the ambulance had left with Haley and what was left of Chris. He sat across from Sully at the table on the deck. He helped himself to a beer and one of Sully's cigars. After lighting the cigar he said "one of these days we have to go fishing together or play a round of golf Sully, because it seems that the only time we see each other anymore is when I am supposed to fix the messes you create."

Sully grinned at his comment and said "fishing maybe, but the only use I have ever had for a golf club is as a weapon."

Weathers laughed and then said "last I had heard you were grooming that kid for a second chance at training, now I have to show up here because you make hamburger out of him, care to explain?"

Sully shrugged and said "the little fucker squared off on me and threw, he should feel lucky that I'm injured right now, otherwise he would be dead. I'm probably gonna need a new nurse."

Weathers shook his head and stubbed out the barely smoked cigar. He leaned forward and was quite serious when he said "I can't protect you anymore son, Macmillan thinks you are a rouge agent at this point, and he is pushing me to get rid of you. You had better get well quick, and get back out in the field."

Sully simply said "I'm ready right now boss, you just give me a job, and I'll do it."

Weathers left without saying another word, but the message of his visit had been crystal clear.

Ron came out and sat next to Sully soon after Weathers had left. He handed Sully a scotch rocks and then asked "what did the boss man have to say?"

Sully answered "he wants me to golf with him, and I can't wait. It's been a long time since I golfed."

Ron had a puzzled look on his face when he replied "I can't believe you golf, I would have bet my life that you didn't."

Sully continued his lie by saying "oh yeah, I golf every chance I get. I'm right around a seven." Sully had no idea what that meant, but he had heard golfers talk about numbers before. He figured that the number was how good they were on a scale of one to ten.

Ron was shocked that Sully seemed to be a golfer because it just didn't fit. He was still having a hard time with Sully giving him the house, and he said "I'm sure you can sense that I don't feel comfortable taking your house as a gift Sullivan, I kinda need a better reason than you told me before."

Sully wasn't exactly sure why he had given away the house, but he had a strong feeling that it was the best thing to do right now. He decided that telling Ron the way he felt was the best explanation. He said "I can't look anywhere in this house without seeing her Ron, the best thing I can do is to get out of this place so I can move on with my life. I don't think I could make it any clearer than that man."

Ron nodded and said "I had a feeling that was the reason, but I really needed to hear you say it. Thank you buddy, but I want you to know that if you ever want this joint back it's yours."

Sully nodded his understanding, the reached into the pocket of his sweat pants. He said "I need you to do me one more favor Ron." Sully placed two things on the table and said "I want you to take these and do whatever you want to with them." Sully gingerly rose from the table and walked into Ron and Janet's house.

Ron looked down on the ring and watch that were Zoe's and sighed. He hoped his friend would be able to find his way out of the dark place he was in.

Sully went to his lair and laid down on the bed. His mind was spinning and his heart ached more than it ever had. He made a conscious and clear decision at that very moment to let his heart turn to stone.

Sully stood from the bed and moved the foot of it away from the fireplace. He used a long match to light the manufactured log that had been waiting for fire for a long while.

While the fire got going Sully went over to the small computer desk and booted up Zoe's laptop. He paged through the stack of CD's until he found the system recovery disk that had been supplied with the computer. He inserted the disk and wiped the drive back to factory settings.

He grabbed all of the disks that weren't marked as utilities that the computer came with, and the stack of printed photographs. Sully went over to the fireplace and threw everything in.

He walked back out to the kitchen table where Ron and Janet had been sitting, watching him. Sully said "why don't we get all of Haley and Chris's shit out of here and packed into their cars, I don't want her anywhere near me right now."

Ron answered "that sounds good to me boss, I really don't want to see you mess her up like you did Chris." It was a joke, but way beyond poor taste.

Sully gave Ron a dirty look and went back to his lair to watch the fire. Sully watched his life with Zoe burn away to ashes, and unconsciously nodded as the fire burned. Having symbolically ended that chapter in his life, Sully was ready to kill again.

Sixteen days later Sully jumped with Ron to finish his airborne qualification. Ron was thrown immediately back into the agent program, and was a full field agent three months later.

Sully had never left his campus apartment during that time other than to help Ron. He was about seventy five percent healed, and that was good enough for the SSO to start using their top field agent again.

For Sully the next five years were a blur. He had successfully completed forty six sanctions over that time, and each one had helped him toward his goal of total blackness.

Sully had become a hermit when he was not out on a mission. He had not gone to Ron and Janet's wedding, and never spoke to Chuck or Terry again. He sold his plane, and had moved the contents of his vault to the safe house vault.

Sully was a killing machine, and that was all he cared about. He had completed several "impossible" missions, but most of the time his targets posed no threat. The hardest times for Sully had been when he was not in the field.

Weathers was impressed with the turnaround in Sully, and finally loosened the reins he had tightly held on him. Rather than a liability, Sully had become the best agent the SSO had ever seen.

Sully focused solely on his job, and had no time for outside interruptions. He had never become close to anyone he encountered, past or present. His goal was simple, kill enough to make his pain go away. What he failed to realize was that no matter how many flawless sanctions he performed it would never erase the thoughts of Zoe that ran through his mind continually.

Three years later he had enough. Janet and Ron had two children, and Sully caught himself constantly driving by their house at night to catch a glimpse of 'the normal life'.

Sully was thirty four years old when he requested a meeting with Weather to discuss his future. He was on a track that was heading toward a major burn out, and he knew that he needed a break.

Sully's mother was in her late sixties now, and he wanted to see if he could be of any help to her. He had sent her around two million dollars to her over the years, and he was curious to see what she had done with it.

It was May sixteenth, two thousand seven when Sully walked into Weathers' office to request a sabbatical from the SSO. He sat across from Weathers and said "I need some time off to recharge, I would be grateful if you could arrange a year or so off for me."

Weathers had been expecting this someday, but not this soon. He said "Mills your duty is up for the SSO, it has been for two years. You are free to leave if you want to, but I would prefer to keep you on the books."

Sully replied "I have no doubt that you will always know where to find me if you need me. I'm not saying this is the end Jim, just the end for a while."

A two thousand three Ford Excursion diesel was the truck Sully had been driving for the past two years, and it was more than large enough to hold what he chose to take with him back to Arizona.

Sully elected to take a handful of weapons, some clothing, and some specialized gear that he had found useful over the years. On his way out of town he stopped by his old house. If Ron or Janet had been home he wouldn't have stopped, but luck was on his side for once, and the house was empty. Sully picked the lock on the front door and walked through the house. It looked nothing like the place he had remembered, but just being there invoked powerful memories and feelings in him.

Sully placed a handwritten note on the table and left the house. He had no real reason to hurry, but the sooner he left Virginia behind him the better he would feel, or so he thought.

The three day drive to Arizona would have taken most people five, but Sully drove straight through, stopping only a few times to nap at rest areas.

Southern Arizona was as bleak as he had remembered, and it was a welcome sight that matched his disposition. The town of Mirage had not grown at all in the sixteen years he had been gone, in fact several of the stores on the main street had closed.

Sully stopped the truck in front of the Diner that used to be Smitty's, but was now named "Danny's". The place had changed over the years he had been gone, but it was still an overdone truck stop.

The hostess station was gone, and Sully's mother was not in sight. Sully sat at the counter and ordered a cup of coffee. He sipped the bitter drink, and asked the waitress if she knew 'D'.

The waitress was a younger woman who was a little overweight, and a lot flirtatious. She leaned over the counter showing off her ample cleavage when she answered "I think she worked here a few years ago, but I don't know her."

Sully nodded at her and left two dollars on the counter before he turned and left. He went to the small house he had grown up in, and knocked on the door. Thirty seconds later a man in his early seventies opened the door and asked "can I help you fella?"

Sully took off his sunglasses and set his jaw before he answered by saying "I was looking for Miss Mills, and I thought she lived here, if I have made a mistake pardon me."

The man looked at him with a skeptical eye and said "who wants to know?"

Sully was not in the mood for the man's attitude, and matched it with his own when he answered with his own question by asking "is she here, or not? I don't have time to mess around with you sir."

There was stirring in the back of the house, and Sully saw an older woman in the background. The man at the door obviously did not like Sully or his abrasive attitude, and he said "unless you tell me who you are, I'm closing this door."

Sully looked past the man to try to see if the woman he saw was his Mother. He gruffly said "I am Sullivan Mills, and I just wanted to say hello to my mother, tell her I was here." With that having been said Sully turned and walked down the sidewalk toward his truck.

He was stopped in his tracks by a familiar voice emanating from the house. Donna called out "Sullivan, is that really you?" She had run out of the house when she heard him say his name, and when Sully stopped and turned around she was running down the sidewalk toward him.

Donna almost knocked him over rushing into his arms. She kissed his cheek and said "I can't believe you are here, I didn't know if I would ever see you again. Come on in the house with me." She grabbed his hand and squeezed it before pulling him into the house.

The house hadn't changed much in the years that Sully had been gone, aside from all of the furniture being new. When sully sat at the table across from his Mother, the man who had barred his entry earlier came in the kitchen to introduce himself. He said "my name is Mark, Sullivan, nice to finally meet the other man in my wife's life."

Mark was a portly, balding, shorter man with large meaty hands, and a slight lisp. Sully had taken an immediate disliking to him when he would not simply tell him that his Mother resided in this house.

Sully was in no mood to deal with this man, and said "nice to meet you Mark, could you please leave me and my Mother alone for a while?"

Mark gave Sully a dirty look, but obliged his request by leaving. Sully had believed the adage that money can't buy happiness, it certainly hadn't for him, but Donna was a different story entirely. She was no longer the sad, pitiful woman he had left years ago. She seemed incredibly happy, and Sully found it annoying.

He sat with her for an hour listening to her regale him with her accounts of world travel. The money had changed her life, and although he should have been happy for her, Sully was getting annoyed by her. He had not said a word since he sat down in her house, and he felt like interrupting her to tell her where the money had come from and how many people had to die for her happiness.

Donna was droning on about Australia or something when Sully gave her a forlorn and knowing look, and then he stood and walked toward the door. She said "where are you going Sullivan, you just got here?"

Sully didn't even turn to look at her, and he was amazed at how the tables had turned. He simply replied "I just wanted to see if you were happy, and I have." He walked out the door and to his truck. Not another word was said as he got into his truck, and drove away.

Sully toured the small town of Mirage looking for a place to live for a while. When he really didn't find anything he drove towards Tucson. When he was near Tucson he stopped at a circle K gas station/ convenience store for fuel. He picked up a local real estate magazine. From there he drove half a mile down the highway to the first dirt road he found. Sully drove three hundred yards down the dirt road and turned the truck off.

Sully opened the back of his truck and pulled out a small cooler, and a folding camp chair. He sat on the chair and had his lunch which consisted of a soggy bologna sandwich, a beef stick, and a beer. He had made ten sandwiches before he left the SSO campus, and this was the last one, thankfully.

He paged through the real estate magazine until he found a young female realtor, Stacy Wosniak, who seemed to specialize in selling cheap properties. Sully dialed her cell phone, and they had agreed to meet two hours later at the Diner in Mirage.

Sully finished his lunch and threw the cooler and chair into the truck. He took his time driving back to Mirage, and continually shook his head as he gazed over the incredible bleakness of the cold and unforgiving landscape which he called home. His final thought was that it matched his soul perfectly.

Sully parked his truck at an abandoned auto parts store five blocks from "Danny's" café and put on his tattered straw cowboy hat. He walked with his head down to "Danny's", taking in all he could along the way.

What he saw was the same thing he had grown up seeing, a depressed border town. The closed stores had changed, but it might as well have been the early nineteen eighties, rather than two thousand seven.

He waited around a corner of the café until he saw Stacy park and walk into the Diner. He recognized her from her picture in the real estate magazine, and laughed to himself. Sully mused 'why do all realtors publish pictures of themselves that show how attractive they could be, rather than showing the public how plain and ugly they really were'.

Stacy wasn't ugly, but she was way less than advertised. Sully entered two minutes after her and sat next to her at the counter. He knew how to be charming, and had used it to his advantage on several occasions, today Sully turned his internal charm knob to full tilt and wooed Stacy to the best of his ability.

By the time they each had finished a cup of coffee, Sully knew that she would do her best for him as long as he kept flirting with her. Stacy invited him to ride in her car as they toured the available properties in the area. When Sully told her his five hundred thousand dollar cash budget, he thought she was going to faint.

When they had exhausted the residential possibilities, Sully said "just for the hell of it, show me some commercial properties. I don't know that I am really in the market for commercial, but I would like us to spend some more time together, if that is alright with you Stacy."

Stacy swooned and said "that would be wonderful Sullivan, I don't think I am ready to let you go quite yet either."

Sully winked at her and replied "I'm glad we are on the same page Stacy." He was making himself sick with the syrup he was pouring over the plain, slightly overweight realtor.

Stacy had to call her broker to find out the particulars on the commercial listings in Mirage. Sully stood outside her Toyota Camry and smoked a cigar while she scribbled down the commercial listings on a notepad.

When Stacy ended her cellular phone conversation with her broker she spent another two minutes scribbling notes into her Day-Timer. She lifted her right hand and curled, then straightened her index finger several times while batting her eyes at Sully. Stacy was beckoning him to her.

When Sully returned to her car she showed him her scribbled notes regarding commercial properties. Stacy leaned too close to him to be professional, and read her notes to him in a seductive voice.

Sully surveyed the list and crossed off the properties he had no interest in. He narrowed it down quickly to an automotive service station, and a gas station. He matched Stacy's sexual advance with his own when he looked directly at her chest and said "I would like to see those two if you don't mind."

Stacy was almost breathless with his reciprocation of her sexual onslaught, and whispered "I will do whatever you want me to Sullivan."

Sully cooled her of for the time being and replied "let's go see these properties first, then we can talk more personally." He was giving her an intense look that promised passion.

The automotive service station was owned by a buffoon who charged un-expecting travelers way too much for simple repairs, and it was not an enterprise that Sully wanted to be involved with.

The gas station had a small apartment attached to it that was cramped, dirty, and bleak. The small store where the sale point resided looked very similar to the living quarters. The gas station had only one redeeming quality, it was the only one for miles in either direction.

The asking price for the fuel stop was three hundred eighty thousand dollars, and Sully had set his own price at three hundred thousand even.

As they toured the dilapidated gas station, Stacy was on Sully's hip, rubbing her body against his whenever the opportunity presented itself.

Sully continued to tease Stacy by inviting her advances and making his own. He had no intention of acting on them, but it was invigorating to be wanted by a woman, even if it was a sex starved big girl.

They left the gas station and Sully told Stacy that he wanted to write an offer of two hundred sixty thousand dollars. Stacy went "all in" and said "I have a real comfy bed in Tucson if you need a place to stay, but I can't promise you much sleep."

Sully smiled at her provocatively and replied "that's more tempting than you could know, but I will have to take a rain check. I'm staying with a cousin of mine here in town, and I promised to cook dinner."

Stacy pouted and replied "are you sure, I'm sure your cousin wouldn't mind missing you for one evening, and I promise not to bite, at least not too hard."

Sully frowned and then said "I'm sorry Stacy, but I got into town early this morning, and I haven't seen my cousin and his family for ten years. It would be rude to run off to Tucson with you the night of my arrival."

Stacy begrudgingly took no for an answer and moved to kiss him on the cheek. Sully turned into her and kissed her deeply on the lips. He held her tightly and whispered "thanks for the offer, some other time we will definitely get together."

Stacy was hurt at the rejection, and drove Sully to his truck in silence. When they reached Sully's Excursion she told him that she would submit the offer as soon as her broker could approve and sign it, and as soon as there was an answer she would call him.

Sully had insisted that the purchase offer expired four hours after it was received by the owner of the gas station. Stacy told him the normal expiration of an offer was one day, but he had played her like a cheap guitar, and she was willing to do anything for him.

They exchanged cell phone numbers, and Stacy left for Tucson to submit his offer. Sully almost regretted not going home with her, but he hadn't been with a woman since Zoe "died", and he preferred to keep it that way.

Sully went to Bronco's, the only tavern in Mirage, and sat at the bar drinking beer after beer. His somewhat sexual encounter with Stacy had injured his wounded heart, and lately he found his solace in alcohol.

Sully was one of the four drunks in the seedy gin mill, and did not care. The world could think whatever they wanted, as far as Sully was concerned. He was in a sinister mood, as he had been for the past several years. As hard as he tried to forget Zoe, he was unable to. His scarred body was a daily reminder of the day he had lost her, and he imagined that he saw her almost daily. He had a broken heart, and a ruptured soul.

Sully's cell phone rang shortly after he had left Bronco's, and it was Stacy telling Sully that his offer was countered with a price of three hundred ten thousand. Sully countered back with an offer of two hundred fifty, all cash.

Stacy was shocked at him making yet a lower offer as a counter, but promised to submit it. Sully drove to the outskirts of Mirage, down a rough dirt road that he used to walk down to go rabbit hunting. There used to be a livestock corral that was always in operation, and it was still there.

Sully striped down to his birthday suit, and washed himself with the water from a cattle trough. He put on fresh clothes and climbed into the back of his dramatically oversized truck. Sully laid on top of the sleeping bag, with his hands behind his head, and closed his eyes. He executed the same ritual he had daily for thousands of days.

Sully replayed the life he had with Zoe, from the very moment he first saw her, to the explosion in Maine. Most nights it helped him fall asleep, but nights like this one happened all too often. Sully laid awake in the back of the truck until the sun came up.

Sully washed his face in the cattle trough. The water was cold enough to scare the cobwebs from his fragmented and depressed mind, and he begrudgingly faced another day in his sad and lonely life.

The call came at nine thirty that his offer was accepted, and Stacy asked when he could have the cashier's check ready. She was shocked when Sully told her that he had cash, meaning green paper money.

It probably wasn't prudent for Sully to drive across the country with seven million dollars in cash hidden in a false floor of the cargo area of his truck, but he really didn't want the SSO to know where he was headed. One million was in cash, and the rest was comprised of two hundred and forty, twenty five thousand dollar cashier's checks. Any wire transfers would have been immediately discovered by the SSO. He was under no delusion that they didn't know where he was, but he tried his best to not be an open target for them.

If it was possible, Stacy was even more flirtatious than she had been the day before. She met him wearing a pink V-neck Ann Taylor blouse that was far too tight around her ample bosom, and showed off almost all of her now unencumbered cleavage, the blouse was accompanied by a tan leather mini skirt and six inch black heels. Stacy had way too much make-up on, and looked like she should be working the streets of Tucson as a hooker.

Sully wore blue Wrangler jeans, and a black short sleeved Walls Henley. As usual his outfit was accompanied by his tattered straw hat, and his boots. He carried a distressed brown leather Coach satchel / briefcase that was bulging with the cash.

A man in what Sully guessed to be in his late forties pulled up in a red Dodge Durango. He had greasy, slicked back hair that looked like he combed it with buttered toast. He was wearing a cheap, ill fitted, dark blue, linen suit that was incredibly wrinkled. The tie that he had worn spoke volumes about the man. It was bright green, and featured large yellow stripes. He introduced himself as Leonard Dewayne, and they all went into the diner to sign the paperwork.

Lenny, as he insisted to be called, started the meeting by handing Sully a purchase contract. The current owner was eager to move away from Mirage, and Sully could definitely identify with that point of view.

With a full cash sale there was no escrow time, only half a day for the title company to get the documents recorded. The three of them drove separately to the gas station. The soon to be former owner, Gus Springfeld, was anxiously waiting for them, and after three hours of orientation, he left Mirage.

Lenny had only stayed until all of the paperwork was signed, and promised Sully to forward the title to him when it was recorded. He left, but Stacy stayed with Sully and Gus. As Gus explained the workings of the gas station Stacy unabashedly threw herself at Sully.

Sully was sad, gloomy, and depressed. He was always grumpy when he hadn't slept, and Stacy's advances were starting to annoy him.

Gus handed Sully a set of keys and said "I hope you do well here Son. I've been feeding this place cash for far too long, and I just can't afford to anymore."

Sully nodded at the man and accepted the keys. He said "I'll give it a go mister Springfeld, I always wanted a place like this, and I have relatives in town. With my cousin owning two cars, I already have a strong customer base."

Gus laughed a hearty guttural laugh until he started coughing, when he was finished he said "best of luck to you Son, I hope you do better with this old place than I did."

With that said Gus grabbed the seed money out of the register, and left. Sully turned to Stacy and said "what do you say I close up early today and take you out to dinner to celebrate my new business venture?"

Stacy closed the small gap between them and forced a huge kiss onto Sully. She pressed her body against his and raised her right knee softly into his groin.

Sully needed to stop her, so he said "Stacy, as much as I would enjoy being with you I can't yet, my wife died not long ago, and that is what brought me back here. I'm sorry, but my heart hasn't healed yet, and I can't see myself being with another woman. Trust me if I was emotionally ready I would ravage you right now, but I'm not, and I have no idea when I will be."

Stacy seemed hurt at being rejected and looked foolish for having thrown herself at him. Her eyes filled with fire as she said "keep your fucking dinner Mills, I'm sorry I ever entertained the idea of having sex with you!" With that, Stacy stormed out of the gas station, and spun gravel as she sped out of the parking lot.

Sully stood in the door frame of the small store and watched her leave. He grinned, shook his head and said aloud "making new friends already."

Sully filled his lonely days by tending to the gas station. He painted and repaired things to the best of his ability. The snack truck came by once a week to replace any expired items with fresh ones, and Sully always wondered how room temperature meat snacks could expire.

Life went on day after day for like that for Sully for the next year. His social interaction was limited to the three or four customers that stopped daily for fuel and snacks. The gas station was a losing venture, but for Sully it was simply a place to hide from the world.

One day when Sully got out of bed, without having slept, there was a large sign blocking the front door to the gas stop. Sully went out the back door and walked around to find that the sign read "Mill's Last Stop." Sully shook his head because he knew it was from his Mother even before he read the attached note. She had been coming by the gas station for two dollars of fuel every other day, when she was in town, ever since Sully had bought the dilapidated property.

Donna was trying desperately to be a part of Sully's life, but he shunned her every time. Sully didn't have a clue as to why he was so upset with her, and his only thought as to why he was alienating her was that it wasn't fair for her to be so happy when he was so miserable.

They say time heals all wounds, but "they" were full of shit as far as Sully was concerned. It had been over ten years since he lost Zoe, and the emptiness in his soul had grown every day. Most days he found it hard to concentrate on simple tasks without thoughts of her interrupting him. Sully had thought that being a recluse would ease his pain, but he was fooling himself, because if anything the loneliness had amplified his heartache.

Sully reluctantly hung the sign over the door to the small convenience store, inviting every passerby to know his name. The worst part was that he had met an old schoolmate at Bronco's, and the name of 'Milly' had been bestowed upon him once again.

Chapter 11

Present Day

Sully finally woke up twenty minutes after the blast. He was dazed and confused. He shook his head vigorously to clear his mind, and evaluated the current situation.

The blast had caused only material damage, and Sully was convinced that it had to have been some sort of humongous concussion grenade. His shoulder hurt like hell, but it was intact and functional.

Sully immediately saw the agent mobile that he had just filled with fuel rolled onto its side and blocking the front door to the "stop". He rushed out the back door, and around the small building to check on the occupants of the vehicle. The passenger was lying in a strange position, and his neck was quite obviously broken. Sully checked for a pulse, as a matter of courtesy, but he knew it was a futile gesture.

"Ace", the driver who had disrespected him, was unconscious, but otherwise intact. Sully slapped him hard across his right cheek, and he woke up as Sully would have, pissed off and ready to fight.

"Ace" asked "what the fuck is going on here Mills, and who the hell hit me?" He was dazed and hurting, but he was still feisty.

Sully was even more pissed off than he had been, because the agent knew his name. He angrily answered "I did, but I think that we need to put that aside right now and get to work." Sully pulled him out of the wrecked car and asked a question he knew the answer to, he said "what agency are you with?"

"Ace" was undoubtedly sore as hell from the roll over, and his attitude showed it when he answered Sully's question by saying "I'm a junior SSO agent. Me and Phil were assigned to find out where you were and what you were up to."

Sully helped him to his feet and said "Phil is dead, the roll over broke his neck. You got a name, or are you willing to settle for shit head?" Sully was pissed at being tracked by the SSO, and was being as antagonistic as possible.

The agent dusted off his cheap suit, and gave Sully a dirty look as he removed what was left of his broken sunglasses. He answered by saying "name's Todd Dinucci, and I need to know what you know about this blast." He was inching his hand toward his pistol as he said it.

Sully was almost twice the young agents age at this point, but he had stayed in top physical condition, as usual. He had noticed the move Todd was making, and sneered at him as he said "I think we need to work together on figuring out what the hell is going on, and it's gonna be hard for you to help if you are knocked out. Keep going for your weapon and see how an old guy can kick your ass."

Todd retuned his hand to his side, because he was aware of Sully's reputation. He knew Sully wasn't bluffing, and was very wary of him. Todd said "there was no fire with that blast, what the hell does that mean Mills?"

Sully unconsciously rubbed his side where the burn scars were as he answered "that's the first thing we need to find out. Scavenge all the gear you can from the car, and I'll go get my truck."

Todd gathered all of the gear from the wrecked car and put it in a pile near the gas pumps. He had even taken the gear from Phil's lifeless body. Almost twenty minutes had passed before Sully returned without his truck. He handed Todd a beer, and said "my truck wouldn't start, and none of the electronics in the store work at all. Check your radio and phone."

Nooch, as he preferred to be called, did as Sully instructed. Both his cell phone and radio were dead. He was curious as hell and asked "what the hell is going on?"

Sully answered him by saying "follow me, Dinucci I have an observation point on the roof. Let's see what's going on in town."

Nooch followed Sully to a ladder installed on the rear wall of the "stop". The adobe building with its high parapet walls was perfect for the three sniper's nests that Sully constructed.

Sully was safely hidden in the nest that faced Mirage and was already scanning the town with high powered binoculars before Nooch even reached the roof.

When Nooch reached Sully's perch he asked "how bad is it? Is any of that shit-hole town still standing?"

Sully hadn't liked Nooch from the moment he had pulled into the station for gas, and although he agreed with the assessment of his hometown, he was ready to beat the young agent's ass. Sully snarled at him before he said "how about you shut the fuck up and grab a pair of binoculars."

Nooch went to the nearest sniper's nest and started scanning the town for damage, and was shocked to see that there was none. He carried his binoculars back to Sully who was still intently scanning through his own. Nooch asked Sully "how the hell can there be a blast that flips my car, kills Phil, and causes no damage?"

Sully never put his optics down as he answered "think a little bit dumb ass, whatever hit us was not a conventional weapon. I think we were close to the blast point. That's why we absorbed the concussion of the blast. If it was chemical we would already be dead or sick, so I have ruled that out, but it seems to have had the same effect as a nuclear detonation."

Nooch was confused and let it show when he said "Mills, I think you've been out in this godforsaken place too long. If there had been a detonation of a nuke we would be fried right now."

Sully was beyond irritated with him when he replied "try your phone and radio again." Sully waited as Nooch played with each item, then he said "they don't work do they. Nothing electronic in the store or my truck does either. I even checked the gear in my bunker, and all of my electronics are hardened against EMP. Whatever they hit us with is severely high tech!"

After letting himself look around stupidly for several seconds Nooch asked "EMP? How they hell is that possible without a nuclear blast?"

An Electro Magnetic Pulse (EMP) is emitted with any nuclear explosion. It renders any electronic device permanently useless for a radius of up to ten miles depending on the kiloton size of the device detonated.

Sully quickly surmised that this device was much more sophisticated than one associated with a nuclear device. A normal EMP has only limited effects on electronic devices that are turned off when the EMP occurs this event had destroyed all electronics on or off.

His mind was running almost faster than he could think. If they were close to ground zero of the event and the whole town was affected by this EMP the radius on this new weapon was well over 25 miles in radius, maybe much more.

The applications for a weapon like this were endless, but Sully shuddered to think of the chaos this weapon would cause if used in Washington D.C., or Quantico, or the Pentagon, etc.

Sully let out one deep chuckle, then answered the young agent by saying "I have no idea how, but it happened. You can bet your ass it's for a reason too. "How" is the last question we should be asking right now, we had better figure out "who" and "why", and we better do it damn quick."

Nooch went from confused to concerned by the time Sully finished talking. He processed everything Sully had said before he asked "what can I do to help?"

Sully answered "the town appears to be totally affected too, the fact that your car flipped makes me think we were very near the center of the blast radius. I can see no visible damage to Mirage, but I can't see any lights or vehicular activity either. Our first priority is transportation, because whoever set this device off is almost definitely on their way to mop up."

Nooch nodded and said "if you're right and all of the cars are dead what are we supposed to use for transportation?"

Sully stood from the snipers nest and started walking toward the ladder as he spoke. He answered Nooch by saying "in case you didn't know, I grew up here. There are a couple of ranches about a mile and a half from here. Let's gear up and go get some horses."

Sully went into the back room of the "stop" where he kept his small arsenal. Ten minutes later he met Nooch by the gas pumps dressed in lightweight desert camo. Sully had on a tan tactical vest that he kept packed to the hilt. He wore a lightweight backpack, a desert camo boonie hat, and military desert boots. He handed another small pack to Nooch that had eight bottles of water in it.

Sully looked at Nooch and shook his head. Nooch looked about as ready for a run across the desert as Frosty the Snowman. He had on his wool blend black suit, complete with tie, his shoulder holster, and black loafers.

Sully said "grab the rest of that gear and come with me, you won't last half a mile out here dressed like that."

Sully led him to the small back room that he had just dressed in and started quickly grabbing gear for him. He asked "what size are your feet?"

Nooch told him and shortly thereafter he was dressed in Sully's tan Dockers, a tan Edie Bauer Safari shirt, Nevado hiking boots, and a tan baseball cap. Sully had him wear his shoulder holster on the outside of the shirt, and then they left.

Sully said "follow me Todd, and try to keep up. If you fall too far behind I'm not stopping, and keep your eyes open for resistance."

He replied "if you don't mind, I prefer to be called Nooch."

Sully had his own battle with nicknames over the years, so he obliged him by saying "Nooch it is, and you can call me Sully."

With that said Sully left the "stop" and headed toward town across the desert. He was moving at a fast jog despite the thirty pound tactical vest. Nooch was keeping up, barely, and although Sully never looked back, he could tell he was having a hard time. Sully could hear Nooch's labored breathing, and his footfalls were getting heavier the farther they traveled.

Sully smiled and picked up the pace. He was enjoying the fact that he was wearing the much younger man out. Sully had been running five miles through the desert twice a week to stay in shape, and it way paying off now. He liked Nooch, despite himself, and knew it would be valuable for him to have a partner right now.

Levi's old llama ranch, the same one that Sully had slaved at as a child was in sight so Sully stopped and retrieved a small set of binoculars from his vest to let Nooch catch up. The ranch was still in operation, and if Levi was still ranching it Sully knew he always kept at least four horses.

Nooch was bent over with his hands on his knees, catching his breath when Sully said "let's move, but at the ranch we have to be selective with the targets, remember these are innocents."

Sully started running the last nine hundred yards to the ranch, with the fatigued Nooch close on his heels. Sully cleared the five strand barbed wire fence like a gazelle, and when Nooch tried the same leap he found himself rolling in the dirt. His right foot had caught the top wire of the fence. To his credit, he popped up onto his feet and continued on.

They reached the barn two minutes later, and Sully stopped at the corner of the structure. He held up his fist as a stop sign to Nooch, and crouched as he looked around the corner. Sully turned to Nooch and whispered "I don't see or smell any hostiles, so you had better be damned sure of any target you choose to engage. You got me Nooch?"

Nooch was well aware of the situation, but he also respected the hell out of Sully and his reputation. He nodded then answered in a whisper "I won't shoot unless I'm positive of a hostile target Sully."

They moved out around the corner of the barn to the entrance, and when they were inside Sully stopped suddenly. He looked at Nooch and said aloud "wait by the door and detain anybody entering. I'll go get our rides, if they are here."

Nooch nodded his understanding and took a defensive position by the barn doors. He heard the sound of horses whinnying as Sully saddled them.

Less than twenty minutes later Sully walked out of the horse barn leading three saddled horses by the reigns. He could tell Nooch that the third was a backup, but that would be a lie. He was hoping that the woman that had reminded him of Zoe would be stranded on the side of the road, and that he could come riding to her rescue like a white knight.

Zoe was on her way back home from Tucson. She had dropped her son off for his first football camp. She was too worried and self-absorbed to worry about fuel until it was almost too late. It was the first time her son, ten year old Sullivan, was going to be away from home longer than overnight at a friend's house. When she stopped and looked at her map, Zoe was shocked to see that her only option for fuel was Mirage, Arizona.

Knowing that it was Sully's birthplace, and that he had moved back there, made Zoe very nervous. Janet visited Zoe about every six months, and they spoke almost daily. Until Sully had taken a leave of absence, Janet was able to tell Zoe everything she could about Sully.

Zoe knew the odds of seeing him were astronomical, but she still took the time to put on a short dark wig she had brought. Zoe accessorized the wig with large dark Donna Karan sunglasses.

She drove slowly through the small town, and it fit Sully's description almost perfectly. As she drove toward New Mexico Zoe started to worry that Mirage didn't have a gas station anymore.

When she climbed the small hill on the way out of town she was relieved to see the gas station at the top of the hill, then horrified when she saw the name "Mill's Last Stop". The odds that it wasn't run by Sully were also astronomical.

Luck was against her in every way when she pulled in and saw Sully in his unmistakable hat and boots. To compound her bad luck, all of the pumps were full service.

Zoe wanted desperately to talk to him and heal his broken heart, but Weathers had made it quite clear to her that even incidental contact with Sully would revoke her protected status. That would ultimately mean that she would be sanctioned, and her son would become an orphan.

Zoe had no choice, her mini-van needed fuel, and Sully's place was the only game in town. She made sure not to look at him, and made her voice raspy and deep when she said "fill it up."

She watched Sully intently for the four minutes it had taken to fill her tank with fuel. By his posture and demeanor Zoe could tell how sad and lonely Sully was, and it broke her heart all over again. As she paid him with cash Zoe wanted desperately to rip off the wig and glasses and tell him how much she loved him.

Zoe longed to tell him what a wonderful son he had fathered, and how she had never been with another man since she left him. It was an impossible situation, but just seeing him made her heart soar, then crash back to earth.

Zoe drove slowly away from the gas station staring into the rear view mirror watching every move Sully made. She was lucky that the desert road was as straight as an arrow, or she would have driven off of it. Her anonymous encounter with Sully had torn open the wounds in her heart that were almost healed.

When the gas station was out of her mirrors Zoe pulled the mini-van onto the gravel shoulder, stopped, turned off the vehicle, and removed her disguise. She thought long and hard about turning around and reuniting with her one and only true love, but again thought of the consequences for her and Sully Junior.

Zoe felt an odd wave of energy pass through her, and dismissed it as extreme heartache. She turned the key to start the mini-van and nothing happened. She tried again several times to no avail. Zoe opened the hood and checked the battery connections, they seemed just fine. She tried her cell phone, and it wouldn't even power-up. Zoe tried to start the van for several more minutes, and then finally gave up.

Zoe went into what used to be the spare tire compartment of the mini-van, and grabbed several weapons and a change of clothes. She had thought it was hard to hide her past from her son, but hiding herself from Sully had been heartbreaking. Especially after Zoe saw how downtrodden and depressed she had made him.

Zoe felt horrible, and promised herself to do her very best to make it right somehow, someway.

Sully walked out of the barn and handed the reins of one of the three saddled horses to Nooch. He saw Levi coming with his shotgun, determined to stop them and yelled "Levi it's me, Milly, and I planned on paying you a lot for these old trail nags."

Levi lowered the shotgun and said "Milly, damn boy I ain't seen you since you were poppin' pimples on that funny face of yours. I heard you was back in town. I need two hundred a piece for them nags, and another fifty a piece for the rigs."

As Levi walked over Sully reached for the wad of money he carried in his front right pants pocket. He counted out two thousand dollars and handed it to Levi.

Levi took the money and counted it, and then he said "It's good to see you Milly, you were the best hand I ever had. I could always trust you."

Sully nodded and replied "thanks for the horses Levi, I will probably bring them back here to board them in the next couple of days, then we can talk about boarding fees."

Nooch had climbed into the saddle of the largest horse, and when Sully had finished dealing with the rancher, he saddled up as well.

He turned the horse one hundred and eighty degrees and said "follow me back to the gas station." Then he used his heels to urge the horse forward. Sully turned the horse around again, and headed for the gate.

The gate latch had been designed to be accessible on horseback, and Sully opened it. When he was through the gate he heeled the horse in the ribs, and was off in a full run, with the extra horse running at his animal's side.

Nooch had only been on a horse a few times, and they had all been trail horses. He urged the horse into a canter to get the feel of the saddle. When he finally felt comfortable with the animal he wrapped the reigns around his left hand, and slapped it on the hindquarter with his right. With his limited riding experience, Nooch was proud of himself for how well he was riding.

Nooch followed the dust trail that Sully was leaving, and a few minutes later they were together at the "stop". Sully had dismounted his horse, tied the reins to a gas pump, and was scrambling up the ladder to the roof. Nooch did the same and was only a minute behind Sully, who was scanning the town with binoculars again.

Nooch grabbed the pair of binoculars he had used earlier, and followed Sully to the roof. Once there he began scanning the town himself. Neither of them saw any unusual activity, and Sully left the roof without saying a word.

When Nooch reached the ground, Sully was kneeling on the ground behind a map he had made in the dirt. Nooch went over to him, and Sully said "let me explain my plan. We are here, and let's assume the gas station to be ground zero of the blast. The Mexican border is only two miles from the heart of town, so I'm gonna assume that any invasion force will come from behind the border."

Sully was pointing with a stick at his drawing on the ground, and he continued "my plan is to head east toward New Mexico, following the highway until we are out of the blast radius. There are several ranches that we can get some vehicles from, then we can head back to town to mount an offensive if need be."

Nooch nodded his head in approval of the plan, and they went into the "stop" to load up on water and snacks that could be put into the saddlebags on the three horses. Sully disappeared into a back room and brought out three loaded rifle cases. When the food, water, and rifles were loaded onto the horses they left the gas station at a trot. It wasn't much more than a mile into their journey when they came across a woman standing next to a disabled mini-van.

Sully was in the lead when they saw the van, and pulled back hard on the reigns to stop the horse. Nooch almost ran his horse into Sully's, but ended up stopping right beside him. The two of them looked somewhat ridiculous in their respective combat outfits on horseback.

They were about two hundred yards from Zoe, and after Nooch looked at her through his binoculars he said "wow Sully that chick is gorgeous!"

Sully gave Nooch a violent look, then he said "easy boy, that's my wife you're drooling over."

Nooch was past confused and rounding the corner headed towards dumbfounded when he queried "what the hell are you talking about Sully? Your wife was K.I.A. (killed in action) over ten years ago, wasn't she?"

Sully shook his head and answered "I never believed that bullshit story and, unless that is a ghost over there, I think I was right." Sully put his sunglasses on before he continued with "go on over there and see what she wants, tell her you are SSO but don't mention my name I won't be far behind."

Nooch was quite a bit more than mildly confused as he urged his horse forward towards the woman by the van. Sully was really staying back for a few seconds to try to find words to say to Zoe.

When he thought that he had a plan in his mind of what to say, he heeled his horse in the ribs and Sully galloped to catch up to Nooch. When Sully caught-up to Nooch he abruptly said "wait here until I signal you." He dropped the reins on the extra horse, and went to meet his wife for the first time in over ten years.

Zoe saw Sully riding toward her, and there was no way to run or hide. She had no idea how he would react to her not being deceased, and hoped for the best.

Sully closed the last two hundred yards toward Zoe forcing the horse to a walk when he really wanted to be going to her at a full gallop. As much as he loved her, and had yearned for her over the years, he had no idea what to say. He finally decided to say nothing, and let her explain.

When Sully was twenty feet from her, he dismounted and walked the rest of the way holding the horse by the reigns. She was wearing a lightweight cotton sun dress with a floral print, and from ten feet away Sully could smell her wonderful aroma.

Sully stopped leaving four feet between them, set his jaw, and stared at her with a mean look on his face.

Zoe meekly said "hello Sullivan, how have you been?" She too had no idea what to say to him, but she was positive she couldn't tell him the truth.

Sully said nothing, and simply stared at her until she looked at the ground. He had an incredible urge to grab Zoe and kiss her like he used to, but he decided to be immature instead. She looked absolutely beautiful, and the years had been much kinder to her than they had to him. It was if she had stepped out of his nightly dreams, and was flesh and blood standing just feet from him.

Zoe softly said "I've been looking forward to this day, and dreading it at the same time. I never, ever wanted to leave you Sully, but Weathers gave me no option. I needed out, I was having a real problem with all of the sanctions I had completed."

Zoe finally looked up at Sully and continued with "Weathers arranged the fake death and a job for me in New Mexico. I've been an elementary school teacher for the past ten years."

When she finished speaking Sully turned around and signaled Nooch to come over. When he got to them, and dismounted Sully started talking to both of them at once. He was methodically laying out what he believed to have happened, and the plan he had going forward. He had only acknowledged Zoe once, calling her "former agent Millstad".

Nooch went to work scavenging through Zoe's van for anything useful. Zoe tried to look Sully in the eye, but after having given orders, he turned to tend to the horses. Zoe went back to Nooch to help look through her van.

Sully had been elated to see Zoe alive, as he somehow always knew she was. His soaring spirits crashed almost immediately after she spoke.

The voice in his head screamed at him to stay away from her, and not let her hurt him again. Sully listened to the voice.

The three of them were horseback and headed east ten minutes later. Sully took the lead because he has a pretty good idea where to go, and so he wouldn't have to look at Zoe. Sully guided them down a power line road that paralleled the highway. He knew that the "stop" was at mile post eighty one, so they would have to ride to at least mile post seventy six to be out of what Sully had guessed to be the blast radius.

Homesteads in this part of the Arizona desert were few and far between, and they rode past mile post seventy four before they saw three rusted mail boxes on the north side of the highway. Sully stopped and quickly dismounted. He cut the four stands of barbed wire and pulled them to the side.

The small mounted group crossed the highway and headed north on the dirt driveway. Six hundred yards up the road was a small working cattle ranch with three pick-up trucks scattered around the main building. Sully led the group to a small empty corral near the shabby metal-roofed barn.

They dismounted and let the horses loose in the corral for water. Sully didn't want to take the saddles off, just in case they couldn't get a vehicle from these people. They walked toward the small house in single file with Sully leading and Nooch in the rear.

Sully was almost to the front porch when a deep voice shouted from a window "stop right there soldier boy. State your business or you can leave, it'd be best if y'all just get on them horses you come here on, and head on out?"

Sully said "Sir there are some big problems in Mirage, and we need a vehicle damned fast." He had said it quickly and in a threatening tone, which was the last thing they needed right now.

The man inside the house was even more forceful when he replied "I ain't got no trucks for sale soldier boy, so you and yours can get back on them horses you put in my corral." He punctuated his position by saying loudly "ain't nothin' here for you!"

Sully turned to leave and bumped shoulders with Zoe, who was advancing toward the house. She disregarded Sully as if he weren't there, and climbed the porch steps. She had changed into Guess blue jeans, a tailored white oxford long sleeved shirt, and hiking boots before they had mounted the horses.

She walked right across the porch to the man with the shotgun, and after forty seconds of conversation, the front door opened and she disappeared inside the house.

Sully walked past Nooch, and went to the corral. He went through the saddle bags on Zoe's horse and took all of the items he deemed useful. He grabbed the reins of his horse, then the horse Nooch had been riding. He walked the horses halfway toward Nooch, and then waived him over.

By the time Nooch walked over to him, Sully was sitting tall in the saddle, ready to go. Nooch looked up at him and asked "are we waiting for agent Millstad?"

Sully looked down and answered "I'm sure as hell not. I'm gonna find a vehicle further down the road. Your choice agent Dinucci." Sully headed back to the highway not caring what he chose.

He urged the horse to a full run on the shoulder of the highway, and headed further down the road. It was over a two miles before he let the horse slow to a gallop. He never looked back to see if he was being followed. Sully saw a large house on a hill off to his right, and spurred the horse back to a run with the heels of his boots.

Sully stopped his horse at the driveway to the house he had seen and looked back to the west. Nooch had decided not to follow him, and that was just fine with Sully. He thought '*be careful Nooch, that lady will ruin your life without a second thought*'.

Sully galloped up the driveway to the large well-kept house, and rode directly to the front door and dismounted. He took off his hat and sunglasses to look less like a soldier, but it did little to soften his hard look. Sully rang the bell and waited for a response.

A grandmotherly looking woman in her seventies answered the door a minute later and said "well hello son, what can I do for you?"

Sully tried to smile at the old woman to soften his face, but it only made his face look harsher. He answered by saying "I was wondering if I could buy, or rent a vehicle from you. There is an emergency in Mirage, and I really need transportation."

The old woman said “oh my, we need to speak to my husband.” Then she invited Sully in and yelled “Abe we have a young soldier here who has an emergency!”

Abe came out of the hallway and gave Sully a thorough once over. He was the same age as his wife, with a stern weathered face. He walked smartly over to him and stuck his hand out. Sully shook it as he said “Colonel Abraham Danies, United States Army, retired.”

Sully stood at attention and saluted, then replied “Sir, Master Sergeant Sullivan Mills, United States Marine Corps.”

Abe said “at ease Mills, follow me to my office. Mabel, find us a couple beers, we will be in the office.” Abe’s office was a small room with a large desk. The walls were adorned with his personal military memorabilia, and it was quite clear that he had served for a long time and was quite proud of it.

Abe offered him a seat in the chair across the large ornate oak desk from him and Sully declined by saying “thank you sir, but I’m really dusty from the horseback ride I just took, and I wouldn’t want to soil your chair.”

Abe smiled a very disarming smile and said “sit down Sergeant, we can always clean the chair.” Mabel came in with two beers in frosted mugs on a serving platter. She set the platter on the desk blotter, put the mugs on coasters in front of each man, and then started to leave.

As she left Abe said “close the door on your way out dear.” She did as she was asked, then Abe focused on Sully and said “tell me what’s going on Mills.”

Sully didn’t have a choice right now other than to kill these two nice people and take what he needed, so he said “Sir, there was a blast in the town of mirage this morning that mimicked a nuclear detonation. It caused very little property damage, but an EMP has disabled all electronics in the town.” He stopped for a reaction, but the Colonel was staring intently at him.

Sully continued by saying “I need to check in, then do forward recon to find out why this device was deployed.”

The Colonel took it all in, then took a long drink of his beer before he said “my guess is that the blast was just a test of a new enemy weapon. Mirage has no strategic importance, and is actually a good pick for this kind of test. You can bet your ass that they are sending an assessment team from Mexico to check the effective range of this new weapon."

He pushed his phone across the desk and said "dial three, seven, nine and you will be connected to a secure pentagon operator. Make your call, then we can talk more." He stood and left Sully alone in the room to make his call.

It took two transfers and five minutes before his call was connected. Sully just finished his ice cold beer when weathers came on the line and said "Mills, I hope this call isn't going to upset me."

Sully smiled and said "I'm pretty sure it will boss." Sully spent three minutes explaining everything that had happened including Nooch and Zoe. He spoke to Weathers like he felt, stone cold and having no emotions left.

Weathers said "I'm sorry about the lie regarding Millstad, but it was necessary at the time. Right now we need to focus on the problem. Wait one second." Weathers put him on hold for two minutes. When he came back he said "I have a C-130 leaving Tucson in twenty, to drop three hummers and a small support team. One of our teams will be airborne in ten, and should be there in less than three hours."

Sully asked "what is my end of it boss?" He was hoping that Weathers would tell him to sit this one out, but it was exactly the opposite.

Weathers said "you are lead on the ground. We need all the Intel you can get about the device, and who set it off. Do whatever you have to Mills, but I think you know the catastrophic possibilities a weapon of this kind represents."

Sully had been thinking of nothing else all day. If this device was perfected it could be used to wreak havoc all over the world. He said "yes sir, what about the other agents on the ground?"

Weathers replied "use Dinucci any way you see fit, and get Millstad out of there, she is a civilian now and shouldn't have been involved in this to begin with. Sully do your best to remember her as dead, we have a very important job to complete."

Sully skirted the subject and said "when I leave the Colonel's house I will be out of contact until I meet the hummer team."

Weathers gave Sully his contact code name and clearance codes, wished him luck, and the line went dead.

Sully left the office to find the Colonel. Mabel saw him leave the office and called him into the kitchen. She said "Abe is out back in the barn waiting for you. Sergeant Mills, he wants to go with you. Please convince him to stay with me, he is all I have in this world."

Sully had no idea what to say to the kind old woman, so he simply nodded at her. Then he walked out the back door, and to the large well kept barn / garage / workshop. The Colonel was dressed in old style olive drab fatigues. He had on a black leather pistol belt that was shined just as highly as his boots.

Sully walked in and said "Colonel, will all due respect sir, this is a covert mission and that's what I do. The best thing you could do to help is to block the highway not letting anyone in from the east. If I could borrow or rent a vehicle, I will be on my way."

Abe said "I have you set up in that Jeep Cherokee over there, take these, and you can always call the house if you need me, the number is programmed in to both of those cell phones, and Mabel can get me on our FRS radios. You need to be sure you don't want me along Mills."

Sully nodded at him and said "yes Sir, what I need to do right now is to be a ghost, and gather Intel until the Calvary gets here. I was first in my class in sniper school, and I need to put those skills to use now."

Sully went to the Jeep and quickly checked it out. It was almost brand new, four wheel drive, and loaded with supplies. Sully tuned to the Colonel and said "Sir I can't thank you enough for all of your help." Sully got in the gold jeep and started it. He stopped at the front of the house to retrieve his saddlebags from the horse that Abe had promised to look after.

He shook the Colonel's hand and gave him the number to the SSO switchboard, and a code that would get him in touch with operations.

Sully headed down the driveway to the highway with one black thought running through his mind over and over. *'Kill as many as you can, kill em' all.'*

Sully drove the five miles back to town at break neck speed. He covered the seven miles to the "stop" in less than five minutes. He had seen no sign of Zoe or Nooch along the way, but he was too far into "kill" mode to give it a second thought.

Sully sped through town at eighty miles an hour, taking in the little he could of what was going on. He drove about five miles out of town to the west until he reached the old, abandoned train depot.

There was an old fashioned wooden water tank for the old steam engines fifteen feet from the edge of the road, it was a tourist attraction.

Sully climbed the tower and used his high powered binoculars to scan to the south look for the invaders. It had been only two hours since the EMP had been deployed, and he saw no forces advancing. He climbed down the tower and assessed the structure of the base of the water tower. His plan was to topple the tower into the highway, shutting off Mirage into his own private kill zone.

The tower was built in the early eighteen hundreds, and showed the pride of craftsmanship indicative to that era. Although it was nearly two hundred years old, the base of the structure was sound and solid.

Sully went back to the Jeep to see what the Colonel has packed for him, and found nothing suitable for the job. The tower would have to wait until later. He raced the Jeep back thru town and toward his gas station. He stopped two hundred yards short of the last turn in the road and grabbed his binoculars again. There was a red and white seventies Ford pickup truck parked by the station.

Sully scanned and saw no one until he carefully scanned the roofline parapet walls, then he saw Zoe with binoculars looking right at him. Sully said aloud to no one "Nooch you stupid mother fucker."

There was no use being coy anymore, Zoe had obviously conned a truck out of the redneck that was going to shoot him. He got back in the Jeep and drove slowly to the "stop". He had his plan in mind on how to deal with Zoe and Nooch.

When he parked the Colonel's Jeep next to his useless Excursion, Zoe started down the ladder. It was a sight in different times that would have led to a day of lovemaking. But that was long ago, and Sully had nothing but blood on his mind right now.

He disregarded her and yelled up to Nooch to hand down the three sniper rifles from the roof. One by one Nooch leaned over the parapet wall and dropped the rifles. They each fell fifteen feet into Sully's waiting hands. Sully put them in the Jeep, and then yelled "Nooch get your ass down here for orders."

Agent Dinucci scrambled down the ladder as quickly as possible. He ran to where Sully was standing and asked "what do you want me to do agent Mills?"

Zoe was standing nearby taking everything in without saying a word until Sully answered Nooch by saying "we have a civilian here, and Weathers has ordered that she be transported outside of the affected are to wherever she wishes. That is your assignment agent Dinucci."

Sully turned slickly on a heel and headed toward the Jeep. A familiar voice stopped him from climbing into the vehicle. Zoe shouted "just wait one second ass-hole I might want a say in what happens here!"

Sully smiled and said "agent Dinucci, you have your orders." He got in the Jeep and looked in the driver's side mirror just in time to see Dinucci grab Zoe by the arm. He said softly aloud "um, not a real good idea Nooch." Then he watched as Zoe dispatched the junior agent in three moves.

As Zoe stormed toward the Jeep, Sully rolled up the window, as if it might help. He heard the drone of the C-130 before he saw it and yelled at Zoe "get in, my team is here."

Zoe got in the Jeep still breathing heavy from the encounter with Nooch, and her ferocity at Sully. Sully drove the Jeep across the desert straight toward the cargo plane that was now in view. When the first parachute popped out of the rear of the aircraft he stopped the truck and got out.

Sully watched chute after chute spill out of the back of the plane, and once he had a good bearing point, he got back into the Jeep and headed for the team from Tucson.

On the slow, bumpy, ten minute ride to meet the team Zoe had calmed herself enough to ask "do I get any chance to explain why I left, or do I go straight into your 'people I should kill' file?"

Sully stared straight ahead while he drove and gave her a short staccato answer by saying "I used to care, but I gave up giving a shit years ago."

Long ago Zoe would have thought that he was just trying to piss her off, but he was nothing like the man she had known and loved. Sully had become bitter, mean-spirited, and unapproachable, and the only possible reason for the change in him was, unfortunately, her.

Zoe longed to tell him about his son and what a wonderful boy he was, and how happy she had been watching him grow. Zoe wanted to tell him how she wrote him letters almost every day, then once a week took them to work and shredded them. Mostly she wanted to tell him that she loved him.

They stopped as the first Hummer landed with a thud, then the other two followed in rapid succession. When a large gear container landed Sully raced toward the first hummer. By the time he covered the six hundred yards in the Jeep, twelve fully equipped soldiers had landed and were retrieving their parachutes.

Sully pulled up and exited the vehicle. He went to the nearest soldier and asked who was in charge. The Private pointed out his First Sergeant, and Sully left to talk to the man in charge.

First Sergeant Jeff Johansen was about Sully's age with a broad open face that made you want to laugh, no matter how harsh his voice was when he spoke. He had three teams of four readying the Hummer's for duty.

He turned to Sully, but before he could speak, Sully said "code name Viper." It was one of the more embarrassing code names he had been given over the years, but not the worst. He gave Johansen the security code that went with the name.

Johansen fished a code card from his left rear pants pocket to verify Sully. When he had verified the code he said "tell me what you need us to do Sir, we are at your disposal."

Sully looked at the detail that had crudely formed in front of him expecting orders. Zoe was shocked to hear how harsh and grating his voice was. It sounded to her as if he hadn't really spoken aloud in years when he growled "thank you First Sergeant. What I need right now is a detail to detain the civilian woman in the Jeep, take a Hummer with a three man team and load all of my gear out of the Jeep. Then have two men escort her to the Eastern road block I have established using the Jeep. There is currently a retired Army Colonel manning that post. You will brief him, and then you can relieve him. Tell your men that the female will most definitely resist. Allow them to use any force necessary to subdue her."

Sully instructed Johansen to deploy a team of four to the west end of town to knock the water tower down to erect a makeshift roadblock. The rest of them would go back to the "stop" and wait for the invasion.

It was hard for Sully to watch three of the soldiers take Zoe into custody. As soon as she started to fight they drew their weapons, and that was that. She was cuffed and roughly thrown into the back of the Jeep.

Sully watched the Colonel's Jeep motor out of sight, and his heart sank because he had a feeling that he would never see Zoe again, and he had handled this meeting with Zoe so badly. Sully thought '*this is exactly why I chose to live alone in the middle of nowhere fucking Arizona. Why the hell did the world choose to find me?*'

The western bound team had left, after all the gear out of the Jeep had been loaded into the third Hummer. Sully climbed into the back seat and guided the driver back to his gas station.

When they reached the "stop" Johansen ordered the three soldiers climb to the roof after they revived Nooch, with Sully's three sniper rifles. Johansen turned to Sully and said "your in charge here Mills, I would assume you have a plan. As soon as you let me in on it we can get to work."

Sully put his leftover feelings for Zoe back into the deepest recesses of his mind, and did what he did best, plan and kill. He looked at Johansen, with a look that would have frightened the hardest criminal on death row, and growled "just take care of Dinucci, and stay out of my way."

Sully moved quickly to the back room / vault of his gas station. He started retrieving the gear he needed for what he planned to do. Sully picked out; four Claymore mines, six fragmentation grenades, four smoke grenades, an M-16 with twenty clips, and his old favorite; a Marine M-40, in a caliber of .338 Lapua Magnum, with an S & B 30x70 micro adjust scope.

Sully quickly loaded the weapons into an extra-large green duffle bag, then into the pickup. Johansen watched him loading the truck, and when he was ready to get in and go, Jeff walked over to him and said "do you want to give me a hint of your plan so that the boys on the roof don't shoot you."

Sully smiled out of the left side of his mouth, which made it look like a sneer, before he said "if your boys can get a clear shot on me you let them take it, and don't ever blame my weapons. I can drive nails with any one of those in high winds at over a thousand yards."

He had talked briefly with Johansen about where his call-in points would be, and then Sully drove away in the pickup towards town. He knew a road that eventually turned to dirt, and headed straight for the border. A month from now it would turn into a river of illegal border crossers. He parked the pickup about a mile from the border, and grabbed all the gear he would need.

Sully still remembered all of the small washes that were popular border crossing points, and he ducked into the second one he came across.

Sully quickly placed three of the Claymore's along the road with trip wires and remote detonators, then he laid down in the rocky sand in a rapidly constructed sniper's nest. He called Johansen on his throat mike, and said "Viper to Eagle eye, I'm at home. Are the neighbors behaving?"

Sully's earpiece crackled, then Johansen came back and said "roger Viper, looks like the Smiths are having a big party, they're stacked up almost to the wall."

The code talk that Johansen had responded with meant that there was a large enemy force about half a mile to his left that was ready to cross the border. Sully called back and told Johansen that when he started firing, as soon as there was return fire he should send the two Hummers, with guns blazing.

Sully had a shooting lane to his left that saw the border fence for over a mile. He was pretty sure that any engaging force would come right where they had chosen to. His reasoning for his position was simple, if he was going to engage the town with a large force, it's exactly the way he would have done it.

It was less than ten minutes later that Sully acquired his first target in his scope. He grabbed a small laser rangefinder that he had set next to him in the small nest he had made. The range finder set the target at four hundred fifty yards, and Sully smiled. At this range the only problem he foresaw was reloading the rifle fast enough.

Sully waited until the first vehicle started to cross the border fence where the insurgents had cut it. If he could take out the driver, it would hopefully block their path. The only variable was if the driver would take his foot off the gas pedal after a bullet went through his brain.

Sully waited until an old military Jeep was ten feet from crossing the border. He had the driver's head clearly in his scope, and set his aim three inches in front of his nose to compensate for the vehicles rate of travel, and the speed of the bullet.

Sully thought through his range to target one more time in less than a second. He took a breath, held it, and squeezed the trigger.

Zoe's blood was boiling as she rode shackled in the Jeep. Things had gone just about as badly as they could have with her encounter with Sully, and she was furious with him for being such an ass. Now, more than ever, she had to make things right with the love of her life.

Zoe would have to bide her time. Her first order of business was to get out of these handcuffs and away from these soldiers. They stopped at a roadblock not far from the ranch where she had killed a man for his pickup truck. Nooch had never heard a thing while she was breaking the man's neck.

The driver of the Jeep got out to talk with the man watching the roadblock, an older man in an ancient Army uniform. The old soldier had been guarding the roadblock. The Colonel saluted the troops, and then got in the driver's seat of the jeep. Zoe was riding in the back seat, and one of the soldiers occupied the passenger seat.

When they reached the house at the top of a small hill, Zoe was yanked from the vehicle by the soldier, while the older man drove the Jeep to a barn and parked it. Nothing was said until the older soldier came back to them. He had extreme presence, and he glared at the young soldier and loudly said "give me the keys to those cuffs, and get your ass back down to the roadblock!"

The young man saluted, shakily handed him the keys, and stammered "yyes Sir" then he hurried down the hill to the roadblock.

The Colonel took Zoe's handcuffs off and softly said "I have no idea why they would treat a civilian the way they were manhandling you. I expect in time you might tell me. I'm Colonel Abe Danies, Army retired."

Zoe put her hand out and replied "very nice to meet you Colonel Danies, I'm Zoe Mills." She had figured that her real name would get her a lot further than the Kathy Jackson alias.

The Colonel closed his right eye halfway and said "I would be pretty foolish to think that the young man who was here earlier is not somehow related."

Zoe nodded and casually said "Sully is kinda my husband."

Now Abe raised an eyebrow and replied "last time I checked, kinda being married is like kinda being pregnant. Let's go inside and have a cup of coffee with my wife Mabel, and sort this out, and by the way, she is one hundred percent my wife." Abe turned and walked toward the side door of the house that faced the driveway.

Zoe smiled, despite her mood, and followed him into the house. The house was a modern day Rockwellian portrait of Americana, and Zoe liked it instantly. Mabel walked over to greet her with a hug and said "it is so wonderful to have another lady in my house, the testosterone level here is usually off the charts. Please dear sit down at the table with me and gab a little bit, brighten an old woman's day."

Zoe had no idea why, but over three cups of coffee and the next half hour, she had divulged to Mabel things she had never said aloud before. She told her everything about Sully, how they met, how they had loved, and how horribly they had parted. The Colonel stood in a corner of the kitchen the entire time, unmoving, taking everything in.

When Zoe finished she was emotionally exhausted, and needed a nap, but she knew that she needed to enlist the Colonel's help, and get back to Mirage as soon as possible. Zoe said "if Sully is right, and a new weapon has been tested in Mirage, a sizeable enemy force will be coming to assess the effectiveness. I need you to help me get back there and help Colonel Danies, they only have a few men, and Sully is going to need all the help he can get."

Danies finally moved from the corner and walked to the table. He loomed over Zoe and said "I've got maps in my office, let's go make a plan."

Zoe smiled at him and nodded, then she followed him to his office.

When Sully fired the first shot all hell broke loose. As he had feared, the driver had a muscle spasm after Sully's bullet had smashed its way through his brain, and had pushed the accelerator to the floor.

Gunfire was going off all around Sully and the desert. They had no idea what, or who they were shooting at, but they all fired at no apparent target.

Sully wasted no time when Johansen barked in his ear, saying "the roast is in the oven." Each of the five clips he had for the M-40 held eight rounds, and Sully was going to make sure that every shot counted.

Sully quickly squeezed off four more silenced shots, and four more men died. He was no longer taking head shots, all of his bullets were aimed at the center mass of the targets. Sully patiently waited for three more targets to present themselves, then ended three more lives.

Sully ejected his clip, then slapped a loaded one into the rifle. He manually moved the first shell into the chamber and settled behind his scope again. As was usual for Sully, everything moved in slow motion during a sanction. He was aware of everything around him, and everything that was going on through the reticle of his scope.

The first thing Sully noticed was that all of the enemy soldiers were Middle Eastern. He made the snap judgment that they must be Al Qaeda, or a very well-funded splinter faction. When it came to killing, Sully never cared about ethnicity, just blood.

Sully saw the two Hummers racing in, and when all of the fire was directed at them, he took the opportunity to change positions. Sully packed his gear back into a duffle bag, and moved swiftly three hundred yards down the side of the road toward Mirage. He was just past the Claymore mines he had set up when he stopped and hid behind a large prickly pear cactus. He improvised a sniper's nest in seconds, and was set to acquire targets in less than a minute.

The enemy convoy rolled toward him, and although he could have taken out the drivers of the vehicles one by one, he chose to let the mines do their job to stop the convoy.

Sully watched the action through his scope, and saw that the Hummer teams were doing well with their roof mounted M-60's. Sully picked enemy shooter after enemy shooter as targets, and he had only missed once by the time he slapped in his fourth clip.

The enemy force was too large for a simple recon mission. Sully counted seven Jeeps, and three two and one half ton military trucks, known as "deuces" all loaded to capacity with enemy soldiers. His best guess was that there were at least two hundred enemy combatants eager to overtake the now powerless town of Mirage.

That number was being whittled down, but not nearly enough. Sully gave up on the code talk when he called Johansen and asked "is there any more back-up on the way?"

Ten seconds passed before Johansen answered "we are it until your team from Langley gets here."

Sully shook his head and responded "that's not the fucking answer I wanted to hear. Pull the team off of the eastern roadblock, and have them come to my position." Sully gave out detailed directions on how to find him, which was a mistake in any combat situation, but he had no choice, he needed backup quickly.

After a long pause, Johansen said "they should be there in fifteen minutes, that's the best I can do."

Sully didn't respond because the time frame was useless. He needed a lot more backup, and he needed it a hell of a lot sooner than fifteen minutes. Now his job was pretty clear, try to take out any ground troops that were ahead of the vehicles.

Four soldiers walked in front of the lead vehicle and Sully waited impatiently for them to get within feet of the first trip wire before he took them out. At that point they would be less than one hundred yards from his position.

His simple, stupid, plan was to take out the four lead men as fast as possible, and then run out into the road as bait to urge the lead truck to accelerate to catch him. If the deuce followed him fast enough, it should trip the first two Claymore mines, and if Sully was alive to find another hiding spot he could remote detonate the third mine he had placed.

Zoe and the Colonel were more than halfway to town when Zoe heard Sully's plea for help to Johansen. Zoe was deathly afraid for his life because if the situation were not hopeless he would have never divulged his location.

The Colonel shook his head and hit the gas when he too heard the radio transmission from Sully. He watched the road intently as he pushed the Jeep Cherokee faster. He kept his eyes on the road as he said "I know right where he is Zoe I used to quail hunt down that same road. We should be there in less than five."

Zoe just nodded instead of answering him as they passed the "stop". She was too busy willing the Jeep to move faster to speak.

The Colonel had a nice collection of military surplus gear, and weapons, so they were equipped as well as could be expected. Zoe wielded an M-16 with six extra clips, a Taurus semi-automatic pistol in a caliber of forty Smith with three extra clips, and four fragmentation grenades. Colonel Danies carried the same compliment of weaponry, and a sawed off pump ten gauge shotgun that held nine shells. He planned to sling the shotgun on his back.

In the part of Mirage they raced through most of the population was out in the streets. The hood of just about every car was propped open, and everyone Zoe saw had a confused look on their face, even the children.

Danies almost lost control of the Jeep when they hit the dirt road, and Zoe saw the pickup she had killed for. They stopped next to the pickup truck just as two loud explosions erupted within a second of one another.

As fast as Sully fired to take out the four lead soldiers, his last shot was off. He knew it when he squeezed the trigger, and the bullet only grazed the soldier's left side. Having exposed his position, he had no time to spare, so he stuck to his plan. He left the sniper rifle and ran out into the road as fast as he could. The dust and sand was erupting into small clouds all around him, and just before he heard the first explosion he felt searing pain in his left calf.

Sully's left leg failed as he tried to take another running stride, and he rolled on his left side with the fall. He sat up and looked down the road as the second Claymore was tripped, blocking the road with the burning wreckage of an enemy deuce. Sully got up and was able to ignore the pain enough to limp to the side of the road and hide himself inside a creosote bush.

As Sully fished the remote detonator, and his berretta pistol from his vest, he saw the next deuce forge a path around the blown up truck heading straight for the third mine. Sully waited and watched to make sure the truck hit the trip wire. As soon as he heard the mine explode he limped as fast as he could to the pickup, which was just over a quarter of a mile away. He was almost there when he heard the gas tank of the first disabled vehicle explode.

Zoe and Abe started out after checking their gear, when suddenly a third and fourth explosion rocked the calm desert day. As soon as they moved out they saw Sully limping toward them. Zoe's heart smiled at seeing him, and it filled her with a warmth long since forgotten.

Sully saw Zoe and the Colonel and got immediately pissed off. She was supposed to be on her way back to New Mexico, yet she was here where she didn't belong, and brought the elderly Colonel along with her.

Sully pressed his throat mike as he advanced and said "Eagle eye this is Viper, where are the party crashers?"

Johansen squawked back "the party is almost over, and most of the guests have left for home."

Sully finished limping the last hundred yards to the truck. He limped to Zoe and the Colonel and said "our eye in the sky says that they are retreating. Watch this road for any stragglers. I'm gonna go check on the rear team." They could still hear sporadic gun fire in the distance.

Zoe had her mouth open the whole time Sully spoke, staring at his left pant leg that was soaked with blood. Sully limped to the pickup truck and slid into the driver's seat. Zoe was right on his heels and blocked the door from closing. She said "let me look at that leg before you go Sully."

Just hearing her say his name made him furious, and he scowled as he said "I need your help like I need a hole in my other leg. Back away or I'm gonna throw this truck into reverse and run you over with the fuckin' door!"

Colonel Danies had walked over and heard Sully's comment. He tried to exert his once unquestioned authority when he loudly said "Sergeant, you will stand down and let this lady examine and dress your wound."

If Danies hadn't been there, Sully was pretty sure he would have run her down with the door of the truck, but he followed orders and stuck his leg out of the truck door. He reached over to the passenger side floorboard and grabbed his med kit. He handed it to Zoe without saying a word.

Danies left them to guard the border road at a pretty good pace for his age. Zoe cut his pants up to his knee and peeled the blood soaked cloth away. Zoe used a field bandage to wipe the blood from around the wound in Sully's left calf. The bullet, presumably from an AK-47, had entered Sully's calf about ten inches below the knee from behind. The entry wound was smaller than a dime and oozed blood. The problem was the exit would in the front of his calf. It was larger than a silver dollar with shredded muscle and pieces of bone sticking out.

Zoe gasped when she saw the wound and involuntarily put a hand to her mouth. Sully let out one chuckle and sarcastically said "shit, that's like a mosquito bite, try being burned on thirty percent of your body sometime if you want some real fun."

Zoe didn't respond as she tended to his wound because she had heard that Sully almost died and was burned badly in her "death mission". She poured some peroxide over the wound and used two packaged field dressings to tightly wrap the wound.

Just then the third Hummer showed up and parked next to the Cherokee. Three young soldiers piled out of the military vehicle and ran to Sully.

The Corporal saluted and said "Sir, Corporal Halo, my squad is at your disposal, what do you want us to do?"

Sully answered "Corporal you're with me, we are going to check on the rear team." Then he pointed at the two other soldiers and said "you two triple time it down that road and find Colonel Danies, then do exactly what he tells you to." Then he looked at Zoe and said "I don't give a fuck what you do, just stay out of my way!"

Sully limped even more now that he had sat for ten minutes and the muscles left in his calf had tightened. He went to the Hummer and got in the front passenger seat. Halo beat him to the vehicle, and as soon as Sully closed his door, the Humvee did a quick U-turn, and was gone in seconds.

Zoe got into the pickup, trying hard to hold back tears, and drove. She had no idea where she was going, but she felt that she had to leave the scene of Sully's brutality.

She finally decided to go to his gas station and see how he was living. She glanced down at her hands on the steering wheel and then the tears flowed down her face. Her hands were still covered with Sully's blood, and the symbolism of blood on her hands was almost more than she could handle right now.

When Zoe arrived at the "stop" she sat in the truck for a minute to compose herself. She climbed the ladder to the roof to introduce herself to Johansen. When she was four rungs from the roof Johansen was there peering down the ladder with a pistol drawn. He said "it would be a pretty good idea for you to identify yourself right now."

Zoe was just about sick and tired of being threatened this day, and it showed in her voice when she answered "I'm Zoe Mills, Sully's wife, and an SSO field agent."

Johansen disappeared from the edge of the roof, but he said "I've heard of you Zoe, come on up."

Zoe finished climbing the ladder, and walked to the south side of the roof where Johansen was kneeling behind a tripod, and looking through a high powered spotting scope. Zoe picked up a pair of binoculars that were sitting on the top of the parapet wall and knelt to steady them on the wall.

The optics Zoe was halfheartedly looking through showed her what looked like ants milling around matchbox cars. All she was able to determine for certain was that there were three Humvee's, which meant that Sully was safe for the time being.

Zoe asked Johansen "where did the enemy go?"

Johansen stood and rubbed his bloodshot eyes. Then he said "what's left of them retreated back into Mexico. We probably took out half of them already, and with back-up on the way, we should be in the clear. You're man is like a one man army, I think he took out about forty by himself."

Zoe replied sarcastically "yeah, he is wonderful at killing, but not much else. He took one in the leg, and it looks pretty bad."

Johansen said "we've got a convoy of eighty men on the way from Tucson, they should be here in less than an hour. I'll radio them and make sure they have a medic."

Zoe left him without saying a word, and climbed down the ladder. She had decided to be nosy, and it wasn't long after she started prowling around the small building that she regretted her decision.

Sully's life was despicable at best. Other than the small store, the building contained three other rooms with no windows. Sully's bedroom looked like a prison cell. It was six feet by nine feet with a small cot, three gun safes, and an old folding television tray with a hotplate on it. Nothing was hung on the dirty grey walls.

The bathroom had no door, and contained a toilet, a laundry sink, and a shower stall so small Zoe could barely have fit in it. It explained the floor drain in the center of the dirty floor.

The final room had a heavy steel door with four deadbolt locks, and a digital keypad alarm panel. The rush of this mission had caused Sully to leave the door open, otherwise entry would have been difficult for even a seasoned safe cracker. The room was the same size as Sully's bedroom and contained Sully's arsenal.

Zoe was sad before, but now she sat on his bed and wept for a full ten minutes. Her actions had not only almost killed him, but now she saw that he was not living a life at all, just surviving. They had a wonderful life until she got pregnant, and she wouldn't give up her son for the world, but how she had shattered Sully's life broke her heart.

Zoe steeled herself against her emotions, wiped her face, and walked out the back door.

Johansen was coming down the ladder and Zoe waited for him. When he was down Zoe went to him and asked "do you have a working cell phone I could use?"

Johansen reached into the breast pocket of his vest and handed her his satellite phone. He saw that Zoe had been crying, and she looked about as distraught as a person could look. He asked "are you alright Ma'am?"

Zoe's answer was a mean snap, when she angrily said "I'm fine, how are you?"

Johansen just shook his head and walked away.

Zoe walked the direction opposite of Johansen while she was dialing Jill's number. When Jill answered Zoe quickly asked "is he okay?"

Jill answered "Zoe, he is fine, how are you, what did the doctor say?"

Zoe took a deep breath and said "they didn't tell me a thing, the first biopsy was inconclusive, and so they did another one. You have to call the hospital and tell them I lost my phone. Have them call you if you don't mind."

Jill said "not a problem Kathy, do you want to talk to the monster?"

Zoe shook her head, as if Jill could see her, as she answered "no I should be home by tomorrow, and then I will talk with him."

Zoe walked back to Johansen without saying a word and handed him his phone. She went to the truck and headed back to the Danies house. She desperately needed a shower and some sleep. She was physically and emotionally drained.

The earpiece in Sully's ear crackled, and then Johansen said "our cousins from the west are here, come and eat some cake with us."

Sully limped over to Corporal Halo and said "leave three men here, and send one with a Hummer over to find Colonel Danies. Get Danies out with the Jeep and leave the others there on watch. Have both teams call in every hour, one at the top of the hour, the other at the bottom." Sully limped back to the third Humvee, and headed for his gas station to deal with Zoe.

His dark mood turned to black when he saw the pickup being driven away by Zoe as he approached. He stopped the truck three hundred and fifty yards from the gas station, and waited until Zoe was out of sight, only then did he drive up.

He had no doubt that she saw him because he made no attempt to hide. He felt childish and stupid, but his mood was an almost uncontrollable rage, and Sully knew it was safer to stay at a distance rather than to have another encounter with Zoe in this frame of mind.

When he pulled up to the back door of his gas station he got out of the Hummer as Johansen was walking over to him. Jeff smiled and said "boy, you are just as advertised and then some. If they hadn't turned tail and run, I bet you could have taken them all out by yourself. Zoe told me you were hit in the leg, are you alright?"

Sully scowled at him and said "get your shit and get the hell out of here, this is your mess now, I'm done. And when you find the rifle and gear I left on the side of the border road, I want it brought here, and put in the Excursion." With that said he limped badly into the "stop" and locked the door behind him.

Johansen got on his cell phone and called in to the SSO. When the phone was picked up by Weathers himself, Jeff was impressed. He told the head of field services all about the success of the mission, and Sully's injury and attitude.

Weathers said "our team touched down in Tucson half an hour ago, and I will instruct them to go straight there, and I will get a nurse on the way. I want you to stay with him until the team arrives."

Johansen shakily replied "ah Sir, that might be a problem. He locked himself in the gas station, and made it quite clear that I should leave. Sir, his order was quite serious, and I don't feel real comfortable staying here."

Weathers let out one jolly laugh, and there was a smile in his voice when he said "you had better get your ass out of there then, I've never known Mills not to follow through on a threat. I will tell the team to meet you a mile from that gas station."

Sully had gone to his small bedroom and took off his heavy tactical vest, and his boots. He collapsed onto the cot and thought for only two minutes before sleep overcame him. The only cogent thoughts he had were about Zoe, and why he had chosen to be so hostile toward her. Half of him never wanted to see her again, and half wanted to tell her how much he still loved her. The only thing stopping him from having a real, productive, and happy life was his stubbornness.

Sully had no idea how long he had slept, but scratching at his door woke him from a deep sleep. Sully forgot about his wounded leg when he jumped off the cot to grab a weapon from his vest. His leg gave out, and he fell hard into one of the gun safes, cutting his forehead on the combination lock wheel of the safe. He grabbed the tactical vest and sat on the bed. He pulled the nine millimeter Beretta out, and two grenades.

Sully sat on the bed and yelled "anybody that comes through that door is going out feet first!"

Ron Rady yelled through the door "quit being an ass-hole and open the door Mills."

Sully was shocked to hear Ron's voice because they hadn't spoken since Sully took his leave of absence. If it was even possible, he got even more upset because Weathers had sent Rady knowing that they had a relationship. Sully thought '*what's next, Janet and Zoe.*'

Sully laughed to himself when he heard Janet say "please Sully, let us in, Zoe is on her way, and we have a doctor from Tucson with us."

Sully sighed, and then replied "I'm not in the mood to see anyone right now, so it looks like you wasted your time, and the government's money."

Janet would not give up that easily, and tried to threaten him by saying "listen here Sullivan Mills, we have a directive from Weathers to make sure you are alright, and we can't report back until we have completed that mission."

Sully laughed on the inside because he truly did not give a shit about Weathers, or any of them right now. He sat on the cot and donned the heavy tactical vest again, and reloaded it with the items he had removed.

Sully opened the same gun safe that had cut his forehead. He took out an antique buffalo gun that he had bought on a whim and never fired. He used the extra-long rifle as a crutch to slowly make his way to the cash register. He grabbed the old barstool he customarily sat on to ring up customers and painfully carried it, while using the buffalo gun as a crutch, to a spot five feet from the back door. The creaky swivel seat of the stool would allow him to cover both entrances to the "stop", even though the front door was totally blocked by Nooch's agent mobile.

Sully once again pulled the Berretta from his vest and held it in his lap. Like the rest of Mirage, Sully's gas station had no power. In the dim light he saw the two glass door coolers that contained Gatorade, soda pop, and beer. He limped over with the buffalo gun and grabbed something for dinner, a lukewarm six pack of Budweiser.

There was no communication through the door until Sully had finished his second beer and thrown the empty can at the door 'time for dessert' sully thought as he opened his third beer.

An all too familiar voice came through the door when Zoe said "Sully, will you please let me in to speak to you? If you do I promise it will be the last time you ever hear from me."

Sully thought about her offer for a few seconds, then decided that, if it could give him the closure he needed, he would allow it. He waited three minutes before opening the door, just to make her think. Sully limped over, without using the buffalo gun, and unlocked the three deadbolts on the door, allowing access to his former one true love.

Sully went back to the barstool as the door opened and Zoe walked in looking better than he ever remembered her looking. He felt lucky that he was not standing, because his knees went weak. He had decided to be cordial, but seeing her in the dim light cast by her battery operated lantern made him want to stand up and whisk her into his arms.

Zoe looked concerned at the pistol he held in his lap and asked "is it safe to come in, or are you going to shoot me?"

Sully put an uncomfortable half-smile on his face and answered "if I didn't want you in here, you wouldn't be. Close and lock the door behind you if you don't mind, I think we need to talk alone."

Zoe closed the door and locked two of the three deadbolts with trepidation. She turned back to Sully, who was taking off his tactical vest, and said "I think I have quite a bit of explaining to do. Where would you like me to start?"

Sully shifted uncomfortably in his chair, and finished the third beer in one long drink. He looked her straight in the eyes and replied "you don't have to tell me anything, I have come to accept the situation, and I don't blame you a bit for getting out of the SSO if you had the chance." He opened the fourth beer before she could answer.

Zoe quietly said "Sullivan, first and foremost I need you to know that I love you. I have from the moment we met, and I will never stop." She looked up from the floor and met his eyes to gauge his reaction. He was staring at and through her at the same time, showing no emotion whatsoever.

It was obvious to Zoe that he was not ready to speak, so she continued by saying "I burnt out Sully, you were in Malaysia for two months, and being alone made me evaluate my life. I just couldn't go on killing anymore. I used you as leverage with Weathers to get out. I told him that if he sanctioned me he would have you to deal with, and he didn't want any part of that scenario.

She paused again to give Sully a chance to speak, but he continued his blank stare. Zoe went on, saying "the mission in Maine was well planned to make sure nobody got hurt, but you must have placed a tracer on me, and you ran straight into the cover blast. I was horrified to hear how badly you were injured, and I begged to be with you, but my bed had been made."

Sully cleared his throat and finally spoke. In a weak, hoarse voice he asked "besides Weathers and Janet, who knew about that mission?"

Zoe looked him squarely in the eyes and answered "Barnes, Carter, and …. Rady." She knew that Ron being involved in the cover-up of her "death" would hurt Sully, but she was going to be as truthful as she could this time.

Sully shook his head and pursed his lips into a disgusted sneer. He said "and the son of a bitch didn't even wash my feet." Then he went back to his blank hateful stare.

Zoe wanted to smile at the dark, sarcastic joke he had made, but there was no joy in her soul right now. She quietly said "I have no right to ask for your forgiveness Sully, but I need to know that you are going to live some semblance of a life. This thing you're doing now is barely surviving, and I know it is meant to punish me, and you need to stop it."

Sully looked her squarely in the eyes and replied "I really think you have given up your right to make demands of me, and if this is how I choose to live, you will just have to deal with it." He was getting angry again, and didn't like the road this conversation was going down. He continued by saying "I think we are done here, you can leave the way you came in."

Zoe was as stubborn as ever, and replied "I'm not leaving here until you let me look at your leg."

Sully laughed aloud and replied "first a demand and now an ultimatum. You always did have balls Millstad, but they aren't gonna help you this time. Now get out, and trust me I won't ask again."

Ron had climbed the underside of Nooch's rolled over car. It had effectively blocked the front door of Sully's gas station, leaving only a four inch gap, at the top, to see through. When the conversation between Sully and Zoe had gone wrong, Ron put the sights of his pistol on the back of Sully's neck, and fired twice.

Chapter 12

Sully woke up in a large bed in an overly frilly room. His head hurt as if he been on a three day drinking binge, when he could only remember having had three beers. He looked around the room and quickly figured out that he was somewhere in the Danies household.

Sully sat up quickly, and instantly regretted it. He felt as if a miniature mariachi band was performing inside his head. He laid back down for a minute, until the band played something el dolce, and went through his memory of the events that had led him here. The last thing he could truly remember was his adversarial conversation with Zoe.

There was a light knock at the door that preceded Mabel Danies. She was carrying a tray that she set on the triple dresser. Mabel smiled at him and cheerfully said "good morning Sullivan, I thought you might like something to eat."

Sully's throat was dry and when he tried to speak his voice was little more than a whisper. He hoarsely answered Mabel by saying "no thank you, but I would really like some water."

Mabel brought him a bottle of water and a glass of tomato juice from the tray. Sully greedily drank from the water bottle until it was half gone, then said "thank you Missus Danies, I apologize for being in your home, it wasn't my idea."

Mabel replied "nonsense dear, you were badly injured when they brought you here, and from what I hear you are quite a hero. I will tell the doctor you are awake." Mabel took the tray and left Sully alone in the room.

Doctor Asher Maxwell had been flown in from Virginia to work on Sully's leg. He was the doctor that had done the majority of work on Sully after the Maine mission. Maxwell's son had been an Army Ranger who was missing in action for over a year in Afghanistan, and he ended up coming to the SSO for help. After the remains of his son were found, Maxwell had become an indentured servant of the SSO.

Maxwell came into the room and shook his head at Sully. He said "every time I get a call about you Mills I shudder to think what you've done to yourself this time." He had a smile on his face as he had said it.

Sully didn't return the smile and said "how bad is the leg Ash?" Unfortunately over the years Sully had gotten to know Doctor Maxwell quite well. His resume of injuries rivaled even that of Evel Knievel.

Maxwell frowned and said "it's bad Sully, but I have no idea of how bad until I can get you to a hospital and get some films. I cleaned and debrided the wounds the best I could under these circumstances, and sutured the wounds as well as possible. The problem is that I removed quite a bit of bone and metal fragments, so I'm sure that I will have to operate again.

Sully scowled and replied "thanks Ash, but no thanks. I'm not going to any hospital, and I'm not letting you cut on me anymore."

Maxwell said "don't be stupid Sully, if I don't fix that leg it will be useless, and no matter how many antibiotics I give you it is going to get a major infection."

Sully replied "Ash, I would never hold you responsible for my actions, you know that. I have just had enough right now, and I'm not having any more surgeries."

Maxwell started to leave the room, then stopped and said "if you don't get that leg fixed soon Sully, I'm afraid the prognosis is quite grim."

Sully simply closed his eyes and lay back onto the pillow. Maxwell let out a heavy sigh and left the room.

Fifteen minutes later the door to Sully's room opened again, and Weathers strode purposely in. He had a stern look on his face, and Sully could tell he was in a foul mood. He stood at the foot of the bed and looked down on Sully. Weathers said "what's the game this time Mills? Apparently you want something from me before you will let Maxwell fix you up. Cut to the chase and tell me what you want."

Sully replied "the only thing I want is to be left alone boss, that's it."

Weathers shook his head and said "you should know that is impossible right now, just about every government agency with an acronym wants to talk to you right now. You get through that and I will leave you alone."

Sully groaned and said "I would really rather just debrief with you boss, and have you do the rest of the dog and pony show."

Weathers shook his head and replied "sorry Mills, not this time, this is way too big, and Macmillan has insisted. I have an ambulance on the way to take you in a convoy to a secure facility just outside of Roswell, and we leave within the hour. There is a complete medical facility there, and as soon as you debrief with everyone, Maxwell is going to fix that leg."

Sully defiantly said "I'll do the dog and pony if I have to, but I aint doing the leg. By the way, who shot the tranquilizer into me?"

Weathers squinted and answered by saying "I don't know why it should matter, but Rady did if you must know."

Sully scowled and nodded at no one, and Weathers left the room. After he left Sully sat up and swung his legs out of the bed and tested his leg. The more weight he put on it the more it hurt, but he was able to walk with a severe limp.

Sully limped slowly to the door, and locked it. He looked in the closet and dresser in the room and found no clothing, other than what he assumed to be Mabel's. He was in only his boxer briefs, and went to the door again.

He unlocked the door and opened it halfway. As he had hoped there was a single guard there and when Sully spoke to him he jumped. Sully said "hey buddy, I limped over here, but I could use a hand getting back to the bed."

The young agent eagerly replied "certainly agent Mills, anything you need Sir."

The young agent rushed into the small room, and Sully put his arm around his shoulder and closed the door. Before the agent even knew what happened Sully had him in a choke hold with both arms. He squeezed as hard as he could clamping shut both of the young man's carotid arteries, and he passed out in less than a minute.

Sully limped back to the door and locked it. Seven minutes later he had changed into the agent's clothing and gear, and had put him in the bed and covered him up. All of this quick action had taken its toll, and his leg was burning with extreme pain. Sully did his best to block it out, because it was time to go.

Sully limped over to the only window in the room and opened the heavy shades. His luck was running as usual, bad. There was no clock in the room, and the agent's watch had told him it was nine twenty five, but it turned out to be a.m. when Sully would have much preferred it to have been p.m.

The window had a different view than he had expected. The window of this room faced the back of the Danies' barn. Sully guessed that it must have been a guest house that he hadn't seen the last time he was here. He saw no guards in view, so he popped off the screen, carefully climbed out the window, and lowered himself to the ground. He closed the drapes, and replaced the screen.

Now that Sully had gained his freedom, as temporary as it might be, he had to get back to the "stop" to get some supplies. He limped to the barn to try to find a mode of transportation. Sully carefully opened the rear door of the barn just a crack and looked inside. The front door was closed, and there was barely any light in the barn.

Sully went inside and closed the rear door. He waited a couple of minutes for his vision to adjust to the abrupt darkness. He had been in the garage only once, and was trying to remember what he had seen.

Unless there was a four wheeler, or an off road motorcycle, in here he was screwed. There was no way he could drive the Colonel's Jeep out of here, there were way too many SSO agents lurking about, and it wouldn't be long until the agent he had placed in his bed would wake up and sound the alarm.

Sully used the backlight of the cell phone he had taken from the agent he had incapacitated to look around the barn. He found nothing he could use for an overland getaway. The cell phone light also showed that he was bleeding at a steady rate from the recently patched bullet hole in his leg.

The Jeep was parked in the barn where it had been before, and Sully opened the back end to see if it had been unloaded yet, and it was empty. Sully stood there going through the options in his mind, and found none. He started to feel light headed, so he crawled into the back of the Jeep to lie down and rest.

Sully had no idea how long he had slept, but he was stirred awake by the loud sound of the barn door being opened, and the bright light suddenly streaming in. He carefully peeked over the back seat to see three agents walk in, methodically searching the garage. Sully felt the pistol against his ribs in the shoulder holster, and thought about it for a second, then decided that he had no beef with these men, they were just doing their job.

Waiting in the Jeep to be discovered was an unfamiliar feeling for Sully, and when he was finally discovered, he surrendered for the first time in his life. One SSO agent ran back to the main house, while the other two pointed their pistols at him.

He said "relax boys, I'm sure help is on the way, besides, I can't walk right now so you can be pretty sure your safe." He had to lie back down because he was so light headed.

Seconds later Weathers arrived followed by; Ron, Janet, Ash, and Zoe. Weathers took the Glock nine millimeter from Sully's stolen shoulder holster without a struggle, and then ushered Maxwell in to examine him.

Maxwell shook his head and said to Weathers "I hope that ambulance arrives soon, he has lost too much blood, and he needs an I.V., and some blood, and you had better line up a couple donors."

Weathers nodded and walked off toward the house without saying a word, Maxwell urged Sully to lie back until the ambulance arrived, but he refused. They only ended up waiting for the ambulance for fifteen minutes, and when it backed up the driveway to the barn Sully was put onto the gurney and placed in the ambulance.

While waiting for the ambulance Sully had locked eyes with Zoe and they stared at one another for five minutes, and in Sully's weakened condition he conveyed to her his sense of loss and longing for her. Zoe broke the stare and had walked away.

Sully decided that he was through punishing himself and when the debriefing was over he would end his sabbatical and return to the SSO.

Killing was not a substitute for love, but it helped him feel nothing. In his mind he finally said goodbye to Zoe, and let her go, forever.

Maxwell had given him I.V. fluids, and a pint of blood ironically donated by the agent he had taken out for his short lived escape. It was a slow moving convoy, and a normal trip of six hours took over ten. Sully slept for most of the trip.

He woke still in the ambulance, and felt that something had changed. He could no longer smell the heavy layer of cheap cologne that always told him Ash was in the room, instead he not only could smell, but he could feel the most familiar essence he had ever encountered. Zoe was on the ambulance.

Zoe saw that Sully was stirring on the gurney and went over to sit next to him. Zoe looked down into his eyes and said "I was hoping we could talk. If you don't want to I totally understand, and I will leave you alone."

Sully smiled weakly at her, and replied "I think it's about time for me to be reasonable. I would like to talk to you Zoe." Sully wanted to hear about her life, and hoped that she had found the happiness he was never able to give her.

Zoe started the conversation by saying "I will never be able to tell you how sorry I am that I left, and that you got hurt so badly. Like I told you before I just couldn't do it anymore, or be a part of it. I have been living as Kathy Jackson Malloy in Madrid, New Mexico. I am a grade school teacher, and enjoy it very much."

Sully smiled at her genuinely and sincerely said "I am very happy for you Zoe, I always wanted a normal life like you have." Then he asked "are you married? Do you have any children?"

Zoe finally lowered her eyes from his gaze, because she was about to tell him the lie she had rehearsed for years. Zoe answered "I was married to a local firefighter, Jay Malloy for two years but he was killed fighting a forest fire. I have an eight year old son."

It took Sully only seconds to do the math. Zoe had become pregnant about eighteen months after she left. Sully put on a fake smile and said "I'm glad you are happy Zoe, that's all I ever wanted." Inside Sully was angry. Zoe had said she never wanted children, and that she would love only him forever. He was disappointed that she had remarried and had a child so soon after leaving him, he felt somewhat betrayed.

Zoe was pretty sure that Sully was lying about being happy for her, and she wished she could tell him the truth. She had asked Weathers for permission to do just that, and he had refused, and then he had threatened her and her son if she did. All she could say to Sully was "I wish things could have turned out differently."

Sully was more forlorn than ever, and nodded his agreement to her and pretended to sleep. Zoe took his hand and held it for the rest of the ambulance ride. It was her way of saying a final goodbye. Not another word was said between them until they reached Roswell, then Zoe kissed him lightly on the forehead and softly said "goodbye my love."

Sully was whisked from the ambulance to a surgical suite in the Roswell complex. Maxwell had convinced Weathers that he needed to operate on Sully's leg before a long series of debriefings could be done. When the convoy had stopped for fuel Maxwell had been taken by helicopter to the base to make all the preparations for surgery.

The surgery on the SSO's top agent's leg had taken over four hours to complete. Cadaver bone, titanium plates, and nineteen titanium screws had been required to patch together the shattered portion of Sully's Fibula. Maxwell and the two assisting base surgeons considered the operation a success beyond their expectations.

Three hours post operatively the debriefings began, and they lasted a total of fourteen hours. Sully was given amphetamines to keep him awake and alert during the non-stop session. When the grilling was finally over, Sully slept for an entire day without waking.

The SSO, and the FBI had teams of military personnel replacing every electrical circuit, and every component in every household and business in Mirage that had been affected by the E.M.P. for days, and the town was almost back on its feet when Sully was returned to his gas station. Dinucci had been assigned to him as a valet until he was back on his feet, and Sully did not object. The SSO had the "stop" up and running by the time he got back with Nooch and his very own shiny new crutches.

They had his Excursion up and running, and the entire station had been re-stocked with fresh junk food and beverages. A brand new, thirty foot, top of the line travel trailer had been placed behind the building as living quarters. Once sully was settled in and had taken a nap in the trailer, he crutched his way to his truck and went to town.

Mirage had not been structurally affected by the event at all, but it was a slow, ongoing process to replace every circuit board even in a town as small as this. Military and contracted civilian personnel were scurrying around the town like an infestation of beetles.

Sully drove by "D's" house to check on her, but there was no car there. Sully figured she was off trotting the globe somewhere and had missed the biggest event that would ever to happen in this small town. Sully went to the IGA market and used a shopping cart to limp around the store. He bought some ugly looking expired steaks, and frozen side dishes for dinner with Nooch as a combination thank you and apology.

On the way back to the "stop" he made a decision. Sully was going to allow three weeks for his leg to heal, then he was going to pack up, and head east. He could not shake the feeling of betrayal that Zoe would have married so soon after she "died". Sully planned on dealing with it the only way he knew how. He was going back to full active field duty with the SSO, so that he would be able to focus on sanctions, rather than Zoe.

After two weeks of boredom, Sully had Nooch start loading up his truck for the drive east. Sully called Weathers and told him what his intentions were, and he was thrilled to say the least. Weathers was going to leave Nooch in place to run the gas station because now it was considered a position of strategic importance.

Sully was walking with only the aid of a cane now, and it was time to go. He left at four hundred hours on a Friday, and he had only one stop of importance on his way to Virginia, Madrid New Mexico.

Sully arrived in Madrid at eleven thirty hours, and drove straight to Kathy Jackson's house, there was no Malloy in the local phone directory. He parked right in front of the house and walked up the sidewalk to the front door. The house was a well-kept older Victorian, that Sully guessed to be no more than two thousand square feet.

Sully rang the bell, not expecting an answer at noon on a weekday, but a woman's voice yelled back to the bell "just a second, I'm coming!"

Sully was confused and disappointed. He thought he might have the wrong address, but that was unlikely. Jill Ling came to the door and Sully recognized her as an operations agent of the SSO. He knew immediately he was in the right place.

Jill was obviously shocked to see him and tentatively invited him into the house. Sully took off his well-worn straw hat, wiped his boots, and entered Zoe's house. Jill offered him coffee, and he accepted the gesture even though he could go for a beer. Jill excused herself to make a fresh pot of coffee.

Sully took the opportunity to prowl around Zoe's living room. He still had no idea why he was compelled to come here, or what he had hoped to accomplish, but he was here for some unknown cosmic reason and he needed to try to figure it out.

It only took Sully a minute to figure out why he was here. There were several pictures of Zoe and her son on the sofa table. Sully had no doubts anymore about why he was here. The pictures showed Zoe posed with their son. The child in the photographs was at least ten, and looked like a twin of Sully when he was that age.

Sully's hands were still shaking when Jill brought him an oversized mug of coffee. She handed it to Sully, who had sat on the sofa still holding a framed photograph of his family. Jill saw the ghost white look on his rugged, well-tanned face, and knew that the lie was over. Jill asked "would you like cream or sugar agent Mills?"

Sully had a blank stare on his face when he answered "no, thank you, tell me about my son." He sipped the tepid coffee in an attempt to project normalcy to agent Ling.

Now it was Jill's turn to turn white. She shakily answered "you mean Van? He is Jay Malloy's son, I don't understand?"

Sully scowled and said "I think it's about time everybody stopped lying to me. I just want to know how their life has been for the last ten years Jill, no more bullshit, please."

Jill bowed her head, and knew that there was no sense in lying anymore. She rubbed her forehead with her right hand, and then said "I guess you do deserve some answers, let's go sit at the kitchen table, I need a drink before I tell you everything."

Sully nodded his head and followed Jill to the kitchen, still carrying the picture. He sat at the table and said "I'll have a double scotch if you have it, with a beer chaser. Otherwise beer will be fine."

Jill opened a bottle of Beringer Merlot for her and set it on the table along with a wine glass, then she poured Sully a triple Glenlevit on the rocks and set it on the table along with the bottle. Jill went to the fridge and brought Sully a bottle of Dos Equis dark beer and an opener.

Jill disappeared into the living room, and returned moments later with a large photo album. She set the album in front of Sully, and then sat across from him pouring herself a glass of wine. She held up her glass and offered a toast. Jill meekly said "to the truth."

Sully half smiled and raised his glass. He replied "I will drink to that" and they both took long drinks. Sully greedily opened the photo album and committed each photo to memory. Sully smiled a genuine smile for the first time in ten years as he looked at photos of the son he never knew he had growing up picture after picture without him.

Jill spent three hours narrating each picture and telling Sully all about his son. Sully's head was spinning, as much from the flood of information he was receiving, and the three double scotches he had ingested followed by four beers. Van was only eight years old in the photo album, when they decided to take a break and eat something.

Sully went out to the back patio of Zoe's house and had a cigar. When Jill came out with a sandwich for him he thanked her, and ate the sandwich quickly.

Sully walked back into the kitchen at fifteen thirty hours and sat back at the kitchen table. When Jill sat down he closed the album and asked "What time does Zoe get home from work?"

Jill was somewhat confused by the question, but she answered Sully by saying "Zoe usually gets home with Van around five o clock."

Sully laid out his plan by saying "I would like you to ask her if she would meet with me alone at six thirty. Do you have a place you could take Van for the night?"

Jill answered "yes, I have my own place not far from here."

Sully scribbled down his new SSO cell phone number on a napkin, and said "call me only if Zoe will not take the meeting." Sully stood from the table and left the house without saying a word, but he carried the framed picture with him. He stopped by the door and took the picture out of the frame, and donned his hat as he left.

Sully drove to the nearest motel, the "Mountain View", and paid for a room for one night. The motel was a rundown motor-court that allowed him to back his truck right up to the door.

Sully grabbed his bag of clothing, and an identical duffle bag that contained several weapons. He made sure that his truck was locked and alarmed, and then he entered the motel room. He took a Glock nine millimeter pistol out of the weapons duffle and set it on the well-worn and scarred triple dresser. He dead-bolted the door, and engaged the privacy lock.

Sully went through the other duffel and took out the clothes he wanted to wear if he was going to meet Zoe. He hung the blue and white striped Wrangler western shirt he planned to wear in the small, dirty bathroom. Sully turned the shower on as hot as it would go and closed the door to the room. He was hoping that the steam would take some of the wrinkles out of the crumpled shirt.

Sully shaved for the first time in a week, and cut himself twice. He laughed to himself, remembering the first date he had with Zoe, when he arrived with a small piece of toilet tissue on his face. He showered quickly, and dressed in everything but the shirt. He wore a black pair of Levis, a black tee shirt, and of course his worn out boots, which he had cleaned with a wet washcloth.

Sully felt the same excitement he had felt long ago when he and Zoe had fallen in love. He was praying that his phone did not ring. It was seventeen twenty (five twenty), and his phone had not rung. Sully took it as a good sign, because Zoe was almost certain to know of his visit, and his offered plan.

Time moved slowly for Sully. He was so filled with anticipation that he could not sit still. At eighteen hundred he left the motel room packing all of his things back into the Excursion. He had put on the shirt and tried to press out the rest of the wrinkles with the palm of his hand. He tucked the shirt into his pants, and put on a long blue and white horse hair belt with a large silver and turquoise buckle, and a large silver tip. When Sully got to the truck he put on his old brown bomber jacket and left the motel.

Sully drove to the local supermarket and bought two bottles of wine, one white and one red. He went to the floral department and picked out a small bouquet of assorted flowers without roses, or a vase.

Sully drove to Zoe's house and parked a block away. The Excursion was about the most conspicuous vehicle on the planet, but Sully didn't have a choice right now. He grabbed a pair of fifty powered Swarovski binoculars and looked intently at the house. It was eighteen fifteen, and the lights were on, which Sully took as a good sign. He caught only glimpses of movement with his limited vantage point, but there was movement.

Sully found himself shaking as he drove the block to her house at fifteen miles per hour. Sully took several deep breaths and grabbed the wine and the flowers. With his hands full he was unable to use his cane, but he had planned on leaving it the truck anyhow. Sully limped to her front door and shakily rang the doorbell with his left hand.

Zoe's heart leapt into her throat when she heard the doorbell. When Jill had pulled her aside, and told her about Sully's visit and his request to meet her alone this evening she started shaking. It was a day she had wanted to come for the last ten years. Zoe had dressed three times and finally decided on a low cut, knee length Chanel red dress, long pearls that drew eyes to her cleavage, and red Dior heels.

She almost stumbled when she went to open the door. Zoe smiled at Sully and said "come on in cowboy, you look wonderful."

Sully shakily handed her the flowers and replied "you look even more beautiful than you do in my dreams Zoe." She took the flowers and stepped aside so he could enter the house.

He limped into the house and Zoe closed the door. She took the two bottles of wine from him and set them on a small table by the door. She turned to Sully and opened her mouth to speak but nothing came out. Zoe threw herself into Sully's arms and whispered "I am so happy that you came here today and found out about Van, I have wanted to be honest with you since before I left, and now I finally can.

He grabbed her chin and kissed her lightly. Sully felt an electric shock run through his body as he did. He softly said "all I ever wanted was the truth, it's about time we got around to it."

Zoe kissed him deeply, and grabbed his hand. Zoe led him into the kitchen where they sat at the table for an hour talking about Van, and their separate lives that they had missed due to the SSO. Zoe got out the picture album again and tuned it to the page he had stopped at earlier.

She stood over his shoulder and narrated the pictures that he pointed at, and told him about their son.

Every time Sully smiled or laughed at a picture or her commentary, it filled Zoe's heart with the love that had been missing for all of these years. She was incredibly lonely for him, but she had Van to help fill the void in her life. Zoe could only imagine the incredible loneliness that Sully had dealt with over the years. She kissed his neck and said "I've missed you Sullivan, thank you for coming here. You are the only thing missing in my life."

Sully turned to face her and respond, but he didn't get the chance. Zoe kissed him passionately and deeply like they used to. They kissed for several minutes, holding and petting one another, until she said "come on cowboy, let me show you my bedroom." She took him by the hand and led him down the hallway.

When she stopped at the first door on the right and started to open it Sully grabbed her and pinned her against the wall. He nibbled her ear and rubbed against her, she moaned and said "come make love to me Sully, please."

He let her break free from his grasp and enter her bedroom, he followed close behind. Zoe let her dress fall to the floor, and stepped to Sully to help him undress. He grabbed her by the shoulders and stopped her. He looked in her eyes and said "don't forget about my burns, they aren't the most attractive things to look at."

She kissed him, and then replied "Sully, I really don't mind. They are my fault, by the way. He took off his tee shirt, and although Zoe thought she was ready, she let out an involuntary gasp when she saw the mangled skin covered by grayish blue patchwork quilt of grafts.

She tentatively reached out and ran her hand over the burns as a tear rolled down her cheek. The mood was damaged, but not yet broken. Sully kissed her deeply and then whispered "come to bed and make it up to me." He sat on the edge of the bed and took off his boots, then slipped off his pants and briefs together and laid down on the bed.

Zoe smiled, took off her red lace brassier, and then joined him on the bed. They made love like neither of them had in years, because they hadn't. Sully and Zoe had never fallen out of love, and in bed they acted as if they had never left one another. They both had voracious sexual appetites, and acted like they had to fill a lifetime in one night.

They took breaks and cuddled and talked until the mood struck them again. On one break Zoe asked Sully about each of the scars on his body that she did not know the origin of. It turned out to be a tour of the world through Sully's life as an assassin. From a knife wound acquired in Argentina, to bullet wounds from Zimbabwe, Sully was able to use his battered body as a world map.

Zoe kissed each and every healed wound over and over as Sully told her how they had happened. Zoe smiled and suggested that they take a shower, but unfortunately he could not because of his leg.

It was four thirty when Zoe drifted off to sleep holding him tightly. Sully was wide awake trying to think of a way to tell her he was leaving. He tried to escape from her arms without waking her, but failed. Zoe held him even tighter and softly said "snuggle with me Sully. I haven't been this happy and content in years."

He snuggled in closely for a few minutes and said "Zoe I'm leaving for Virginia this morning." He got the reaction that he expected, Zoe rolled away from him and pretended to sleep.

Sully quickly dressed, and kissed her before he started to leave. He said "I have to get approval from Weathers before we can be together. I can't be with you if it would endanger you or Van."

Sully stopped in the living room to look at the happy pictures in frames. He reached into his coat pocket and returned the photo he had taken earlier to its frame. He took a long look back, but Zoe was not coming out to say goodbye. He left the house as sad and lonely as he had ever been because now he knew what he was missing.

Sully drove to the motel and showered with a garbage bag duct taped around the cast on his calf, changed clothes, and checked out. The drive back to the SSO was long and sad for Sully. He drove almost non-stop to get there, and get the answer that would shape the rest of his life.

Sully stopped at a motel with only one hundred miles left to go. He checked in and took a shower. He had gotten the cast wet this time, but he knew that after he spoke to Weathers, his next stop would be the medical center. Before he dressed he called in to Weathers office and told them he would be there in about two hours. Stephanie told him that Weathers would be waiting for him.

The meeting with Weathers weighed heavily on his mind as he slowly drove past Ron and Janet's house. When it was his home he had a lot of great memories there. Now it only made him sad to look at it.

Twenty minutes later he was at Weathers' office. The night he had spent in Mirage not sleeping, combined with the long drive, had exhausted Sully and aggravated his leg.

He was thankful to have the cane as he limped into the outer office. Sully thought he must have looked pretty bad, because Stephanie came from behind her desk to help him. Sully's strength and pride were exhausted, and he put an arm around her shoulders to allow her to help him into Weathers' office.

Stephanie let him go and quickly returned to her office, as Sully slumped into the chair across from Weathers. He weakly said "hi boss, how's it going?"

Weathers shook his head before replying "if you feel like you look, I think I should get on the phone to the M.E."

He did have a grey pallor to his face. Sully was so tired that his breathing was labored, and it was hard for him to keep his eyes open. He replied "I just need a nap and a meal, and I'll be fine Boss."

The intercom buzzed, and moments later Stephanie came in with a cup of chicken broth and a bottle of water. She placed it in front of Sully without saying a word, and left.

Weathers said "why don't you tell me why you're here before you pass out Mills." Even hard ass James Weathers looked concerned about his welfare. He continued by saying "I guess that night you spent with Zoe really wore you out."

Sully sat forward and sipped the broth before replying "she is why I am here. I want to know if there is any way you will let me retire and be with her."

There was a heavy tension in Weathers' voice when he said "I had a long meeting with Macmillan and Spies about this, and the only option we have for you is that you live on campus with Zoe and your Son, otherwise it is too much of a liability. I'm sorry son, I wish I had a better option."

Sully sipped on the broth and said “what about contact with Zoe? I will go back to full active duty if you allow me monthly access to my family.”

The smile on Weathers’ face told Sully the answer before he said “We can arrange that with some terms that we can discuss later. Why don’t we get our top agent over to the med-center? Welcome back son.”

There were tons of details to be ironed out, but Sully smiled as he was helped to the ambulance’s gurney, but that was the easy part. He couldn’t wait to call Zoe and tell her the news, but right now he needed to get healthy.

Sully had successfully modified his deal with the Devil, and as long as he killed for the SSO he could have a partial life with Zoe and his son. It was the happiest he had been in years, but somehow Sully knew it wouldn’t last.